FIGHTING THE
FALL

Also by JB Salsbury

Fighting for Flight
Fighting to Forgive
Fighting to Forget

To my Goddaughter:

He broke your heart, but don't give him the power to break you.

Fight on and never give up.

I love you.

PROLOGUE

Las Vegas
Fourteen years ago...

I walk into my home office for a reason. My eyes scan the room, but…what the fuck was it? As if my mind's on perpetual vacation, I reach back and try to grasp at my thoughts from only seconds ago. Something led me here. A growl of frustration rumbles in my chest along with the heat of anger, which tenses my muscles.

Four months of neuropsychologists, occupational, speech, and physical therapists, and another therapist for comprehension, problem solving, and brain shit. I'm drowning in 'pists and getting pissed the shit isn't working.

They said I'd be back—that a brain can heal over time—and yet I'm still stumbling around like a dumb shit. I squeeze my eyes shut. Think, dammit. My hands rake through my hair and pull as if I can yank the answer from my skull. There's a mantra, a coping mechanism they teach in rehab. Slow down, backtrack, and give yourself permission to fail—no. Fuck no.

With a shove to the bohemian-bullshit mantra, I move to my desk and check my phone. Gripping it, I glare into the lifeless gadget, hoping it'll remind me why the hell I walked in here.

I search my mind.

Blank.

Fuck it. I shove the phone into my pocket and head to the kitchen, the one place I'm guaranteed to remember why I'm there. Food. Besides, if D'lilah catches me in my office, staring around the room like an Alzheimer's patient, I'll never pull off the act that I'm healthy enough to fight again.

My phone vibrates in my pocket. I check the caller ID, and a tiny swell of satisfaction warms my chest. I must've gone in my office to get my phone, expecting this call. *Bullshit.* I grind my teeth at the tiny voice in my head that won't stop reminding me what little progress I've made.

"Hey..." *Shawn. It's Shawn.* His name runs through my head, but I've learned the hard way that my brain damage keeps it there rather than letting me speak the word. "Sh..." *Fuck!* "What's up?" My jaw clenches, and the fire of frustration heats my skin.

"Cam, you got a minute?" The UFL owner sounds serious, but that's pretty much his M.O.

The plan was for me to continue my training after Shawn received an okay from the gaggle of 'pists. *Maybe he's calling with good news?* I pull back my shoulders and move to the window that looks into the backyard where my wife sunbathes by the pool while my toddling twins play in the grass nearby.

I can't fuck this up, so I concentrate hard to bring the right word to my lips. "Yeah." A breath of relief slides from my lips.

"I spoke with the doc today about clearing you to fight."

I wait for him to continue, but after a few uncomfortable seconds of silence, it's clear he's waiting for a damn invitation. *But why? Good news?*

My muscles jump with excitement at the possibility of returning to the octagon. "And?"

He blows out a long breath, but I refuse to believe he's calling me with anything but good news. "It's a liability."

"I'm...I'm..." *Dammit, fuck!* "Liability?"

He grunts and it sounds like agreement. "There's more."

No, no, no.

"He's worried about how many more hits your brain can take. He...Fuck, Cam, there's just no easy way to say this."

He can't mean it. He can't. I want to tell him that he can't do this! Fighting is my life. I can't lose it. I will not lose everything over something I had zero control over.

"Saying..." The words, they push from my gut, rip at my throat, and die at my lips. "I'm out?"

"It's a damn tragedy. A fighter like you lost because of a broken fucking tooth." At least he has the decency to sound angry about all that I've been robbed of. "I get that you moved to Vegas for the UFL, brought your family along, and you need an income. I'd like for you to stay with us, Cam. There's a lot of money in promotions."

Promotions? Is he fucking crazy? "I'm a fight...fighter." God, I sound like a babbling idiot. My chest tightens with humiliation.

"I know you are."

His words drip with pity, and I pace the living room to match the beast inside me that thrashes to roar its protest.

"I can fight." My brain is a scramble of nonsense and black holes, but I know my body, and I'm good to fight.

"Cam." His voice is low. "You're all over the place, you know that. Doc says you're making improvements, but you'll probably never be back to where you were before the infection. It's been months, and the aphasia is still obvious in your speech."

"Just words, Shawn. I can..." *Fight.* "Fight."

"I'm not tryin' to be a dick, but we can't pussyfoot around the facts. You're impulsive, have memory lapses—"

"Don't need a rundown…livin' it." My heart pumps blood into my muscles, fueling for a fight. *I'm being fired? Demoted?* "I can—"

"Fight. I know, but think about your family. Does D'lilah want you to fight?"

She's expressed her concern about my safety, but seems more interested in my paycheck. Not that I blame her. I dragged her from her modeling career in New York City to set up house in the desert. Things looked promising. I was on the cusp of a legendary career, in line for my first title fight, and then…the seizure. She went from a kept mother of young twins to nursing a grown man who needs his damn chin wiped after being fed.

My cheeks warm with humiliation, but it only increases my drive to get back all that was taken from me. "Doesn't matter. Fighting comes first."

"Jacked-up priorities, man. Don't get me wrong. I'm grateful for your loyalty to the organization, but as a friend, I have to make you aware of…"

As if summoned by my thoughts, D'lilah comes in from the backyard. Black string bikini, long legs, and all that blond hair. She looks at me and, seeing I'm on the phone, mouths "watch the kids" before heading to the bedroom. I nod and move to stand in the doorway to the backyard. My twins, Ryder and Rosie, tumble around the grass. Three years old and Ryder already knows to be gentle with his sister as he wrestles her to the ground in a flurry of blond hair and toddler limbs. The sound of their giggling permeates the air and warms my chest. A smile pulls at my lips.

"…make the decision."

Oh, what? "Yeah." I'm not sure what I'm answering, but I hope it makes sense since I don't have a damn clue what he just said.

"So it's settled."

Fuck. Pay attention! I answer the unheard question the same way I have for the past few months. I lie. Pretend I'm not as scattered upstairs as I really am.

"I'm no…*not* giving up." The twins squeal, and I move back into the kitchen so I can hear Shawn.

"I'd expect nothing less." I hear papers rustle on the other end. "But in the meantime, I'm taking you off the roster, and you're headed into promotions."

I slam my fist onto the granite countertop. "No!"

"Not up for discussion."

My breath comes faster, fists clenching.

"I'll need you to come in and sign papers. Shit…" More rustling papers and a long sigh. "I'm sorry about how this turned out…"

My arms are heavy, and I blink to focus through a blur of fury. *That's it? It's over just like that?*

"…on the fifth and—are you writing this down?"

I head back to my office on autopilot, grasping for something, anything that might make him change his mind. But my head is like an empty well, dark and thick with silence. Sliding into my desk chair, I grab a pen and scribble on my palm. "I'm, uh…so the eighth."

"Fifth. You using a planner as the therapist suggested?"

"Mm-hm." My eyes scan the area, but quickly give up. I don't even know where it is. *Did I even bring it home?*

He rattles off the date again along with a time, and I mark up my palm, vowing to transfer the words to paper when we get off the phone.

"You'll do great with fight promotion, and maybe someday…"

He can't even say it because he doesn't believe it. I can hear the lie and the disappointment in his voice.

"Right."

I hang up and sit in the silence of my office. My blood drums, and the stress only furthers my confusion. The octagon is my first love, the only place I truly feel alive. My life is fighting. *What the hell do I do now? Sit behind a motherfucking desk all day?*

My gaze swings around the room as a feeling of urgency pricks at the back of my neck. I scrub my face, shoving my hands up through my hair. This isn't happening. My legs ache for a workout. My muscles coil and ready to light up a heavy bag. They can't take this away from me.

I've never fallen, never dropped to my knees in defeat, and this is no different. They can keep me from the octagon now, but they can't keep me outside it forever.

Panic races my heart and shoots adrenaline through my veins. One hit broke a tooth, one infection caused a seizure, and one surgery destroyed my brain and ended my career. Twenty-four fucking years old and it's over.

With my head in my hands, I will my pulse to slow. The heels of my palms press deeply into my eyes, and I savor the ache that it brings.

"Shit. What am I gonna do?" I drop my hands and stare blindly at the smeared mess of letters and numbers on my palm.

I forgot to transfer what I wrote on my hand, and it was only minutes ago. No wonder the UFL thinks I'm a liability. They're worried I'll walk into the octagon on fight night and within seconds forget what the hell I'm doing there.

They're probably right. I'm dizzy with the impact of the truth.

One of the kid's cries filters into my office from the back-yard. Maybe one of them fell and got hurt. The cry gets louder and triggers my internal alarm. Something's wrong.

I head to the kitchen and crane my neck over the sink, and my gaze rakes through the yard, but I don't see the twins. I shift my body weight to peer out the window towards 'Li's lounge chair and—no D'lilah.

Where is…? Oh no!

I was supposed to be watching them. My body responds on instinct. I race to the backdoor and outside, blood pounding in my ears. My eyes scan, searching the area. My glare swings to movement under the patio table. Ryder is hunched over, his face bright red from screaming, and tears flow down his cheeks.

I crouch and hold out my arms. "Come here, buddy."

He screams louder, his eyes fixed on a spot behind me. I turn, expecting to see what's got him so upset, but there's nothing there. "Are you hurt?" He doesn't seem to be injured, but his piercing cry sounds like pure pain. *What the fuck is going on?* His little arm rises and points over my shoulder. "I don't underst—Wait, where's…?

My heart stills; my breath freezes in my lungs. *Where's Rosie?*

In slow motion, my vision shifts to the pool. The water ripples distort a tiny figure at the bottom. Dressed in pink. Lifeless.

I move and dive. Cold water rushes up my nose. My eyes scan, hands search. I grab her, pulling her up with me, surfacing for the life-giving air.

I gasp for it.

She doesn't.

Out of the pool, I lay her body on the table. My mouth on hers, I blow. Nothing.

I press on her chest. "One, two…come on."

Mouth again. Breathe.

The back door slams. "Cam, what…?" The guttural roar of my wife's screams shreds through my skull. Words, questions, all of them are distorted by her wailing.

"Call 911!" I work harder. Water drips from my hair to her face that's no longer flushed pink with life, but tinged with gray. God, please. Don't let her die.

"No! Come back, Rosie!" I pump her tiny chest. "One, two, three…"

Breathe.

More screaming. D'lilah's and Ryder's cries mix in palpable agony. Rosie's body jerks from the force of my hands. I put my ear to her heart. Nothing. Her mouth. Nothing.

"Don't give up!" A sob chokes me. Push. "One, two, three…"

Breathe.

"Rosie, please!" I push over her heart. Again. Again. "One, two, three…"

Breathe.

"Fight for me, baby."

Breathe.

Breathe.

Don't let go.

I press my ear to her chest. Nothing.

Please, God…no.

My legs wobble.

Knees buckle.

And for the first time in my life…

I fall.

ONE

Present Day

EVE

"I hate you. Like honest to goodness from the depths of hell kind of hate."

A slow grin pulls at Raven's mouth. "Liar."

We're in another standoff, this time in my kitchen and way too friggin' early in the morning. I should've known she didn't just drop by to say hi as her sweet, innocent voice explained when she came knocking at my door at the butt-crack of dawn.

"Thanks for the coffee, but the answer is still no." I rip open two packets of sugar and dump them into the liquid gold she shoved into my face when she walked in. "Why are you up so early anyway?"

She points to her swollen belly. "I have a human tornado playing jump rope with my guts. Hard to sleep with Cirque de Bebe going on behind my belly button."

"That's disgusting. I'm never getting pregnant." I keep my eyes on my coffee and hope she doesn't see the disappointment that weighs heavily in my chest.

"Come out with us. This fight means a lot to their camp, and we need to show Blake and Rex our support."

I groan at her stubbornness. "Nice try. I know you're trying to set me up *again*."

She pins me with that blue-green glare, but I don't miss the twitch of her lips. *She thinks this is a joke?*

I point in her face and scowl. "You promised you'd back off and stop dragging me out with a gang of hot dudes. They don't do it for me, you know that." Such. A. Lie.

She loses the battle with her mouth and grins.

I cross my arms over my chest. "What's it going to take for me to get you to understand?"

Her eyes sparkle with restrained laughter, her eyebrows raise, and she curls her lips between her teeth.

"It's not funny." I glare at her cute, pregnant, happier-than-a-dick-in-jelly expression. God, she's pissing me off. "Newsflash. I'm gay!"

The tension in her face explodes, and a burst of laughter shoots from her lips. A quick snort-suck of oxygen and she dissolves into body-racking laughter. She holds her belly, taking in deep breaths. "Stop…making me…laugh. I'm gonna pee."

"I'm not trying to make you laugh." I stomp and throw a dishtowel at her head. "I'm being serious."

She hops from foot to foot, shaking her head to send her dark wavy hair cascading over her shoulders. And—*surprise, surprise*—she's still laughing.

I cock my hip and wait. "Go ahead. Get it all out." I roll my hand through the air. "Laugh at my expense like a good best friend."

She sniffs back her tears of laughter and swipes at her eyes. "I'm sorry. It's just you act like you really believe it, and it makes it so much funnier."

"Rave, I don't act like I believe it." I throw my arms out to my sides. "I am gay!"

Her eyebrow lifts high above one eye. "Really."

Is she kidding? I look around, exaggerating with my hands out and eyes wide. "Are you listening to me at all? That's what I've been telling you."

"Fine, if you're gay, how many women have you slept with?" She leans a hip against the counter, waiting.

I muster up a nasty evil eye because she knows the answer to this question. She just wants to hear me say it. "How many has nothing to do with—"

"Nope, no backpedaling. Just answer the question."

I clench my teeth and straighten my shoulders. "None. But that doesn't mean—"

"Right. And how many women have you been on a date with?"

Ugh! I want to scream and throw a fit; she's so frustrating. "Exactly."

"These questions are irrelevant." I take a pretentious sip of my coffee, pinky in the air and everything. "I hate men, so there's your answer."

Her eyes go soft and she tilts her head. "Hating men doesn't mean you're attracted to women."

True. Vaginas actually gross me out. I shudder and cringe. The thought alone makes me gag. I'm not even a big fan of my own as often as the little slut gets me into trouble. But there's no way I'm telling Raven that.

"Eve, you've been hurt badly. But just because there's a barrel of bad apples out there doesn't mean that no good ones exist."

"Easy for you to say. You're married to a seriously rad guy. Jonah's smokin' hot, funny, and has good taste in music." I tick the qualities off on my fingers. "He's sweet, rich, and worships the ground you walk on."

No one has ever shown me that kind of care, not unless they were getting something in return. Is it possible to find a man who doesn't have an agenda?

A soft smile tugs at her lips, and her eyes go all fucking love-drunk and dreamy. "He is all that, but can you honestly say that Jonah was all those things before we started dating?"

Jonah was a playboy and a heartbreaker, still hot and rich though, but he became a new man when he met Raven. I'm not surprised. The woman is steps away from sainthood, always has been. She radiates goodness so much that it all oozed over a dude like Jonah Slade and turned him 180 degrees. I could never be so lucky. I'm not the kind of woman a man changes his stripes for.

"So who's to say there's not a man out there that would be willing to be all that for you? Not a perfect guy, but a perfect-for-you kind of guy."

"I don't know, Rave." *They all walk away.* It must be physiologically impossible for a man to stay with me long term. It's been this way since birth, starting with my dad. With no brothers or sisters and a selfish bitch for a mom, Raven's the only one who's never left.

"Come on. I miss hanging out with you." Her aquamarine eyes go puppy dog. "Pleeease? It'll be quick and painless. I'm not setting you up; it's just an opportunity to hang out somewhere other than the gay bars."

I nod a few times. "Yeah, that's probably a good idea. I think the chicks there are sick of me anyway. Last week I dropped half my paycheck into the jukebox on Justin Timberlake songs. Not their usual Alanis man-hater Morissette."

Raven's back to the look she had earlier, threatening to burst. "You're so not gay."

"What?" I sip my coffee and shrug. "Timbo's hot, ya know?"

"Not gay." Her sing-song tone is soaked in a smile.

"Am too." *No, I'm not.* "I can appreciate a good-looking man. And his voice is…damn, it's like sex and maple syrup."

Not that I remember sex, it's been so long since I've had it I'm sure I've forgotten how. Warmth spreads throughout my body at the prospect, but it quickly cools at the thought of the last man I let go there. Vince. Con-artist, manipulator, controlling, possessive, and yet I was undeniably attracted to him. He made me feel irreplaceable. Until the day I wasn't.

He used me to get to Raven and would've raped and possibly killed her. If I'd been smarter, paid closer attention, he may've never gotten to her. As if living with that guilt isn't enough, I have the strangest feeling that if he weren't incarcerated I'd open myself up to him again. A sharp pain twists in my gut.

"So you're saying you'll come tonight?" She shifts and leans back against the counter, her hand rubbing circles on her baby bump.

How can I say no? I nod.

"It'll be fun. No pressure to choose guy or girl. Just be..." Her face pinches in concentration. "Gosh, what would you call it if you weren't attracted to men or women?"

"Asexual."

Her face glows with a genuine smile. "Perfect. You're asexual. Until further investigation."

I'm not gay. I'm stupid. I can't trust myself around most men. Nice guys aren't the problem. No. They're safe. It's the other ones: the bad-in-a-bad-way bad boys. Those are the ones I need to stay away from.

As much as I'd love to have what Raven has, the risk is too great. I can't watch the back of another man as he walks out of my life. I wouldn't survive it.

———

CAMERON

Sitting in a conference room listening to a dozen grown men bitch and throw a fit is another example of how much work needs to be done. I curse Taylor Gibbs for the zillionth time today for fuckin' up the UFL and turning its warriors into whining babies.

"You've gotta be shittin' me. You're dropping this bomb on fight night?" Blake Daniels glares at me as if he's trying to burn holes through my skull. "Why now?"

The rest of the table of Vegas-based UFL fighters follows up with similar questions and complaints.

I lean forward, elbows on the table, and grind my teeth against the words that are bursting to be said, but I've worked to damn hard for this and need to prove my competence. "This is the fucking Universal Fighting League. It's what we do. We train and move fighters through the program. In order to do that, we need new bodies in here. I've given you the list of fighters that will be joining us here in Vegas. If you don't like it"—I jerk my head to the door—"get the fuck out."

"He's right." Owen—the head trainer and, from what I can tell, the self-appointed leader of this crew—stands up. "We could use a revival. Some fresh meat and a little competition would do us some good."

More groaning. *What the hell?* I rub my eyes and try to wipe what I'm sure is a look of absolute disappointment from my face. Whatever happened to fighters welcoming a challenge? *Shit.*

"I agree with Cam and Owen." Jonah—the Heavyweight Champion and, from what I can tell, one of only two people these fighters listen to—speaks up. "Things have been lax since Gibbs left. The Fade and his camp joining us here will keep us on our game."

"Fine." Blake smiles like a guy who's made a decision that's going to be painful for someone else. "After the ass beating I give him tonight, he'll stay out of my way." Tonight's fight has a lot more to do with him earning back his reputation than it does kicking Wade's ass. And I curse Taylor, *again.*

"Blake." Layla, my assistant and Blake's better half, speaks up from my side at the conference table. "I think what Cam's trying to say is that he wants you guys to work together so—"

"Fuck that, Mouse." Blake shakes his head. "Ain't happenin'."

The room rumbles again with protest. I get it. Blake's been burned, and now he doesn't trust me or the organization. But getting it doesn't mean I like it, and I've lost my patience. "You spoiled little jackoffs. Do you have any idea how lucky you are to be here?" No one answers. Pathetic.

"We're done." I push up from my seat and nod for Layla to grab her shit and follow me out of the room and back to my office.

A thought occurs to me when I'm just into the hallway. I freeze mid-step, and Layla must not be looking because she slams into my back with a squeak of surprise. I swivel around to face the room. "There are fighters out there that would kill to be in your place."

Like me. I'd give anything to have this back, to step into that octagon, trained and ready to represent the sport with honor. These guys don't have half the respect for this organization that we had. We were the pioneers of mainstream MMA, fought back when gloves weren't required and there were no rules. Now they whine because they have to share, and some of them don't even fucking show up for meetings.

"And where the fuck is Rex?" A growl bubbles up in my throat. He bailed me out by taking this fight with Reece, so I push back my rage. I'll let his absence slide this once. "I expect you guys to fill him in on what we talked about."

"You got it, Cam." Owen's standing, leaning against the wall, arms crossed at his chest, glaring at the team. "I'll take care of it."

I nod and turn from the room. Halfway to my office I can hear Owen giving the guys a lecture about manning up and good sportsmanship.

In my office, I throw a stack of papers on my desk harder than I need to. They scatter and mix with all the other shit that needs dealing with. My head pounds and spins in a fuzzy loop of what's next: nothing I'm not used to. I reach in my empty pocket for the small spiral notebook. Shit, it's not there. Where did I leave it?

I don't remember taking it to the conference room, but that doesn't mean I didn't. Dropping down into my desk chair with a grunt, I shove my hands through my hair. Retracing my steps, I'm pretty sure I had it this morning when Layla and I met about today's agenda. But after that…Fuck!

Stress always makes it worse.

I've only been CEO for a couple months, and I don't see the kind of progress I was hoping I would by this time. There's still so much to do, which is why I need to find my damn notebook.

"Layla!"

"Yeah?" Her voice is closer than I expect, and I look up to find her across my office, shoving papers into files.

"Have you seen my notebook?" My hands move over the desktop as if I'm reading braille. "I could've sworn I had it—"

"There." She's points over my shoulder to the other side of my L-shaped desk. "By the phone."

I swivel around and there it is. Right where I left it, I guess. I wouldn't really remember. "Thanks."

She makes a noncommittal mm-hmm sound and resumes what she was doing. Only good thing Taylor Gibbs did as CEO was hire Layla. She's saved my ass on multiple occasions, and although I'm sure she's starting to notice that I'm often forgetful, she never mentions it but instead swoops in and saves me time and time again.

Meeting with the whiners. Check. Weigh-ins. Check. I'm flipping through the pages and checking off things I've completed when I feel her eyes on me.

I don't look up from my lists, but hear her feet on the carpet and finally the sound of creaking wood as she takes a seat across from me. "You got something to say?"

"Can I ask you something?"

"As long as you make it fast." Her silence brings my eyes to her contemplative expression.

"I noticed you're not married." She tilts her head to my left hand that is very much without a wedding ring.

Not anymore. "And?"

"Nothing really. Just surprised."

I lean back in my chair as irritation pinches my brows. "Surprised."

She shrugs. "Yeah, I mean you seem like a decent guy."

I'm not. "You seem like a decent woman and you aren't married." I nod to her empty left ring finger.

She grins. "That's because I just got divorced. Marriage jumping isn't my thing."

This feels like one of those you-share-I-share conversations that I do not participate in. I find if I can bite back my impulsive outbursts and stay zipped people eventually give up.

She twirls a strand of her long blond hair. "Ever been married?"

I lock my jaw and wait, but she doesn't fucking budge and stares with expectant eyes. Something tells me we'll be here all day if I don't give her something. I'd lie, tell her I've never been married, but if I plan on digging in here for the long haul, I'm going to have to give her enough to keep her satisfied.

"Once."

Her eyes light up as if she just realized we belong to the same super-secret club. "Really."

What is it about sharing that creates this weird expectation from people? As if simply telling another person about your past allows them some special access into friendship. I don't do friendship.

I flip through my notebook and hope like hell this conversation is headed toward *The End*.

"Any kids?"

My hand freezes mid page-turn, and a whisper of pain echoes through my gut that would usually be followed by a cringe, but not anymore. I clear my throat and refocus on my notebook. "I have a son."

"Oh, that's cool." She's silent for a few beats that are probably uncomfortable for her but don't bother me at all. "I have a daughter."

The rumble of an old hurt reverberates against my shield. Ten years ago those words would've bled me alive, but not anymore. "Mm."

"How old—"

"Look, I really have a lot to do." I'm still studying the pages of my notebook like a complete asshole, but honest to God it's as if we're about to bust out some knitting needles and tiny sandwiches.

"Sure thing." She hops up and moves toward the door when she turns suddenly. "Oh, I forgot. We're having a party after the fight tonight. The Blackout. You should come."

"Thanks, but"—I flip a page and another—"I think I'll go home after the fight. Long day."

"Suit yourself. If you change your mind, we'll be there." She's gone with the soft click of my office door.

After party. Haven't been to one of those in a while, at least not many I remember. The little flashes I've managed to retain carry good feelings of camaraderie with the team. I groan and lean back in my desk chair. My goal is to get back into the octagon, but until then I need to run this organization and put it back on its feet. The fighters got screwed by Gibbs and are having trust issues. I get that. Maybe showing up at this party is a smart move after all. Just for one drink. Should be painless enough.

I scribble at the bottom of the notebook page: *After party tonight @ The Blackout.*

My phone vibrates, and I shift to pull it from the pocket of my jeans. "Cameron Kyle."

Dead air followed by a feminine giggle. "Hellooooo?"

"'Li, now's not a good time." Shit. She's hammered.

"We need to talk." There's a too-happy smile in the sound of her whine. "It's important."

I'd bet my balls it's not. It never is. "D'lilah." I lower my voice. "You're drunk. My guess is whatever you have to say isn't all that important, but if it is, then you call me when you're in a state to remember this conversation. Not gonna waste my time saying shit I'll have to repeat tomorrow."

The tinkling of ice in a glass and the slurp and smack of her lips sound in my ear. "The twins' birthday is coming up."

Typical. She always goes for the direct hit. "Point?"

"My point, dear husband—"

"Ex."

"Right. We need to throw Ryder some kind of party." More tinkling of ice.

"He's a little old for a party. He wants to hang with his friends and buy cigarettes on his eighteenth birthday like all the other eighteen-year-olds."

"He smokes?"

I'm too damn tired of her mother-of-the-year-act to even roll my eyes at her attempt. "It's fight night, 'Li. Gotta run."

"Wait, but…"

I wait. Nothing.

My thumb hovers over the end button. "We done?"

"For now." The call disconnects.

Ryder's birthday coming up must be triggering her drinking. The weeks she's not boozing I barely hear from her at all, but this last week alone she's called nearly every day. I can't be mad at her for the woman she's become; after all, it was me who did this to her. After promising her the world, my brain blew up and took all my promises with it. Her addiction dulls the pain of all she'd lost. And then after Rosie…I tried to fix things between us, but some things aren't fixable. Or forgivable.

I push aside the past and focus on the now. I've got my first fight as CEO of the UFL. Biggest ticket the organization has seen in years and one step closer to getting back into the octagon.

The final step to finding my way back to the man I was: a man who never gives up and never falls.

TWO

EVE

I'm in my element. The air around me vibrates with music, raising goose bumps on my skin, while the steady buzz of liquor in my veins moves me to the beat. The musky scent of bodies, booze, and sweet perfume dances in the air. I keep my eyes closed and drown in the presence of bodies and the occasional wandering hands, but my mind is focused on the beat. There could be six hundred people on the dance floor, and it wouldn't matter. Right now it's just the music and me.

I remind myself to thank Raven for inviting me to this party. Although there's no live band, the DJ seems to have a direct link to my brain because he's spinning all my favorite songs. Since Blake and Rex won their fights, the guys are all smiles and shoulder punches, quite the opposite of what I'm used to seeing at the lesbian bars where everyone is pissed about something. Come to think of it, they do a fair amount of shoulder punching as well.

With a swirl of my hips, I toss my hair and grin at the freedom of dance. Yeah, I definitely needed this tonight. Two strong hands lock my hips in place. I roll my eyes at the familiar feeling of some douchebag as he grinds his tiny hard-on against my ass. Poor guy. If that's his calling card, he's in for a long line of rejections.

I swerve and turn to move out of his hands, but he doesn't release his grip. Asshole. Just as I'm about to grab his fingers and bend them backwards, he lets me go and steps back with such force that I stumble forward and right into a brick wall of muscle.

"What the fu—oh hey, Jonah."

His only response is a glare directed over my head. I turn around and see who I assume is Mr. Short-Distance-calling-card frozen wide-eyed, staring at my bodyguard. A slow shake of Jonah's head sends the message, and the guy slinks back into the swarm of dancing bodies.

I mouth "thank you" to Jonah, and he grabs my arm and ushers me off the dance floor, depositing me into a seat next to Raven.

She leans into me. "Having fun?" One eyebrow lifts as she dares me to say no.

No way am I giving her the satisfaction. I rock into her shoulder and search the surrounding tables for my drink. I could've sworn I set it here when I went dancing. Trying to place myself, I whirl around and—*ah-ha!* My drink was moved to the table behind me. Warmer and a little watered down, the sweet liquid is refreshing against my dance-parched lips.

Raven yawns. "I think we're going to take off."

"What? Why? It's only..." I do a booty tilt and pull my phone from my back pocket. "Eleven-thirty."

"I'm a pregnant lady in a nightclub, Eve."

I shrug. "Eh...good point."

"You ready?"

This is the first time in a long time that I've had fun at a club. I'm not ready for it to end. "Nah, you guys go ahead. It's a cheap cab back to my place."

Her eyes narrow but tinge with the hint of concern. "You sure you want to stay? Blake and Layla are leaving too, so that'll leave you with Mason and the boys."

"No biggie. Besides"—I take one look over my shoulder at Blake and Layla, who have had their hands all over each other all night—"my guess? If Layla wasn't already pregnant, she probably would be tonight. Being conceived in a bar is a sad story to have to tell Junior."

As if on cue, Blake tilts in toward Layla and devours her mouth. I watch for a second, wondering what it would be like to be kissed like that again. To have someone who needs me so badly that he can't help but touch me in public, consequences be damned.

Jonah drops into the seat next to mine, robbing me of the view.

"Yo, Slade. Where's Rex?" I twirl my straw between my fingers. "Shouldn't he be celebrating his own victory?"

"Didn't want to come." He scans the room, always looking like a watchdog. "Too tired, went home."

That doesn't sound like Rex at all. He's usually the laid back one who would go along with anything the group was doing. Not to mention The Blackout is like his second home.

"That's weird." I take another pull from my straw.

"Yeah, I'm not sure what's up with him, but..." His gaze moves toward the entrance of the club, and one of his two dimples pops. "Holy shit. He came."

I follow his stare to find another fighter making his way toward us. I'm assuming he's a fighter due to his size, probably a heavyweight like Jonah because he's close to Jonah's height, but he has Jonah beat on the width. This dude is huge!

He struts with the confidence of a prize-fighter through the room and toward us. His black pants fall perfectly down long legs and stretch taut across his thighs with each stride. I bet those thighs could throw some power behind that body in the bedroom. *Wait, what? No!* I want to move my eyes away, but instead they travel up to his crisp white, button-up shirt that's tucked in against a flat stomach. It would look too dressy, almost stuffy if it weren't for his sleeves that are rolled up in a casual sexy way. His shoulders are broad, and as his thighs do to his pants, the fabric pulls tight at his biceps. If he flexed hard enough, that thing would shred.

A warm and foreign feeling of lightheadedness floods my system. Damn, maybe I'm drunker than I thought?

As he gets closer, I blink as his face comes into view. *Please be ugly; please be ugly.* I squint through the club lighting to focus.

Aw, dammit. A thick square jaw leads to full lips that are held in a tight line. High cheekbones showcase a dark pair of eyes held in a permanent glare. Framing that deadly expression is chestnut hair cropped short on the sides with just enough length on the top to bury hands in and sideburns that lead into two-day-old facial hair that screams rugged and I don't give a fuck.

"Damn." The word falls from my lips on a whisper just as he steps up to a standing Jonah to exchange a fist bump.

"Glad you made it." Jonah pulls Raven up, tucking her under his arm, and the familiar flare of envy fires in my chest.

Blake and Layla join the greeting committee just as Caleb and Mason seem to appear out of nowhere to do the same. *Who is this guy that just his presence alone calls a crowd?*

And why am I insanely irritated that no one is introducing me to this guy? Fuck it. Whatever. I have to pee.

I shove up from my seat and move around the group, disappearing into the belly of the club and toward the restrooms. Every step I take intensifies my pout. I don't know why I care. I mean sure he's handsome in a way that makes Justin Timberlake look like a girl, but I'm off men forever, especially superhot ones that don't simply walk into a room. That guy prowled. He looks like the kind of man who, when faced with something he wants, doesn't ask. He takes. A warm rush of excitement turns in my belly.

"No, no, no!" I slap myself in the face and push through the door to the ladies' room. "Asexual. I'm asexual."

I have to be. Because being attracted to a man seems to scramble my brain cells and leave me stupid with zero sense of self-preservation. Bad things happen to a woman when she lets go and gives her heart the freedom to roam.

Not me. Not anymore. I'm locking it away where no one can touch it.

I throw back my shoulders in resolve even as the tiny voice in my head says I don't stand a chance.

—

CAMERON

One drink and I'm leaving.

After the fight, the press conference and subsequent questioning sucked up every ounce of my good mood, not that there was much there to begin with. Gibbs might be gone, but that doesn't keep reporters from drudging up the shit he caused and forcing me into a tight spot during questioning. I have to paint on the face of a CEO, when inside I'm a fighter who's forced to sit around and listen to one too many mamma jokes.

The last place I want to be is a fucking nightclub, and if it weren't for the scribbling in my notebook, I would've forgotten to come. For the first time in a long time, I'm cursing an event I remembered and pissed I didn't forget.

I haven't been in a place like this since I was...well, since I was the age of the people I'm surrounded by. Back then, I thought I was hot shit, but now I feel like someone's dad who was sent along as a chaperone.

"Cam, here ya go." Mason brings me a beer from the bar.

"Thanks, man." I try to force a peaceful expression, but it doesn't come easily, so I give up and move to conversation. "Blake, great job tonight." I hold up my beer and tap bottles with the fighter. "You stayed on your feet. Textbook KO. Proud of you."

"Thanks. I know you doubted me, but that's cool." He takes a swig of his beer. "I had enough confidence for the both of us."

"Caleb, you're up next." I nod to the country boy. "You ready for a fight?"

"Like you have to ask." He shakes his head, grinning.

This is a good group of fighters. They're talented and hungry, and outside of Blake's justifiable attitude toward UFL upper management, if we could infect some of the other fighters with this drive, we might have a chance of saving the organization.

"Yeah, well—"

"Excuse me." A woman bumps me from behind. "Coming through." She pushes past me to reach for the table and snags a half-empty drink. She holds the watered down concoction up and locks eyes with me with a sneer. "Don't mind me."

Did she just roll her eyes?

"I wouldn't want to crash in on the hero worship." She brings the drink to her lips.

"You sure that's yours?" I motion to the cocktail glass.

She cocks a hip and stirs what's left of her drink into a whirling pale purple vortex. "What kind of question is that? It's in my hand, isn't it?"

My eyes dart to Jonah, who appears to find something funny. I swing my gaze back to the woman, and something about the way she's scowling makes me curious to how far I could push her.

"You left your drink alone on a table?"

"I do it all the time." She dips her head to take a sip.

My hand shoots out and grabs the glass from her. "No."

Her jaw falls open, and her eyes grow wide before they narrow. "Hey! That's my dri—"

"You can't drink this." I hand the glass over to a passing cocktail waitress to take away.

"What the fuck?" Her glare follows the cocktail server until she's out of view, and then she swings it back to me. "Who the fuck are you?"

It's ridiculous, but even while this girl looks at me, probably wishing I were dead and yelling fuck in my face, I can't help but think she's a funny little thing.

"Oh." Raven moves to stand between us, and something tells me she's doing it to protect me. "Eve, this is Cameron Kyle, Jonah's new boss."

Apparently Jonah's wife has some sway over this Eve girl as her expression relaxes a bit.

I nod. "Nice to mee—"

"You owe me a drink."

"Saved your life. Way I see it you owe me a drink."

Her shoulders pull back a fraction, accentuating her curves, of which she got more than her fair share. A hot pink top hugs her body to her waist where the hem meets a pair of blue jeans so tight it's impossible not to imagine her naked. As hot as her body is, that's not the most eye-catching thing about this girl. It's her face, round and angelic, framed in golden blond hair with a thick curtain of bangs that touches her eyelashes, but nothing about the way she's looking at me is angelic. She's walking the thin line of becoming enraged. I can't tell through the music, but if I had to go off expression alone, I'd bet money she's growling.

"Puleaze." She cocks a hip. "Saved my life?"

I shrug and pull my gaze away from her. Staring too long could give her the wrong idea. "How long was your drink sitting on the table?"

Her eyebrows drop low over her big blue eyes. Aw hell, I'm staring again. "What does that have to do—?"

"Did you even buy that drink yourself or did some guy bring it to you?"

"I'm a woman." Her sweet face contorts with disgust. "I never buy my own drinks."

"Yes." I take her in again from hips to face. "I see that, but being a woman doesn't mean you act like an idiot."

She gasps, and someone nearby giggles while most of the guys cough on their laughter.

"Desperate dude wants to get laid"—I motion to her—"and sees a hot chick."

Her mask of irritation gives way to a blush.

"She leaves her drink on the table." I throw back a gulp of beer. "You connect the dots."

"He's right, Eve." Jonah's smiling.

She pins him with a glare. "Hey! I left my drink with you guys." Her accusing finger points back and forth between everyone.

"So you get drugged, dragged, and bagged, and it's their fault?" She can't be that stupid. We're in Vegas. This kind of shit is on the news every day. She's not answering my question, but nothing about her silence says she's conceding. "You're smart; you buy your own drinks from now on."

Her glare gets impossibly tighter. "I am smart." She pushes the words through clenched teeth.

"Accepting a drink from a stranger then leaving it lying around? Smart is debatable." I take a swig of my beer and realize on some level that I'm a fucking asshole. People skills aren't my thing, and my inability to think before I speak ticks people off more often than not. Especially women.

I expect to look down at the fragile little doll to find her tearing up, lip quivering, the usual shit I see on a woman's face after they've ventured into a conversation with me, but when I drop my chin to look, I find something entirely different. Sure, her expression is still tight with a fuck-off-and-die scowl, but there's something else there that stirs my blood. A longing behind her glare that makes my chest thump and my fingertips itch to get at her.

"As *pleasant* as it was to meet you, I'm in need of a drink." She throws a heavy section of her long blond hair over her shoulder and stomps off toward the bar. With her distance, I'm able to shake the fog that had my slacks growing tight. "Interesting girl."

"Don't be too hard on her, Cam." Blake grins and leans against a barstool. "She's in an...experimental phase."

Everyone shares a small laugh and secret looks. What am I missing?

"I don't get it."

"To put it bluntly?" Blake shrugs. "She thinks she's gay."

"Huh." No fucking way.

THREE

EVE

This is exactly why I hate men. They breeze in all *blah, blah, blah,* throwing out compliments like hot chick, all brooding glare and crazy hot body.

So what's a girl to do? She falls all over herself in an effort to get close. Close enough to touch him, to feel the heat of his body against hers, the weight of him on top of her. She says and does all the right things, hoping that he'll just hold her while she sleeps, whisper that he loves her, and promise never to leave. And she's so buzzed off all he's offering that she actually believes for once—for once in a fucking lifetime of promises—this one'll keep his word.

What a crock of shit!

I slide through the crowd and redirect my path from the bar to the dance floor, determined to regain my good mood. The DJ spins some sick remix of Wiz Khalifa's "Work Hard, Play Hard." It hits hard and the bass causes the air in the room to vibrate, exactly what I need. I move to the music, faking it at first until I really start to *feel* it. Bodies bump and glide against mine until I'm hypersensitive to every touch and my blood drums through my veins as if to the beat. The friction of bodies against my skin bathes my arms in goose bumps and unleashes a sensual heat throughout my torso. I'd blame it on the alcohol, but I know better.

My libido has been hibernating since Vince, but it's wide freakin' awake now thanks to the pushy and condescending UFL boss-dude. My mind conjures up his image against my will: the way his huge body towers over mine while he's telling me what I can and can't do. A shiver of excitement races up my spine for no good reason at all. And so it begins…

Fucking hell! It's hot in here. Having totally lost my mojo on the dance floor, I push through dancing bodies to the bar. Snagging an empty barstool, I grab a cocktail napkin and dab the sweat from my chest and neck.

"What do you need?" The bartender leans over the bar, ear aimed at me.

"Something strong and icy." I fan myself with the soggy napkin.

He nods and gets busy making me a drink. I scan my surroundings to make sure Cameron—ugh, even his name is hot—doesn't catch me buying my own drink. I know men like him. They thrive on power, and seeing me do exactly what he suggested I do would be like bowing down and admitting failure. Ain't happenin'.

"That'll be eighteen." The bartender drops a huge pint glass filled with what looks like iced tea in front of me. *Wait, eighteen dollars?*

"There better be gold flakes in that ice, *compadre.*" This is another reason I never buy my own drinks. They're flippin' expensive.

He rolls his eyes. "You said strong, sweetheart. Long Island ain't cheap." He offers his hand, palm up.

I hand over a good quarter of my grocery money and glare at the bartender who, by the look of his grin, finds this mildly entertaining. Whatever.

Hoping the food-for-a-day priced cocktail is worth it, I take a sip of my fancy tea. My throat flames and my stomach warms.

"Holy shit!" How could something that looks so innocent be so damn dangerous? It tastes like gasoline. I mix it up and try again. It's a little better. A few more sips into my drink my lips go numb. Mission accomplished. Hopefully my head will be next.

Someone from behind presses in to get to the bar. "*Negra Modelo.* No lime."

That voice. My head whips to the side, my back goes ramrod straight, and I glare. "You."

He frowns back. "Don't you mean *thank* you."

"Are you following me?"

The corner of his mouth moves in a way that makes my stomach dip, and my hands grip the bar to keep from toppling toward him.

"No." He drops some cash on the bar just as the bartender delivers his beer, and then Cameron brings the bottle to his lips.

Damn, his hands are huge. I wonder what it would feel like to have those hands on my body, touching, protecting, possessing. A shiver of need runs up my spine, and I go back to my atomic tea. Gulp after gulp, I swallow straight booze, holding my breath like a kid with cough syrup. This guy is a dick. A huge one. Does he have a huge—*no! No, no.* I shake my head, wanting to kick my own ass for being such a slut, even if only in my head.

"Which lucky stiff bought you that, doll?" He nods to my drink.

Doll? That was sorta sweet, but I hold my scowl and refuse to give him the satisfaction of knowing I bought my own drink. "It was the guy down there." I tilt my head to motion down the bar. "The one with the red shirt on."

He turns and spots the random dude I just pointed out about four stools down, and then turns back to me. "Oh yeah?"

"Mm-hm." I take a long pull from my tea and stifle the urge to recoil from the liquid fire.

"Hope his girlfriend doesn't mind him buyin' drinks for other women." I hear the chuckle he tries to hide in his bottle as he takes a sip of his beer.

Leaning forward, I peer down the bar and—shit, he's right—the guy in the red shirt has a beautiful brunette on his lap and his hands all over her.

I shrug and drop my lips back to my drink to hide my hot cheeks.

"You know." He leans down to speak into my ear, and the spicy sweet scent of his aftershave filters to my nose. "It's pretty fucked up to let guys buy you drinks, *especially* if you're not interested in *men*."

The heat of his breath against my ear paints goose bumps down my arm, and I fight the urge to groan. He's like a light switch to my sexuality, turning me on by simply talking.

"I might be interested. I'm just…undeclared."

He turns his big shoulders toward me and leans an elbow on the bar. "Explain that."

"It's none of your business, but if it means you'll leave me alone"—*Please don't leave me alone*—"then I'll tell you."

Void of any playful expression he nods for me to continue. *Does this guy ever smile?*

"I'm not attracted to men or women." Such. A. Lie.

His eyebrows drop low over his already tight eyes. "I don't believe you."

"Why does everyone keep saying that?"

"You don't give off the vibe." He tips his chin back to take a long swig off his bottle, and I watch the powerful cords of his neck contract as he swallows.

Act unaffected.

I shrug and slug down another gulp of my tea. Funny, I hardly taste the booze at all now. "If I were into men, I'd be throwing myself at a guy like you." *What? Why would I say that?*

Challenging a man like this is lunacy. I'm drunk. That's got to
be it.

"Maybe you're playing hard to get." The set of his eyes makes
it look as if he's glaring, but the corner of his mouth is pulled up
just enough to contradict. Not a smile, but a taunting. It's predatory, dangerous with just enough soft to lure in his prey. His eyes
drop to my mouth. My cheeks flame and I look away.

"Or maybe I actually *am* hard to get." Oh my gawd! It's as if
I've been taken over by a phone sex operator. Why do I insist
on poking the bear?

"Sounds like a dare, Eve."

Is it just me, or was there a growl in the way he said my name?

I take a deep breath, hold my head high, and swivel my barstool to face him. My knee brushes against his rock hard thigh,
and another wave of arousal washes over me. I need to stay away
from this guy. He's fishing with superhuman pheromones.

This is the moment, the line drawn in the sand and a
choice to make. But how do I turn and leave when every cell
in my body screams for me to plow through and right into bed
with this charming asshole.

My chest aches, my heart's memory clearly stronger than
my libido's. One-night stands. All the men I hoped would fill
that black gaping hole in my chest and never did. Even now, as
fucked up as it is, I still hold out hope that this guy, every new
guy, could be the one. *What is wrong with me?*

I swing my gaze to his. That mouth. Those eyes. I'm
screwed. *I wish.* Ugh!

"Well, I better get going. It's late and I have to work tomorrow." Or more accurately, if I don't get out of here soon, I'll
get him on his back and climb aboard begging. I slide off my
stool to land on unsteady legs.

His hand grips my elbow to hold me up. "Easy, there." He
eyes my tea. "Long Island?"

"Yeah, but I'm fine, just lost my footing." Or lost my mind in his presence.

He leans down, eyes fixed on mine. "Fuck, Eve. You drivin'?"

"Yeah, or…" Wait. I came with Raven. I press my fingertips to my forehead. "I didn't drive. I was going to take a—"

"I'll take you home."

"What? No." I move to pull away, but he doesn't release his hold. That'll ruin my plans for strategic avoidance. That last drink has me a little wobbly on my platforms. And shit! That last drink took my last twenty bucks. "I'll see if one of the guys can give me a ride."

"Yeah?" He tilts his head. I stare drunk and unabashed at his handsome face.

A soothing warmth envelops me. "Yeah."

"Good." He finally releases me with a nod and turns back to his spot at the bar.

I roll my eyes at his back and decide to take my chance to get away while I can, but at the same time I'm a little disappointed that he let me go so easily. It happens all the time, and for some reason, I find myself a little surprised each and every time it does.

They let me go. They always do.

Unless they're getting something from me.

The great thing about being asexual is I have nothing to offer.

—

CAMERON

I must be under more pressure than I thought. That's the only conclusion that would explain why I'm standing in a bar and so turned the fuck on I can't concentrate. It makes sense. With all the heat I'm getting from the board about putting the

UFL back on track and positioning myself to get back into the octagon, it's no surprise my body is looking to work off some steam. My reaction to Eve is nothing more than a red-blooded male's response to stress. Sex is a cure-all in most cases. I pinch the bridge of my nose and close my eyes.

I offered to take her home? Since when do I care about how a woman gets home?

Yeah, I better get the fuck out of here before I catch another glimpse of her that I won't be able to drag myself away from.

"Cam, you leaving already?" Mason snags my attention just before I step away from my barstool.

"Long day."

Caleb strolls up with a girl under his arm, but in a quick scan, I don't see Eve. I thought she was going to hunt these guys down for a ride. Maybe she changed her mind and decided to take a cab. What the hell? Why do I care?

"You think I'll get a shot at Santori this year?" Mason has his elbow propped on the bar and a longneck between his fingers.

"You tell me?"

We launch into talk about who'll be fighting whom in this new season, and it takes the edge off of the Eve-induced disorientation I was experiencing earlier. Caleb hands me another beer. So much for leaving after one drink.

"You think after tonight's fight Wade will go after Blake for a rematch?"

"Personally? I think he'd be stupid if he—"

Mason turns away as if someone tugged at him from behind. I down the rest of my beer and take advantage of his diverted attention.

"I'm takin' off." I shake Caleb's hand and move to give Mason a visual *see ya* when a flash of blond hair catches my eye.

"You're right, Mase. I could probably hang out a little and just drink wa—" She yawns. "Water."

Mason shifts on his feet and has removed his arm from the shoulders of the girl he was with. "Are you sure? Or um…" He looks around, and his eyes land on me, just as Eve's do the same.

Mason's narrow, while Eve's go wide.

"Cam, you're takin' off, right?" He hooks Eve around the waist and guides her toward me. "You mind dropping Eve off at home?"

Ah, I see. Eve's looking for a ride, but Mason's in the middle of negotiating a sleepover with the little brunette.

"No, that's not…You don't…" Eve's words die when my hand comes down around hers.

"Let's go."

FOUR

CAMERON

This is stupid. I should put her in a cab and leave. The words came out of my mouth before my brain was able to get on board. There's something about this girl that calls to me, one very specific and demanding part of me. There's no denying it after watching her on the dance floor, her body fluid and seeping sex vibes. Who am I kidding? Even when she's telling me to fuck off, she's all-consuming.

With a quick chin lift to the guys, I put my palm to the small of Eve's back to guide her out through the crowded bar. In the short distance between the club and my car, I struggle to sort out my body's reaction to her and what the hell I plan on doing about it.

With a face like a doll and the body of temptress, this woman stirs my blood. She's pissed off: bitter, stubborn, and disillusioned. But one thing she certainly is not is *gay*. It's evident with every blush of her cheeks, her tiny intake of breath when I get close, and then there's the way her gaze burns into mine. It's hot as hell, but there's an innocence to her, too, that tugs at something deep I can't even name

"Can you slow down?" Her shoes click against the asphalt, and I realize I've been so stuck in my head that I'm practically shoving her to my car.

"Shit, sorry." I slow down and I know—*I know*—I should drop my hand from her back, but it feels too good give up.

I pull my keys from my pocket, hit the fob, and walk to the passenger side.

"Wow, nice ride."

"Thanks." I pull open the door and motion for her to hop in.

She complies, dropping into the black leather seat. I catch her running her hands along the fabric and mouthing the word *wow* as I shut the door.

I head to the driver's side, pulling out my phone before folding inside. Before I get the car started, I'm instantly caught by two things: her delicate female scent filling the small space and her not-so-feminine snort-giggle doing the same.

Strapped into the seat, she's turned toward me, laughing.

I look around the space then back to her. "You find something funny?" Maybe she's drunker than I thought.

"From the outside, I didn't think you'd fit in this. What kind of car is this?"

"Maserati." I shift in my seat, figuring out pretty quickly what she's referring to. "You saying I'm too big for my car?"

"No, I mean it's a hot car and you're like, you know…" She holds her hands out and shrugs as if it's an obvious connection. "It's a great match, but aren't you a little cramped in here?"

I never really thought about it. Being six-foot-five, I'm cramped everywhere. But now that she mentions it…"Yeah, a little. But like you said, it's a hot car."

She nods and her laughter dies. "It's like these jeans. They might cut off all circulation to my brain and squeeze my ass so tight that it goes numb." She grins and makes a sweeping motion down her body with her hand. "But they're hot."

"Can't argue that." I fire up the engine and move the car through the lot to the main road, ignoring the sudden swelling between my legs at the mention of her jeans. "Where to?"

"Oh, take a left here." She settles back in her seat. "So president of the UFL. What's that like?"

"Headache, but it's gettin' easier."

"What did you do before you took over for that asshole Gibbs?"

"Fight promotions." I suck at the tell-me-about-your-life conversations. I have no desire to shed my skin and bare my soul, but a non-answer would make me a dick, and for one very particular and very naked reason, I want this girl to like me.

"I wouldn't have thought that." She gazes at the lights passing by her window. "I would've thought you were a fighter."

A suffocating weight settles in the small space between us. It's a painful subject, but it's only painful for me. "I was once."

A tiny gasp and she turns toward me with her whole body. "I knew it! Did you fight for—oh, crap, turn here." She points and I make the turn. "Did you fight for the UFL too?"

"Yeah, but that was a long time ago."

"Psht. How long ago? You can't be that old."

Halted at a stoplight, I turn to her. "Fourteen years."

Her eyes go wide on me. "Really. How old are you?"

I'm not ashamed of my age, but something about her surprise makes me think I should be. "Thirty-eight."

"Damn." She whistles and tugs her tight top down over a sliver of exposed skin. "You're a lot older than I am."

Somehow I never stopped to think about how old she is. I mean she's in a bar, so at least she's legal. "A lot as in…?"

"What, me? Oh I'm uh…twenty-four."

Fuck. She's closer to Ryder's age than mine. Reality hits me like a bucket of ice water on my nuts. What the fuck am I thinking?

This is what happens when I let myself go and forget that I don't have the luxury of floating the way the wind blows. My gaze darts to the small notebook that sits in the center console. That's where I need to stay: regimented, scheduled, and focused.

When I let loose, I end up having dirty thoughts about a twenty-four-year-old girl who is also now in my car. In my defense, she looks much more mature in all the right places.

"Take the second right and my house is on the left." She points her directions. "I bet you were a heavyweight, huh?"

I nod, grateful for the subject change, but not interested in continuing this share-fest. Especially when I know where it might lead.

"There it is." She points to a small duplex on the corner. It's modest, and we seem to be in a decent part of town, but I can see right away that a few of her windows are open. Not that it's my business to care.

The click of her seatbelt rings in my ears, signaling it's time to part. I pull into the driveway but don't get out.

She fidgets with her keys. "I appreciate the ride."

"No problem."

"And um, thanks for all that stuff about leaving my drink."

I shake my head. "Hold up. Did you just say thank you? Did I hear that right?"

She grins and tilts her head. "Yes. You were right." Her big eyes meet mine and she leans in. "Thank you."

Okay, she needs to stop with this sweet bullshit immediately or else…*or else what?*

"No more accepting drinks from strangers." I try to keep eye contact, but when I do, the heat in her gaze draws me closer. Leaning one elbow on the center console, I'm sucked into her stare. In the dark, the dashboard lights bathe her hair and skin in a soft blue glow. Fuck, she's even more beautiful than I thought. "Go on now, Eve." Why the hell did that sound like a warning?

"Mmm." Her eyes flash with need.

I groan and drop my head, but only for an instant before my body demands I keep looking. "Go inside." Or I'll kiss you or fuck you. Most likely both.

"I don't want to." The sound of her denim-clad legs rubbing together slices through the car straight to my dick.

This can't happen. She's young, most likely inexperienced, and naive. Damn, looking at her now, my excuses seem pointless. I need to convince her to leave the car. Push her away.

"I thought you were having a sexual-identity crisis."

I expect her to get mad or embarrassed. Instead, the tip of her tongue darts out to suck her upper lip between her teeth before she releases it. "I think I've been cured."

Fucking hell. Her upfront style of seduction is such a turn on; this car has gone from cramped to painfully uncomfortable. I shift in my seat, hoping to give my hard-on some room, but it's pointless.

If she had any idea how close I am to burying myself so deep inside her tight little body, she'd watch what she says.

This is stupid. Impulsive. Selfish.

Fuck it.

"You sure you want this?" I reach out, fork my fingers into her hair, and groan when she lets the weight of her head fall into my hand. Just that tiny tilt of her head says it all. She's giving herself over to me. "Come here."

Her eyes flare with need, and she leans in while I guide her lips to mine. The first brush of flesh on flesh, so fucking sweet, makes my body ache for more. I tighten my grip in her hair and her lips part. Perfect.

Our tongues glide together hot, slick, and so fucking wet it ignites a fire to strip her naked. Who knew this mouth spewing sass and saying fuck could taste so damn sweet.

The leather seats creak as she pushes her torso closer, reaching over the center console. Her chest heaves, and her hot breath licks against my lips in frenzied bursts. Her hand runs up my thigh to my zipper. Eager, she wants this as badly as I do.

I break the kiss with a gentle but firm tug to her hair. "Inside."

Her heavy-lidded eyes fix on mine, swollen lips parted. "Fuck...yeah."

All breath and desire and damn if my dick isn't pushing painfully to get at her.

She drops back to her seat, pops the door open, and before she can close it, I'm out and rounding the front of the car. At the door, she fumbles with the keys, and I press in behind her. I drag her hair off her neck and nip at the tender flesh below her ear.

"Cameron." Her body goes limp against my chest.

"Open up." I flex my hips, grinding against the top of her ass.

A few more fumbles with the key and we're plunged inside the darkness of her living room. I kick the door shut and the sound spins Eve to face me.

"Where's your room, doll?" I take a step toward her, almost expecting her to retreat, but instead she comes at me.

She hops and I catch her by the ass just as her lips crash against mine. Her tongue invades, hands bury into my hair, and legs tighten around my waist. She rolls her hips, rubbing herself against my hard-on. I growl into her mouth and turn to press her back into a nearby wall. My hips move on their own, thrusting but unsatisfied with the friction alone. Fuck, I need more.

I shove my hand up her shirt, ripping and pulling against the flimsy fabric. She leans back so I can get her shirt and bra off. I pin her hips to the wall with mine, and with her legs still wrapped around me, I squint into the darkness.

"Aw fuck, baby." My eyes devour her naked torso: long sleek hair falls over her shoulders to frame full breasts and creamy skin that call for my mouth. I cup one, running my thumb over the tip and warm at her responding shiver. "You're perfect."

A tiny gasp falls from her lips. "Thank you."

I lean forward and close my lips around her nipple.

She groans and pumps her hips against mine as much as she can for being wedged between me and the wall. "Bedroom."

Oh, hell yeah.

I push back, and her arms and legs clamp around me. "Where?"

"Back hallway, door on the right."

With her round ass in my hands, I follow directions until we're in a dark room, but the white comforter on the bed stands out like a big X that screams "fuck here." I toss her to the bed and unbutton my shirt while she peels off her jeans. "All of it. I want you bare."

She shimmies her panties down to her ankles then kicks them across the room. I pull a condom from my wallet and drop my pants. Her eyes go wide as I roll the latex on.

"You sure about this, Eve? Once you give me the okay, I don't think I'll be able to stop."

"Yes. Even if only for tonight." She pushes up and brings herself to the edge of the bed. Her chin tilts back, and she hits me with the full force of that angelic face. So innocent, so fucking beautiful. "I want you." Her eyes go to my dick. "All of you."

With a knee on the bed between her legs, I lean forward, and she scoots back so her thighs cradle my hips.

"All of me?" I nip at her lower lip and push inside in one thrust.

A sexy-as-fuck moan rumbles deep in her throat.

I thrust again, harder. "You got it."

And in this moment, for one night, I'm hers.

FIVE

EVE

Here I go again. Or better yet, there he goes again. With my knees tucked up to my chest, arms wrapped around my shins, I watch him get dressed. The cool air washes over my naked body, making me shiver, but I refuse to cover up. Discomfort is the least I deserve for what I'm doing to my heart.

It's dark, but I can make out the sleek lines of his powerful body as he slides on his pants one leg at a time. Buttoned and zipped, he grabs his shirt off the floor, gives it a firm shake, and pulls it over his massive torso decorated in tattoos on both ribs in a flurry of black ink. Waves like water and intricate patterns. I don't have time to study exactly what they are. As soon as the condom came off, he said he had to go.

The hollow ache in my chest is a harsh reminder of how stupid this was. I knew what I was getting myself into, understood this was going to be a one-night stand, and I begged him for it anyway. But I'm not like other girls, and now that the butterflies and orgasms have faded, my heart rages at what I've done. I'm such an idiot.

He moves toward the bed where he left me sated and now completely sober. With a sigh that I don't think he wanted me to hear, he sits at the very edge of the mattress, keeping his distance. Fuck. That burns. His eyes are narrow, and there's a hint of a pity in his expression. If I didn't know any better, I'd say that's the look of regret. The ache in my chest blooms in a suffocating rush.

"Eve, I—"

"You don't have to say anything." I use my voice to disguise the heaviness in my chest. "One-night-stand rules. No apologies. No expectations. Two satisfied participants." I grin. It's fake.

"Right. Well, um…thanks. That was fun." He pats me on the arm. Fucking pats me as if I'm a kid he just bought ice cream for! *There ya go, kiddo. Enjoy!*

I resist the urge to groan and bury my face into my pillow. I got what I wanted: one night of ah-mazing sex with the hottest guy I've ever seen. Why do I feel so sorry for myself now that he's leaving?

Because I want more. I always want more. That's my problem. I want to be the girl that a man can't live without.

He stands to leave, and rather than follow him out, I memorize the look of his back as he disappears through my bedroom doorway. I force myself not to look away and burn the image into my head with hope that it will penetrate this time.

How many do I have to throw against a wall before one sticks? The internal grind of guilt and humiliation is my own form of self-mutilation.

I pull my comforter over my body and close my eyes. Tomorrow is a new day: an opportunity to start over with improved determination.

Tonight I'll lick my wounds as a reminder of why I need to stay away from men like Cameron. I'll beat myself up for all the reasons I should've said no even with the knowledge that given the chance to do it again I'd have said yes.

—

CAMERON

Re-energized.

A few hours with a good-looking woman will do that to a man. After leaving Eve's, I was able to rack up a few solid hours sleep; then I was up at sunrise and out the door for a run. The best of Social Distortion playing in my ears and the bright desert horizon in the distance, it was as if I'd left thirty pounds of pent-up tension behind.

Sweat soaked and starving, I dig through my refrigerator for some eggs when the scent of warm sugar and cinnamon wafts up from my chest. The moisture and heat from my skin intensifies the trace of Eve I haven't yet washed off. I breathe in deeply and groan; the smell of her lotion alone brings me back to being between her legs. Fuckin' heaven.

"Dad?"

I peer around the open refrigerator door to find Ryder fresh out of bed but dressed for the day. His hair, the exact shade of blond as his mother's, sticks up all over, making him look like a human firecracker. He studies me for a second, eyebrows pinched. "You lost?"

"No, I'm looking for the eggs." It seems like a ridiculous conversation, but Ryder's whole life has been a front row seat to the Fumbling Brain Damaged Dad Show. I resume my hunt in the fridge. "Hungry?"

"I'll grab a protein bar on my way out."

I give up on the eggs and grab two protein bars from the pantry, tossing one to Ryder. "It's Sunday."

He catches it on the fly. "Yeah, I know. But Theo got new skins on his kit, and we wanted to jam before he has to be at work."

The older he gets, the more he's been avoiding our Sunday routine. When he was a kid, he had no choice but to join me, but now that he's older, he has the freedom decide what's best. Doesn't mean I have to like it.

I notice then that there's a tiny smudge of black makeup below one eye, and his fingernails are painted black. "What did you do last night?" I motion to his arsenal of emo-punk dead giveaways.

He glares at me, his pale blue eyes bloodshot. "I was about to ask you the same thing."

"After party." I take a sip of my coffee, focusing on my son, but my mind goes back to Eve: her body, warm and welcoming, wrapped around mine. The sounds that fell from her lips ring through my skull, and I turn to hide my dick swelling at the memory.

"Some party." Ryder motions to the side of my neck; his lips tick into a knowing smile. "Did you get assaulted by a vamp?"

I hold up my stainless steel coffee mug but can't see shit in the reflection. My gut tightens at the memory of her mouth at my throat while I was thrusting inside her tight little body. Goose bumps break out on my skin and my neck gets warm. Had to have left a mark. Great.

The last thing I need in my already fucked-up head is the complication that a woman brings, especially a girl like Eve. She's young, and if her dance moves and party skills are any indication, she's not giving up her wild Vegas nights any time soon. I don't have the energy to keep up with a girl like her. Not with everything else I have going on in my life or the fourteen years I've got on her.

But fuck, the sugary scent of her hair, sweet taste of her skin…What I wouldn't do to taste her everywhere.

Last night is a perfect example of what happens when I lose focus and follow my dick rather than logic. Once she led me into her house, the need to be deep inside her took over, and foreplay was non-existent. Not that she seemed to care. If

I'd had my way, I'd spend hours pleasuring every inch of that body: full hips, round ass, and gorgeous breasts that fill two hands. I groan and get Ryder's questioning eyes.

"Vamp...ha-ha, smartass." No use in throwing out some made-up story about falling down the stairs or wrestling with a vacuum cleaner. Ryder's no idiot to the ways of bachelor life.

"Mom called last night," he says through a cheek-full of protein bar.

Perfect buzz kill subject. I drop my chin and bite down on the string of curses that are pushing to be said. "Figured she might. Everything okay?"

He coughs out a humorless laugh. "Is anything ever okay when it comes to her?"

Fuck, I hate this. After D'lilah and I got divorced, she really took a turn for the worse. The drinking and partying were out of control, and I threatened to fight for full custody. She checked herself into rehab when Ryder was eight. Unfortunately, her sobriety only lasted until she checked out. I had no choice but to make good on my threat. I'd lost one child I couldn't save. There was no way I'd risk losing another.

"She's doing her best, Ry."

"Her best is shit."

"You know your mom." I force back what's really on my mind. Like the fact that she thinks she can pick and choose when to come and go from his life. His birthday's around the corner, and she hasn't given a shit about more than half of them. "Cut her some slack. She's having a hard time dealing with..."

"I know. But she's not the only one who lost Rosie. I don't see you getting shit-housed every day."

If it were possible to curl up and die, I would've done it the day I pulled my baby girl's body out of that pool, but I knew I needed to make up for what I'd done. I didn't take my brain damage seriously enough. If I'd worked harder in rehab rather than throw all my focus into getting back into the octagon, she'd still be here. I'll never forgive myself for that.

My chest is heavy and my skin clammy. The urge to comfort Ryder pricks at my throat, but I know my limitations. Talking this out with him will only bring out the anger and shame: all of the crap that makes my legs threaten to give way beneath me. I can't go there, won't allow myself to feel anything even close to what I felt that day.

It's survival. Necessity. I have to stay on my feet.

SIX

CAMERON

"Mornin', Layla." I stop off at her desk and sort through new messages. "World still turning after the fight on Saturday?"

"Seems to be." She hands me the hour-by-hour schedule of my day. "You've got a lunch meeting with Jonah and Owen and then two more on site this afternoon."

Lunch. I forgot, not that I should be surprised. I'd planned to sit down with the guys and talk game plan to make sure this intro of new fighters runs smoothly.

"Looks good." I thank her and move into my office only to sit down and see her sit down across from me. She's smiling, and I don't have a good feeling about what the smile is about. "What?"

"Did you have fun at the after party?" There's a casual anticipation to her voice that makes me leery. She can't possibly know about Eve? They're not even friends. Are they?

I tug at my shirt collar to hide the memento from last night that marks my neck. "I did. You?"

"I heard you gave Eve a ride home."

She doesn't pussyfoot around the subject, I see. Not good, the last thing I need is my employee knowing I slept with a twenty-four-year-old girl. "She had too much to drink." I shrug, playing it off. "You guys left. I was her only option."

She twirls a section of hair. "A cab would've been an option."

I pin her with a glare that only widens her grin. "You trying to get at something? If so, get to it. I've got a busy day."

"Just thought that was super cool of you."

"Thanks, because that's what I live for. To be *super cool.*" I shake my head and flip through my notebook. Hell, it's like being in grade school again with these women. "Happy to hear my life is gossip-worthy."

"Oh well, Mason told Blake"—yep, grade-school he-said-she-said bullshit—"that she didn't even put up a fight, which is kinda surprising since Eve's, ya know, off men."

I take a grateful breath that my nosey assistant actually believes that Eve really is off men. Blake, Layla, Eve, this circle runs a little too tight for my taste. It's good that last night was limited to just that. One night of fun with lasting memories of her luscious body. I can't ask for more than that.

"If you—"

The intercom on my desk phone buzzes. "Mr. Kyle? There's a man here to see you."

I press the orange talk button. "A man? Gonna need more than that, Vanessa."

"He says his name is Rusty Faulkner."

Faulkner? What the fuck is he doing here?

"Says he's here to talk to you about a fight."

"Holy shit." My old rival in more ways than one. We both fought for the UFL back in the day, but he never honored the sport, always treated it like a free ride to becoming a celebrity. For him, it was always about the show, and less about the fighting. Just the sound of his name has my muscles bunching.

He's been lying low for years. Opened an MMA training gym in Portland, or so I hear, but he hasn't been turning out any exceptional fighters as much as he's producing fame-hungry actors.

"Who's Rusty?" Layla mouths.

"Douchebag." I grab my notebook and hit the intercom. "I'll be right down."

A click sounds from the speaker. "I'll let him know."

I scan my schedule for the morning. Free until lunch. Perfect.

"What do you think he wants?" Layla's up, her yellow legal pad tucked under her arm and a pen behind her ear.

"Come with me." I stand and head toward the lobby. "Whatever it is, it ought to be good."

Passing through the training center, I ignore the voices of fighters talking shit back and forth. Heated, but harmless enough. As long as they don't kill each other, I'm good.

Walking down the hallway toward the lobby, I can already see the telltale white Ferragamos propped up on the coffee table. "Well, I'll be damned."

Lounging against the leather couch, feet up as if he fucking owns the place, is Rusty Faulkner. Other than his hair being a little thinner than I remember, he hasn't changed a bit with his black suit, red tie, and neck dripping in gold jewelry.

"Rusty, what brings you to Vegas?" I move toward him and he stands.

"Fuck me sideways." He shakes my hand. "Cameron 'Kyle-Driver' turned big dick promoter and now the Prez. You're dippin' your stick in everything, huh?"

I ignore his attempt to get me riled. After I stopped fighting and started promoting, this dick bag treated me like shit stuck on his shoe. I was a better fighter and a great promoter while he dropped off the radar after he retired. And now I'm CEO. Asshole can't stand to be one-upped by a washed-up fighter with a fucked-up noggin.

"You show up in my house, represent a past I'm not interested in relivin', and now you're talkin' shit?" I cross my arms over my chest, afraid that if I don't lock them down I might take a swing. "Speak your peace."

"Cut to the chase, huh? Don't want to talk about old times? Relive the glory days." His eyes slice to Layla. "You Kyle's woman?"

She juts out her chin and shakes her head. "No, sir, I'm Layla, Mr. Kyle's assistant."

"Assistant. Very nice." He draws out his words, making his implication clear.

"Easy. Layla's man is Blake Daniels. Not sure if you caught his fight this weekend, but you'd be smart to keep your opinions about Layla to yourself unless you want Blake in here mopping the floor with your corpse."

He raises his eyebrows and shrugs. "Business it is." His eyes scan the room before coming back to me. "Right here in the lobby?"

I don't answer and wait. The more I'm around this guy, the more I feel as if he's got something to say that's just gonna piss me off.

His beady brown eyes narrow on mine. "I've been training."

"You come all the way here to tell me that?"

"Rumor has it you're coming full circle. Going back into the cage?"

It takes everything I have not to give away my shock. How the hell does he know that? No use in covering it up, but the board strictly said they didn't want talk of the possibility until they made a decision. Something about a media nightmare. "Not sure what you're talking about, but if I ever had the opportunity to re-enter the octagon, I'd take it."

"So you need a challenger." He scratches his jaw and shrugs. "I'm interested."

"You shittin' me?"

This little nugget of good news almost makes it worth all I had to do to get here. I'd pay money for the opportunity to kick this guy's ass, but to get paid to do it is better.

"Not even a little. You and I were lined up to fight back before you quit."

My body tenses. "I didn't quit." The words are shoved out through clenched teeth.

"Uh…" He scratches his chin. "Pretty sure you did. I was at the press conference."

He knows exactly why I had to walk away from fighting. He fucking knows it!

I'm breathing heavily as I step into his space. As expected, he doesn't back down and a slow grin spreads across his ugly mug. I'm giving him what he wants, falling right into his trap, but fuckin' A if I give a shit.

"I'll take the fight. You pick the date and—"

"Cam." Layla's at my side, her hand on my forearm. She looks from me to Rusty. "Would you mind giving us a second?"

The asshole completely ignores Layla's question, and my fists clench ready to teach the dick a lesson in manners.

She jerks her head to the side, and I follow her out of earshot of Faulkner.

On tiptoes, she leans in. "What are you doing?"

"What does it look like? I'm taking the fight."

Her gaze swings up to the ceiling where she stares as if she's trying to gather strength, and then swings it back to me. "I see that. But why not give him an answer later? You don't call these shots, Cam. The board does."

Good point. "Knee-jerk reaction."

"I get that, but right now you're CEO. Not a fighter."

Fuck. I take a deep breath. "Agreed."

"All right." She pushes back her shoulders and cradles her legal pad to her chest. "You good?"

Brain damaged, not incompetent. I glare my response.

She nods, sharp and quick. "Good enough."

We move back to Rusty, and he doesn't even try to hide his greedy eyes as they move over Layla's body. Sick fuck. I'd give anything to have Blake walk in while this shit's going on.

"I'll meet with the board first and then give you my answer." Not that it matters what they say. I'm taking this fight.

"Gotta be complicated, eh, Cam?" He pulls a card from his breast pocket and throws it on a nearby coffee table. "Here's where to find me."

I stare at his back until he disappears from view. This is the fight I'm looking for, everything I've ever wanted dropped directly into my lap. No way am I backing away from an opportunity to return to the octagon and prove I'm not a failure. I mean what's the worst that could happen? *One more punch to the head kills me, that's what.* Fuck. So what do I do?

As soon as the question filters through my brain, the fighter in me rages his answer.

I will fight Rusty Faulkner.

SEVEN

EVE

Mondays suck balls. If I ever become president, the first thing I'm going to do is make Monday illegal. Not really sure how I'd do that, which is probably why I'll never become president, but I add it to my mental bucket list anyway.

I'm sitting in the tiny office that I share with three other managers. It always smells like dirty socks and farts. No matter how many cans of Febreze I spray in this place, the smell only seems to get worse.

"You want to grab a bite before the lunch rush?" Dion, the cook, who I swear is trying to poison me, pops his head into the office. He offers a plate piled high with pasta.

"Do I look stupid to you?" I do my best Joe Pesci impersonation from Goodfellas, but the effect is lost on Dion. "I'm not eating your poison pasta." I shoo him away and catch his laughter as he heads back to the kitchen.

It's no joke. One of the other managers wouldn't give Dion the day off, and he ended up on the toilet all night. Dion won't admit it, but rumors spread around the restaurant that massive amounts of laxatives were to blame.

I groan and push up to welcome the lunch rush. I've worked in this POS restaurant since I was sixteen, and the longer I work here, the more it feels like a black hole sucking my life away one year at a time. As pathetic as it is, feeling sorry for myself isn't going to get me through my shift any faster.

By the time I make it to the hostess stand, people are already showing up for lunch.

"Eve, Cristof called in sick." One of the waiters tosses me a note as he heads to his section to greet a new table.

I read the damn message and crumple it up. "Shit." Guess that means I'll be running food in a skirt. I hate this job.

After a quick trip to the back to tie on an apron, I take my place at the line and wait for orders to show up in the window. It's not long before the kitchen is slammed with orders. Garlic, oregano, and fresh pizza dough swirl though the air as orders scream through the kitchen printer. I roll up the sleeves on my starched white shirt and wish I hadn't worn my fitted BCBG button down, but rather my Target special. I'm so sick of all my nice clothes smelling like a damn Italian food festival.

"Order up!"

I nab the ticket from the line and layer plates on a large tray, hoping I'll be able to bring this table their order in one trip. I dip low and hoist the massive platter on my shoulder then swerve around staff and negotiate my way through the tables. I grab a stand, bend at the knees to lower the tray, and peek up at the table of guests. "Hope you guys are hung—"

A dark scowl hits me right between the eyes.

Holy fucking shit.

He's here.

Cameron is sitting at a table for four with Jonah and Owen.

I expect his eyes to widen with recognition, but instead they narrow in that signature glare that I feel between my legs.

The cool air burns my eyes. *Blink, dammit!* I do and then wave pathetically. "Hi, uh—"

"I was hoping you'd be working today." Jonah stands and gives me a chaste side hug. "Any chance you could hook us up with that scampi on the dinner menu?"

"That shit's the bomb." Owen shoves a piece of French bread in his mouth.

"Uh—"

"You remember Cam?" Jonah sits down and nods to the gorgeous man I know all too well.

In the light of day, he's even better looking than I remember—if that's possible. He's dressed in a similar shirt—rolled-up sleeves and open at the neck—but this one in a deep blue.

My gaze slides up his corded neck, traces the lines of his jaw, and settles on the fiercest brown eyes I've ever seen. I couldn't tell in the dark, but here in the light, even through his glare, they're almost the same color as his hair.

"Yeah, uh, hi again. Thanks again for the lift."

He nods in greeting and then turns his attention to Jonah.

That's it? I mean one night of meaningless sex surely deserves a little more than *that*?

The tension in the air is thick as a million things that could be said are not.

He engages in conversation with Owen. "Like I was saying, I'm hoping with the addition of these new fighters we'll…"

Clearly he hasn't lost his ability to speak in complete sentences since I last saw him. I tune out his voice and continue to stare stunned.

Is me giving up my body to him not worth a single-word reply? The whisper from my past says it's worth less than that, but I ignore it and move straight to the tray.

Deliver their meals and then get the hell away. I refuse to check the ticket to see who ordered what and drop the plates on the table. Out of the corner of my eye, I notice Owen and Jonah exchanging uncomfortable looks, but Cam has his eyes dead set on me. I try to avoid him, but it's hard as he's pinning me with a scowl so intense that it charges the air.

With the last of the plates off my tray, I grab it and kick closed the stand to make a hasty exit. "If you need anything—"

"Could I get another tea, princess?" Owen reaches over the table for the linguine he must've ordered.

"No, but I'll send over your server. I mean"—I fix my eyes on a scowling Cameron—"unless you're opposed to communicating with a woman."

He doesn't even flinch but continues his death stare.

I swing my gaze to a very confused-looking Jonah. "Oh, I can't get you any scampi." I narrow my eyes at Cameron who still hasn't taken his off me. "We're out of garlic."

Scooping up the tray, I stand and head back to the kitchen and into the stinky office. There's no way in hell I'm going back out there. Not after the way he just brushed me off as if he didn't have his dick in my body less than forty-eight hours ago.

I'm not asking for a damn marriage proposal, but a little common courtesy would be fucking appreciated.

And there I go with my inflated expectations. From now on, I should expect to be kicked in the gut by men, Then maybe I'll start being thankful for the constant brush-offs.

—

CAMERON

"There something you need to tell us, Cam?" Jonah pushes his food away, as if his plate is covered in dog shit, and turns toward me.

Fuck. I could've handled that better. That was awkward as hell. Seeing Eve again, her long hair pulled back off her pretty face and wearing a black tight skirt and white oxford, lookin' like a Playboy centerfold, I was lost for words. Struggling between what I wanted to say and what I should say, nothing came out. Not even a hello or nice to see you again.

Eve—here, hot, and staring. Those big blue eyes looked through me, picking apart my soul, as if she knew the number of times her image has infiltrated my thoughts.

"What do you mean?" I force a bite of lasagna even though I've lost my appetite.

"Oh, I don't know, maybe like how you clearly fucked my wife's best friend, and now you're treating her like disposable pussy at her own restaurant."

Well…shit.

"Cam, man." Owen's growl means business. "Please tell me he's wrong."

How did I not know how close Eve was to these guys? Slade's wife's friend, yeah, but best friend? Not good.

"She drank too much. I gave her a ride home."

"Don't treat me like I'm stupid." Jonah's jaw ticks. "I've done it enough. I know the look on a woman's face after she's been fucked over."

No one fucked anyone over. We're consenting adults, and these guys thinking they have some right to know what I do on my own time is pissin' me off.

I drop my fork to my plate, and the clang of metal to ceramic gets the attention of the people at the table next to us. "You mind backin' off my shit, Slade?"

"This isn't business. It's personal." His eyes move to the door Eve disappeared behind then swing back to me. "You know nothing about her."

"I know enough." Not exactly true. I know she's gorgeous, fucking crazy in bed, and she's old enough to make her own damn decisions.

"I don't believe this shit." Jonah slams his clenched fist on the table and everything shakes.

Owen doesn't take his eyes off me. "Easy, J. Making a scene will only make things worse for Eve."

"No more." Jonah leans toward me, and I can almost feel the rage coming off his body. "You stay the fuck away from Eve, or you and I are going to have problems."

Is he threatening me?

"The fuck you say?" I turn toward him. "I don't answer to you or anyone. I'll do whatever the hell I want." And if that means another chance at Eve's warm body, I'm taking it.

"I'm not messing around, man. I don't want to, but if you hurt Eve, you and I are going to have issues."

"Fine by me." I have no intention to hurt the girl.

We're staring each other down when my phone vibrates in my pocket. I grab it without looking and accept the call. "Yeah."

"Cam?" A female whimpers and sobs.

I don't need to check the caller ID to know who it is. "D'lilah, calm down. What's going on?"

I've learned to speak softly to 'Li when she calls like this. If not, she really loses it. Jonah and Owen pin me with death stares.

"I need you come over?" She's slurring.

"Shit, 'Li. Now?"

Another sob. "I don't want to be alone."

"Yeah, I'll be right there." I hit end and grab my wallet. "I've gotta run. Emergency." I throw enough cash on the table to cover our lunch, the tip, and then some.

"Midday booty call." Owen looks disgusted. "Classy."

I don't acknowledge his shitty conclusion or the fact that Slade looks halfway to beating my ass. I turn and head to my car while fighting the urge to look back and see if Eve is watching me walk away.

EIGHT

CAMERON

I speed down the highway on a familiar route that takes me to my old house. After Rosie drowned, I wanted to sell it, but D'lilah refused to let it go. Said it had too many memories. For me, it only held one memory that I was more than happy to leave behind.

I couldn't look at a single thing in that house that didn't remind me of what I caused and all I lost. It's one of the reasons that our marriage fell apart and D'lilah ended up a walking liquor bottle.

Fifteen minutes later I'm pulling into my old driveway. Pristine lawn, trimmed shrubs, and a wide concrete path lead to an atrium surrounding the front door. From the outside, no one would ever guess the devastation that lives within.

I slide my key in the door, and before it's all the way open, I can hear her crying. Fuck, what's it going to be this time. Whatever it is, I'm sure it's my fault.

"'Li?"

"I'm in here." Sniffling and small whimpers come from the living room.

I round the corner to see her curled up on the couch. With the vaulted ceilings and overstuffed furniture, she looks tiny in this space. I cross to her and drop to the opposite end of the sofa. Her blond hair is piled high on her head, eyes puffy and bloodshot, and her lips are swollen from crying. Even now, after all the heartbreak combined with her unhealthy lifestyle, I can still see a sliver of the woman I married. She was so gorgeous, so full of life, and now…I look around the room, unable to stomach how broken she's become.

"House looks good." Pathetic, but I can't think of what else to say. We both know why I'm here. She has no one, burned all her bridges and chased away every friend she ever made.

"Cleaning lady." Her voice is small and fades with another sniff.

"You wanted to talk?"

"Yeah." She pushes herself up a little and straightens her wrinkled tee. "Ryder doesn't want anything to do with me."

"He's a grown man, 'Li. Nothing I can do to help you there." She can't possibly be surprised that after fourteen years of being ignored by his mother he'd want nothing to do with her. I wish I could muster up some pity for the woman, but it's as if there's a sheet of glass between us. I can see her and hear her, but even with her pain so obvious, I can't bring myself to console her.

"I think I'm sick."

"Can you be more specific?"

She shrugs and wipes at her nose with her shirtsleeve. "I can't eat, never sleep. I'm…" A sob rips from her chest. Her body shakes with each wave of sorrow, and the smell of hard liquor seeps from her body. "I don't know what's wrong."

"You're a drunk."

A gasp cuts off her crying. "No—"

I hold up my hand. "Don't waste your time. You're not fooling me or anyone else."

She blinks and drops her chin to her chest.

"Not tryin' to hurt you, 'Li, but think of this from Ryder's eyes. You've been choosing booze over our boy since…" The twinge of discomfort in my chest reminds me of how far I've come.

There isn't much that causes me to cringe anymore. There was a time, back after I fell, that I could cry. I'd watch Ryder toddle around the house, calling out for his twin sister, who was never coming home. I'd hold D'lilah in my arms as she wept and cried out to God. The pain was so intense, like having my heart ripped from my chest on repeat.

Then one day I pulled myself up. It was time to stop rolling around playing victim, and I was ready to take back by force all I'd lost starting with the octagon. I stopped caring, refused to feel, and that shit worked wonders. So I don't envy D'lilah and all she's wrestling with. I gave all that up years ago.

After what seems like forever, her tears finally dry. "I'm sorry, Cam. I'm such a mess."

"You think it might be time to get some help? Try rehab again?"

She pushes up; her blue eyes bore into mine. "You want to lock me up?"

"Your life. Your call. I'm thinking that if you want to know your son you need to show him you're willing to put all this shit"—I motion to the empty wine glass on the table—"aside and put him first."

"Ha!" Her eyes narrow. "Typical, Cam. That's your answer to everything, isn't it? When people become a burden, you send them away."

My jaw clenches. "Fuck you." Too late to bite down on my impulse, I brace.

"Fuck me?" Her voice is loud, shrill. "It wasn't my head that exploded and made me stupid was it, Cam? Fuck *me*? *You* walked away when the backdoor was wide open." She coughs on a sob. "Our little girl…"

"I'm not doing this with you." I push to stand and prepare to leave, unable to believe I actually left a business meeting for this shit. Not that I wasn't more than happy to escape the Jonah-Owen standoff. "You think I don't wake up every morning of my life aware of the mistakes I've made. I live with those regrets every hour of every fucking day."

"You son of a bitch—"

"You wanna blame me, I get that. But don't forget, 'Li, you'd be living on the streets, sucking booze out of half-empty beer bottles in trashcans if it weren't for me."

She crumbles in on herself, and I watch the fight drain out of her. "You're right."

Well, that's something, I guess. "No shit."

She cringes at my response, sighs, and drops her head back on the couch. "I miss my son."

She needs comfort, but my anger for her abandoning Ryder when he was so young keeps me distant.

"I'll quit."

"You serious?"

"I'll try." She shrugs. "But do you think you could get Ry over here maybe? Just for dinner?"

"'Li—"

"Please, Cam. He'll do it for you."

Shit. I stare at the broken woman before me and contemplate stomping out of the house and leaving her to her crap, but the backdoor catches my eye.

I scroll to Ryder's number and hit send.

"Dad, what's up?"

"I need you to come by your mom's house."

"Can't. I've got plans."

"They can wait."

"No way. I've had plans with these guys for a week now."

I pinch the bridge of my nose and pray for calm. "It won't be a late night. Push back your plans 'til nine."

"Dad, this isn't fair. I—"

"Ry, please." Is it too much to ask for a little help?

Silence.

"Ry?"

"Yeah, I'm here."

"Stop by the grocery store on your way; put it on the card."

"Fine." A long sigh.

"We're having dinner here tonight, so grab some steaks while you're there."

"Whatever."

"Thanks, man. Later."

He doesn't say goodbye.

I hope this little family dinner doesn't blow up in my face and make things worse for Ryder and his mom. Dinner. Just one dinner.

And suddenly I have a powerful urge to drown in warm sugar and cinnamon.

———

EVE

It's late and I'm watching DVR episodes of "Say Yes to the Dress." My eyes burn either from exhaustion or crying. Who knew watching women pick out their wedding dresses would be so emotional? I sniff and wipe my cheeks with my comforter that's pulled up to my neck.

"I'm never getting married." I sound like such a baby.

After seeing Cameron at work today, I've been in a funk. Another reminder of all the things I'll never have. Sure, I could probably find a husband who'll beat the shit out of me and call me names, but what's the fun in that? I roll my eyes at the direction of my thoughts.

I scroll through recorded shows but quickly tire of the same ole crap. I should go to bed, but I can't get my brain to slow down enough to sleep.

How could he not have more to say? Even a "hey, how are ya" would've been better than his silence. Not that I deserve more. He probably thinks I'm a whore. I mean I basically acted like one. He tried to say something before he left that night in my room, and I wouldn't even let him do that. I wonder what he would've said if I hadn't cut him off with my ridiculous rules-of-a-one-night-stand speech? From the look on his face today, I'm guessing it would *not* have been "Let's do this again sometime."

I pushed him away after we had sex, and today at the restaurant, he treated me no better than I deserved, even left without saying goodbye. *Shocker.*

My doorbell rings. I jump. Who the hell would be here—I check my clock—after midnight?

I dip deeper into my bed, pulling my comforter up to my eyes. This neighborhood has seen its fair share of yellow tape, and it would be just my luck. My heart races and my body heats. A knock at the door. Crap, it's a psycho murderer.

Do I even have a weapon? There's a baseball bat in my closet, if I could—the doorbell rings again.

"I'm gonna die. I'm gonna die. I'm gonna die." My palms sweat. I can't just lie here and do nothing. I drop out of my bed to the floor and crawl to my closet.

A loud knock sounds on the door.

"Shit! Okay, think." I take a few deep breaths. The door is locked, so that should buy me some—oh crap. I left my front windows open. If I call 911, I'll be dead before the cops get here. I'm going to have to fight. Blood pounds in my ears as I grab my bat and tighten my hands around the grip. I hold it at the ready as I creep through the dark toward the front door.

Another knock. I squeak and cover my mouth, hoping the psycho didn't hear me. Tiptoeing, I move through the living room to the front door.

"I can do this." I reach out and slowly twist the lock. Fuck, fuck, fuck. Here goes nothing. With one quick move, I hurl open the door. "Die, motherfucker!" I swing hard, but in a flash, the psycho whips out a hand and catches the bat before it makes contact with his head.

"Fuckin' shit, Eve!"

I freeze, my chest heaving as adrenaline fuels my nervous system. "Cameron?"

He yanks the bat and manages to pull me closer to him before I release my grip. He opens his mouth to say something, but his eyes lock on my chest and no sound comes out. I do a quick mental assessment, grateful that I'm wearing my favorite pair of lacy boy shorts and a newer white tank that isn't covered in stains. His eyes drag down my body, narrowing as they go until they're nothing more than tight slits. My thighs warm and my tummy tumbles at the predatory way he takes me in. Inviting me to play while pushing me to run.

"I thought you were a murderer!" I hiss through my teeth.

"Murderers knock on doors?"

My mouth gapes at his *duh-dumb-shit* tone even though he makes an excellent point. I slide my gaze down his broad chest, trying to figure out how to answer. I've never seen him dressed so casually before, but the man can rock a pair of jeans and a cotton tee just as well as he can the dress shirt and slacks. I remind myself that he blew me off today, in front of Jonah and Owen. In my damn restaurant. I meet his glare with a scowl that I don't mean.

"What are you doing here?" I chastise myself for sounding so breathy.

"Needed to see you." His words are clipped and guttural.

"You saw me earlier and you had nothing to say." Anger builds within my chest, but so does the urge to strip him naked and pounce. "You expect me to believe you've suddenly found your voice."

"You're mad."

"Ha! I'd have to care to be mad." I'm such a hypocrite. I've been over here crying into my bedding, feeling like a pathetic loser, and now I'm acting as if I couldn't give a flying fuck.

He advances, taking two long strides toward me as I take double that to step back. "Had my share of crazy women today, babe. Not in the mood for back talk."

Did he just…? Crazy *women*?

"I don't give a shit. You show up at my house after completely ignoring me, and you think I'm going to fall back with my legs open?" If that's what he thought, he'd be right. Nausea coils in my stomach.

"Be lyin' if I said I wasn't hoping for that."

Heat flushes through my body, anger mixing with arousal. "You're a fucking asshole!"

He kicks the door shut behind him, and it's only then I realize he's backed me into my house. My breath hits in bursts. He's treating me like a booty call, but I like it. I'm sicker than I thought.

"You tried to take my head off with a baseball bat, and I'm the asshole?"

He keeps advancing, herding me like livestock toward my bedroom.

"I want you to leave." Fuck that was painful to say when my entire body screams the opposite.

Another step, his eyes drop to my chest. "Not what it looks like to me."

I chance a quick look at my boobs. Shit! I could win a wet T-shirt contest without the water. "It's cold." I shrug, but he sees right through my lie, and a wicked grin tugs at his perfect lips.

"Had a fucked-up day." Another step. "Want it to go away." And another. "Only way I know how to do that is between your thighs."

A tremor of arousal races through my body and collects deep in my belly. Even if he turns away after tonight and all I ever did was offer him relief through my body when he needed me, isn't that worth it? I have something to offer him that might keep him coming back. That's not love, but it's like love's second cousin. Close enough to the real thing.

I'm taking my last few steps backward when my legs hit the side of my bed. He steps in close, and the spicy scent of his aftershave teases my body to life. Blood pounds through my veins, in my heart, and between my legs. I want this.

He dips his chin and places a lingering kiss to my forehead. "My doll."

My chest swells with warmth. Needed *and* his.

One finger traces down the side of my face to my jaw and down my neck to my nipple. He swirls it around and chuckles when the flesh grows impossibly tighter. "Cold my ass."

I can't help but giggle. There's a voice deep down that says I'm screwing everything up, that sleeping with him again is ruining any chance I had with a man like Cameron Kyle. Teach others the way you deserve to be treated? I'm teaching him that I'm a slut. Men never date *the slut.*

And yet…

He hooks the hem of my tank and pulls it up. I lift my arms and nearly groan as he removes my top in a slow drag against my body.

"That's my good girl." He tosses the shirt to the side and makes quick work of his own tee.

The light from the TV casts shadows that seem to intensify his muscles. I don't remember him being so big the first time we hooked up, but that may've been due to the fact that we attacked each other, not giving any time for visual appreciation.

I flatten my palm against his chest and push up to his shoulder mesmerized by the feeling of his soft, inked skin before raking my nails down his bicep. My fingers fumble with his belt, but he doesn't intervene. He stands there, hands to his side, allowing me to undress him. His pants open but need a shove to drop from his thighs to pool at his feet. He toes off his shoes and steps out of his pants, standing in nothing but a black pair of boxer briefs.

Dizzy with all that stands before me almost gloriously naked, I sit on the bed. My eyes take the time they need to memorize every inch of his body, knowing that this is most likely the last time I'll get to see him like this.

"Enough." His deep, gravelly voice calls my eyes to his. "Open your legs."

I don't consider anything but total cooperation, and I walk my feet apart against the carpet floor.

He shakes his head. "Wider."

I brace my weight with my hands against the bed behind me and push my legs wider.

A low rumble vibrates from his throat. Approval? "Put your feet flat on the bed."

I scoot back and do just that.

He sucks in a short breath through his teeth. "Fuck yeah. There it is." Now it's his eyes that eat me up from top to bottom. He steps in close and slips his hand into the front of his briefs.

In unison we both moan as he touches himself.

My body melts into the bed. I have the urge to rub my thighs together, but I know closing my legs will displease him. And all I want to do is make him happy.

I lick my lips, my hands clenching against the bed sheets. I'm so anxious to get at him, to touch him and feel the heat of his body as it covers and impales mine. My lungs fight for more oxygen, lightheaded by the visual he's providing.

"Eyes up here."

I force my gaze to his.

"Good girl." He bites his lip as he continues to stroke himself. "Tell me what you want, Eve."

"You." His body, time, attention, affection—everything. God, I sound so desperate.

"Say please."

"You first."

He pulls his hand from between his legs and glares. "I don't beg."

Fear toys with my head, tells me that I'm pushing him away, even though the hunger in his eyes says the opposite.

"Neither do I." I tilt my head, hoping he sees confidence rather than insecurity.

"Fair enough."

A slow smile pulls at my lips.

He steps between my legs and dips two fingers inside my panties. I catch my breath as the euphoria of finally being touched rocks through my body. I arch my back to force him deeper.

His fingers retreat. "Uh-uh."

"You are so frustrating!" I drop back to lie flat on the bed.

"But you like me here, tempting, frustrating. You know it'll end well."

No. It won't. Because ending means he'll be walking out, and I'll be left alone to sort through my regret and second-guess everything.

NINE

CAMERON

I don't remember consciously deciding to come to Eve's. After Ryder and I spent most of the night stocking D'lilah's kitchen and sobering her up, he went out to stay at a friends and I went home to crash.

Sleep never came. Instead, I stared at the ceiling and thought about all the shit D'lilah and I had been through. I tried to pinpoint the day I fell out of love with her and couldn't. Fact is I'm not sure I ever really loved her as much as I loved the idea of her.

That's when the visions of another blonde tore through my mind: Eve with her sharp tongue and innocent good looks, her soft body that soothes without even trying. Antsy, sleep was out of the question, so I took a drive that brought me here, in her bedroom and so fucking ready to lose myself inside her.

I thrust my fingers into her over and over, bringing her close until she's writhing and desperate. The first time we were together was an explosion, a crash between two people racing to the finish line. Tonight I plan to take my time, enjoy and devour her until I'm completely stuffed and stumble out of here exhausted.

"Cameron…"

I close my eyes and drop my head at the sound of my full name from her lips. How can something I've heard my whole life suddenly sound so wanton, so fucking sexy?

Her teeth work her lower lip, and my mouth waters to taste it. I lean over her, making sure to hold most of my weight with my free arm. Her knees lock to my hips, as if she's got me where she wants me and I'll have to fight to get free. But there will be no power struggle. I'm exactly where I want to be.

Running my nose along her cheek, I inhale and take her scent deep into my lungs. My hand works between her legs, and she pulls in a breath.

"Fuckin' beautiful, Eve." I nip at her lower lip.

Her hands rake into my hair, fisting so hard my scalp stings. My breath quickens as she pushes me to the point that my dick throbs. I tilt my head and moan at the first touch of her sweet mouth. She opens to me, her tongue darting out and sliding against mine. Wet, hot, we find our rhythm and drink from each other, savoring. Damn, if I'm not careful, this woman's kiss will destroy me.

I travel from her lips down her jaw and trace her collarbone with my tongue. Every part of her tastes so fucking perfect. Delicate and delicious. For a second, I want to kick my own ass for not taking my time with her the first time, but as my mouth meets her full breast, my thoughts scramble.

"These are…" I kiss the tender underside, one and then the other. *Mine.* "Gorgeous."

"Please, stop teasing." She grinds down on my fingers. "Don't make me wait."

I know this is wrong for so many reasons, but risks have never stopped me before. And now, this close, the taste of her on my tongue, the sound of her soft moans in the air, there's no way this isn't happening.

"We can go fast this time, babe, but I plan on taking my time with you for the rest of the night." Her eyes flash with something I can't name before I dip my head and suck one firm nipple deep into my mouth. She cries out, the sound of audible pleasure ricocheting off the walls. I growl in approval and clamp down with my teeth.

She shoves hard with one heel against the bed and I allow her to roll me to my back but refuse to release her nipple.

"Oh my...I'm gonna..." She rocks her hips against my hand. Faster. Harder.

I reach down and free myself from the confines of my boxer briefs and stroke while I do the same to her.

Hungry for her mouth, I swirl my tongue around to soothe my bite and release her breast. "Mouth."

She complies immediately, dropping her chin to crush her lips to mine. One hard kiss, and then she's gone. What the fuck? I blink and see her standing at the edge of the bed. Her hair is wild around her face, and she shimmies her panties down her legs, never once taking her eyes off mine.

I lift my hips and do the same, kicking my boxer briefs to the floor. She bends to her side table, opening the top drawer, and tosses a square foil packet on my chest.

Condom. In her side table. Jealously mixed with fierce possession flares behind my ribs. I have no right to feel it, but I'm not the kind of man who shares his women, and the idea that Eve has slept with anyone besides me makes me want to rip these fucking walls down and light this bedroom on fire.

Rational? Probably not.

I scoot back on the bed and roll on the condom. She crawls toward me on the king-sized mattress, throwing a sexy sway in her hips.

She straddles my waist and leans down, her lips held just a fraction of an inch from mine. "I'm glad you came over." She grips my dick and guides me in.

I fist the comforter at my sides to avoid grabbing her hips and slamming her down onto me. "Happy you let me in." I tilt my hips, accentuating my meaning.

She smiles against my lips before she opens hers over mine. I cup her jaw then fist her hair and hold her to me. Her hips rock against mine and the pressure builds deep in my gut. Kissing her while I'm buried deep, feeling every roll of her pelvis and her thighs clamped tightly at my hips, I need more.

I break the kiss and flip us to her back without breaking our connection. Her legs immediately wrap around me, locking me in place so tightly it's hard to move.

I rub the outside of her thigh. "Shhh...Love you holding on, babe, but you don't need to worry." I drop a single kiss to her forehead. "I'm not going anywhere."

Her body freezes as her legs convulse around me. "What did you say?"

A small smile tugs at my lips. "I'm not going anywhere."

Her bottom lip quivers and her eyes turn glassy.

Oh fuck. What did I do? "Whoa, Eve." I brush her thick bangs back off her forehead. "Talk to me."

She shakes her head fast, blowing me off.

"Answer me." I pull back and thrust in deep and hard.

She gasps and moans. "Don't stop."

My chin drops, and my eyes slam shut at the desperation in her voice. I have a split second to decide. Stop this and make her talk, or give in to our bodies' demands and talk afterward. She reaches down and grabs my ass with two hands, digging in her fingernails.

Decision made, I thrust into her hard. We'll talk afterward.

Pushing up to brace myself, I throw my weight behind my body. I'm relentless, needy for what this girl does to me. Her body erases my thoughts, helps me to forget all the shit. With her, it's just us. No past, no future, just now.

Over and over again I pound into her tight body until her legs clamp against my sides and she cries out, pulsing around me. I slow down while she rides out the aftershocks of her orgasm and her arms and legs fall limp to the bed.

I pull one of her legs up and rest the back of her knee at my shoulder. She's sated and stares up at me through sex-fogged eyes.

"You okay?"

She bites her lip and nods.

I dip down and press a kiss to her lips. "Arms up, babe."

Her arms go over her head and push against the headboard; every rock of my hips she meets with a push of her own. Tension coils in my lower back, pressure building and on the cusp. I chase down my release and slam into her with a frenzy that shocks even me.

But not Eve. Her face is relaxed. Big blue eyes stare up at me as though I'm not a failure, as if the world starts and ends with me. She looks at me as though I've never failed, fuck, as if I *couldn't* fail.

My orgasm explodes in a blinding euphoria, and I groan into her neck. "Fuckin' A, woman."

Our chests press together, hearts racing, bodies intertwined. Like two people morphing into one, even our breathing is identical. What is that? Something inside clicks, and even though it should be obvious, it feels like nothing I've ever experienced before. Much more than an orgasm, but what?

I crush her body with mine, and she doesn't let me go. For the first time in a lifetime of heavy, I feel...light.

—

EVE

There's no way I'm sleeping. No friggin' way. The sun is coming up, and I haven't closed my eyes once since my last orgasm. Why? Oh gee, let's see. Maybe because I'm still riding the high from four hours of earth-shattering sex? Or huh, could it be the fact that I've never been so sexually satisfied in my life, and yet I'm still hungry for more? No, that's not it either.

I know exactly what it is that's keeping me from drifting off. I don't want to miss a second of what's happening right this very second. The sunrise peeking through the windows confirms my excitement.

Cameron stayed the night. As in *all* night.

Not only did he stay the night, but he's sleeping. As if things couldn't get any better, they do. He has his front to my back, his arm wrapped around my waist so tightly that his hand is tucked between my hip and the bed. Holding me. Holding *on to me* while he sleeps.

He said he wasn't going anywhere and he didn't. After he disposed of the last condom, I fully expected him to get dressed and walk out, but he shocked the shit out of me when he crawled back into bed, pulled me to his body, and with a toss of the sheet to cover us, fell asleep.

The heat of his breath tickles my shoulder, and I pray that the sun doesn't wake him. I pretend that he's mine, that we're in a committed relationship and this is how we wake up every morning. My mind takes me to a fantasy where I'm the priority in his life, so much so that he can't even sleep without having his hands on me. If only I could be that for him.

A low grumble vibrates against my back, and his arm squeezes tighter around my middle. It's hard to breathe, but totally worth it.

"Shit, what time is it?" His deep morning voice against my ear sends goose bumps down my arm, but they quickly fade with the realization of what's about to happen. Fantasy over. He's leaving.

"Early." I can see my phone from here and know it's almost five-thirty in the morning, but I keep that information to myself, hoping it'll buy me some more time.

"Mmm." He groans and stretches flexing his hips into my ass, but never releases his hold on me. "Slept like the dead."

I'm grateful he can't see the sure-to-be-ridiculous embarrassing smile that sweeps across my face. "Me too." No, I didn't, but what I did was better.

He nuzzles my neck. "Smell fucking amazing, Eve."

My tummy flips, and I tilt my head for him, welcoming his lips as he brushes featherlight kisses over my bare skin.

"You work today?" More kisses and the rough drag of his stubble along my shoulder.

"Um…not 'til four." If only he didn't have a million-dollar fighting league to run, we could stay in bed all day. "You?"

He groans and drops to his back, releasing his hold, which I immediately miss. I roll over and prop my head on my palm to watch him scrub his hands over his face and push up into his sex-messed hair.

"Yeah." He turns to look at me, and I fight the urge to bury my face in my hands.

I must look like shit: no makeup, hair all over, bloodshot eyes from no sleep. My cheeks heat and my chin dips to my chest as I shimmy my fingertips through my bangs. "I look like crap."

With a gentle tug on my hair, he gets my attention. "No, you don't." He pushes his fingers through the long strands to my nape. "Have breakfast with me."

My stomach drops and tumbles with excitement. "Breakfast?"

"Yeah." He stares up at me, his eyes the color of chocolate, they're so dark. "You eat breakfast, right?"

"I do." I nod, probably a little too eagerly.

"Right, so let me buy you breakfast. It's the least I can do after you let me barge in on you."

Wait, is he trying to pay me back for last night? Rather than kicking some cash to his whore, he's buying me food. Would I care if that's what this was? Nothing more than a perk after a night of amazing sex?

"Sounds great. Let me get dressed and freshen up."

I move to exit the bed, both excited and frustrated at myself for feeling that way. He hooks me by the neck and pulls me down to his lips. A warm, soft kiss and I'm melting into him, my body jump-starting at the memory of his mouth all over me just hours ago.

"Smell good. Taste even better." He kisses me one last time, and I slide off the bed and head to the bathroom dizzy.

I'm going to do this. His intentions may not be the same as mine, but I can pretend. Booty calls, one-night-stands with the occasional meal, it's more than what I'm used to, and if I can get the occasional night in his arms while he sleeps, it'll all be worth the eventual meat grinder I'll be putting my heart through.

TEN

CAMERON

After Eve disappeared into her bathroom, I threw on my clothes and went to the tiny kitchen in her duplex. This place must've been built in the seventies with its original avocado green gas stove and refrigerator. There's a small table that seats four with mismatching chairs and well-worn lacquer. I don't know Eve that well, but something about the funky way her place is decorated suits her.

The sun is already up over the mountains. June days in Vegas are pretty long, and sunrise comes earlier than I'd like. Especially this morning. It's been so long since I've held a woman in bed. And even on the rare occasion where I have, it's never felt like that. Her soft curves fit against me as if she were built to be there. If I didn't have to go to work, I never would've let her go.

I splash cold water on my face and run wet hands through my hair. Searching for a paper towel, I find what looks like a month's worth of mail stacked on the counter. Patting my face with a dishtowel, I finger through the envelopes. Bills, bills, and…bills. Credit cards, utilities, department stores, and many of them have the telltale past due pink paper flashing through the address window.

I squint and study the typed name on every bill. "Yvette W. Dawson. Huh…" That's quite a grown-up name for such a young and vibrant girl.

My phone vibrates with a new text. I check it and punch out a quick reply to Ryder, telling him I'll see him at dinner. I have three missed calls from D'lilah and no messages. Fuck. I should call her back, but chances are she just needs an ear, and I can give her that later.

"I'm ready!" Eve comes into the kitchen with her head down and her hands in a purse. "Lip gloss…where the hell…"

She says more, but I'm not paying attention. My eyes are glued to her toned legs showcased in cutoff denim shorts and a pair of those sandals women wear that make them six inches taller. She's poured into a tiny tank top that enhances her breasts, and my dick is wide awake and aching to get at her.

"…at Paris, Paris."

"I'm sorry." I clear the rumble from my throat. "What did you say?"

Her eyes narrow. "Where were you just now?"

"Buried between your tits." *Shit!*

Her breath catches. Good job. Think before you speak, asshole. I want to smack my forehead, but I'm fixed on her wide eyes and pink cheeks.

"Sorry, I…" Have brain damage.

"It's okay." She adjusts her purse on her shoulder and flashes a genuine smile. "I appreciate your honesty."

Subject change or we're getting naked. "I'm driving. You ready?"

She nods and grabs her keys to lock up. We're out the door and moving to the truck when I hear her footsteps fade to a stop behind me.

I turn around and she's standing there staring. "What?"

"That's yours?" She points to the pick-up that she's looking at as if we're about to board Cinderella's pumpkin.

"My granddad's, but he can't drive anymore."

Her expression softens. "Oh, I'm sorry."

"Don't be. He's happy it's being used. Now move it. I'm starving."

She steps to the hood and runs her hand along the bright red paint. "What is it?"

"'69 Ford F100."

Her head turns from side to side. "Wow, Raven would shit if she saw this."

"Yeah?" I unlock her door.

She slides in. "She's a sucker for classic cars."

I move to the driver's side and fire up the truck, and the cab fills with the familiar sound of Hank Williams.

"From a Maserati to an old pick up playing country music." She slides on a pair of sunglasses. "I gotta say, very few people shock me anymore."

"Maserati's for work. Fast, efficient—"

"Hot."

I peer at her from the corner of my eye. "If you say so…"

"So the truck is for…?"

"Taking things slow. Lounging."

"Huh." She nods. "Makes perfect sense to me. And the music? You don't strike me as a honky-tonk guy."

"My granddad loved country music, and after I got the truck, it never occurred to me to change the station."

She slides her shoes off and puts her feet on the dashboard. Her soft tan legs on display are tipped with bright pink toenails that are cute as hell and dangerously distracting. "I like it."

"Some of the country shit isn't too bad."

She giggles and allows a few seconds of comfortable silence settle between us. "So where are we going?"

"I know a great dive. Coffee's for shit, but it does the job."

We cruise to the café in silence. I'm sure there's something that needs to be said, but I can't figure out what that is. Fact is I'm not entirely sure I know what the fuck I'm doing. I want to see her again. I don't have the time to invest in dating, but she seems okay with what happened last night. Ideally, I'd like her to be available when I need her. *Does that constitute as an open relationship? Will she fuck other guys? 'Cause there's no way in hell I'm okay with that. Is that something we need to talk about?*

The silence in the cab trails along, and I scrape for a conversation subject.

"Slade tells me you're best friends with his wife?"

"Yeah, Rave and I were inseparable all through high school and after, until she hooked up with Jonah." There's a sadness in her voice.

"You and Slade don't get along?"

Her head whips in my direction. "What? No, I love Jonah. He's a great guy and he saved Raven's life."

I heard all about what happened last September in the mountains. Both Jonah and Raven are lucky to be alive.

Eve is quiet. Thoughtful. Her gaze slides to her window. "I just miss her."

"She the first of your friends to get married?"

"Ha. More like my only friend."

"So you have all your other single friends to hang out with."

She turns to me, her face serious. "Not my only friend to get married, she's my only friend, period."

I don't believe that shit for a second. Eve's funny, sweet when she's not yelling fuck in my face and swinging a baseball bat, and, hell, even then I'd say she's pretty damn cute. "Raven's your only friend?"

She nods and ducks to hide beneath a thick panel of blond hair. "Never needed more than her."

Why do I sense that should be followed up with *until now*? I keep my mouth shut and figure our relationship, whatever it is, doesn't dictate that we know the deep intimate details of our lives.

Once inside the diner that looks like something out of a malt shop in the 50s, we're seated at a small booth in the back. The scents of bacon grease and strong coffee fill my senses. Pressed for time, we take a quick peek at the menu and order.

The waitress brings our coffee, and at the first sip, it's like liquid coal down the back of my throat.

Eve rips open a half a dozen sugar packs and pours in creamer until her cup is almost overflowing. After her first sip, she smacks her lips together and grins. "Not bad."

I chuckle and watch her take another sip.

"Raven and I know a place in town that serves the best coffee. They get the beans raw and then roast them on Sundays in this big roaster thingy; anyway, it's the best coffee in Vegas. I'll take you there next time…" Her eyes get round and her cheeks flush. "Um…not that I expect there to be a next time, or whatever, but…" She gives up and dips her chin to hide behind her coffee cup and bangs.

Next time. Yeah, I want more of Eve. But I'm not sure what goes on between us needs to be made public. There's the age difference, the fact that my heavyweight champion doesn't approve, and the icing on the shit cake is the media. I get photographed out with Eve, and she becomes fair game for the paparazzi. It's not an impossible obstacle for committed couples, but that's not the path we're on.

"Eve, I need to ask you to do me a favor."

"Okay." Her eyebrows drop low over her questioning eyes.

"Whatever's going on between us has been great." I tilt my head and try to get a read on her expression, but she's giving nothing away. "I'd like to do it again sometime." All right, probably not the most romantic proposition, but at least it's out there.

Her expression is blank. Did she not hear me? Shit. Maybe I should've planned that a little better.

———

EVE

He wants to do it again? My stomach growls, so I know I'm not dreaming. He said *again*.

I give myself a mental slap. Must not get my hopes up.

"Okay, is that your favor?" Sex as a favor. I can do that. A sexual favor. My heart drops into my stomach. Oh no, I am his slut.

He runs his long, powerful arm over the back of the booth, showcasing his enormous biceps. "No, but it's probably in our best interest if we don't let Jonah and Raven know what we've been up to." He takes a long pull from his coffee.

My heart sinks lower. "What exactly have we been up to?"

He lifts an eyebrow. "You know what we've been up to."

One-night stands and booty calls. The heat of shame flares at my neck and chest. "Oh."

He wants to keep our sexual escapades a secret. My stomach feels full regardless of how hungry I am. Vince wanted to keep us a secret too. I bought all his lies about why our relationship needed to stay private, but the truth was completely different and almost got us killed.

No one keeps secrets unless they have something to hide, and he wants to hide me. He's ashamed. Or maybe he has a girlfriend. I mean, if I'm going to have to pretend that we barely know each other when Jonah and Raven are around, then I deserve an explanation.

I stir my coffee, unable to look him in the eye. "Mind me asking why?"

He blows out a long breath. "Jonah and Owen didn't seem too pleased with my taking you home the other night."

"So you're afraid of Jonah?"

He glares. "Fuck no. I'm not *afraid* of Jonah. But I'm trying to get the UFL back on two working legs. I can't afford any drama in my business right now." He takes another gulp of coffee.

His job. Even though my chest pinches at his reasoning, I guess it makes sense. After all, I'm just a piece of ass to him, someone he can screw and buy breakfast for. The UFL is his life, and a lot of people rely on him.

God, I feel sick. "Sure, my lips are sealed."

"Appreciate that." His eyes move over my shoulder, and the waitress appears with our breakfast.

She sets a stack of pancakes in front of me that's over six inches tall. I motion to his plate. "Here, have a pancake. I can't eat all these."

He forks one off my plate, and my heart clenches at how we must look to an outsider: like a real couple who orders for each other and shares what's on their plates. The smell of warm dough, butter, and maple syrup makes my mouth water, and I'm suddenly ravenous after our calorie-burning activities from last night.

"Eve Dawson, is that you?"

I drop my fork and whirl around at the familiar voice. "Mrs. Lutich!"

A smile lights her face. "It is you!"

I jump out of my seat, and she wraps me in a warm hug. She's always given the kind of hugs that feel like a warm blanket. The kind I'd want to hang out in it all day.

"I haven't heard from you in over a year." She pulls back and studies my face. "You haven't changed a bit."

"Neither have you." She must age, but I swear her sweet face and perfectly highlighted, shoulder-length blond hair look the same as they did all through high school.

"You stopped emailing me." One eyebrow lifts over her stylish glasses.

"I'm sorry. Things got crazy; life happened."

"Well, that's good. It's supposed to happen." Her eyes move to Cameron, and I remember my manners.

"Oh, I'm sorry." I motion to him, and he slides out of his seat. "Cameron, this is my high-school science teacher, Thia Lutich."

He shakes her hand with a warm smile that, if I'm not mistaken, makes her blush. "Thia, it's nice to meet you."

"Mrs. Lutich, this is my, uh…" What is he exactly? "My friend, Cameron Kyle."

"Mr. Kyle, it's nice to meet you. You look familiar. Did you go to North Mountain High too?"

"No, ma'am. I grew up on the east coast."

"Cameron is the new president and CEO of the Universal Fighting League. You probably recognize him from the newspaper."

His body goes rigid. Was I not supposed to tell anyone that we're friends? I thought he said only Jonah and Raven, but maybe I misunderstood? Dammit.

Mrs. Lutich studies him. "Hmm, I don't follow sports, but maybe you're right. Anyhoo, I don't want to keep you two from your breakfast, but when I realized it was you, I had to say hi."

"Yes, I'm glad you did." I give her one last hug, not wanting to let go. I didn't even realize how much I missed her until now.

After my mom left, my dad blamed me. He was angry and insisted on exercising his anger frequently. It wasn't until Raven and Mrs. Lutich that I realized love was shown in ways that didn't leave marks or make me cry. "I'll write you soon."

"I hope you do." She waves to Cameron and strolls out of the restaurant.

"Nice lady."

I slide back into my seat. "She's amazing. I don't know what I would've done without her."

"Amazing you guys stayed in touch all these years." He forks a piece of sausage into his mouth.

"The first two years after graduation I was religious about keeping in touch." The waitress stops at our table to silently refill our coffee. "Thank you." I rip open three sugars. "This last year I stopped. All the stuff that happened with Raven...I knew she'd want to talk about it and—what?"

Sometime between the waitress refilling our coffee and now, he's managed to put down his fork, lean in, and hit me with a glare that has my nerves prickling. The air between us is practically charged with his anger.

"How old are you?" His words are spoken so low they rumble.

Oh shit, oh shit, oh shit. I think back over what I said and a tremor of panic skates up my spine. "What do you—?"

"Simple question. How old are you?" He emphasizes every word.

I told him I was twenty-four that night at The Blackout. Shit! My teeth rake over my lower lip, and I move pieces of pancake around with my fork.

"Yvette."

My eyes dart to his and my stomach plummets. "What did you call me?"

"Answer me." His jaw pulses.

I set down my fork and pull my purse into my lap like a shield. My heart races, and my stomach twists in knots. There's no getting out of this. I look him in the eyes, and it's almost impossible to see the whites through the tiny slits of his glare. "I'm twenty-one."

"Fuck!" He shoves his plate hard enough that it slams into mine.

"I'm sor—"

He holds up his hand. "You lied to me."

I swallow, my throat dry and achy. "Yes."

"Why?"

"Would you've given me a chance if you knew my real age?"

"Given you a chance?" He leans in. "By that do you mean would I have fucked you?"

I shouldn't be surprised at the callousness of his words, but I hold my breath and nod.

"No."

"That's why I lied."

"Dammit, Eve. I'm seventeen years older than you. We can't do this. You're…Fuck, Eve, you're closer to my son's age than mine."

My breath freezes in my chest. "Son?"

"Yes, I have a seventeen-year-old son."

I swallow hard. "I didn't know that."

"Of course you didn't." He pins me with a scowl. "We haven't exactly spent our time together talking."

Heat rushes to my cheeks. "Right."

He shoves two hands through his hair. "This is my fault. I followed my dick rather than common sense."

"Ouch."

He recoils from his own words, but shakes it off and meets my eyes. "I'm thirty-eight years old."

I shrug. "I don't care."

"Well, I sure as shit do!"

"I messed up, but it's not like I'm a minor. My age is just a number. I've lived on my own since I was fifteen. Paid my bills with my own money since then too."

"Right. You're doing stellar job at that."

What in the hell does that mean? "What did you say?"

"Your bills, Yvette W. Dawson, are not being paid with your own money or any money for that matter."

My entire body heats, and I know my face is bright red with anger and embarrassment. "You fucking snooped through my mail?" This is unbelievable. What else did he go through? "I may have fudged my age by a few years, but I would never go through your mail."

"You can't compare the two. Your lie got us naked. My snooping only pissed you off."

"No. I'm way more than pissed off." I'm furious! More accurately, I'm humiliated, but whatever.

Digging in my purse, I manage to scrape up some crumpled dollars and a handful of coins. "I should've known: rich good-looking guy like you, who's all growly and controlling in bed, going through my shit. You know what?" I point at his face. "This is why I should've stayed gay." I drop money on the table, sending change rolling off and bouncing on the floor. Good. He can pick them up. "I'm outta here."

He grips my wrist. "Eve, sit."

"No way, stalker." As the words fly from my lips my insides are screaming that I'm going to push him away. He'd walk away sooner or later. Why not give him a shove off? Fuck, even that feels like a knife to the chest.

"Hardly a stalker, doll." His voice takes on a warm tone, and his thumb rubs circles on the inside of my wrist. "Let me explain. Your mail was lyin' out on the kitchen counter."

It's as if there's a purr underscoring his words. My knees go wobbly, and I sit to avoid falling. Where am I gonna go anyway? We're at least fifteen miles from my house, and whatever money I had before I dropped it on the table isn't enough to get me home.

"I'm still mad at you."

His expression relaxes a fraction of *not at all.* "Feeling's mutual."

I glare, and for some reason it releases the tension in his jaw. Not a smile by most standards, but closest thing I've seen on the man. Minutes ago he was ripping into me about my age, and now he's calm. Bi-polar? Not that I'd be surprised. He's way too hot to be mentally stable. Now that we've just thrown my age, his son, and his snooping into the mix, there's no way we'll hook up again.

And another one walks away.

—

CAMERON

Huh? That's it? I expected tears. D'lilah always busts out with the waterworks when we fight, but not Eve. I need to break things off with her. Shit went from simple to complicated, and complications are something I don't need. But even as the words "this is over" sit on the tip of my tongue, I can't force them out.

I like this woman. She's young, clearly has some things to learn about budgeting her money, and naïve about who she takes drinks from, but she's not immature. It's in her eyes: the hardened way she looks at me when I expect her to be vulnerable. Like now.

Women are emotional, crazed with it, and after treating this woman like a slam piece, I just blew her off because of her age and gave her shit about being in debt. I'm no genius, but I think that qualifies me for the Dickhead World Records.

After forcing her to take back the money she tossed on the table, I pay the bill and we're back in the truck. She's quiet, which is good because it gives me time to figure out how the hell I'm going to handle breaking things off. I can't continue to sleep with a twenty-one-year-old girl. Can I?

My phone vibrates in my pocket. I pull it out to see Ryder calling.

"Ry, what's up, man?"

Throat clearing. "It's me."

"D'lilah?" What the hell? "Where's Ryder?"

"Oh, he's here. Um…I'm at your place. You weren't answering my calls last night and I worried, so I drove—"

"You drove?" Drunk.

"Yeah, and when I got here, no one was home. I used the hide-a-key and stayed on the couch. Ry just showed up. My phone died, so he let me call you from his."

I guess it's good that she didn't try to drive home after she realized we weren't there. "Everything okay?"

"Yeah…I was upset last night. After you guys left, I got sad and I was thinking about…" Her voice cracks. "Her birthday is coming up, and I just miss her so much."

"Hang tight. I'm on my way." If she could just hold it together until I get home so Ryder doesn't have to coddle his own mother…

"Where were you last night, Cam? I needed you." More crying.

"We'll talk when I get home." I pull up to Eve's duplex.

"But—"

I press End, exhale hard, and turn to say something to Eve that'll smooth over our conversation at breakfast, but the look on her face freezes the words in my throat.

Her eyes are wide, face pale, lips parted and staring right at me.

"Eve?"

She blinks rapidly, her lips close, and she grabs her purse. "I gotta go."

Before I can say goodbye, she's out of the truck and halfway to her front door. At a slow crawl, realization filters in. My phone call from D'lilah. I try to think about what Eve might've heard that upset her. Talking to another woman after we spent the night together was probably enough.

I move to chase after her and explain, but maybe this is for the best. It's not smart for us to continue seeing each other. There are a thousand reasons why I need to stay away, but only one reason why I don't want to. I can't get enough of her. I suppose it's better that she hate me. Because if she doesn't lock me out, there's no way I'll be strong enough to leave her alone.

ELEVEN

EVE

"Is yellow the only unisex color out there? Because I'm not gonna lie." I point to the pukey fabric swatch. "That looks like barf."

Raven and I have been sitting at her dining room table, going through catalogs and flipping through fabric and paint samples for the last two hours. I'm trying to be helpful, but not seeing or hearing from Cameron in almost a month is starting to affect my mood.

He did say there'd be a next time. I guess I'd hoped it would be sooner than later. A tiny voice in my head laughs that I'd give him another chance after he took a call from another woman after spending the night with me. I was pissed for a day, but when he didn't come knocking the next week or the following two, I pretty much forgave him. That's me, Doormat Dawson.

Raven holds the fabric up to the light, and her teeth tug her lower lip. "Well, crap." Her hands drop back to the table, and her head quickly follows. "Ugh...this is hell."

"Oh don't be so dramatic." I flip through a few pages of a catalog when I feel her eyes on me. I turn to find her scowling. "What?"

"Dramatic? I was about to decorate my baby's room in the color of puke. What's wrong with me? The baby isn't even born yet"—she throws her arms out to her sides—"and already I'm a terrible mother." Her face twists in disgust, and her eyes get glossy.

Okaaay. What the hell? "That's it. Who are you and what've you done with my best friend?"

Her lips tick with what might be a smile, and she takes a long breath. "Sorry, it's just…" She shakes her head. "Forget it."

"Oh, no, ya don't." I twist my stool to face her. "You already opened the door. There's no going back now. Spill."

Resting her elbows on the bar, she shoves both hands into her hair. "I don't know what I'm doing. All I ever wanted was a family, and now that I'm finally getting one, I'm terrified I'll end up screwing it up. I don't know how to be a mom."

"Who does? I mean I think the most important part is you love your kid." I shrug and flip a few pages of the Pottery Barn Kids catalog. "You already have that, so the rest is just details."

"You're probably right. Gosh, I feel like I'm going crazy. Jonah's being so stubborn, and my emotions are all over the place."

"Stubborn about what?"

She pushes back and puts both hands on her belly. "Don't get me wrong. I love Jonah, and he's so protective, which is awesome, ya know?"

"But…?"

Another deep breath. "He took away the Nova."

"What?" He took away her car? What? Like she's a kid who's been grounded? "Why?"

She shakes her head. "He's worried about the baby and me. I totally understand. I mean he lost his dad in a car accident, and the Nova doesn't have airbags and only has lap belts."

"So what? You're stuck at home and work with no car? That's bullshit, Rave!"

Her eyes widen and she shakes her head. "Oh no, I'm driving his truck, and he takes the Impala or the Camaro."

"But that Nova is like…well, it's your first baby."

"Exactly. And we're coming up on a year since…" Her voice is soft and heavy with emotion. "So much has happened, and I don't know. The Nova was the only thing I ever did that I'm truly proud of. Just driving it and listening to music, it was freedom to me."

This all makes sense now. Jonah was her savior, swooped in, took her from her hell, and saved her from a life worse than death. But not everything about her life was horrible before him. She loved her independence, and that car signifies all she accomplished on her own, gave her a sense of purpose when she had none. I love that Jonah wants her safe, but it's just like a man to disguise control in the name of protection.

"You still have the keys, right?"

She nods and sniffs back tears. "Yeah, but I promised Jonah I wouldn't drive it. But, Eve"—she turns to me—"you know he's never going to let me drive that car again. He'll never let me take the baby in it." Her voice cracks. "God, I'm sorry. I must sound like such a whiner."

"Not at all." I push her hair off her shoulder and tuck it behind her ear. "I totally get it, but I say fuck it, take the car out for a spin if you need to, just around the block."

"He'd be so pissed."

"Not if he never found out."

She directs a tiny smile at me. "Yeah, I guess you're right."

"So…" I push a color swatch toward her. "Lavender. Not pukey and unisex. If it's a boy you can add chocolate brown, a girl you can add pink or white."

She picks it up for a closer look and then nods. "It's perfect."

We make sandwiches for lunch, and Layla stops by to give her color suggestions. She's been in a funk lately after her friend Mac disappeared. The cops investigated and said because she apparently left a good-bye note and there was no sign of foul play they had to conclude that she left because she wanted to, but Layla swears something's wrong. She cries all the time. I blame the pregnancy hormones.

"She's right." Layla squints and purses her lips. "It's barfy. Although, in the right light, it looks a little like the color of a Twinkie."

"Exactly." I point to Layla. "Twinkie vomit."

"Mmm…a Twinkie sounds so good right now." Raven rubs her pregnant belly.

Layla gets a faraway look in her eyes. "Yeah, it does."

I look back and forth between them as they sit in their own little junk food fantasies. "Hello?" I snap my fingers and get their attention. "Jeez, you two sound like stoners."

"Mmm…munchies." Raven's smiling, and from the look in her eye, I'd guess she's imagining every piece of furniture in this place is some form of snack cake.

"You know what? Forget it. I say go blue. Just commit. You know Jonah's got some seriously testosterone-dominated sperm. It's a safe bet." I'm so exhausted with this conversation. I never knew pregnant women could be so neurotic.

"That's what I've been telling her." Jonah lopes into the kitchen and ruffles my hair as he passes by on his way to Raven.

"Why don't you guys just find out the sex? Save yourselves from the unisex color debacle," Layla says.

"I saw the ultrasound." Two dimples carve into Jonah's cheeks. "We're having a boy."

"That was the baby's umbilical cord." Raven shakes her head.

"Hey, I know what I saw, baby." He pushes his wife's hair to the side and kisses her neck.

The front door opens, and Mason comes strolling in wearing workout shorts and a T-shirt with the sleeves cut off. "What's up, ladies? Whoa—you workin' on girl shit in here?" He eyes the scattered decorating paraphernalia.

"Trying. What do you think, Mase?" I flip him the piece of fabric, and he snags it out of the air. "What does this color remind you of?"

He squints at it then tosses it back to me. "Barf."

I turn wide eyes to Raven, eyebrows up. "My job here"—I bow from the waist down—"is done."

"Baywatch and I are going to play some b-ball." Jonah kisses Raven's cheek. "Oh, who's going to the Fourth of July deal this weekend?"

Mason nods and Layla raises her hand then drops it.

Jonah eyes me. "Eve, you going?"

"Why would I go? I don't even know what you're talking about."

"It's a UFL deal. You should come."

Butterflies explode in my stomach. UFL party? That means there's a chance that Cameron will be there. I want to go, any excuse to accidently run into him on purpose, but what if he's with that other girl? I don't think I can handle being in the same room with him while he acts as if we're total strangers.

"Nah, I'm cool." I run my sweaty palms over my thighs. "Besides, it's a work thing, so—"

"Come with me."

Everyone in the room turns to Mason, who's standing casually with his arms crossed over his chest, accentuating his very swollen and very tan arms. He meets my eyes and gives me a half smile that's really sweet, but doesn't stir my blood like Cameron's predatory scowl.

"Mase, you don't have to—"

"I've been hitting on you for-fuckin'-ever, trying to be creative, and none of that shit worked. Now I'm just straight up asking. Go out with me."

Layla, Raven, and Jonah must be as shocked as I am as they've all gone completely silent.

Warmth crawls into my cheeks, but I push it back. God, he's such a great guy. He has been throwing out cheesy lines since I met him, and although he makes me laugh, he's not my type. My type is a man who treats me like dog shit, apparently.

The words filter through my head and leave a bitter taste in my mouth. When was the last time I gave a nice guy a chance? I don't think I ever have. And Mason is gorgeous in a beach-boy kind of way, all sun-bleached hair and white smile. If Cameron does show up at the party with another girl, at least I won't feel like a total jackass if I'm there with Mason. That's if he shows up at all.

"Sure, I'll go with you."

His expression goes slack. "No shit?"

I shrug. "Why not?"

"Rad." He nods a few times, a slow smile spreading across his face. "I'll pick you up."

"Come on, Baywatch." Jonah walks by and smacks him on the back of the head.

"I'll call you." He winks before he turns to follow Jonah outside.

"You're going out with a guy." Raven pins me with a knowing glare. "You're so not gay."

If she had any idea what my mind and my body have been up to...

"Mason's cute, but I didn't know he had the power to turn a gay woman straight." Layla pulls at her lower lip, hiding the smile that her eyes can't.

"Real funny." What have I done? Besides leading Mason on and potentially pissing off the CEO of the UFL. Yeah right, like he cares.

I've never been anything more to him than a booty call. If he is at this party, I bet he won't spend a single second worrying about my being there with Mason. And I'll spend the entire night wishing Mason was him.

Fucking great.

My phone rings in my purse on the table. "Oh, I better get that." I'm the on-call manager tonight, and it would be my luck to get called in for something stupid like them running out of toilet paper. "Hello?"

"Yvette."

My chest gets heavy and I swallow hard. "Hey, what's up?" I hold up one finger to Raven and Layla and mouth "I'll be right back" to avoid them overhearing our conversation.

"Did you miss a deposit?"

I hurry to the back door and step outside. "No, Dad. I've never missed a deposit. You know that." My shoulders slump and I close my eyes, knowing what's coming.

"It didn't come through, honey. I swear. I need you to put more in."

Dammit. He must've gambled, drank it, or both. "I don't have any more until payday."

"How's that possible? You've gotta eat, right?" He chuckles.

"Dad, you're asking for my grocery money?"

"You've got rich friends, Yvette. I have no one. And you promised you'd help me out when I need it. I need it."

This is so fucked up. My stomach roils, and I muster up the courage to say no. "I put the money in your account. It's not my fault you ran out." I hold my breath, close my eyes, break out in a sweat, and wait.

"Always so selfish…"

Here it comes.

"Just like your mother. She should've listened to me when I told her to abort you, but the selfish bitch had you anyway."

Every word chips away at my soul, destroying what little confidence I'd managed to build since our last call.

"...gave you life, and you repay me with nothing. Every breath you take on this earth you owe to me."

I don't want to believe him, but I can't think of a reason to refute him. My head hangs low between my shoulders.

"...you spend all your money on food to feed your fat ass..."

He's wrong. Right? My chin trembles.

"...I never loved you..."

I cringe and tears spring to my eyes.

"...horrible daughter..."

He's right. My mom left when I was seven because I was too much of a burden, and he was left to raise me alone. I do owe him.

"...never hear from me again, you selfish bitch."

My heart leaps in my chest. "Dad, wait!" *Don't leave me.*

He's silent.

"If you can give me a few days, maybe I can scrape something up. It won't be much, but I'll try."

"I'll come by to pick it up."

"Wait, Dad—"

The phone disconnects. Shit.

I take a moment to pull myself together before going back inside. Just like every other time I give in to my Dad's demands, I feel sick. Used. Dirty. But the little girl in me rejoices that I've managed to keep him around. It's only money, right?

As long as I have something he needs, he'll never walk away.

TWELVE

CAMERON

Things are coming together. For the first time since I took this position, the UFL doesn't look like a sloppy mess. The guys aren't killing each other, they're fired up and training harder to get on the big-card fights, and I'm seeing a revival of UFL pride within the organization.

With the holiday weekend approaching and the party on Friday to kick it all off, I'm feeling damn good about the progress I've made.

I'm headed to the weight room for a workout before I go home when I see our intern, Killian. He's a great kid, and from what I've seen, Blake and the guys are going to turn him into an exceptional fighter. At seventeen, Killian's managed to pick up on some basic holds and submission techniques. Which is why seeing him on all fours, his hand braced on his belly, gets my attention.

"Killer, what's up?" I move toward him, and he pushes up to his knees, his face red. "What the hell happened to you?"

"Nothin', Mr. Kyle. Just some of the...new guys playin'... around." He's sucking in air, but trying to act unaffected.

I admire that.

"Don't lie to me, kid." He's obviously had his helping of ass kickings and cover ups throughout his life, but I won't tolerate being lied to.

His shoulders drop along with his chin. I put out my hand to help him up, but he shakes off my offer and pushes to standing. He's taking deeper breaths and looks me in the eyes. "Reece and his boys were just razzing me."

"They put their hands on you?" Adrenaline rockets through my veins. This isn't the first time I've had issues with that punk Reece. Razzing is one thing, but bullying and assault is another.

"No, sir." He doesn't meet my eyes.

"You lyin'?"

"No, sir."

"Killer, I'll give you one more chance to tell me the truth."

"I...There were too many of them, or I think I could've taken 'em." He's practically whispering. "Pretty sure they were just messin' with me."

Fuck. I get what's happening. This kid wants respect, he's looking to be accepted into the fold for being a man, and that'll never happen if he's ratting out the punks to the boss.

"Who're you training with?"

"Blake, sometimes Rex and Caleb." He bends over and picks his glasses up off the ground. When he puts them on, one lens is shattered. "Damn, that sucks." He takes them off and studies them with a fire brewing behind his eyes.

Killian's the kind of kid who'll end up being exceptional given he's shown some direction, but he also has that quiet crazy look that given the wrong direction could land his ass in prison.

"I'll pay for new lenses." Or I'm taking it out of Reece's paycheck, that little fuck. "If you're interested in earning some cash, I'd be happy to upgrade you from intern to employee." I see big things happening with Killer, and being an official employee of the UFL should earn him more respect from the guys.

His eyes grow wide, and the battle raging behind them fades. "I...I mean..." A broad smile spreads across his face.

"Yeah, uh, yes. Sir, yes. Please." He shakes my hand. "Thank you."

"No problem. When summer break is over, we'll move you back to part-time, but you'll remain on the payroll. Who're you training with?"

His eyebrows pinch together. "Um, Blake. You already asked me that, sir."

Shit. I did? "Right, well, I'll talk to the guys you've been training with about getting more sparring in, getting you ready."

"Ready for what?"

"Ready for whatever you decide to do after graduation."

His entire face lights up, and that slump in his shoulders is gone. "Thank you, Mr. Kyle."

I nod and move to continue toward the weight room.

"Are the rumors true?"

I stop and turn. "Rumors of what?"

"You being challenged to return to the octagon by Rusty Faulkner?"

I should've known having that conversation in the lobby would come back to screw me, but I've got nothing to hide. "It's true."

"They're saying he's wants to put you out of commission. Permanently."

They? "Not sure who you've been talking to—"

"It's all over the Internet. His camp, even Faulkner himself, they're posting on all the MMA sites. Says all it'll take is one hit."

That media-hungry motherfucker. He's pitting me against the public before I've even officially accepted his challenge.

"Faulkner's a no-good piece of shit. He'll say anything to get me riled."

Killer rubs the back of his neck, his eyes fixed on everything but me. "But…it's true, right? One more concussion could be lights out. You quit because the doctors said you were unfit to fight."

Not exactly accurate, but that's the story I've been selling since the day Rosie drowned. "That's about right. But times have changed. I'm meeting with the board to see if they'd be supportive of me going back into the octagon. I think my coming out of retirement could be a big ticket." I shrug. "Can't see why they'd say no."

"That would be so fucking cool. I saw footage of your fight in '98 against Kiro Tumbo, and honestly, the only way Faulkner stands a chance is if he can avoid your takedown. If he can't, and we know he can't, it'll be over by submission, first round."

I can't fuckin' believe this kid. "You're seventeen."

"Yeah."

"You were one year old in 1998."

"Uh-huh."

Amazing. "You see any of Faulkner's old fight footage?"

"I have. It's unimpressive, you know, all the showboating he does."

I really like this kid. "Think about what you want to do after graduation."

I give him a fist bump, head to the weight room, and smile when I hear his whispered "fuck yeah" from behind me. He's a good kid, on the path to becoming a good man, as long those fuckin' bullies leave him alone.

Speaking of bullies, Faulkner's clearly trying to piss me off enough so that I'll fight him. Not that he even has to try.

The more I think about it, the more I want to beat his ass in the octagon.

EVE

As if dressing for a date isn't hard enough, but dressing for the guy who *isn't* the guy taking you out is awkward. I don't want to lead Mason on by making him think I went to all this work for him, but it's been so long since I've seen Cameron I want to make an impression.

It's stupid. Cruel even. I'm setting myself up to be hurt again, but that doesn't stop me from putting together the most kick-ass Fourth of July outfit ever. If he does show up to this party with a girl on his arm, I want him to see me at my best. I want to wear an outfit that makes him forget about our age difference, forget that I lied, and most importantly, I want him to ache to be close to me again.

Pulling some lip gloss and gum from my everyday purse and into my red clutch, I see headlights pull into my driveway. My stomach flutters. Don't freak out. There's a good chance Cameron won't be there tonight.

"I'm such a bitch." Here I'm getting excited over a guy who wants nothing to do with me when a very sweet guy who's interested is hurrying to my door. "Karma is going to kick my ass for this one."

I open the door just as he arrives. "Hey, Mase."

He stills, and his eyes move up from my feet to my hair. "Whoa, Eve, you're like...hot."

Sigh. There's a part of me that would've loved for that compliment to light some kind of fire, but it falls flat. "Thanks, you look...really handsome."

Jeans that fit just right, blue and red plaid short-sleeved collared shirt, blond shaggy hair, he's like Malibu MMA Ken.

"You ready?" He jerks his head to his waiting Tundra that's the color of the ocean.

I lock up and follow him to the passenger side door, which he opens for me. I should fall for him. I should.

He fires up the engine, and "Don't Push" by Sublime blares through the speakers. He turns it down. "You feel like grabbing a bite to eat?"

"I thought this shindig was being catered."

He shrugs and turns out onto the main road. "It is. I'm just trying to get some alone time with you." A slight twist and he flashes me a half smile that is really, really cute.

"You're so honest."

"And that surprises you." His expression loses its humor.

"I'm a single woman, Mase. This isn't my first rodeo."

"Ex do a number on you, then?" The muscle in his jaw ticks.

God, he's really so damn sweet.

"You could say that."

He doesn't respond, and we travel the rest of the way to the party in silence. For a moment, I consider what my life would be like with a guy like Mason. We've hung out a few times in a group, and I've always enjoyed his company. He's funny enough, definitely hot, and safe. If I could trick myself somehow, convince myself that he's what I want, what I need, I would.

The truck lurches to a stop in a fancy neighborhood, the street lined with cars.

"Hang tight." Mason jumps out of the driver's seat and hurries around the front of the truck to open my door.

Guilt coils in my chest, but I push it back and paint on my most appreciative smile. "Thanks, Mase."

"My pleasure, beautiful."

I fight the urge to roll my eyes at his obvious schmoozing. Funny, when Cameron calls me beautiful, I melt into a puddle of goo.

He hits the fob and leads me down the sidewalk. It's seven o'clockish and warm since we still have a couple hours before sunset. I hope we don't have to hoof it too much longer. Showing up sweaty won't do anything for my look.

I notice Jonah's truck and Blake's Rubicon parked ahead when Mason leads me with his hand on my lower back to turn up a long walkway to a killer house. It's not what I'd expect in this posh neighborhood. Dwarfed by its multi-leveled neighbors, this house is modern and sleek. It's all brick and glass with exposed metal beams. The landscaping is simple with an almost Asian-prayer-garden flare. Trickling water leads to a pond that's surrounded by those cool-looking green stick bushes. Dark and airy, peaceful simplicity, in a word… masculine.

"This place is incredible. Does it belong to one of the new guys?" I've heard that a few of the new fighters have had pretty successful careers and whoever owns this place is loaded.

We reach the enormous wood door, and Mason ignores knocking to push right inside. The sound of music, voices, and laughter filters out from the depths of the house.

"Pretty sick pad, huh?" Mason shuts the door and to my surprise grabs my hand to lead me further inside. "It's Cam's place."

Oh shit.

THIRTEEN

CAMERON

This party was a good idea. I remind myself to thank Layla again for setting this all up. The smell of fried chicken, mac-n-cheese, and baked beans makes my mouth water. Going with an all-American menu was fuckin' brilliant. As soon as the sun goes down, the firework show should begin. It's being put on by the country club, who also does its own party for the Fourth, but my generous financial contribution had them setting up the pyrotechnics with a perfect view from my backyard.

"Sanderson," I call out to Mike Sanderson, a member of the UFL board as he and a woman I'm assuming is his wife, saunter out into the backyard. He makes his way to me, hand out, and smiles. "Glad you could make it."

"You went all out." He grabs my hand in a firm shake and introduces me to his wife before sending her to the bar for drinks. "You thought any more about Faulkner's challenge?"

"I have." Been planning for this fight for fourteen years. "Just waiting on the approval from the board."

"We've met. Discussed." He shrugs and swings his gaze in a slow rake around the backyard before coming back to our conversation. "It'd be a Supercard."

"It would. Set up the prelims with rivals. Promote the fuck out of it. We're talkin' record-breaking numbers. Huge money."

"Rival Bout. I like it." His wife comes back with two drinks, hands one off to him, and then waves to another woman she recognizes and excuses herself.

"The rest of the board see things like we do?"

"They're…less convinced. Fact is we need you. With your medical history, combined with the possibility of concussion, we need to ask ourselves if one fight is worth the possibility of losing a great CEO."

"Gotta get hit hard enough for that to happen, Sanderson. He won't get near me."

"I appreciate your confidence, but you can't guarantee—"

"I can. Give me the fight. I'll prove it."

He glares and his lips pull up on the sides. "Stubborn son of a bitch."

"I want that fight." I laugh and throw back the last of my beer when a flash of blond catches my eye.

Is that…? My blood pounds through my veins. The mingling crowd obscures my view, until she emerges. Holy fuck. It's Eve.

She's here, at my house, and looks better than my fantasies have recalled. Her straight blond hair falls around her bare shoulders; I know those thick bangs, even with her sunglasses on, frame the biggest pair of sky-blue eyes. It looks like she was poured into a blue and white dress that seems as if it's made out of elastic bandages. Her long legs are tipped with bright red heels that beg to mark a man's back. Fucking gorgeous.

"…meeting next week. We should—"

"Give me a minute?" I hold my hand up to Sanderson. "I need to go say hi to…"

What. The. Fuck.

She's coming this way. But she's not alone. My teeth clench and my fists get tight. She's with Mason, and not just accompanying him. She's holding his motherfucking hand.

"Cam, man. Great party." Mason's talking to me. I know he is, but I don't pay him even a second of my attention as my eyes are firmly set on Eve.

Mason drops her hand only to throw his entire arm over her shoulder to hug her to his side. "You remember Eve from The Blackout."

She pushes her sunglasses up on her head and fuck me... those eyes. "Hey, yeah. Nice to see you again."

Sanderson clears his throat at my side.

"Mike Sanderson, Mason Mahoney and Eve Dawson." I still haven't stopped looking at her, and just like the first night, the more I stare, the harder it is to look away.

Mason and Mike talk about something, but it's white noise compared to the thump of my pulse in my ears. I knew I missed her, wanted to show up at her house a dozen different times, but I held back, knowing it was best for us both to end things. But now, now I'm gearing to rip Mason's arm from his body if he doesn't fucking drop it from her. He must feel her soft hair against his arm, her even softer body pressed to his ribs.

"What are you doing here, Eve?" The rumble in my chest makes it more of a growl than comprehendible words.

She pins me with a glare that goes straight to my dick, and fuck if I don't want to provoke her into a fight.

"She's with me, Cam." There's a smile in Mason's voice.

I turn my frustration on him. "Is she?"

"Cameron." Eve's voice is stern, but even still the way she says my name makes me want to pull her head back and devour her mouth. My fingers itch to tangle in all that long hair. I flex my hands. *Think before you act.*

"Yep, lucky me, huh?" His fucking pretty-boy ass smiles even bigger. "I'm gonna take my girl to get a drink, and..."

Eve looks up at Mason, her eyes huge and her jaw loose on its hinges. She doesn't seem to like being called his girl. A trickle of satisfaction tempers my anger.

We exchange a few mumbled words and a head nod before he guides her, his arm still slung over her shoulders, to the bar. I can't help but watch the entire thing unfold, my eyes glued to their connection.

What was she thinking showing up to my house on the arm of one of my fighters? My guess is she's trying to make me jealous, but that seems so beneath her. She's young, sure, but from what little I know of her, she's above this petty shit.

I excuse myself to go inside, making a quick run to my office. My stash of high-end liquor is locked up there. I pour three fingers of Remy XO into a crystal tumbler and drop into my leather club chair.

What's a man supposed to do when tempted with a woman like Yvette Dawson? Young, gorgeous, and every single thing I need to stay away from.

———

EVE

I've had too much to drink. I told myself that I shouldn't let my nerves dictate how thirsty I got, but knowing that Cameron is within range, feeling his eyes on me, I just kept throwing the drinks back.

Luckily the backyard misters are maintaining a pretty decent evening temperature. I scouted out a little bistro table and chairs away from the bulk of the party so I can lounge in the fresh air and try to clear my head.

As nice as Mason has been tonight, it's pretty obvious he thinks my acceptance of this date *means* something. Referring to me as his girl in front of Cameron would've gotten him an elbow to the ribs if it weren't for the obvious jealousy painted all over the hotshot UFL CEO's face. But the knowledge that Cameron might still be interested in me, even now that he knows how old I am, has been doing a number on my heart all night.

Why can't we just be honest with each other? Yeah, maybe we're not the perfect match, but we're clearly attracted to one another, have explosive chemistry when we're naked, and don't find the other insanely annoying. That's more than most couples can say.

I drop my head back and close my eyes. It's almost completely dark. As soon as the fireworks are finished, I'll hit Mason up for a ride home, explaining that I've had too much to drink, which isn't a lie, but it's not really the problem either.

"What are you doing here?"

I jerk upright, searching the dark corner where the voice came from. "Cameron?"

He takes a few steps out of the shadows. His eyes drill holes in me. He looks mad. No, not mad. Furious. "Answer me."

Okay, maybe I was wrong about him having feelings. At least, not the good kind.

"Mason invited me."

"Why did you come?" His voice is so deep, demanding, nothing like Mason's sweet cajoling tone.

My body responds immediately. Heart pounding, skin warming, womb tingling. "Had nothing else to do."

He tilts his head, studying me. "Try again."

"It's true." I shrug and lean back with a slow cross of my bare legs. Hold on! I'm being seductive. I'm trying to seduce him?

"You expect me to believe that your coming here tonight has nothing to do with me."

"I don't care what you believe, but yeah, that's the truth."

A wounded expression crosses his features before he reins it in. "You and Mason."

I should tell him it's none of his business. Or hell yeah, me and Mason, what're you going to do about it, asshole. "No."

"No?"

I shake my head.

"He know that?"

The rough edge of his voice makes my toes curl. "He's not really in tune to my subtle hints."

A low growl rumbles in his throat. "I'll interpret."

God, this is so confusing. It's as if he's jealous, but why? "I haven't heard from you since the night you showed up at my place to get me naked. Now you want a say in who I hang out with?"

His hand pushes through his hair, which looks almost black in the dim light, and he groans. "Fair enough." He crosses to me and drops down on the seat next to mine. Elbows on his knees, he scrubs his face with his hands. "Fuck."

"I uh...I like your house." Generic, safe, and totally lame subject change.

He turns his head, and there's a slight tilt to his lips that look far from amused. Sexy hair, thick jaw, full lips, and eyes that even when they're smiling look as if they want to devour me.

My heart pounds. This is so wrong. I'm around Cameron for ten seconds, and I'm visualizing all the things I'd do to him if we were alone, but Mason only makes me want to punch him in the arm and give him a wedgie for being obnoxiously sweet.

The silence between us is thick with tension. "The party was a good idea." I motion to the crowd that is now gathering outside for the fireworks. "Don't think Gibbs ever did anything like this for his fighters."

I feel his eyes on me, and when I turn, I almost recoil at the intensity behind his stare. "Can you stop acting like we're two old friends shooting the shit when you know good and fucking well you're thinking the same thing I am."

My mouth falls open and I force it shut, only to have it drop open again.

"I've had my hands and my mouth all over every inch of that gorgeous body, doll. You think I can't read you? Know what you're thinking about right now?"

I swallow hard. "What am I thinking about?"

"Same thing I am." His eyes move over my body in a slow caress, and he leans in close. "Us naked, our bodies tangled together sweat-soaked from fuckin—"

"Dad!"

My head jerks toward the direction of the voice, heart pounding, and body jacked the hell up from what Cameron was describing. *Pull it together, Eve.*

A boy, no not a boy, a man but one who just recently made the transition, is headed toward us. He's tall. My guess is he's close to six foot, and he looks like a lanky, lighter shade of Cameron.

"Oh my God." I cover my mouth when realization sinks in. This has to be his son.

The kid approaches, his blond hair sticking out all over like a rock star, and he's wearing a pair of black skinny jeans and a faded black concert tee that looks one size too small. It's not the kind of style I'd expect from an offspring of Cameron's, but this kid rocks the look.

"Dude, we've got a problem." He looks at me and then back to Cameron with questioning eyes.

Cameron groans. "Ryder, this is Eve." He meets my eyes in a meaningful and what seems like apologetic way. "Eve, my son. Ryder."

I shake the kid's hand. "Nice to meet you."

"Yeah, you too." He flashes a knockout smile, and I'm not surprised to see he looks even more like his dad than I thought. "You must be the vamp."

Vamp?

"Ry." The nickname comes out as a warning, but Ryder chuckles.

"I don't mean to interrupt, but um…Dad, can you come here for a second?"

"You can talk in front of Eve," Cameron says.

Warmth explodes in my chest. Two one-night stands and a breakfast and he's comfortable with me being witness to a conversation he's going to have with his son? I refuse to let my heart go to all the places it wants to and decide Cameron knows his son best and whatever he has to say is most likely not a big deal.

Ryder's eyes shift between Cameron and me, and he decides with a shrug. "Okay." He looks at Cameron. "Mom's here."

I suck in a breath.

"Fuck!" Cameron jumps up from his seat and storms off without saying goodbye. No see ya later. No I'll be right back. Just gets up and takes off to go see his ex-wife.

Ryder gives me a halfhearted smile as if he's taken notice of his dad's rude departure. "Nice meeting you, Eve."

"You too." My response is soft, but it doesn't matter. By the time the last word is out of my mouth, he's gone anyway.

Talk about emotional whiplash. One minute he's talking about us, and then *poof!* he takes off to be with his ex. This shouldn't be surprising. It's what I expect and probably deserve. My head tumbles with questions, feelings, and emotions I can't even name. I rub my temples, trying to make it all stop and only manage to give myself a headache.

This was a mistake. A huge one.

Boom! The sound of fireworks and the follow up of collective ooh's and ah's fill my ears. I inch closer to the crowd for a better look. One after the other, fireworks launch into the sky and light up the crowd of faces in every color of the rainbow. I find Mason standing with Blake and Layla, but I stay where I am, afraid of getting too close and having him touch me in some way.

God, I'm a royal bitch.

Mother Nature alerts me to the fact that I need to make a stop before we go. Now's probably a good time.

I wander through the living room, passing big leather couches and a flat screen TV that's bigger than my refrigerator. The house is basically empty save for a few of the caterers picking up empty cups and plates.

I get the attention of a girl as she's heading to the kitchen. "Is there a bathroom nearby?"

She jerks her head toward the hallway. "Over there."

"Thanks." I turn down the long hallway, and all the doors are closed except one door at the end that's cracked. "Bingo."

I avoid taking in too much of the house as I scurry to the bathroom door. It seems the more I learn about Cameron the more I like him, and noticing his excellent taste in decor won't help. Head down I push through the bathroom door and stop dead in my tracks.

Oh shit. Not the bathroom. I'm in a bedroom, a gigantic bedroom that has its own sitting area with a couch. And on that couch is Cameron, but he's not alone. He's sitting, leaning in towards a woman. Fuck!

FOURTEEN

EVE

"Shit, I'm sorry." I point over my shoulder. "I thought this was the bathroom."

The woman, most likely Ryder's mom, studies me with bloodshot eyes. Her shoulder-length hair is pushed back off her face as though she's been running her hands through it. Her nose is red and her face puffy, but there's a beauty behind all that, and it's strangely familiar.

"Eve," Cameron says, but I don't take my eyes off the woman at his side. "Give me a second and I'll be—"

"Oh my God!" I take a few steps into the room. "I know you."

The woman jerks and watches me through cautious eyes.

Cameron clears his throat. "Eve—"

"I worshipped you." My heart races with my impending fan-girl freak-out. "I had all your magazine covers pinned to my walls."

A tiny smile curls her lips.

"You're D'lilah Monroe." Butterflies explode in my stomach.

She nods and sits up a little taller.

"I fucking love you." I close the distance between us. "I mean I wanted to *be* you. You're so beautiful." Time has aged her, but she's still supermodel material.

She sniffs and tucks her hair behind her ear. "Thank you. That was a long time ago."

I look at Cameron, who's observing me through narrowed eyes. "This is amazing." I point to D'lilah. "She was my role model growing up." I swing my gaze back to her. "Why did you give up modeling?"

Cameron stands. "Eve, please, give us a—"

"Cam." D'lilah grabs his hand, and he looks down at her.

My jaw clenches, and my stomach gets hard as a wave of jealousy washes over me.

She blinks up at him. "It's okay."

He nods and drops back to sitting.

I swallow against the thick lump forming in my throat. The star-struck fog dissipates with awareness. Cameron was married to D'lilah Monroe, the most beautiful and sought-after woman in the world.

All of a sudden I'm the slut in the room. The other woman. My dress feels too tight, my boobs too big. I cross my arms over my chest and take a step back. "I uh…I'm gonna"—I point with my thumb over my shoulder—"find the bathroom."

"You don't have to go." D'lilah looks up at me and pats the couch next to her. "Come sit. It's been so long since I've talked about my career; might be fun to reminisce."

Cameron has his head buried in his hands. This is clearly uncomfortable for him, and it's not a fucking party for me either. "Oh, no, I can't—"

"Dad." We all look to the door where Ryder's head is popped in through a crack. He looks at me. "Oh hey, Eve, you're in here too, huh?"

I give an awkward wave. This is so uncomfortable.

"The caterers need you to sign an invoice."

Cameron pinches the bridge of his nose. "Where's Layla?"

"Your name's on the credit card, so it has to be you."

Cameron's eyes move between D'lilah and me. He's obviously stressed out about leaving her alone. Or maybe leaving her alone with me? Either way, I hate his discomfort.

I take a couple steps toward him. "It's okay. We'll talk fashion from the nineties until you get back." What? No! What am I doing?

He looks at D'lilah. She nods and smiles. Whoa...that smile. The fan girl in me jumps up and down, clapping her hands.

He groans and pushes up off the couch, his eyes on me. He mouths "Be right back" and passes me to meet Ryder at the door they close as they leave.

I have a seat next to D'lilah, and my hands knot together in my lap. "So, uh...Vogue. What was that like?"

I pray Cameron comes back quickly. Every second sitting on a couch with D'lilah Monroe solidifies the truth. I had no chance with Cameron, and with a supermodel as competition, that fact is carved in stone.

CAMERON

I'm in a hurry to get back to my room. After signing invoices and explaining where the recycle can is on the side of the garage, I move through the house to relieve Eve of her babysitting duties. The fireworks ended and people are headed home, stopping me to say goodbye. I rush through goodbyes, worried about leaving the girls alone in my room for too long.

D'lilah showed up drunk and in tears. Knowing Eve and all her sass, who knows what kind of trouble she could be getting in with my ex-wife? I should've had Ryder sit back there and play ref.

I finally get halfway down the hall, preparing myself for the worst, when a sound I haven't heard in years filters out from behind the bedroom door.

D'lilah's laughter. And not the girlie kind of laughter, but the deep booming guttural laughter of the uncontrolled kind. My breath catches in my chest, and I freeze, taking a moment to enjoy the sound of it. Only a woman like Eve could bring out that kind of response in a woman who hasn't smiled in over ten years. The light hum of Eve's giggle goes straight to my chest. A warm pressure forms behind my ribs. What the fuck?

If I could, I'd toss D'lilah's ass in a cab and pin Eve to my bed or bend her over my couch until her legs give out. I scrub my face. What the hell is this girl doing to me?

I put my hand on the doorknob when I hear Eve's voice.

"I can't believe you lived with Telle Sailor."

"She swore peeing in the shower fought athlete's foot." D'lilah's voice is light, lighter than I've heard it in years.

"Eww, really?" Eve goes silent. "Wait, does it work?"

"Totally."

They both burst into another round of hysterical laughter. As much as I'd love to let this continue, if I don't get my mouth on Eve, I might explode.

I push open the door, and both their smiling faces turn to me. D'lilah's eyes brighten; Eve's smile falls. "Ladies, seems like you two are hitting it off well."

"You'll never believe it, Cam. She still has my first Seventeen Magazine cover. I told her if she brings it by I'd sign it for her."

My gaze swings to Eve, who's trying hard not to look at me. "That's great, 'Li."

D'lilah takes a deep breath. "Well, I better go."

"Ryder can give you a lift. He's on his way out to meet some friends."

"Eve, you're not coming with us?" she says.

Go with her and Ryder? They really did hit it off.

Eve swings her gaze to me. "Oh, ah…" She shifts uncomfortably. "I'm gonna hang out here. I have friends out there waiting for me."

She means Mason, but last I saw he was in the middle of a competitive game of pool where big money was at stake. He won't be looking for her for a little while, just enough time for her and me to have a little talk.

"Oh, okay." D'lilah's eyebrows drop low, and her smile droops like the weight of reality just showed up and sat right on her good time. She stands and turns to Eve. "Thank you. I haven't talked about the past in so long."

Eve shrugs. "Sure thing. Anytime you want to pass on anymore supermodel secrets, I'm game."

"Ryder's out front. Car's running."

D'lilah nods and with a sad smile trudges out of the room, closing the door behind her.

I run my hand through my hair. "Sorry about—"

"I can't believe you were married to D'lilah Monroe." She blinks at nothing and shakes her head.

"It was a long time ago."

Her eyes find mine. "You care about her." She sounds disappointed.

"I owe her."

She sighs and drops her gaze to the floor. "You owe her *and* you care about her."

"I guess."

She cringes, but nods. "She looked…sad."

"She is, and she upsets easily, which upsets me."

"Because you care about her," she says under her breath.

"I care about you." Shit. Why the hell did I say that?

Her eyes dart to mine, jaw slack.

"I don't *want* to care about you." Dammit, slow down and think. I could say all this better if I knew how the hell I felt. "But the thing is you keep poppin' in my head and starring in my dirtiest dreams. What you did tonight with 'Li…" I shake my head. "I don't want to stay away from you anymore." Even as the words come out of my mouth, I feel the truth behind them.

Her hand flies to her throat, and her chest rises and falls faster.

I tilt my head and study the strong woman who I'd swear could never get brought to her knees, and now she's on the verge of crying. "That doesn't sit right with you, does it, Eve?"

Her head moves slowly from side to side.

I want to prove it to her, pay her back for showing up here tonight, pushing her way into my life, and, by making D'lilah laugh, further planting herself in my soul. Marking her spot in a permanent way.

This is happening. I've been denying it for weeks, avoiding the little voice in my head that keeps telling me this woman means something. I've made the argument with myself that twenty-one is too young, wrestled with the idea that we're in two different stages of life, and listed the reasons why we'd never last. But here I am, mere yards from my bed with her and thinking the couple feet that separates us is way too much.

"So um…just so we're straight, you're thirty-eight, have an easily upset-able ex-wife, and a seventeen-year-old son. Is there anything else I should know?"

Yes. "Not really."

"That's a lot to digest."

My gaze slides up her luscious body. "Too much?"

She rakes her teeth along her lower lip, and her eyes flare. "No."

I take a step toward her and run my thumb along her lower lip to release it from her teeth. Those big eyes, flushed cheeks, full lips. "Missed touching you, doll."

"After you found out how old I was, you never came by." Her eyebrows pinch together. "Is our age difference *too much* for you?"

"Yeah."

Her head jerks a tiny bit.

"But only when we're not together. I can justify staying away because of our age difference. But now..." I hold out my hand, and she presses her palm to mine. I run my thumb over the tender skin at the underside of her wrist. "Being so close to you, seeing you with Mason and hearing him call you his girl..." Fuck, even thinking about it now is making me crazy. "I want you."

I thought it was what she wanted to hear, but her face twists with what looks like confusion. "So you see me with Mason and now you want to fuck me?"

Her words are like a blow to my gut. That's not what I meant.

"Eve, I—"

She pulls her hand from mine. "That's fine, Cameron." Her voice is hard. "Honestly, I wish I could shut you down and turn you away, but I can't. It sucks, it really does, but the truth is I'll be whatever you want me to be. You want to show up at midnight for a quick fuck, spend the night, take me to break-fast, or not..." She shrugs; her big blue eyes are steely and set on mine. "That's fine. I can't say no to you, and if that makes me your slut, then I can live with that."

"My *slut*."

She nods. "You've been honest with me, and it's only fair I do the same." She runs her hands through her hair and gathers it over her shoulder. "I like you, more than I should and probably more than you like me. If a fuck buddy is what you're looking for, I can be that."

I cringe at the casualty of her words and how easily she dismisses her worth. "Stop talking."

"You call me doll. I'm a toy to you." She tilts her head, and I don't see a hint of disgust as she speaks of her worth. "Don't worry about hurting my feelings. Honestly, it's better that I know where we stand, because the wondering is what'll make me crazy and that's—"

I hook her behind the neck and tug her to me, covering her lips with mine. Lucky for me I caught her off guard and mid-sentence so her mouth is open and my tongue slides in. She moans and leans her weight against my chest. My free hand moves down to cup her ass and hold her up and close.

Her breasts melt against my chest, and her tiny hands fist into my shirt. She thinks I'm using her for sex. I suppose I was, at first, but the night I left her place after The Blackout, I knew it was more than that. How much more, I didn't know, but now with her in my arms, her ass in my hand, and my tongue in her mouth, I'm one hundred percent sure I'm making her mine.

I scoop her up by her ass and turn to place her on my clothes dresser. Standing between her legs, I slide my hands up the outside of her thighs to the hem of her dress. She's convinced she's nothing more than a place to bury my dick, but she's wrong. And I'm going to prove it.

Pushing her dress up, she rocks from side to side so I can get it out from under her ass and to her hips. I look down to her soft thighs, which cradle me between them. They lead up to a pair of bright blue lace panties, and as hot as they are, I'm itching to see what's underneath.

"The door." She's breathing hard, her words sputtering on panting breath. "Is it locked?"

I run my hands up and down her thighs, willing her to relax. "Don't fuckin' care." Ryder and D'lilah are gone. Anyone else who walks in can watch or fuck off.

My fingers find their way beneath her panties.

"What if Mason—*oh God…*"

"Relax. He's playing pool." I lean in and suck her bottom lip into my mouth, allowing my teeth to scrape against it upon release. "What I have in mind won't take long."

Her legs lock around my hips, ankles hook behind the backs of my knees. "Don't stop." She braces her weight with her palms behind her, and her eyes flutter closed.

"Look at me." I bury three fingers to my knuckles.

She opens her eyes, but it takes a few seconds for the fogginess to clear.

"I want you to listen very carefully." I cup her breast then pull one strap off her shoulder to pop one full breast out from her bra. One hand between her legs, the other toying with her nipple, I have her at my mercy. "You're not my slut." I roll her nipple between my fingers, and she groans so fucking sexy I feel it in my balls. "You're not my fuck buddy."

"Cameron—"

"Tell me you get me." I plunge in three fingers and clamp down on her nipple. "You're not Mason's or anyone else's."

"More…" The word fades into a moan.

"I know you want to come, baby, and you will, but first we need to get some shit straight. When we're straight, I'm gonna lay you back and eat until I'm full."

"Oh my—"

"But not until we're clear."

She's writhing against my palm, arching her back and offering her breast. My dick is straining behind my zipper, but tonight isn't about my getting off.

"You're worth more to me than a quick fuck." I lean down and kiss her forehead.

"Whatever you want, just promise you won't stop."

A tiny grin pulls at my lips. "Whatever I want…"

"Mmmm…"

"Tell me you're not a slut."

She shakes her head. "I'm not…a slut."

It doesn't sound like she believes it, but we haven't got all night.

"Lie back."

She adjusts and drops back to her elbows while I drag her ass to hang off the edge of the dresser. I slide her panties off and toss them aside then drop to my knees. Placing a kiss on one ankle at a time, I rest one of her long legs over my shoulder, followed by the other. Her high heels dig into my back, and I groan at the pleasure-pain.

My hands cup her ass, and with my thumbs, I open her up to me. "Fuckin' starving for this, baby."

I lick long and slowly. Her tender flesh, so soft against my tongue, is heaven, and I delve in deeper for more. Mmm… so damn sweet. Her thighs quiver against my shoulders, and I bury my fingers back inside her tight body.

Her head drops back to the wall; hands fist into my hair. She pulls me closer, grinding down on my fingers while I use my lips, tongue, and small grazes of my teeth to bring her close.

She's moaning my name, and her legs clamp down hard on my back. I growl as she pulls me in, draws me deeper into her body. Sensing she's ready, I suck hard and hold on with my teeth.

A rasping whimper falls from her lips, and her body tightens up. She calls out my name and rips at my hair as the orgasm thrashes through her. She's pulsing against my mouth, and my eyes drop closed in an attempt to control the urge to seek out my own release. To sink inside and mark her so deeply that any man who comes close can smell me on her skin.

That sounds insane in my own head, but it also sounds right. What the hell am I getting myself into?

FIFTEEN

EVE

Cameron slides me off his dresser to my feet. Still coming down from my release, I lean back against the solid furniture so I don't topple over. He snags my panties from somewhere and slides them up my legs then wraps me in a hug. "You okay?"

"I…yes? Yes." I can't think or breathe right. After a few minutes between my legs, he's left me a stuttering mess of buzzing skin and tingling girlie parts. "I'm good, yeah. Thanks."

His low chuckle vibrates against my chest. "My pleasure."

An obvious symbol of his lack of receiving pleasure digs into my stomach. I slide my hand between us and grip him from the outside of his jeans.

A hiss seeps from between his teeth, and he pulls his hips back. "Not tonight."

The nauseous roll of rejection turns my stomach. "Oh, but I thought—"

"You're my slut? Fuck buddy?" He drops a soft kiss to my forehead. "Not tonight, Yvette."

A flash of disgust makes me cringe at his use of my full name, but it quickly disappears when his words sink in. He doesn't want me to reciprocate so I don't feel used. I've never been with a guy who wasn't more concerned with getting off than he was about me. And fuck if my eyes are welling up with tears at the thought of Cameron putting his own needs aside. For me.

I suck it back and peek up at him. "That's the nicest thing anyone's ever done for me."

He blinks and his expression hardens. "That can't be true."

I push out an uncomfortable laugh. No need to air out all my garbage here and now. "Nah…it's not, but that's really cool of you."

"Need to go make an appearance out there. Don't know who's left, but I—"

"Oh shit!" I cover my mouth. I totally forgot about Mason. How long have I been back here? "I need to go." I straighten my dress and do my best to wipe the I-just-came-hard look from my face. "Do I look okay?"

He glares at me, but doesn't answer.

"What?" I smooth my hair and press on my cheeks, hoping the heat I feel in them still will soon recede. "Is it bad? He's going to know what we've been up to."

"Fuck him." Cameron's words are growled.

"I came here with him."

"No, you came *there*"—he nods to the dresser—"with me."

He's so hot and so frustrating. I cock my hip and glare. "What do you want me to do? March out there and announce to everyone that you just had your mouth between my legs?"

I don't want to remind him about keeping our hookups a secret. If it were up to me, I'd be screaming that we're together to anyone who'd listen. But there's this new feeling I have; it's like worry or concern when it comes to Cameron. I want to make things easy for him. I'm also not excited about hurting Mason, but I knew going into this date that was a possibility. All the more reason to keep this between us for now.

"I have to find Mase." I move to the door in a hurry. He must be so worried, probably thought I left and didn't say goodbye.

"Make it fast." Cameron's deep command stills me at the door. "He drops you at home, and then I'm picking you up."

Warm flutters race through my belly, and my blood pounds faster through my veins. "Sure thing, boss."

I move down the hallway, out through the living room, and into the backyard with a huge smile on my face. I scan the remaining partygoers, grateful to find Mason in a group of people talking. Sneaking up undetected, I sit on a tall chair and wait for him to see me.

It only takes a minute or so before his eyes lock on me. He excuses himself and comes over. "I feel like such a dick. I've been so wrapped up in this bet we made playing pool, I've completely neglected my date."

I smile, and this time it's not fake. "Don't worry about it. I knew enough people and had fun hanging out with them."

"I looked for you when the fireworks started."

"Yeah, sorry. I went to the bathroom and got to talking to an old friend." It's not a lie. Not really.

He reaches out and brushes his thumb along my cheek. "Hot?"

"Hmm?"

"Your cheeks are red." His eyelids drop low and communicate much more than his words. He tucks my hair behind my ear and sifts his fingers down its length.

I pat my cheek. "Yeah, it's a little warm outside."

And then I feel it.

If I didn't know better, I'd think gravity had doubled its weight as the air around me turns oppressive. I blink and turn toward the source, but not even gravity can compete with what's pointed my way.

Cameron is staring with a glare so intense it sends goose bumps up my arms and a shiver racing down my spine.

"Damn, Eve." Mason rubs his hand up and down my arm. "You feelin' all right?"

My instinct tells me to throw Mason's hand off to protect him from the terrifying man who hasn't taken his eyes off of us. "You know, now that you mention it, I'm not feeling that good."

"Well shit, you should've grabbed me so I could get you home." His eyebrows are pinched together with concern. "Come on." He helps me from my chair and wraps a hand around my waist to guide me out.

Waving a quick goodbye to everyone outside, we move toward the house and right to Cameron, whose eyes are fixed on Mason's hold of my waist. Shit, this isn't good.

"Cam, sick party. We're gonna take off." Mason moves in for a handshake, but Cameron only glares.

I clear my throat, and Cameron's eyes dart to mine. I tilt my head to Mason's extended hand and toss him a glare of my own. *Shake his hand!*

He slides his gaze to Mason and thankfully reaches out to grasp his hand. "Thanks for coming."

"We'd stay longer, but my girl's not feeling—shit, man." Mason pulls his hand away from Cameron's, shaking it out and laughing. "Can't fight with a broken hand. Damn."

The tiny hint of a smile twitches the corner of Cameron's mouth. "Oops, don't know my own strength."

I shake my head, vowing to punch him in the gut first thing when he shows up at my place—after I kiss him, and ravage his body.

Cameron's eyes fix on mine. "Drive home safely."

I nod. "Thanks for having me."

He runs two fingers across his bottom lip. "Thank you for coming."

My face ignites in a furious blush that has Cameron grinning bigger than I've ever seen, which isn't all that big.

I pull at Mason, and he takes the cue and accompanies me to the front door. "That guy's moody as shit," he says under his breath.

"I guess so." As irritating as his little show back there was, it was equally sexy. And there's a twinge of satisfaction knowing that I can affect a man like Cameron in a way that makes him want to break another man for simply touching me.

It's a short and quiet ride back to my place. I don't know what Mase had planned for the end of the night, but I'd be willing to bet it didn't involve a sick date. I can't bear to look at him. I feel so guilty, but I convince myself that his disappointment in my sudden illness is better than the rejection I'd dole out if he tried anything with me.

He escorts me to my door. "Hope you feel better." His big arms wrap me in a hug. "Get some sleep."

"Thanks for everything." I give him a small smile and push into my house then lean back against the door and take a long, deep breath, listening to the rumble of his truck as it backs out of the driveway and fades down the street. Cameron should be here soon. I need to get ready.

I race back to my room, stripping off my shoes, dress, and jewelry. Standing in my panties and bra, I rip through my drawers and closet, looking for something that looks as if I'm not trying too hard.

Pink maxi dress, flip-flops. Done.

I'm in the bathroom, brushing my hair when I hear the knock on the door. Ponytail in hand, rubber band hanging from my mouth, I swing open the door.

My heart plummets into my stomach.

"Dad?"

SIXTEEN

EVE

My dad's at my front door at almost midnight. It doesn't take supernatural ESP to figure out what he's doing here, which I'm sure has zero to do with dropping by to wish me a happy Independence Day. With his gambling, drinking, and mooching off me, this is more like a reminder of his Dependence Day.

He's dressed in his usual casino slum attire: wrinkled shorts, a faded collared shirt, and a pair of scuffed Sperry topsiders. "Yvette, honey, I was hoping you'd be home."

Yvette, honey.

There's a tingling in my chest that accompanies his term of endearment. I can't help it. Never have been able to. I hate the man and, at the same time, so desperately want him to love me. No matter how many times he comes looking for a handout, all it takes is the hope of a promise that he'll change and I'm his puppet.

"Hey, Daddy." My voice doesn't even sound like me, but rather the five-year-old girl still desperate for her father's attention.

"Sorry to drop in on you like this, but"—he runs a hand through his too-long salt-and-pepper hair and smooths the front of his shirt—"I'm hurtin' for cash, honey."

I lean into the open doorway. "I only have enough to scrape by until the next payday."

His smile falls, but he schools his expression and throws me a sympathetic grin. "So you have *some* money. You said on the phone you'd part with a few bucks to help out your old man." He goes for casual and friendly, but it's coming off as desperation verging on anger.

A whisper of panic trickles in.

"I guess I could part with some."

I step back to open the door, but before I'm able to invite him in, he storms past me and into the kitchen.

I press my lips together, holding back all the things I should say, but know I never will. Kitchen drawers and cupboards slam in a symphony of disappointment as my dad searches for his loot. I ignore the crippling pain that twists in my chest at watching him frenzied for money. My money.

"Help me out here, Yvette. Where do you keep your emergency fund?" He rips through my things, digging through envelopes before scattering them to the floor.

I'm on autopilot, registering on some level that this is necessary if I want to keep my dad in my life. My throat is thick with shame, and I crumple into a chair.

He whirls toward me. "Don't just sit there. Where's the money?"

His patience is waning, and I mentally prepare for the onslaught of verbal insults.

"Dad, I'll get the money. You don't have to rip my kitchen up."

"You say you'll get it." He crouches down to look under the sink, pulling out and tossing aside the cleaning supplies and buckets I have stored there. "But you're over there sitting on your fat ass."

And so it begins...

I push up from my seat and drag my chair to the fridge. He's so busy ransacking he doesn't see that I'm reaching up into the cupboard above the large appliance to pull down a small cash box. I step down off the chair, and the movement catches his attention.

"'Bout time." He takes the box from my hands, opens it, and his face lights up. "You lyin' little shit." He wraps his swollen red fingers around the stack of paper money. "No money, my ass."

"It's thirty-nine dollars. I needed that to last me another week." I hold out my open palm. "I can try to get by with twenty and you can take the rest."

He turns slowly, his eyes narrowed. "Your friend is some kind of a multi-billionaire after she blew her dad's head off." He points to my face. "Don't you get any ideas. I'm broke, remember that." He shakes the money before shoving it into his pocket. "You hit her up for a loan."

I grind my teeth. "Give me half."

"Ha, no fuckin' way."

I reach for his pocket.

He anticipates it and grabs my arm then twists it behind my back. "Tough girl, huh?" He shoves me hard.

I stumble, lose my footing, and crash to the tile floor on my knees.

"I'm thinking Dominic Morretti had the right idea. No reason for a woman to be broke in Las Vegas, Yvette. Not when you can make a grip of money on your knees. Figure you're doin' it anyway; may as well get paid for it."

Pain spears through me, but I don't cry. His overused insults have lost their sting. The sound of his high-pitched laughter accompanies the shuffle of his feet until the silence announces he's gone.

What the fuck am I going to do now? I slump down against the wall and contemplate all the things I should've said or done, starting with not answering the door. I lie there for a long time, exhausted and ashamed, until I realize the place isn't going to clean itself.

I push up off the floor and take in my kitchen that has been tossed by my own dad. I fork my hands into my hair and concentrate on my breathing. Okay…I've been through worse and survived. Surely I'll get through this too.

Headlights shine in through the front window. I peek out, hoping he didn't come back to search the rest of the house.

"Oh no."

Not Dad.

But a sleek, black, Maserati.

———

CAMERON

It's almost midnight when the last of the catering vans pulls out of my driveway. Wrapping this party up took longer than I expected. I can't believe I never thought to get Eve's number.

I fire up the Maserati and hit the freeway to Eve's house. My foot falls heavy on the gas as visions of seeing her leave with Mason flash behind my eyes. His arm wrapped around her body, the same body that fell apart beneath my mouth just minutes before. Eve. What is it about her that makes me react like some lust-drunk kid?

Figuring it all out is a waste of time. Hell, I can't even remember what I'm doing tomorrow much less dissect my thoughts. I pull up to her house and kill the headlights. The place is dark. I hope she didn't fall asleep. If so, I'm waking her ass up.

I knock on the door and it drifts open. Unlocked and left cracked? Adrenaline fires my blood. I push in. The only light comes from the kitchen. "Eve?"

"Oh, um, I'm in here." Her voice's rough, but hurried.

I move into the kitchen to find her slamming closed drawers and cupboards. She whirls around to face me, sending her hair in an arc that cascades over her shoulders. What the hell is going on in here?

"Hey, I'm…are you ready?" Her eyes dart to a drawer she must've missed, and she reaches over to quickly slam it shut. "Let me grab my things." She ducks her head and tries to skate past me.

"Hold on." I snag her arm to stop her, but a hiss slides from her lips, and I release her. "What the fuck's going on, Eve?"

Wide eyes swing to mine. "Huh? What makes you think something's going on?" Her voice is higher than it was before, a telltale sign that shit ain't right.

I turn my back on her and wander around the small kitchen. It doesn't look much different than it did the last time I was here, except now there are random items sticking out of mostly closed drawers.

"Find what you were looking for?" I meet her gaze and watch panic flash behind her eyes.

"Mm-hm?" Jeez, she's a terrible liar.

I make a show of shoving things back inside, buying time and hoping she'll come clean and that I won't have to force her to confide in me.

She keeps her lips zipped, which doesn't surprise me.

"Who did this?" I lean back against the counter and cross my arms over my chest. I'm not moving an inch until she explains to me why she was racing around her kitchen shoving shit in drawers and looks spooked out of her mind.

"Nothing, I'm ready to go if—" She points over her shoulder.

"Didn't ask what, I asked *who*."

Her mouth tightens and her eyes get hard. "Leave it alone."

"So you admit there was someone here?"

"Cameron—"

"Mason do this? Go through your place and leave you scared as shit and lying to me?" My voice gets louder with every word as my temper takes hold.

"Don't worry about—"

"I'll pay the little shit a visit right now." I push up off the counter and head for the door.

"No, wait!"

I ignore her, my vision clouded with red.

"Please, don't."

I reach the front door the same time her hand clamps around my elbow.

"It wasn't him. It…Please, just know that Mason didn't do anything."

"Start talking."

Her hand releases me, and she takes a few steps back until she's halted by the wall. She slides down and pulls her long pink dress up to drape it between her cocked legs.

"Someone break in? If so, we need to file a report."

"No." Her head rolls back to the wall. "Don't call the cops. I did this to myself."

"Did what?" My fists clench tight.

"Mason dropped me off—"

"Already know this. Now I'm losing my patience."

"He dropped me off, and I was getting ready for you to pick me up when…" She slams her head against the wall. "*Fuck!*"

My pulse is raging in my ears. "Tell me!"

She shakes her head. "I don't want to."

"Someone was here, fucked up all your shit, and you're protecting them?"

"Not protecting them. I'm protecting me."

I rub my forehead, praying for patience. "Who was here, Eve."

"No—"

"Yvette!"

Her head whips around to face me. "My dad, okay? Happy now?" She motions to the kitchen with a firm flip of her wrist. "He showed up and cleaned me out, including my emergency stash."

"Say again?"

She shakes her head. "Please, don't make me. Like I'm not humiliated enough."

"You're tellin' me"—my voice vibrates with the force of my anger—"your Dad busted in and robbed you."

"Ha." She smiles, but it doesn't reach her eyes. "When you say it like that…"

I rein in my temper. Blowing up in her face and punching holes in the walls isn't going to help anyone. With a deep breath, I stand and hold out my hands. She stares at them for a few silent seconds before placing hers in mine. I pull her to her feet, and she rushes straight into my chest, catching me off guard when both her arms circle my waist.

I hold my arms out and fight off the immediate discomfort of being hugged like this. Slowly, I lower one arm to her back followed by the other, which only tightens her grip.

Fighting I know. Drive and determination as well. But comforting another person is…I take a deep breath and she melts into me further. Huh, not good, but maybe not too bad either.

"Get your shit. We'll talk in the car."

She tilts her head back to look in my eyes. "Do we have to?"

"I'm assuming this isn't the first time this shit's happened."

Her chin dips, which is all the confirmation I need.

"Definitely talkin'. Now go on. I wanna get the hell out of here before I do something I regret."

With slumped shoulders, she drags herself to her bedroom and comes back out with a backpack slung over her shoulder.

"That it?"

She nods, and we lock up and head to my place. We're barely out of the driveway.

"Start talking."

She takes a long breath and slumps deeper into her seat to prop bare feet on my dashboard. The length of her cotton dress pools around her thighs to expose her legs, and I'm dying to slide my palm from ankle to thigh.

"My dad is a drunk, and he's addicted to gambling. He's destroyed every relationship he's ever had and feels like, since we share DNA, I should fund his habits. End of story." Her gaze slides to the side window.

"He show up like this often?"

She shakes her head and her chin drops.

My gut burns with frustration. "In one night, you've met my son and my ex. I've got my shit out flappin' in the breeze. It'd make me feel like less of an ass if you do the same."

Her eyes move to the front windshield. "It's not the same thing."

"The hell it's not."

With a long sigh, she drops her head back to the seat. "I've been giving him money since high school. It started when he got so in debt he was homeless, living on the streets and begging for change." She shakes her head. "Funny thing is I gave him money back then because I was embarrassed. I didn't really care if he had to dig in garbage for food, but the thought that someone I know might see him or find out I was the daughter of a homeless man…"

"So you kicked him a few bucks here and there?"

"Something like that."

"Eve."

"I opened a checking account for him and deposited half of my paychecks."

"That's a hell of a lot more than helping him out, Eve. That's supporting him."

"Not back then. I didn't make that much." She pulls her hair over her shoulder and picks at the ends. "But now, yeah."

I can't believe she's giving him the money she earns so he can blow it. Now all those unpaid bills make sense.

My hands grip the steering wheel. "So what was tonight about?"

"He spends what I give him too fast, and when he doesn't win at the tables, he comes looking for more."

"Why did you let him in?"

She shakes her head, opens her mouth to say something, but doesn't and slams it shut. "Why do you care, Cameron? I mean...can't we just hang out without sharing our life history with each other?"

What? That's my line. I concentrate on the reflective paint lines on the freeway in front of me. Why the fuck do I care? She's a grown woman. Who she gives her money to isn't my concern. And yet, why do I feel as though it is?

"You're a woman. A dude shows up to rough you up in your house, rob you. Any man who's worth his salt would ask questions. Simple as that." That's such bullshit and I know it.

"You're a good man. But trust me. I've handled my dad on my own for as long as I can remember. I'm okay."

The hell she is.

Eve's dad has a healthy daughter, who lives and breathes and makes a life for herself. His blood runs through the veins of this strong and vibrant woman, but rather than nurture and appreciate her, he takes advantage of her love and her hard work. If he only knew what it's like to lose a child, to hold her lifeless body in his hands, to mourn the loss of a future, the chance to see her spread her wings, become a woman, start a life of her own...My chest cramps. I've lost everything that this man has, and any man who doesn't appreciate his daughter deserves to rot in hell.

But it's none of my business.

SEVENTEEN

EVE

My palms are sweaty. Moving from Cameron's ginormous master bathroom to his bed, I wipe my hands on my boy shorts, grateful that he has his nose buried in some kind of planner so he doesn't get wind of my nerves. I'm finally getting something I've always wanted, someone whose basic instinct is to protect me. And now that I have it, I want to run like hell in the opposite direction.

If he knew that I let my dad in, allowed him to search my house for money, sat silent while he hurled insults at me until he found my emergency cash, would Cameron still feel protective of me? Or would he see me as he did the first night we met? The girl who plays dumb in order to get a man's attention? Fuck, is the truth really that far off?

I force my mind to quiet, refusing to ruin any time I have with him by overthinking. His attention on something other than me provides the perfect opportunity to gawk. He's leaning back against the headboard, shirtless, sheet pulled up to his waist, but low enough to show the muscles of his lower abdomen that form a V, like a runway pointing down with a sign that screams "kiss, lick, and sit here." My eyes devour every inch of his exposed skin. For a guy with a desk job, he sure as hell has the body of an athlete. I round the side of the bed, taking in his ribcage, and my jaw drops as I get a closer look at his tattoos. From his hip up, his ribs are waves of water, but not done in bright blues, but rather variations of black and gray that decorate the cuts of his muscles.

"Eve?"

My eyes dart to his, which are narrowed on me. "Huh?"

I drop my chin and study the empty spot at his side: big overstuffed pillows, luxurious chocolate brown sheets that I'm sure cost a fortune, and an equally decadent looking comforter. It's too good: all of it, him, this room, and these sheets. How can I take what I know I'm not worthy of? Shut up, Eve! I'll never convince him that I'm good enough if I don't at least act as if I'm good enough.

He pulls back the sheet and I smile, crawling in and—*ohhh, yeah.* These sheets are amazing, like spun silk and other amazing things that I've yet to experience. My head hits the pillow, and a deep moan vibrates from my chest.

"Trying hard to make tonight about you, babe, but you strut in here in those tiny shorts and that damn top, and you're making it impossible to keep my dick in check." There's that tiny lift to his lips, but his eyes are all glare.

My heart beats faster, and butterflies swirl in my belly and head south. "Tonight's all about me, but um"—I stretch and a yawn falls from my lips—"it's after midnight, so tonight is technically tomorrow morning." I nuzzle into the soft down pillow. Damn, I knew I was tired, but this bed is like an instant sleeping pill.

He hits the light, and we're plunged into darkness. "True, but we're both beat, and I've been wanting this body in my arms since I saw you walk into the party."

Strong hands grip my waist and tug me across the bed before his arms engulf me and press me to his chest. My eyes roll back in my head at the feeling of comfort and safety the simple act brings.

"Go to sleep." His hold on me tightens. "I'll fuck you for breakfast."

My eyes fly open with the force of my laughter. "I love you when you sweet-talk me."

His body goes tense at my side.

No, no! That's not what I meant. "I love *it* when you sweet-talk. *It.*" Oh shit. My muscles go rigid. It's not like I said "I love you". Well maybe technically I did, but there's no way he thinks that, right? Shit, shit, shit!

My skin flames with embarrassment. It's probably best if I pretend it never happened and hope he chalks it up to a long night. I take a shaky breath. "Good night."

His hold on me loosens along with the tension in his muscles. "'Night."

I blink into the dark room. Leave it to me to go and fuck everything up. I should've kept my mouth shut. My dad was right. I'm better off seen and not heard. I'll try to remember that from here on out, that is, if Cameron keeps me around after tonight.

—

CAMERON

The alarm blares in my ears and finally pulls at my eyelids. There's no way it's already morning. It seems like I fell asleep minutes ago. I rub my eyes and can't help but feel as though I'm missing something. I turn to the clock and slam the thing off. Six-thirty in the morning. I grab my pillow and roll over. I'll catch a little more sleep before—a yawn forces a big inhale. Mmm…sweet and spice.

I blink open my eyes. Eve. Did she get up and leave? She didn't have a car or money, so if she did, she's on foot. I sit up and look around the room. Empty.

I run my hands through my hair and move to the bath-room. My eyes fix on the backpack that hangs from a hook by the shower. I take a deep, relieved breath. She's still here.

While in the bathroom, I brush my teeth and wash my face then head out to find her. Maybe she woke early and went to watch TV. The house is silent until I hit the kitchen where mumbling voices filter in from the dining room. As I get closer, they become more distinct: Eve and Ryder. The clinking of silverware to plates fills the gaps in their conversation.

"How were you able to get into The Joint? I thought they were twenty-one and up?" Eve says through what sounds like a mouthful of food.

"They are, but we know a guy who hooks us up. As long as we don't drink the booze, he lets us in." Ryder's going to clubs under age. Not exactly new information, but it pisses me off anyway. The last thing he needs is a criminal record to set him up for the future.

"You guys go, but you don't drink?"

"We go for the music mainly. Some of the guys drink before, but I'm usually the designated driver."

"You're a lot more responsible than I was at your age." Her low chuckle says that we don't even know the half of it.

His age, so four years ago? Shit, these reminders of her age are like little sucker punches to the gut.

"Nah, I'm not a big fan of liquor. Makes good people act like jackasses."

Eve hums her agreement. "What bands do you like?"

"Traverse is my favorite. Been trying to see them for years, but it's impossible to get into their shows."

"I saw them last summer."

"No kidding. What were they like?"

"Ah-mazing. Cy Castro's voice in real life is even better live than on the album."

"That's what I've heard." A utensil clanks on a plate. "Shit, I'm so jealous."

"When they come back to town, I'll try to get you tickets."

"You could do that?"

She must nod. "Mm-hm. I know a guy who does security for all the big shows."

She knows a guy? And why the motherfuck does that little slice of news make me want to break something?

"Really? That would be so fuckin' cool."

"Pass the syrup?"

"Here."

"Thanks. If you like Traverse, you'd like my friend's band, Ataxia."

"I've heard of them. I think the lead singer fights for my dad."

"Yeah, Rex. The band's more mainstream than Traverse, but they have a similar style. They play at The Blackout all the time. I could pull some strings, get you in."

"Really?"

"Sure."

"That's so kick ass."

A few seconds of silence pass and I move to enter.

"You're way cooler than the other chicks my dad dates."

Oh fuck.

Eve coughs or chokes. She clears her throat. "Um…other chicks? Wow. Thank you? I think."

"Oh no, he's not dating anyone now. I just mean since he and my mom got divorced."

I release the breath I was holding. She's already worried that I'm playing her. Ry's clarification was helpful, but I'm sure it was enough to get into her head.

Thankfully, she changes the conversation back to music, and I quit my eavesdropping and move to the living room.

My stomach churns with unease. Listening to them talk is like being in the room while Ry and his buddies hang out. The bands, the shows, the venues, it's like a foreign language that only the two of them understand.

I told myself I wasn't going to let our age difference affect our hanging out, and here I am considering cutting her loose. Even as the thought passes through my head, my body jolts to stop that line of thinking.

No, we'll be fine. I can look past the seventeen years that divide us, at least for as long as this thing between us lasts. Yeah, this can—

"Hey, when did you wake up?" Eve's voice calls my eyes to her. She's standing there in pair of baggy sweats and the same top she slept in, but now wearing a bra. No wonder Ry was able to have a coherent conversation. No way would he have been able to form complete sentences if she hadn't.

"Just now."

"I made French toast." She gives me an uneasy smile. "I hope that's okay."

Her nervousness is so damn cute. "Smells good."

She motions over her shoulder to the kitchen. "You want some?"

"Be great, babe."

Ryder comes dragging into the room, his eyes looking as if they haven't seen sleep in days. "Mornin', Dad." He passes me to the hallway, rubbing his belly. "Eve's breakfast blows your egg whites and protein shakes out of the water. I'm gonna have to take a nap before I go out today."

"Where are you going today?"

Ryder stops in the open mouth of the hallway and turns. "It's Sunday." He shrugs as if it's the most common thing ever. "Me and the guys jam on Sunday.'"

"Right." I run a hand through my hair, hoping Eve doesn't pick up on my forgetfulness like Ryder's expression proves he does. At least the kid is used to having to repeat himself to me.

Eve's eyes follow him until he disappears behind his door, a small grin on her face. "Nice kid."

Kid. Fuckin' hell.

"You fed my boy." Damn, that came out harsher than I wanted.

Her smile falls. "Oh, yeah, I mean when I woke up he was here, so I asked him if he was hungry." She crosses her arms over her stomach and gnaws on her lower lip.

This is stupid. I'm thirty-eight years old and way too tired to deal with shit like jealousy and mistrust. Especially over my own son.

I grind down on my jealousy. "Nice of you."

She seems to relax, drops her arms, and smiles.

I push up, walk over, and lean a hip against the counter. "You sleep okay?"

Like last night, she rushes to my side, her arms coming around my waist. "Slept great."

I place my arms awkwardly around her back. It comes a little easier than it did last night, but not by much. "You work today?"

She tilts her head back, flashing those big eyes behind dark lashes. "I wasn't supposed to, but I got called in for a manager meeting at ten. I'm going to try to pick up a shift after that, you know, after last night." Her cheeks pink and she dips her chin.

She's picking up a shift after her dad cleaned her out. My chest warms with pride at her work ethic and determination. How many twenty-one-year-olds would pull themselves up like this rather than beg for handouts?

Her finger traces the swirls of the tattoo on my bicep. "I should be done by lunch. If you don't have plans, maybe we could do something?" She sucks in a tiny breath, but doesn't release it.

"I have to go to the office for a few hours, but I'll call you when I'm done."

She nods quickly. "Yeah, of course, I figured you'd have plans. I just, I don't know, I was just putting it out there in case you wanted to, but if you don't, then I'm—"

I press my thumb against her lips. "Shhh. I didn't say I didn't want to, but before things go any further between us…" Fuck, how do I get this out without sounding like a dick? I take a few seconds to go over the words in my head before they fly from my lips. "The UFL gets most of my time. I've worked hard to get where I am, and there will be days that I'm at the training center from sun up 'til sundown. I want to spend time with you, but I can't give you all of me." Even as the words resonate in my head, I hear the truth behind them. There will always be a part of me that lies tucked away from prying eyes. I'll never be capable of anything beyond a surface relationship.

"I understand." She brushes her hand along my jaw. "You're lucky I'm pretty low maintenance." A small frown tugs at her lips before she catches herself and forces a smile. "So on to breakfast and then you can take me home."

"I have a better idea. Breakfast." I swipe her thick bangs off her forehead. "Shower." I run my hand down her back and cup her ass. "Grab a little dessert before you get dressed." Her body shivers in my arms, and I press her against my hardening body. "Then I drop you at home."

She licks her lips, her eyelids drop low. "I lo—er"—her eyelids flutter, chasing away the dreamy look—"I like that plan."

I kiss her forehead. "Feed me." I smack her ass, and she giggles into the kitchen.

This isn't stupid. This is two adults having a good time. A little voice whispers I should break it off, but when I picture Eve with anyone else, imagine her back at her place with scumbags like her dad showing up, it makes me crazy. I'll live in the now, take advantage of the fun that we have together until she starts hinting that she needs more. Then we can go our separate ways as friends so that I'm available if she needs me. Because no matter what, I'm keeping Eve in my life, even if I'm not able to really let her into it.

EIGHTEEN

EVE

I've become that girl. The kind I hate. The one who floats around with a ginormous smile stretched across her face, as if she's privy to an inside joke no one else gets. The girl who says hi and makes eye contact with everyone she comes in contact with just to make sure she gets her I'm-happier-than-you point across. Yep. That's me. And I'd slap myself stupid if I weren't so damn happy about being that girl.

After feeding Cameron my famous French toast, we took a shower that could've drained the Hoover Dam. I had no concept of time as we got lost in exploring each other's bodies, hands, lips, and tongues; we feasted until we were stuffed. I got to study every intricate tattoo, trace every sinew, and taste that VI admired the night before. Along with a lot more. My tummy tumbles at the memory, my skin still tingles from his touch, and my thighs ache from holding myself around him while he drove into me.

A long sigh falls from my lips. Yeah, I'm totally that girl.

I arrive at work a few minutes early to see who's on the schedule and what the projections are for how busy the lunch rush will be. I'm prepared to beg for a shift, banking on tip money to get me through the week until payday. Flipping through reservations at the hostess stand, I'm sidetracked by the front door opening.

"Hey guys, we're not open until—oh, Mr. Cavat." I smile, all teeth and aching cheeks—owed to Cameron—at the two men who enter. My district manager. What's he doing here? "What brings you by?"

He's usually only here at the end of the year for tax purposes. The rest of the time he keeps his finger on the pulse of the restaurant through email.

"Ms. Dawson, this is Seth Gamboni." He nods to the man at his side who's dressed in a collared shirt and black slacks, more business casual in comparison to Cavat's power suit and tie. We exchange hi-how-are-yas.

"Is everyone here?" Cavat swings his gaze around the restaurant.

Everyone? He's here for the meeting? We have impromptu manager meetings from time to time, but the GM has never been a part of them.

I motion for them to follow me to a private room off the main dining space that we use for large parties. The three other managers are in there, waiting. I take a seat with them, assuming this is Cavat's show.

He drops down in a chair at the end of the table and clears his throat. "Thank you for being here on such short notice."

We all mumble a "no problem" and wait for him to continue.

"I'll make this quick." He flicks a hand toward Seth. "This is Seth Gamboni. He's going to be here observing for the next week."

Observing? What the fuck? I take a quick peek at the facial expressions of the other managers and see they must be having the same reaction.

"I'd like for him to work with each one of you closely. If he has questions, answer them. If he offends you, get over it. We're doing an audit of every restaurant in the Nori family of restaurants, and it's your turn." He leans back in his chair, almost as if he's waiting for a response.

We all sit silent.

"He'll start today and be here every day on varying shifts until this time next week."

Everyone nods.

"Questions?"

"Why an audit?" The words fly from my lips before I have a chance to bite down on them.

"Because I said so." Cavat smiles, as if he thinks treating me like his kid is hysterical.

Asshole.

I shrug off his belittling. "No, I mean was there a complaint? Are there concerns about how things are being run?"

Cavat and Seth look at each other and then turn back to us.

Seth straightens his big, shiny watch. "Just keep doing what you're doing, Ms. Dawson, and everything should be fine."

My stomach drops. Why does the way he said that make me feel as if things are far from fine? I've been working here since high school, and I'm sure I haven't always been the picture of employee perfection, but I always get the job done.

He covers a few more minor issues like new uniforms and a change to how we report our numbers before he finally dismisses us. As much as I'd hoped Cavat would leave, he ends up sticking around for lunch. I begged a few of the servers for their shifts, but go figure, with the presence of the GM, no one wanted to be labeled a slacker and take the day off.

Shit. My smile wiped clean from my face, I decide to go home and dig through old purses for money. With Seth in the restaurant all week, my chances of picking up a shift are minimal. Looks like those extra stubborn pounds I've been trying to shed will come off by involuntary starvation. I groan. Fabulous.

———

CAMERON

Days have passed since I've seen Eve. Although we've talked on the phone a few times, it's been brief, and my body's beginning to register her absence. It's not that I haven't gone long stretches of time without female companionship. I have. But Eve's like a habit I can't break. No amount of time spent with her ever feels like enough, and mere memories of her sweet body have made me hard hours and even days after we've been together.

What the fuck is up with that?

With a two-hour break in my day, I plan on hitting the weights hard with hopes of exhausting myself along with the drive to see Eve. She works the closing shift at her restaurant tonight, and I'm not some needy prick who's going to show up at the end of her shift and drag her back to my bed. Or shit, maybe I am. I scribble a note in my planner to find out what time Eve gets off and then head to my car to get my gym bag.

It's hot today, hovering around 110 degrees, but thankfully my car is parked in one of the three covered spots reserved for the CEO and VIPs. I'm in my trunk, grabbing my shit when I hear angry voices from across the lot.

"You touch my ride, you little punk ass bitch?"

It's Reece and one of his boys being difficult as usual. They're in Killer's face again, most likely about something completely made up. Lopez has his phone up, is he videoing this? Fucking juveniles. I can't figure out why they have it out for Killer, but it's getting old.

"I didn't go anywhere near your car, man."

I hang back at the sound of Killer's voice. If he wants to be accepted as an equal, he's going to have to stand up for himself. It won't do him any good for me to swoop in and protect him. I'll watch how he handles himself, and if Reece takes it too far, I'll make sure to stop it.

"Nice try, slut. There's a mark on the side of my car that wasn't there this morning." Reece looks back to Lopez, who's making no attempt to cover up how hilarious he thinks this is.

Man, these guys need to get their asses kicked. Not in the octagon, but in a straight-up bare-knuckled street fight.

"What's your problem, Reece? Every day you find some reason to get all over my ass about something." Killer's standing his ground, taking the high road rather than falling into Reece's trap. Pride swells in my chest.

"I bet you'd like that, huh Fill-ee-man." Reece looks over his shoulder, laughing along with his sidekick. "You hear that? He wants me all over his ass."

The door to the training center opens, and Blake storms out. He doesn't say a word, but stands a few feet back, muscles tense, glaring at Reece and Lopez.

They don't seem affected by his sudden presence and continue to laugh and taunt. I know Blake's got a soft spot for the kid, so I move closer in case he loses his shit. "Reece, Lopez, unless you're out here washing cars, I'd suggest you get your asses back to training."

Reece turns to me; his humor morphs into a scowl. "You're always getting on my shit when this fucker scratched my ride."

Killer props his hands on his hips and shakes his head. "I didn't touch your fuckin' car, dude."

I swing my gaze to the car and squint to fight the glare. It's a two-door compact of some kind, painted cobalt blue with fucking glitter. On the hood, in white letters that form an arch it says *Money, Power & Bitches.*

"You have that done?" I point to the hood of his car. "On purpose? Or is that some kind of joke your boys played on you?"

Blake's low chuckle sounds from behind me, and Killer rolls his lips between his teeth.

"Yeah, right." Reece shifts on his feet and gives Lopez a chin lift as if what I said was supposed to be funny.

He did that to his car on purpose? I blink and rub my hand down my face. He drives this humiliating piece of shit and has the nerve to give Killer a hard time?

"Reece, you can't park this thing anywhere near the training center. Ever. From now on, you hitch a ride, take a bus, cab it, I don't give a fuck, but I don't want that"—I point to the offending vehicle—"anywhere near my doors again. Understood?"

His face contorts with anger. "You can't do that."

"I just did."

"My contract says—"

"I can terminate your contract for lewd and indecent behavior. That"—I motion to the hood of the car—"is the definition of lewd and indecent."

His jaw drops open. "I spent two grand to get those decals made and put on."

"Are you shittin' me? That's the stupidest damn thing I've ever heard."

"'Money, power, and bitches' is my creed. I have the freedom to put that shit on whatever I want."

Blake moves up so that he's at my side. "Dude, you put 'Money, Power, and Bitches' on a *Toyota*, dumb shit. Pretty sure that makes you the stupidest motherfucker around."

I'd usually reprimand Blake for being confrontational, but he's right. This guy's a fuckin' douchebag.

"I'm gonna help you out, Reece." Blake absorbs Reece's glare like it's nothing. "I'm thinkin' you need a new creed." He rubs his chin. "Hm...Ah!" He snaps his fingers. "I got it. How 'bout this? 'Broke ass with a little dick.'"

A laugh shoots from Killer's mouth, and I'm doing everything I can to not join him.

Blake turns to Killer. "It's good, right?"

151

Reece rushes Blake, but the fighter expects it and shoves Reece so he tumbles onto the asphalt. He bounces back. Blake goes for him, but Killian steps in his path while I wrap one arm around Reece's neck from behind.

"Chill the fuck out. Both of you."

Blake's grinning, but his fists are still clenched as though he's ready to dance whenever I give the go-ahead. Reece struggles in my hold.

"Take this to the octagon, boys." I growl my warning before releasing Reece with a shove. He stumbles forward and gives Blake and Killer the finger before ripping through the front door of the training center.

"I fuckin' hate that guy." Blake's back to calm.

"He's a dick." Killer shakes his head and puts out his hand to Blake. "Thanks for having my back."

Blake shakes and gives him a chin lift. "Reece been at you for long?"

Killer's eyes dart to me for a split second before he shakes his head. "Nah, not really."

He's lying to Blake? Huh.

I scoop up my gym bag that I dropped in the scuffle. "I'm hitting weights." I don't stick around for the convo, but my guess is that now that Blake's on to Reece's bullying, he'll keep a closer eye out for the kid.

Three strikes and he's gone from this organization. If it were up to me, he'd have been gone at one.

A quick change into my work-out clothes and I'm headed to the weight room. I push inside and head straight to the treadmills to warm up. There are a few fighters working out, a couple at the weights, one at the treadmills, and another at the stair climber. I take the treadmill close to Rex, and he turns his head to acknowledge me.

I nod to him, thankful that Rex hasn't been in any mood for conversation lately, and start a slow jog. There've been whispers about what's going on with the fighter's sudden mood swing, but the fact is I could give rip what's going on in his personal life. As long as he's a competent fighter with a decent attendance, that's good enough for me.

Cranking my machine up to a sprint, I pound out a punishing run that should knock me out cold and keep my mind off of a certain pretty blonde that I can't seem to forget.

NINETEEN

EVE

I lock the door to the restaurant at eleven on the nose, grateful that the night has finally come to an end. One of our cooks was off his game so food was being sent back and items being taken off bills for the majority of my shift. Usually it wouldn't be a huge deal, but with Seth, the GM watchdog, following my every move, I fucked up more times than I can count.

No matter how many times I explained that I'm a horrible test taker, that pressure screws me up and his breath at my back every second only makes matters worse, he just smiled and said, "Pretend that I'm not even here."

Impossible.

My stomach growls, reminding me that I've been living off one meal a day for the last few days. Funny, I'm working in a restaurant surrounded by food and starving to death. The good news is my pants fit a little better, but as much as I'd like to be thinner, I enjoy food way too much and marked anorexia off of possible diet options a long time ago.

I'm printing sales figures and adding totals, but everything is a cluster and coming up over by just under one hundred and fifty dollars.

"Crap." I start over and count the money, even going as far as to add the evening's sales by hand, thinking maybe it's the computer, but still. "One forty-eight sixty-three over." Shit.

We've been off before, but as long as I've worked here at Nori, I've yet to have an overage I couldn't figure out. My head pounds, and my eyes cross as I go over the numbers again and again come up with the same result. Somehow, with all the refunds, we must've screwed up somewhere. Whatever happened won't be figured out tonight. I glance at the digital clock on my desk. Shit, it's past midnight.

I finish up, putting the correct amount of cash into the deposit envelope and move to put the overage in the safe with a sticky note when my stomach grinds its hunger again.

God, I'd give anything for a cheeseburger. My mouth waters, and I can almost taste the meat and cheese combo on my tongue. *If only I had some money…*My gaze dips down to the envelope in my hand filled with bills and change.

They'd never know. I mean, as far as the computers are concerned, we never made this money. *It's stealing.* But for a good cause, right? I mean I don't have any money and the restaurant has money that it doesn't know it has. Would it be so wrong for me to take it? Just this once? I've worked here since high school and have never been on any extended vacation. I mean, hell, if I added up all the vacation time this place owes me, I'm sure it'd be quadruple what I have in my hand.

I lean back into my chair, contemplating the possible consequences of my actions if I choose to slink out with this money, and before I can think of a single one, my stomach growls painfully.

Must be a sign. I grab my purse from the bottom drawer and hit the lights in the office. Moving through empty restaurant and out the door, I scurry as if someone's going to jump out and catch me.

With my head down, I make way to my car when I notice a familiar car parked next to mine. I look up and my steps freeze just feet away. Leaning against my car, arms crossed at his chest, long powerful legs crossed at his ankles, is Cameron.

My hand clutches my purse to my side. "Hey, what are you doing here?" I internally scold myself for sounding more defensive than happy to see him. He can't possibly know what's in my purse.

It's been days since I've seen him, and our quick telephone conversations do little to slake my desire to see him in the flesh.

He shrugs. "Passing by, saw the place was closed for the night. Thought I'd hang out and see if I could speak to the manager."

My stomach jumps and goes warm. He came all the way here just to see me?

"Did you have a bad experience? Like to make a formal complaint?"

He pushes off my car and takes two steps toward me. *Close, but not close enough.* His eyes set in their usual glare, he shoves his hands into the pockets of his dark washed jeans. "Mmm..." He rubs his fingers across his lower lip, as he did the night in front of Mason. His eyes burn through me. "I have no complaints about my...*experience.*"

His presence combined with his insinuation become too much and I drop my gaze. A tickle of caution pricks at my subconscious, reminding me that I'm not the kind of girl who shies away from flirtation. I'm not timid, demure, or easily swayed by just any man. But there are a few who have brought me to my emotional knees, and both of them I dislike. Immensely.

His feet move into my line of site, and I pull my gaze up to settle on his face. How is he even more beautiful than I remember with all that thick dark hair, his fierce jaw, and full lips that I know are as powerful as they are soft?

"What're your plans tonight?" He reaches out and brushes my bangs off my forehead.

Such a tiny gesture, but the sweetness of it makes my eyes flutter. "I was going to grab a bite to eat."

His eyebrows pinch together. "You hungry? I'll take you to dinner."

I look around at the empty parking lot then move my eyes back to his. "Now?"

"You hungry *now*?"

"Very."

"Then yeah. Now."

"But it's the middle of the night."

The corner of his mouth lifts so slightly it's barely noticeable. "It's Vegas, babe."

"But I'm in the mood for a bacon cheeseburger." I lick my lips. I can almost taste the greasy goodness. "With green chilis." My stomach grumbles in agreement. "And onion rings. Not the battered ones, but those breadcrumb ones." I hum low in my throat. "Oh, and a chocolate milkshake or an ice cold beer will also do." I tap my lips, thinking. "Hm. Maybe both."

So lost in my food-fantasy I don't notice the way he's staring at me until I focus on him. His glare isn't as tight as it usually is, and his mouth isn't the straight—but full and kissable—line it usually is. It's as if someone pulled the starch from his expression, not completely relaxed, but tender.

Silence builds between us and I shift on my feet. "Or not, ya know...I mean whatever you want is fine too."

He tilts his head, still not speaking.

"There's an IHOP down off of—"

"Shut up, Yvette."

God, I hate that name, but hearing it growled from Cameron's lips makes it more than tolerable.

"I'm sorry, it's just...Did I say something wrong?"

His lips tilt, tilt, and holy shit, tilt some more, lighting his entire face, the entire city of Vegas, probably the whole damn atmosphere with the most brilliant smile.

"Far from wrong, babe." He grabs my hand and tugs me to his chest. "I dig a woman who knows what she likes and asks for it."

My cheek is pressed to his chest, the cotton of his shirt soft against my skin while I'm engulfed in the earthy scent of his cologne. "Oh, well…that's good. I thought maybe I came off as a demanding bitch."

His chuckle rumbles against my torso. "I know just the place." He pulls back. "One question first."

I wait while he studies me.

"You didn't eat dinner."

My eyebrows lift slightly. "That's not a question."

"Eve."

"It was too busy to take a break."

"That's fucked. You need to eat."

"But if I had, then I wouldn't get to have dinner with you."

He winds his arm around my shoulders and moves me to his car. "Excellent point." There's that tiny pull of his lips again.

The first night I met this guy I'd have sworn he was incapable of anything other than a scowl. I was wrong. And every time he gives me even a hint of that, my insides lurch to get at him.

This is bad, not at all what I planned for. I'm falling hard for a man who is going to destroy me. That is, if I don't push him away first.

CAMERON

It was in my notebook. That's the excuse I've been feeding myself since I pulled into the parking lot of Eve's restaurant. I stick to what's written and never diverge. Simple as that.

None of me showing up like a fucking stalker is about me needing her. I don't need. I want. I enjoy. I even enjoy a lot, but need? Never.

So walking into the Peppermill with Eve under my arm and the sweet smell of her hair scrambling my senses, I remind myself that this is a fun-for-now kinda thing. I'm sure whatever pull that powers through my veins when it comes to her will someday fade. But why focus on the end when the now is so much fun?

"This place is crazy busy." Eve tilts her head back, the length of her sleek ponytail brushing against my arm across her back.

"Food's good. They're open all night. Makes sense."

"Do they have cheeseburgers?" Her eyes are bright, and studying her in better light, I notice she looks…something. Tired or…I can't put my finger on it, but there's something about her face that seems unwell.

I slide her out from my arm and face her head on. Brushing her bangs aside, I study her face. "You feelin' okay?"

Her eyes dart everywhere but to me. "Fine." She shugs and finally gives me her eyes, forcing a smile.

"I've got a teenage son, Eve. You think I don't know when I'm being bullshitted?"

Her eyes grow wide for a split second before she catches herself. A few steely seconds and then she drops her shoulders on a sigh. "Fine. You want honesty?"

"Fuckin' appreciate it, yeah."

"Well, first I'm tired. I've been working ten hours on my feet, and I don't know why, but it seems like tonight was asshole appreciation night, seeing as every fucking person who walked in had at least one asshole in tow. Some three or more." She ticks off a finger on one hand. "Although this is not unusual, it sucked huge donkey balls seeing as our GM's little troll spy was up my ass all night, following me around like I had magical dick-growing pills stapled to my back."

I'm already pushing back the urge to laugh, and I can tell she's just getting started. I rub my upper lip to hide the smile that's breaking free and nod for her to go on.

She moves to another finger. "That little pecker corrected everything I did, one time in front of a customer." She stomps her foot and throws out her arms. "Who does that?"

"Assholes." I'm sitting hard on my urge to keep my amusement in check.

She points at my face. "Exactly. And finally, we were so busy that I never got a break. No biggie, I work without breaks from time to time, but this means that I didn't get dinner and hence the fact that I could eat the ass out of an alligator right now." She's done, staring while waiting for me to say something.

"Alligator ass." My throat aches from trying not to laugh. "Gross."

"What?" She throws her arms out to her sides. "You asked!"

A laughter born from deep in my gut explodes from my lips. The force of it sends my head back and then forward where I almost double over. I've never been around a woman like this, one who can look as though she belongs on the runway but speaks as if she were raised in a gym with a bunch of guys.

On that thought, my laughter fades. From the little I know about her, I can probably assume her way with words was probably a defense mechanism she came up with early on. She'd mentioned the night her dad cleaned her out that he left with a few parting words. My guess is he's not thanking her for her generosity. Fucking prick.

I suppose after years of being shit talked to, she'd learn to defend herself with words. The cramp in my side, from laughing, moves up to my chest. As hot as I find her attitude, it sucks to know how she came to have one.

I often wonder what it would be like to have my daughter back: seventeen years old, hanging with her friends, making college plans, dating. What kind of woman would she have been? Tender? Outgoing? Athletic? I swallow back the emotion bubbling to the surface. No use dwelling on shit that'll never be.

I grab Eve's hand and lead her to the hostess. There's nothing I can do that'll bring Rosie back, but if my taking care of Eve can soften the blow of all her shit-for-brains dad has done to her, well, that's something.

TWENTY

EVE

I'm standing in front of the coffee maker, tapping my fingernails and waiting until there's enough in the pot to fill my cup. It's seven-thirty in the morning, and I can already feel the heat of the day coming through my kitchen window, which means summer's in full swing.

Warmth hits my back, and I jump in surprise but calm when two huge hands slide around my belly.

"You been up long?" His lips at my ear remind me of his hot mouth between my legs last night, and a shiver races down my spine.

"Not long." I lean back into his hard body and warm as his hold on me tightens.

He brings his mouth to my neck to nip and then soothe with a soft kiss. "How're you feeling?"

My cheeks heat. Last night after I ate and had a few beers, I was eager to show my appreciation. Not for the meal, but for the fact that he keeps showing up. And I did that by begging Cameron to go rough. He let go, gave it to me in every way I'd asked and new ways I'd never thought of. It was gorgeous, punishing, and beautiful at the same time. And although my body is a little tender, my heart is fuller than it's ever been.

Which scares the ever-loving shit out of me.

"I'm good. You?"

He chuckles low and warm against my skin. "You fucking kidding me, doll? The way you let me in last night? No rules, no objections. Shit." He squeezes me hard and drops a long, lingering kiss below my ear. "Blew me away."

My whole body warms at his approval. I grab his hands to loosen his grip and spin in his arms to face him. He's dressed in the black T-shirt and jeans he wore last night, the hair around his face is a tiny bit damp, and his scruffy jaw smells like soap.

I run my hands up his arms and lock them behind his neck. "I was thinking…" My stomach flips and flutters at what I'm about to say, but it's important I get this out while we're together. "This thing between us…"

He blinks, and his jaw goes rigid. *Shit.*

"Do you think we're to a point where we don't necessarily have to keep it a secret from everyone?" I brace for his reaction, expecting him to tell me that we need to keep things quiet for the sake of his job or some other excuse that will hurt but I'll accept.

His hand cups my jaw, and he runs his thumb along my cheekbone. "You ready to go public?"

I blink up at him, shocked at the sincerity I see in his eyes. "Am I…? Fuck yeah, I'm ready to go public." I slam my mouth closed. *Eager much?* I mentally groan.

The corner of his mouth jumps a tiny bit. "Not sure you fully understand all we'll be takin' on."

A cloud of worry settles over my brief excitement. "Explain it then."

"Media attention, reactions from your friends—"

"*My* friends?" I've already told him I don't have a lot—or any—friends.

"The Slades."

Well, except them. "I'll talk to them. They just want me to be happy and"—I shrug—"being with you makes me happy."

163

"Our age difference is going to be a problem for a lot of people. I'll do my best to shield you from that, but you need to know there's gonna be talk, and that shit will not be pleasant."

"Do you not know me at all? I can handle a few harsh words, Cameron. But I do love"—his eyes change for a split second, like shutters automatically dropping down over them before he realizes it and pushes them away—"the fact that you want to protect me from that." I rake my fingers through his hair.

"All right then. Public it is." There's worry in his eyes, but he's giving me what I want, so I ignore it.

I'm sure he's concerned about how the announcement of our hanging out is going to go down. I just hope he's not too worried that he backs out.

"I'll talk to Raven today."

He leans in and kisses my forehead. "I'll talk to Slade at the gym."

Oh crap, this is really happening: a real public relationship or at least the most *real* and public relationship I've ever had. My heart beats faster and my palms get sweaty.

He pulls his phone from his pocket, and once it's in his hand, I hear it vibrating. His eyebrows pull together before he locks down his jaw.

"I gotta get this." He releases me and turns away, moving out into the living room. "'Li, what's up?"

My stomach plummets. The front door opens and closes. He's taking a phone call from his ex-wife and moving outside for privacy. So whatever he has to say he doesn't want me to hear.

A weight of jealousy mixed with curiosity presses in. I fill up my coffee cup and move to the wall closest to the front door to see if I can pick up words or maybe a tone. The low rumble of Cameron's voice comes through. I lean closer, close my eyes, and concentrate.

"…sounds good. I'll see you after I get off." He pauses. "I'm at home, why?"

My gut lurches into my throat. He's not telling his ex-wife where he is. Why the motherfuck not?

"Ry said he was going out with some friends last night." Another long pause. "Look I gotta run. We'll talk when I come by later."

My eyes fly open, and I race as fast as I can with a cup of hot coffee back to the kitchen. Awareness overtakes me as he strolls back inside. I'm standing in my kitchen, wearing an old tee and sleeping shorts while the guy I'm dating, kinda, I guess, is talking to and making plans with his former supermodel turned seriously fucking gorgeous older lady, D'Lilah Monroe. Who, by the way, he lied to about where he was. What the fuck is that?

He leans a hip on the counter and looks up at me. "What're your plans today?"

Oh, I don't know, probably sit around and fantasize about all the many ways you're able to break my heart. "Work. Lunch shift."

He grunts. "I need to get to work, but I'll call you later." His eyes narrow on mine and he tilts his head. "Oh fuck. What happened?"

"What? Nothing. What're you talking about?"

He pins me with a glare and allows a few seconds of silence to tick between us. "You want this shit, you work for it. And by work, I mean you do not fucking lie to me if something is pissin' you off."

"Rich coming from you."

His head jerks and he blinks. "Repeat that."

"I find it laughable that you expect honesty while you're lying to your ex-wife about where you are."

His eyes flash with anger. "You were listening."

"I thought you wanted this." I motion between us.

"I do. But with 'Li things are...complicated."

I don't want to know, I really don't, but I have to ask. "Are you still in love with her?"

"No."

His answer came so fast, as if he didn't require even a fraction of a second to consider the question. My pulse calms. A little.

"Oh, well." I take a sip of my coffee. "I, uh, wasn't expecting you to be so certain."

"Well, I am." He moves closer and hooks me around the neck to pull my face to his. "I didn't tell D'lilah where I was because, like I told you before, she upsets easily. I got a half million things to do today, which now includes swinging by her place to show her how to work the TV, which I've done about ten times already. Last thing I need is her busting out the waterworks to further complicate the complicated day I already have lined up."

I lick my lips, wanting so badly to lean in and shove my tongue into his mouth. "That makes sense."

"Yeah, it does. And when I'm over there tonight, I'll talk to her about us. Then I won't need to lie to her anymore."

Us.

"That would be good. But um...I don't want her to be upset."

"Sweet of you, babe, but the woman upsets over fucking everything. She'll get over it."

"Right."

"In the meantime, you talk to your girl Raven. I'll pull Slade aside today and lay it out for him too." He cringes slightly, as if the very thought of talking to Jonah is an unpleasant one.

"Deal."

He covers my mouth with his and kisses me so deeply that I have to brace myself against the counter to keep from falling. When he breaks the kiss, I sway.

He nips at my lip. "Stay on your feet, babe." And with a wink, he leaves.

—

CAMERON

My morning has been overloaded, and getting a late start only made matters worse. While waiting on the board to make their final announcement about the possibility of me returning to the octagon, I've got future fights to set up, promo shit to approve, and enough in-house auditing BS to last me a fucking lifetime.

I flip open my notebook and check again to make sure I have the free half hour I need. Yep, open. I write *going public* in the empty space. "Layla, you mind grabbing Slade for me?"

She doesn't answer, but I overhear her on the phone talking to Killer, who now owns the title of Locker Room Manager. "Cam needs Jonah to his office ASAP. What? Oh, Axelle's great." A long pause. "Sure, I'll let her know. Thanks."

"Killer's sending him over." She moves from her desk to the chair across from me but doesn't sit. "You need me in here to take notes?"

I shake my head and lean back in my chair. "No, this is some personal shit that needs to be settled."

"Uh oh. That sounds intense."

I'm hoping after he hears me out it won't be, but it's possible. "Nothing to worry about."

Her eyes narrow. "You sure? I mean should I have Blake come sit at my desk?"

I know what she's asking without her saying the words. She thinks whatever I have to say is going to set Jonah off. She's right. But fuck if I need a moderator or a bodyguard.

"I got it."

"You feel like letting me in on what's going on?"

I shake my head. "What is it about women always needing to be the first to know?"

"Don't ask me. It's in our DNA. We can't help it." She props her hand on her hips. "So? You gonna tell me?"

"After I talk to Slade, we'll talk."

As far as I can tell, Jonah is the only person who looks after Eve like a father. It makes sense now, after the day we had lunch and he'd clearly sensed what was going on between us, that he'd be protective. He'd alluded to the fact that I didn't know anything about her. My guess is that he was talking about her father.

That being the case, I'm going to have to pull back my pride and come at this like I'm asking permission. The thought makes my jaw lock, but I'd expect no less from a man interested in dating my daughter.

Shit.

As soon as the words filter though my brain, I cringe at how easily they came.

"You needed a word?" Jonah's standing in the doorway to my office.

"That's my cue." Layla turns and passes Jonah on the way to the door. "Hey, Jonah."

He nods to Layla, and she shuts the door behind her.

I stand and motion for him to grab a seat. "Won't take long."

He glares at me for a second too long, proving his point, and then sits. Things have been quiet between the heavyweight fighter and me since that afternoon at Nori. I can tell he's still not over it, but I'm hoping what I have to say will help.

I take a deep breath and sit back in my chair. "It's about Eve."

"Fuck." He shakes his head, but doesn't move his eyes from me. "I told you to stay away from her."

"Couldn't do that."

"Yeah? Well now we've got problems." His jaw ticks.

"Let me explain." I lean in, resting my crossed forearms on my desk. "I like her."

His eyebrows pinch together, further enhancing his already pissed-off expression.

"She's uh…different."

"You fuckin' kidding me with this, Cam? You *like* her? She's *different?* Do you have any idea what that girl's been through? She needs…" He shakes his head. "No, she deserves better than that."

That's the second time Slade has referred to Eve's past. I register on some level he knows more about her than I do, but that's overshadowed by jealousy that another guy holds her secrets.

I have no right to want that part of her. Deep secrets are often embedded in a part of our souls seldom shared with others. Lord knows I've got secrets of my own that I protect. Eve's no different, which is not a surprise. I sensed it in her early on. But her hiding them doesn't keep me from wishing I knew them.

"You're right. Eve deserves better. But I'd be an idiot to turn her away."

He leans in, his temper obviously working to get the best of him. "She's twenty-one. You takin' advantage of a—"

"I'm not taking advantage of her." *Am I?* Does spending time with someone because you like the way she makes you feel equal taking advantage? Thoughts for another time. "I don't know what else to say besides we're hanging out and we're not going to hide it anymore. I know Eve's dad is a fuckin' prick, your wife is the closest thing she has to family, and you've taken on the role of her protector."

"You know about her dad?"

"Fuck yeah, the dude's up in her shit, causing problems. Wouldn't mind the chance to face off with the dick."

"You get that chance, call me. I want first dibs."

"Can't promise you first, but I'll keep him planted 'til you arrive."

"Good enough."

The tension in the room fades.

"Bottom line? Eve's not comfortable hiding our hanging out from you guys."

He cringes, as if somehow those words mean something. "Yeah, I can't imagine she is."

"I told her I'd square things with you, she's gonna talk with your woman today, and once you two are in the know, we'll share."

He takes a deep breath, leans back in his chair, and rubs his jaw before dropping his hand. "You sure you know what you're doing? This whole thing sounds like a recipe for bad shit."

"Not sure what you mean by that, but fuck you very much for your confidence." He's not wrong to be worried. I've never loved anyone outside of my kids, and after Rosie…Well, I'll never set myself up for that kind of pain again.

"All right, man. She's a grown woman. If she wants to hang with your ugly ass, that's on her."

"You care about Eve the way you say you do, you won't make this shit harder than it has to be."

"Yeah, I'd have said the same shit if I were in your shoes." He stands and extends a hand. "I'm good."

I rise and shake his hand. "Nice to know."

"If you hurt her"—he leans forward, his palms on the desk—"I'll kick your ass."

"If I hurt her, I'll *let* you kick my ass."

He doesn't look completely sold, but he's holding it in well. That should make Eve happy. And even though I don't love the woman, I do enjoy making her smile.

I should call her and tell her the good news. Bringing my phone out of my pocket, I scroll to her number.

"Cam, your teleconference starts in three minutes," Layla says from her desk.

I stow my phone. It'll have to wait until later, if she doesn't hear it first from Raven, who no doubt will be called by Jonah the second he gets a chance.

"Go ahead, Layla." I pick up my desk phone. "Patch me in."

Work first, play later. That's the way it is, the way it'll always be.

TWENTY-ONE

EVE

I cruise into work just on time, a spring in my step and belly full of food after grocery shopping. That overage from last night not only set me up with a stocked kitchen, but I was also able to make a small payment on my past-due electric bill.

Happier than I've been in a long time, I called Raven on my way to work, and she agreed to meet me for coffee at the end of my shift. I can't wait to tell her about Cameron and me. Hell, I still can't believe we're officially um…dating? Or…doesn't matter what it's called. Fact is we're letting people know that we're together, which is more than I could've hoped for.

Throwing smiles to anyone who'll look my way, I head to the back office to lock up my purse. Life is good. So, so good. And it's been so long since I've had good I'm going to rub everyone's face it in for as long as it lasts.

I push through the office door and freeze. "Oh, Seth, you're here." Fuck. I was hoping the GM's lackey would work the night shift. Oh well, not even he can bring me down. Not today.

"Ms. Dawson." He knows my first name, I've asked him to use it repeatedly, but he continues to speak to me like the creepy bad guy from "The Matrix." I roll my eyes and move to the filing cabinet to stash my purse.

"Before you do that, have a seat." He motions to the chair on the other side of his—or rather my—desk.

I huff out a long breath that I make sure is loud enough for him to hear. He's going to lecture me and waste my time about something like making sure the silverware is double polished instead of single.

"What's up?" I take a seat, my purse in my lap, and wait.

He stands up, moves around the desk, and sits on it at an angle with one foot still on the ground. "Is there something you'd like to share with me, Ms. Dawson?"

I clutch my purse tighter. "Um…no?"

He nods, crosses hairy forearms over his wimpy chest, and tilts his head. "You sure?"

My mouth goes dry, and I force a casual shrug. "Pretty sure, yeah."

He narrows his eyes. "Anything eventful go on here last night after I left?"

"Not really. Eduardo stayed late because you let all the kitchen guys take off early, so he was stuck with dish duty."

"So you don't have anything you'd like to share? About last night?"

He can't possibly know, can he? "Can we cut the twenty questions, and you just get to the point?"

"The deposit from last night."

I suck in a breath. *Holy fuck.* How does he know about that? He left at least an hour before I did. Unless…"What about it?"

A quick smile of pity appears before he wipes it away. "Honesty will avoid formal charges, Ms. Dawson. Think about that, and let me ask you again. Do you have anything you'd like to tell me about the deposit last night?"

My mind races and my face heats. He set me up. That's the only way he'd know about the overage and the only reason I wasn't able to figure out where the extra money came from. Asshole.

"I was short on money this month. We got slammed last night, so I never got a break to eat dinner." I shrug.

He nods for me to continue.

I swallow hard and bite the inside of my mouth. Last night, I was so hungry and so desperate it didn't feel as wrong as speaking the words feels now. "I took the money."

"Hm." He studies his khaki pant leg. "So you admit to stealing?"

"Yeah, although I wouldn't call it *stealing*. I've been working here since I was sixteen. There've been nights where we get slammed, and I have to work through my break. If it's that big of a deal, you can take it out of my next paycheck."

"Ms. Dawson, there's nothing that justifies stealing. That money didn't belong to you. No matter how you twist it in your head, stealing is stealing."

"Okay, fine. I apologize. When I get my next check, I'll reimburse you. Now, can I get to work so I can earn a paycheck that'll keep me fed so I'll no longer have to *steal*?"

"I'm afraid we're going to have to let you go."

Everything goes still: my breath, heart, every muscle in my body. Even my eyes refuse to blink.

"You can go ahead and collect your things, and we'll have your final paycheck, minus the amount you took, ready for you in two days."

Is this a joke?

I blink as blood returns to my brain. "Hold on. You're firing me?"

"Yes. You're being let go, but because of your honesty, we won't press charges."

"But I've given my life to this restaurant. I've worked here since I was a kid."

"Don't think of it as a bad thing; think of it as a chance for new opportunities."

"Are you fucking kidding me?" My voice booms and echoes off the walls. "I have no work experience outside of Nori. I'll never get hired after being fired for something like this."

"I'm sorry. If you needed money for food, you should've come to me. I could've requested an advance on your paycheck. Stealing is never the answer."

"So write me up, slap me on the hand, but don't fire me."

"This is something we can't overlook."

"I can't fucking believe you're doing this to me." I can't afford to lose this job. My house, car, utilities, if I don't get them paid soon, I'll lose everything.

"I'm sorry."

"No, you're not!" Dammit, I need to calm down. I drop my gaze to my lap and take a deep breath. "Mr. Gamboni, please, I need this job. I'll do whatever you ask. Just give me another chance. Please."

He shakes his head. "Sorry, orders are from Cavat. I'm just doing my job, Eve."

Oh, now he knows my damn name. Fuck this.

I grab my purse and stomp around the desk. Inside the top drawer are a few of my personal items—nail file, lip gloss, bottle of aspirin—that I shove in my purse. I snag the pen he has tucked into the breast pocket of his shirt. "This is mine too." After dropping it in my purse, I storm out of there and slam the door behind me.

"*Sayonara*, assholes." I head out to my car and point it toward the Slade's house.

My coffee date with Raven at four-thirty just got upgraded to a tequila date at ten a.m.

"Fuckin' dicks!" I throw back another shot of tequila and cringe against the flame that slides down my throat.

"I'm so sorry, Eve." Raven's sitting next to me on the top step of her pool. She's wrapped in a cool fifties-style black halter maternity swimsuit, her hair piled on top of her head and black oversized sunglasses shading her eyes.

I called her after leaving Nori, and she got out of work to hang out with me. I guess Guy has been trying to get her to back off on her workload anyway since she's getting closer to her due date. The second I stormed in her house, she tossed me a bikini and handed me a bottle of tequila. Best friends don't get best-*er* than that.

I put the shot glass down by the bottle on the pool deck. "I don't know what I'm going to do now. I can't put Nori down as a reference. What if they ask why I was let go?"

Raven's eyebrows drop below her frames. "Why didn't you come to me? I had no clue you were hurting for money."

"I can't ask you for money, Rave. It feels so wrong. I mean we came from nothing, ya know? I know you have like zillions now, but I need to find my own." I flick the water a few times. "Although, looking back, I guess coming to you would've been a better option. Hindsight's a dirty whore."

She doesn't say anything, and I'm grateful for that. I can't believe I did something so stupid. What was I thinking?

"Maybe you should try to fight it. I've heard of companies getting sued for not making sure employees get breaks." Raven munches on a plate of grapes.

"Even if I had the money to hire a lawyer, which I don't, they'll never give me my job back." I shrug. "I don't know. Maybe that little troll Seth was right. I could use something new."

"Too bad you don't know crap about cars. I know Guy would love a mechanic to take over for me. Then I can just lock myself up at home and become the perfect little princess, safe in the tower while I await the birth of my baby." She chucks a grape to the far end of the pool.

"Oh boy…"

She turns her shades toward me, and even behind the dark lenses, I can feel her scowl. "More like oh *men*. I tried to get him to let me take the Nova to work the other day so I could change the oil on it, and you would've thought I was asking him if I could shove razor blades up my nose."

"I don't see what the big deal is. If he'd give just a little, you wouldn't be pulling so hard in the opposite direction."

She grunts and inhales another cheekful of grapes.

"Um…speaking of men. There's the thing I wanted to talk to you about, you know, before I got fired."

"Oh, yeah." She finishes chewing and swallows. "That's right. What is it?"

I push off the step and wade into the shallow end of the pool. "Turns out you were right, and I, uh…I don't think I'm gay."

She tilts her head, and this time shoves her sunglasses up to her head to shoot daggers in my direction. "No kidding."

"Ha-ha." I take a deep breath. "I've been kinda seeing someone."

Her eyes go wide, and a big grin pulls at her mouth. "That's awesome. Where did you meet him?"

"That's the funny part. You introduced us."

She blinks, and her eyebrows pinch together. "Huh Oh!" She snaps and grins. "Mason. I mean, technically I think Jonah or Blake introduced you, but it is Mason, right? You were at the party with him the other—"

"No, it's not Mason."

"Oh." Her expression turns sour. "Who is it?"

"It's, uh…Cameron."

Her entire expression goes slack.

"Unexpected, I know. We just...We slept together, and I thought that's all it would end up being, like a seriously amazing one-night stand, but..."

"Eve—"

"He showed up, and we slept together again, and holy shit, it was like..." I make an explosion sound and slap my palms on the water. "He kinda blew me off after that, but then when I went to his party, we hooked up again, started talking, and here we are."

"Eve, but he's kind of—"

"Don't freak out, okay? I really like him, and at first I thought he was just using me, but he's taken me out a couple times, and I don't want to hide this from you or anyone anymore."

"Old."

"What?"

"Don't get me wrong. Cameron Kyle is about as handsome as they come, but isn't he forty or something?"

"No, he's not forty!" I flick water at her. "He's thirty-eight."

"Big difference."

"Jonah's older than you."

"Yeah, but not by"—she counts on her fingers—"seventeen years."

"Age doesn't mean anything, Rave. And you know I've always had a thing for older guys."

"True."

"Please, just be happy for me. It's been a horrible day, and I could use a little good right now." I tilt my head to the tequila bottle. "I mean good outside of Señor Patron."

"Of course I'm happy for you." She waddles across the shallow end and hugs me as much as she can with her pregnant belly between us. "I just don't want you to get hurt again." There's pain in her voice.

My chest cramps. I hate that she feels responsible for what went down between Vince and me. "Rave, I'm fine. I'll never get hurt like that again. I'm walking with my eyes *open* from here on out, okay?"

She pulls back and smiles. "Okay. So let's celebrate. You get a shot. I'll go grab a carton of ice cream." She claps her hands and exits the pool to the outdoor kitchen freezer.

God, I love her. A wave of sadness hits me. We've been everything to each other for so long, but once that baby comes, things will never be the same between us. She's the only family I've ever had. Jonah's taken a piece of her, and whatever's left needs to go to her baby. I breathe deeply through the cramping in my chest. This is life; people change and they move on. Everyone does it, and soon it'll be Raven's turn to walk away.

It'll be okay.

I'll be okay.

I have to be.

———

CAMERON

"'Li, you have to turn on the TV here and the cable box here. If you want to watch a DVD, you have to hit input until it says HDMI." I'm pointing to all the different buttons on the new remote I got. I thought it would be easier for her since each button clearly says "TV On" and "TV Off," but I was wrong. She's still not getting it.

I don't remember her being so dense when we were younger. Then again I was more about her image than I was about her as a woman. Being married to a model gave me some exceptional bragging rights, but I never really searched to know her well beyond her gorgeous looks and public personality. If I had, I doubt we ever would've gotten married.

"Oh, so here." She presses "TV On." The television flickers to life.

"Yeah."

After a few more lessons with the remote, I'm ready to get home and call Eve. I never got the chance to tell her about my conversation with Slade this morning. I'd hoped to call her on my way to 'Li's, but ended up on the phone with Ryder.

"Any plans for the big day?" She picks at the ends of her hair.

Ryder's eighteenth birthday is coming up, and the poor kid always has to share it with Rosie, even though she's not around to celebrate with us. Except for the couple times D'lilah was in rehab, she's a mess when the twins' birthday rolls around. It starts about a week before and escalates until the day of, something I'm really not fucking looking forward to for my kid.

"Ry wants to hang with his buddies this year. I'll take him out to dinner the weekend after."

"Oh, that would be great. Can, uh...? Can I go with you guys?"

Since we'll be celebrating the week after, she should be in decent condition to be out in public. I'd hoped to bring Eve along, depending on how things go between us until then. She gets along well with Ryder, and now that I think about it, she hit it off well with 'Li too. Eve's like a catalyst for all things happy. She can talk music with Ry and fashion with D'lilah.

"Yeah, I'll talk to Ryder and see where he wants to go. We'll work out the details."

"Thanks, Cam." She turns and flips through channels.

"You good?" I push up from the couch and fish my keys from my pocket.

"You're leaving?" It's obvious from the look on her face that she doesn't want me to go. The woman has lost every friend she's ever had because of her drinking, and it's got to be lonely living in this big house alone, haunted by memories.

"Need to get home; have shit to do." Just the thought of spending a lot of time in this house with her gives me the sweats.

As if on cue, my eyes slide to the backdoor that leads to the pool. The sound of Rosie's laughter rings through my head, and I pinch the bridge of my nose to push it back. *Stay on your feet.*

"I'll be in touch."

She smiles and sinks into the couch with her glass of wine and the remote. Her idea of quitting ended up being a switch from hard liquor to wine.

I quick walk my ass to the car, feeling like I'm being chased by ghosts from the past. Once in the car, I hit Eve's contact info on my phone while backing out of the driveway. It goes straight to voicemail. Huh.

No text messages, but I have one missed call from Slade. I hit his contact info and wait for the ring.

"Cam," Jonah answers sounding pissed, but that's not unusual.

"You call?"

"Just dropped your woman off at your place. Your boy let her in."

"Eve?" Fuck, stupid question.

"I certainly motherfuckin' hope so, man."

"You feel like tellin' me why?"

"Girl's drunk as shit."

What? My dash says it's only eight o'clock at night. She was working until late afternoon. "What the hell did she get up to?"

"Sat by the pool with my girl all day, hit the tequila girls-gone-wild-style. Fed her, hydrated her, but she's still drunk as shit."

This doesn't sound like Eve. The night we met she was pulling from that Long Island and cringing as if she were drinking battery acid.

"Not *all* day." I lay a little heavier on the gas. "She worked until this afternoon."

"That's not the story I'm hearin'. She showed up early."

"Any clue why she's feelin' the need to get hammered hanging out with a pregnant woman all day?"

No answer.

Fuck me.

"Slade, what the fuck?"

"Think you need to talk to your woman."

Shit. "Right."

"Later."

I hit End and point the Maserati toward home. Even if her day was filled with girl talk and booze, why would she want to be brought to my house?

This can't good.

TWENTY-TWO

EVE

"I love this song! Turn it up!" I bob my head to "21st Century Digital Boy" by Bad Religion while lounging in a super comfy black beanbag chair in Ryder's room.

As soon as Jonah dropped me off, Ryder let me in and dragged me to his room to check out his extensive music collection. I was expecting shelves lined with CDs, but this guy has a full-blown music database on his computer that's hooked up to one of the most intricate sound systems I've ever seen.

Ryder drums to the beat on his bed with actual drumsticks while I'm slumped into a beanbag chair, foot tapping, and singing into my thumb. I haven't been here long, but I'm slowly feeling my buzz recede and hope I'm sober by the time Cameron gets home to avoid making a complete ass out of myself.

"Do you like Alkaline Trio?" Ryder yells over the blaring music.

"Love them!"

He leans over and moves the mouse, clicks, and "I Wanna Be a Warhol" comes screaming through the speakers. I close my eyes, sing, and smile at how easy it is to get lost in a good song. I have a shitty voice, but damn if belting out the words to a song doesn't make me feel like Celine Dion.

"Eve, guitar solo!" Ryder smiles big, his hair isn't all spiked out today, and he's not wearing any of the eyeliner that I've seen on him in the past. He looks a lot like his mom, almost pretty, but with a rugged edge that is all Cameron.

I roll out of my beanbag cocoon and jump to my feet, air guitar hands in place.

"Here it comes! You ready?"

"Yeah, dude!" I nod and motion to my invisible guitar. "Can't you see?"

He laughs but doesn't break the constant beat with the sticks. The guitar solo rings through the speakers and I shred it out on my air guitar. Knees bent, arms straight, and leaning back like I'm Flea from the Chili Peppers, I jump up on the bed, grateful that I'd slipped off my shoes earlier, and bounce while jamming out, air guitar flying, to finish off the song with everything I have left. As the last chord rings out, I drop to the bed, breathing hard and laughing my ass off.

Damn, that was fun.

"Good job, punk rock girl."

I hold up one hand and bring my thumb to my lips. "You've been a great crowd, Las Vegas. Thank you and good night." I swing my arm to dangle my fist off the bed then open my hand to mimic my dropping of the mic.

The deep sound of Ryder's laugh fills the room but is abruptly cut off.

"What the fuck's going on in here?"

I push up on my elbows to find Cameron standing in the doorway, his jaw hard, muscles bulging, fists clenched. I cringe away from his hard glare.

"Listening to some music." Ryder drops his drumsticks, and now I can see there's something else he's inherited from his father. His scowl. And it's pointed directly at his dad. "What did you *think* was going on?"

Wait. Finally sobering up a little, my brain kick-starts and realization dawns.

"Hold on." I roll off the bed and stand between where Ryder's sitting and Cameron's standing. I turn my gaze to the doorway. "I came over to see you, but you weren't home, so we've been hanging out waiting until you got here."

"Eve, my room. Now." His eyes fix on Ryder. "Need to have a word with my son. Then I'll have a word with you."

I rest a hand on my cocked hip. "Are you pissed?"

"I come home and you and my boy are in his room with the door shut, and you're lying on his bed, breathing like you just ran a marathon. What do you think?"

"Holy shit, Dad, are you fucking kidding me?"

"Eve, go."

"I was playing air guitar and jumping on the bed!" Anger flares in my blood.

"I fucking told you, woman, go to my room. Now!" He roars in my face, which only escalates my anger.

"Stop treating me like a child!"

"Stop acting like one."

"Don't tell me what to do! You're not my dad!"

"Yes, and thank fuck for that."

I sway back on my heels, blood drains from my head, and I get dizzy. "What?"

He drops his chin and shakes his head. "That's not what I meant."

"No, I know exactly what you meant." I head to the door of Ryder's bedroom. "Bye, Ryder."

"Later, Eve."

I move to slip by Cameron, but he snags my upper arm. "Please." He doesn't look at me. "Stay."

I don't say anything. Truth is I have no way to get home, and if I'm being honest, I really don't want to leave. Yes, what he said was shitty. What he's assuming and accusing me of is even shittier, and what he said about the whole dad thing was the absolute shittiest. And even still, I want to stay.

"Ryder, man, I'm sorry."

I blink up at Cameron, who's fixed on his son. His expression has relaxed some, and if I'm not mistaken, I'd say there's regret in his eyes.

"Whatever, Dad."

Cameron mumbles a string of curse words under his breath, before addressing his son again. "Long night. Birthday coming up. Lost it."

It's then I see Ryder's expression soften. Something Cameron said spoke to him, but what was it? Birthday maybe?

"Right, I understand. It's cool." He pushes up and moves to his computer, giving us his back, and then grabs a set of keys. "I'm going out."

At Ryder's dismissal, Cameron tugs my arm and guides me to his bedroom. He shuts the door behind us and leads me to his bed where he deposits me. I sit cross-legged and stare at him as he stares back from his standing position at the edge.

"What happened?" He looks as though he's settled in, not moving an inch until he gets whatever information he's looking for.

"I already told you. I came here to see you—"

"Not that. What happened today? Why were you at the Slade's sippin' booze all day with a pregnant woman when you should've been at work?"

"Just sayin'…you totally sound like a dad right now." And what is it about the parental tone he's using that makes my belly flip and my insides turn to liquid?

"I am a dad. Don't change the subject."

"No, *you* don't change the subject. What happened in there?"

He props his hands on his hips and drops his chin to his chest. "I'm a dick. I'm sorry. Won't happen again."

I blink and stare, searching for the right words, but I'm shocked at how quickly he fessed up and owned his mistake. "Oh, well...good."

Eyes back on me, he shrugs. "Your turn. Why were you drinking with Slade's wife?"

Aw hell. I knew I was going to have to tell him I got fired, and it wouldn't be a big deal if I could leave it at that, but a man like Cameron is going to want answers, and I'm ashamed to tell him the truth.

"Bad day." I dip my chin and pray he lets it go at that.

"Explain."

God, he's bossy. "I um...got in a bit of trouble at work. That guy I told you about? The one doing the internal audit? He pulled me aside when I got there this morning."

Please, let that be enough.

"And?"

Dammit.

I throw my hands up and let them drop hard on the bed. "I got fired."

Silence.

"He pulled me in when I got there and he let me go."

He props his hands on his hips. "They have good reason?"

Yes. "Not really."

I drop to the closest pillow and hope to miraculously pass out to end this conversation.

"You need to file a complaint. They can't fire you without good reason."

Why does he insist on making me go there?

I turn my face into the pillow.

"Judging by your reaction, my guess is they had good reason."

I nod into the down-feathered cushion.

"Share that."

I shake my head.

"Can't help you if I don't know the details, doll." His calling me doll in that low rumbled voice has the power to make me do whatever he asks.

"Don't need help. I'm good." The words are mumbled so deeply into the pillow that I'm not even sure he heard them. The bed shifts, and then the heat of his hand strokes through my hair.

"Whatever happened was obviously bad enough that you went to seek comfort in your girl and the bottle. Not gonna lie, but you boozin' doesn't sit well with me. First, I know you don't like the taste, and second I already got one drunken woman riding my ass all the time. But having said that, I understand why you'd want to numb the shit from you being let go."

I roll over and fix my eyes on his, which are no longer *totally* glaring. "You do?"

"I do. I also know you're freaked the fuck out to have no money after your dad took you for all you're worth and you're livin' off tip money."

I turn my head away and heat rushes to my cheeks. He cups my jaw and turns me to face him. "Talk to me."

"I haven't been living off tip money." I'm so ashamed to be having this conversation that the words come out barely a whisper.

"What have you been living off of?"

I shake my head. "Nothing."

His eyes go wider than I've ever seen them, which isn't all that wide, but it's shock he's feeling, I'm sure. "You fucking with me?"

"No. I've been eating at work every day."

"Shit, Eve, that's one meal a day."

I nod.

"You can't live off that."

"I did, up until the other night. I um…borrowed some money from the restaurant. The till was over. I honestly didn't think anyone would notice. I was so fucking hungry, I hadn't eaten all day, and I acted out of total desperation. Stupid, I know."

"Why didn't you come to me?"

I peek at him out of the corner of my eye. "We being honest?"

He nods.

"Because I want you to like me. And I already feel like you know enough about me *not* to like me. I didn't want to give you another reason."

"You think asking me for money would be a strike against you?"

"Cameron…"

His eyes go soft.

"I know guys like you: rich, powerful, handsome. Women throw themselves at you for a variety of reasons, but money is a huge motivator. I didn't want you to think of me like that." The kindness in his expression is drilling holes in my chest. I can't take it and turn away. "Besides, I can do this. I've managed to take care of myself my whole life. I don't need or want anyone's help."

He cups my face again, twisting me to him, but this time before I can even register his face, his mouth presses tight to mine and my eyes drift shut.

I tilt my head and part my lips to swallow his answering groan as his tongue glides into my mouth. The taste, like clean water and Cameron, floods my senses. I shove my fingers into his hair, holding him to me. Heat in my belly spreads south, and I push up on one arm, desperate to get closer. He grabs

my hips, drags me across his lap, and I turn so that I'm strad-
dling him.

All my worry and anxiety from the day work to further fuel
my need. Like exercising for stress relief, I'm drowning in
Cameron as therapy. I roll my hips, grinding down on the hard
length that stands between us.

"Fuck, doll." He holds my hips still, but tugs at my waist-
band. "You make me crazy." He drags his lips down my throat.

I moan and drop my head to the side. "Good crazy or bad
crazy?"

He pulls back and meets my eyes with a heavy lidded glare,
but he doesn't speak.

Oh no. That's gotta be bad crazy.

—

CAMERON

My fingers dig into the flesh of her hips. I'm out of control
when I'm around her. Reacting to every irritant, jealousy rises
up out of nowhere intent on destroying whoever's in sight.
First Mason, tonight my own kid. How the hell does she manage to fuck with me without seeming to have the slightest clue
she's doing it?

Good crazy or bad crazy? Shit…both.

I don't take my eyes off hers, and she drops her gaze under
my stare.

"Never mind. I think your non-answer is my answer." Her
hands slide from my neck down my arms.

"I was married to D'lilah for six years. In all that time,
including the time we dated, I never went to battle with another
man for her."

She looks up at me, blinking. "But she's D'lilah Monroe? I bet men were throwing themselves at her left and right."

I nod. "They were. And sometimes right in front of me. It's funny. Lookin' back, I think I was numb to it, accepted the fact that marrying a supermodel would come with that kind of attention."

"Had to be hard on a marriage."

"That's the fucked-up part. It wasn't. So fuck, what does that say about my feelings for her? It's not that I didn't care about her; it's just I didn't care enough. Only thing I ever fought for was my career. Take my wife, yeah, it sucks, but I'll live. Take away my fighting, and I hit my knees."

"Hit your knees?"

"Yeah, I fall. One thing I don't do is fall. Not anymore, not ever."

"So you hit your knees when you quit fighting?"

I'm not ready to share Rosie with Eve, so I lie. "Yeah. I picked myself back up and vowed I'd never let that shit happen again."

"Makes sense."

"Then I meet you, and I'm all over the place, wobbling on my feet." The words pour from my lips before I'm able to register what I'm feeling. The whole thing is…"Crazy."

Her eyes widen and her lips part.

"Not sure that's good crazy or bad crazy, but it's fucked up."

"The kind of fucked up you can live with?"

I run my hand up her back and tangle my fist into the long tendrils of her hair. "Come here."

She leans in, and I pull her bottom lip between my teeth before sliding my tongue into her soft hot mouth. So fucking good.

Between her hips rolling and the firm tips of her breasts brushing against my chest, my rational thinking dissipates fast. I roll us so that her back is to the bed and she has her legs wrapped around my waist.

"I, um…smell like chlorine and sunblock. I need to take a shower."

Fuck. That sounds perfect.

"I'm all over it, doll." I lift her off the bed and carry her with her legs wrapped tight to the bathroom. Setting her down, I pull my shirt over my head and step to her to help her do the same.

She's still in her black pants and white oxford that she wore to work this morning. Her eyes devour my chest, drifting from my side to my arms, studying my tattoos while she unbuttons her blouse to expose a bright white lace bra. I bite my lip to dull the urge to run my tongue in the valley of those perfect breasts and lose myself in the sweet and creamy smell of her skin while pushing inside her body.

I lean over and crank the shower on. When I turn back to her, she has her shirt off and bra loose. I watch in awe as she slides the straps down her arms, revealing herself to me.

"Damn." I suck in a breath as she hooks her thumbs into her pants and slides them, along with her panties to the floor.

I kick my pants off and pull her into my arms so fast a giggle escapes her lips.

"Laugh while you can. What we're about to do will be anything but funny."

Her eyes flare, and a tiny grin tugs at her lip. "Promise?"

I smack her ass, expecting her to giggle, but fuck me…she moans. I rub the tender spot on her backside and she presses in deeper, asking with her body. I swat her again, this time with more force.

"Yes." She drops her forehead to my chest.

I grind down against my urge bend her over the countertop and fuck her hard. "Shower."

She slides past me, and if I didn't know better, I'd swear she pressed in to rub those beautiful tits along my ribs as she went. Tempting, teasing, this girl pushes every single hot button I have while creating some of her own.

I follow her into the shower where she steps beneath the streaming water. She tips her head back, and the water cascades down her face and along the long column of her neck. Beautiful.

Lathering up a bar of soap, I tug her free from the spray. "I'll wash you."

She doesn't speak, but simply nods and waits. I turn her to face the stone wall and push her long hair to the front to expose her shoulders. Starting there, I rub bubbles into her skin, pressing in circles with my thumb to relieve the tension I feel she's carrying there.

Her head lulls to the side. "Mmm, that's nice."

"Quiet." It's instinctual. I can't even explain to myself why telling her what to do turns me on, but her trusting me, turning herself over to me in compliance, is hot. And the way her body sways on her feet, I'm willing to bet I'm not the only one enjoying this game.

I move from her shoulders down her back to her hips, every place my hands touch eliciting a small moan of approval. I step in close, pressing my front to her back while my hands wrap around to cup her breasts. She braces herself, both palms pressed flat against the wall. I slide my hand up to her neck, her chin, and cup her jaw, twisting just her face to meet mine. I push my tongue deep into her mouth, and she welcomes it with an eager thrust of her own.

My other hand slides down her belly to between her legs. "Open."

She follows my instructions and widens her legs so I can get between them.

"Tilt your hips."

She does.

"Little more."

Pushing against the wall, she arches her back, tilts her hips and offers what I've been asking for.

"Good girl."

I play, prime, and then in one long thrust, I'm in. One hand on her hip, the other wrapped around and filled with her breast, I move.

She meets me stroke for stroke, putting pressure on the wall to leverage herself against me. "More."

My hand comes down on her ass. "Not yet."

She groans and drops her head forward. Her long wet hair is spread over the slope of her back, which leads to the dip and flare of her hips. My eyes set on our connection and the pressure builds. The sound of our breathing mixes with the steam and sits heavily in the air.

I grind and roll against her, back and forth with deliberate strokes until her legs quake. I wrap my arm around her chest and pull her back to me, knowing that when it hits her, she's going to lose her footing.

"I've got you, babe."

Her head flies back and a long deep moan vibrates so deeply in her chest that I feel it against my arm. I hold her there until she comes down. Her head drops back to my shoulder and her body goes limp.

"Hands back to the wall."

She tilts her blue eyes to me, and a tiny grin lights her sated face. "'Kay."

I lift one eyebrow and she giggles. Fuck, this woman is cute as hell, sexy as shit, and breaking me down with every flutter of her long lashes.

She resumes her position, and I move slowly until she's backing up to chase me down. Her back dips, arching to take me in completely.

"That's it, baby."

It doesn't take long before I'm walking the line. I try to slow down, prolong my completion, but the sound of her moans is impossible to ignore. She twists her neck to look back at me, those big eyes half covered by sex-hazed lids. Our eyes locked, her teeth pull at that full bottom lip and the visual hits me in an erotic assault.

I power into her again and fold forward to growl into her neck. Perfection. My legs go wobbly, but I resist the urge to drop as the aftershocks roll through my body. Fuckin' hell, this woman.

Wrapping both arms around her waist, I pull her back to my chest, keeping us connected.

"That was beautiful." Her arm comes up to reach behind my neck and hold me to her.

"You're beautiful."

Her breath hitches, and she goes tense in my arms before she relaxes again. "I'm on the pill. Just in case you're wondering."

"I know."

"How?"

"Been in your bathroom, babe."

"You snooped!" She smacks me playfully on the forearm.

"I find it fucking hilarious that you leave shit out all over the place and when people see it you accuse them of snooping."

"I didn't leave them out!"

"They were right by your sink."

"Oh, well that's probably true."

"You good?" I back away at her nod, and she shivers.

Finishing up our shower, I wrap Eve in a towel before grabbing my own. "I'll grab you a shirt to sleep in."

"Oh, um…I'm staying the night?"

"Not unless you don't want to." A hollow cramp aches in my gut. What the fuck is that?

"I thought maybe I should go home."

The cramp gets worse. "Why exactly would you think that?"

She drops her gaze and picks at the towel. "I don't know. I guess I just don't want you getting sick of me too soon."

Is she fucking crazy?

I cross to her and tilt her chin to get her eyes. "Babe, what you just gave me in that shower…You think I'll ever get sick of you?"

"Oh, so…it's about the sex. I mean that's cool if it—"

"No, it's about you. You give it to me the way I like, listen when I need you to listen, but fight me when I need you to fight me. And I fuckin' love it when you fight me, babe. I'm thinking I'd like to get in there while you're pissed at me. Watch you come unglued while I'm buried deep."

Her eyes slide closed. "Damn."

"You want that too."

"I do."

"Spend the night with me, Eve. I'll pick a fight with you in the morning."

She bursts into laughter, and the sound loosens something in my chest, making it, I don't know, lighter.

That's what Eve does. She makes everything a little lighter, even when she's being a pain in the ass, and I dig that about her. I've lived a lot of my life under the heavy weight of failure—as a father, a husband, and a fighter—and then this girl breezes in all shit talk and 'tude, and fuck if she doesn't lift some of that weight.

TWENTY-THREE

EVE

Waking up jobless isn't as bad when I get to do it in Cameron's bed. I'm tucked to the front of his body, his big arm heavy over my waist, and everything seems hopeful from here.

The newly risen sun barely filters in through the thick wooden blinds. It must be early. I turn my head to the clock and groan. It's early.

After a few minutes of staring, sleep doesn't come, and I push out from under his arm. He rolls and I take a minute to admire his back. I have no idea how often this guy works out, but he's clearly friendly with the inside of a weight room.

In nothing but one of Cameron's tees, I tiptoe out into the hallway and softly close the door behind me. Maybe I can whip up another breakfast masterpiece. It would be a good way to apologize to Ryder after the way his dad treated him last night. If he's even here.

I dig through the kitchen and pull out some bacon, eggs, and a few veggies for omelets. The ones I make are never as pretty as the pictures, but they taste pretty good. As quietly as I can, I find an empty bowl, a cutting board, and a knife.

With the lack of distractions in the quiet house, a vision from last night assaults my mind: Cameron standing in the doorway looking every bit the predator and ready to kill. My insides clench at how his jealousy hit me in very private and personal places. It made my stomach flutter and my skin flush with the excitement.

It's wrong. So wrong. There's nothing normal about a woman who gets excited by her boyfriend's jealousy. I'd never try to make him mad on purpose, but it doesn't change the fact that it feels good—no, it's hot as hell—to know I'm important enough to him that he'd get upset at the thought of me with someone else.

A soft knock on the front door shakes me to the present.

I check my phone for the time. "It's not even eight." Who the hell would stop by so early on a Sunday?

Seconds pass and I hear the knock again. I better get that before they start ringing the doorbell and waking the whole damn house. I swing open the door, and butterflies flutter in my stomach. Fan-girling still.

"D'lilah Monroe!"

She steps back and almost stumbles. "Oh, you're here?" Her gaze runs down the length of my torso and back up.

"Yep." I am, but what the heck is she doing here? I open the door wider. "Come in."

She moves through the doorway, but she does so with timid steps. "Hey, Eve, right?"

"Yeah, shhh…the guys are still sleeping." I wave her to follow me into the kitchen. "I'm making breakfast. You hungry?"

"Uh…"

She doesn't answer, so I turn and find her face pale, especially in contrast to her hot pink shirt and matching shorts.

"Here." I pull out a barstool from the island. "Have a seat. You want some coffee?"

She drops to her chair and nods. "Sure, if it's not too much trouble."

I busy myself with the coffee while putting pieces of what I know about Cameron's ex-wife together. My experience with divorcees is limited, but her surprise visits seem to happen more than I'd expect.

The room is heavy with silence and a strange tension I didn't feel the first time we met. I grab a couple coffee mugs and some milk from the fridge then dig through the pantry for sugar.

"So you're"—she fidgets with the mug, and her fingers tremble—"spending the night?"

My face gets hot and my palms sweat. Cameron hasn't talked to her yet. "Yes, I am." I clear my throat and keep my eyes on cracking eggs. "I've spent the night a couple times." I don't lift my eyes to see her reaction, but I can feel the shock that charges the air between us.

"That's um…surprising." Her voice shakes.

This is ridiculous. From what Cameron's told me, they've been divorced for going on ten years. Not that I'd be surprised if she still had feelings for him, but I'd expect her to be a little less obvious.

I take a deep breath and turn toward my childhood idol. "It's not a big deal, D'lilah. We're adults and don't have to clear the status of our relationship with anyone."

She blanches. "Not a big deal? How can you say that?"

Is she for real? "Um, pretty easily. I mean we're consenting adults, and frankly, I'm uncomfortable talking to you about this. If you don't approve, take it up with Cameron."

"Take what up with me?" Cameron's booming voice comes from the entryway to the kitchen. He's wearing workout shorts and a faded blue Tap-Out tee, his hair sticking up in a sexy way that I know is from my hands being buried in it last night. "'Li, what are you doing here?"

I step back from the counter as he pins her with a glare and crosses to his ex-wife.

"It's Sunday." She slides her trembling hands off the countertop and into her lap.

"I'm aware of what day it is. What I'm not aware of is why I wake up in my house to find you in my kitchen on a Sunday."

D'lilah's back goes rigid. "So you know she's spending the night?"

"Do I know?" He tilts his head and studies her face. "You fucked up?"

A gasp shoots from her lips. "No, I am not fucked up."

He runs his gaze over her. "Shit, 'Li, you're shaking."

"Don't change the subject, Cam."

"How long since your last drink?" There's a tiny hint of that softness in his voice that I've heard before when he speaks to her.

She blinks. "How long since you've been allowing this girl to do God-knows-what under your roof?"

It's official. D'lilah Monroe has lost her damn mind.

"Mom?" All eyes swing to Ryder, who stumbles into the kitchen in workout shorts similar to Cameron's, shirtless, and scratching his scalp through wild blond hair. "What are you doing here?"

D'lilah's staring at her son, Cameron's scowling at her, and Ryder's looking back and forth between them. Suddenly feeling very out of place, I sidestep the group and move to disappear from the room.

"Eve. Don't take another fucking step." Cameron's growled words freeze my progression.

"All righty."

"'Li, who I have spending the night in my house isn't your concern," Cameron says, his tone vacant and borderline angry.

"I disagree." She motions to me with a flick of her hand, and for the first time I'm seeing more of the confident diva I expected in D'lilah Monroe. "I know you guys want to live like a couple of playboy bachelors, but, Cam, allowing our seventeen-year-old son to have sex with his girlfriend under your roof is irresponsible."

Oh fuck.

Everyone in the room goes still, with backs ramrod straight, and stares at D'lilah for a few silent seconds. Ryder clears his throat, but doesn't swallow the high-pitched groan of restrained laughter. I slide my gaze to him, and he throws his head back in a booming roar.

"Fuckin' hell." Cameron braces his weight on the counter, drops his chin to his chest, and shakes his head.

She moves her eyes through the room, confusion etched on her pretty face. "What?"

I step forward, and Cameron turns his narrowed eyes toward me.

I ignore him and look at D'lilah. "I'm not spending the night with your son."

"Eve." Cameron's warning me, but against what? Upsetting her? What's worse? Her thinking her son is having sleepover dates or her ex-husband?

"Cameron and I are dating." There. I said it. "And I'm twenty-one years old. Not underage. But I've been told I have a baby face if that makes you feel better."

Her jaw goes slack for a second before realization tightens her expression. She glares at Cameron. "Is this some kind of a joke?"

"'Li."

"You do see what you're doing, right?" She motions to me with a forceful swing of her arm. "Look at her!"

What in the hell is she talking about? Yep, she's definitely off her rocker.

"Mom, calm down." Ryder moves to my side in a way that feels like support.

She keeps her glare on her ex. "Tell me you see it, Cam."

Cameron looks at me with a blank stare, as if he's doing it to make her happy but not really looking for anything. "D'lilah, you need to get your ass home."

Her shoulders slump. "I can't believe you don't see it: her youth, hair, face. Look at her, Cam. *Really* look at her."

Everyone stares at me, and I watch in shock as something registers on Ryder's face. But what?

"Holy crap." Ryder's looking between his mom's face and mine. "That's some freaky shit."

Cameron doesn't say anything.

She slaps her palm on the granite countertop. "She's me fifteen years ago!"

"What?" Pain twists in my chest. I stare at Cameron, who's staring right back at me, and I can see it. As if the words were written across his expression, he agrees with her.

It makes sense. I've idolized her most of my life. All those years of studying her image in magazines, I never saw it until now. Even our face shape and coloring is similar. Nausea rolls through my belly. Is that why Cameron's with me? Searching for something he lost, or maybe an attempt at a second chance?

"Oh my God." I cover my mouth and shake my head.

"Ry, take your mom home," Cameron says with a growl so fierce I feel it in my blood.

Ryder groans. "Come on, Mom."

"No, it's Sunday. I'm going with you guys."

Cameron's eyes snap to hers. "What?" He spits his question through gritted teeth.

For the first time since she showed up, she looks scared. "Cam, don't—"

"You show up here, upset my woman, and now, without warning, you decide you're ready to step up and be there?" Cameron leans over the breakfast bar. "Go the fuck home!"

"We all made that promise before—"

"Do not talk about that like you give a fuck, 'Li. It's been too long, and I'll be damned if I'm gonna…" He blinks as if he just realized he's in mixed company. "Just go home."

Her eyes widen and fill with tears.

"No, not this time. You do not get off the hook by crying."

An eerie silence fills the room, as if whoever talks first loses.

"Get her home, Ry." Cameron moves toward me, snags my hand, and pulls me from the kitchen, down the hallway, and to his bedroom. He slams the door shut then pins me to it.

"Cameron—"

His mouth comes down on mine in a brutal kiss that's so heavy with emotion it tightens my chest. He pulls my lips between his teeth, lashing his tongue against mine. Hands at my hips, he holds me in place, grinding his hard body against my soft one. This isn't the kiss of seduction or one of sexual need. The sear of his lips screams of emotional release, the physical expression of an angry confession.

I want to give that to him, be that for him.

My hands fist into his hair, pushing myself up while pulling him deeper into me. Legs turn to jelly, and I force myself to stay upright and pray he doesn't let me fall. He bites my lower lip and a gasp slides from my throat.

That was a side of Cameron I've never seen. The way he spoke to D'lilah was vicious and unrelenting. I don't know what happened between them, but abandoning a five-year-old boy in favor of alcohol is enough to make anyone angry. I still can't help but feel sorry for her.

"What she said about you," he says against my mouth and runs his teeth along my jaw to my neck. "Don't let that in."

"But she's right." I tilt my head while he drags his stubbled chin from my earlobe to my shoulder. "I look like her. You must've realized it on some level before now."

"I didn't." He nips at the tender flesh near my collarbone. "You're nothing like her."

"Our looks, neediness…" I groan and hate what has to be said. "God, Cameron, you probably picked me because I'm her."

His fingers dig into my skin. "You're not her."

"No, I'm like the drag-queen version of her."

His lips still against my neck.

"You know, pretty enough, but missing the most important parts."

He pulls back, his lips twitching. "You got all the important parts, doll. Tasted every single one of 'em."

I sigh heavily. "Not those parts, just the knockout parts. She's tall with long legs and a striking smile. She's a fucking supermodel for crying out loud." I shrug. "I'm average height, curvy, and normal."

"Nothin' about you is normal, Yvette. And you're ten times the knockout D'lilah ever was." He dips to press a kiss to my forehead. "Perfect height so I get the sweet smell of your hair without even trying." His fingers flex into my bottom. "Fuckin' curves to fill my hands and mouth; my dick gets hard just thinking about 'em."

"Really?"

"Yes, really. I'm at work, have the taste of you on my tongue from the morning, thinking about that ass pressed against me." He sucks in a breath. "It's like puberty all over again."

A giggle burst from my lips, and I drop my forehead to his chest.

"Tell me you're okay with all that shit that went down." His strong hand sifts through my hair. "I'm happy to lock you in this room until I'm convinced you're good about us."

Us. My heart jumps. Will I ever get used to hearing that?

"Is D'lilah good with us?" I trace his hairline to his strong, corded neck.

"Don't give a shit."

It's a sweet answer, but it's also an obvious lie. Whatever dynamic there is between D'lilah and Cameron, it's fragile. And he cares.

Compassion saddles my panic. As badly as I feel for Cameron's ex, I don't want her causing problems for us. Our age difference causes enough strain, and adding a volatile ex-wife could seal our fate. For whatever reason, he feels he needs to take care of her. He'd said that night at the Fourth of July party that he owed her.

So what I need to figure out is if it came down to him choosing between D'lilah and me, whom would he pick?

—

CAMERON

I'm loading the dishwasher after another one of Eve's gut-busting breakfasts when Ryder drags his Doc Martin clad feet into the kitchen. After he escorted D'lilah to her car, he must've taken a shower and gotten ready to go out for the day.

"How'd it go with your mom?"

He hops up to sit on the counter. "As you'd expect—crying, apologizing, explaining how unhealthy it is for you to date a woman my age."

"I'm sorry, Ry. Last night from me and this morning from your mom, bet you're getting sick of everyone accusing you of shit you didn't do, huh?"

"I should've expected it with Mom. Fourth of July when I took her home, she kept talking about how Eve was such a *sweet girl*. I didn't put it together. Makes sense now."

I shake my head, shocked at how quickly I assumed the worst and jumped all over Ry's shit. "No excuse for that."

"I get it Dad. Eve's four years older than me, and in less than a week, she'll be three years older than me. That's gotta mess with your head. Mess with anyone's head. Mom's going off the rails because my birthday's coming up—"

"Eve's young. Her age was a concern in the beginning, but when I'm with her, I forget."

A slow grin pulls at his lips. "I bet you do."

"Ry."

He holds up his hands. "Just an observation. She's not hard on the eyes; that's all I'm sayin'."

"You finished." Fuckin' insane shit that the woman I'm dating is also datable to my kid. I lean to look behind him toward the living room to make sure we're alone. "You know I haven't talked to Eve yet about Rosie."

He lifts an eyebrow. "This thing between you two serious?"

"Not really." Or is it? "I mean I don't know yet."

"No sense sharing the past with someone who you don't see a future with."

How the hell did he get so smart?

He hops down from the counter. "Right, well, I'm outta here."

"Ryder. It's Sunday." He's been blowing me off for weeks, and after the showdown in the kitchen this morning, I'd think he'd want to go with me.

"Yeah, I know, but I made plans and…" He shrugs.

I never wanted to be the kind of parent who forced things on their kids. What's important to me isn't as important to him, and I should respect that. "You sure you don't want to come?" I give him one last chance and hope he gives the right answer.

"Yeah." He keeps his eyes to the floor and skirts by me. "See ya this afternoon."

With a deep breath to push past the heavy weight that presses against my chest upon hearing Ry's answer, I head back to my room. Eve's on the couch, folded over and putting on her shoes. Her hair hangs in long damp strands over her shoulders.

"How was your shower?" I move to her but sit in the club chair rather than on the couch next to her out of fear that I'll pull her into my lap and drag her to my bed.

Her eyes are bright and sparkle in my direction. "I've had better." She bites her lip, and I groan as a smile twitches its way to the surface.

"Good to know."

She finishes with her shoes and sits up with a double slap to her black-slacked thighs. "If you don't mind dropping me off at the Slade's, I've got to scour the Sunday paper for a new job."

Shit. With all the drama that unfolded this morning, I forgot about her losing her job. "Damn, that's right."

"I don't even know how to apply for a job. It's been so long." She gathers her hair at her nape, twisting and flipping until it's in a nice tight ball.

I lean forward, and my fingers itch to push her wet bangs back from her eyes.

"But first." She motions to her oxford shirt and black pants. "I'm going to burn my uniform clothes. Then I need to polish up my resume, and by polish, I mean write one. I have to call my landlord and beg him not to evict me then get online and figure out what the hell I'm going to do with my life." She flashes me a bright smile that's so bright it's dark.

"Let me help you with some of that."

"You gonna give me a job?" Her sarcastic smile turns hopeful.

I never thought about giving Eve a job, but I'm sure I could find something for her to do until she gets on her feet. I'll give it some thought, but until then…"Maybe, but first let me pay your rent for the month, get you caught up on bills, put you back in the black."

Her eyes get so big they look as if they might pop out of her pretty face. "You tryin' to Sugar Daddy me?"

I shrug. "I wouldn't call it that, no."

"I can't, but thanks. It's too weird, and we've just starting hanging out. It's a sweet offer, and I know a million different people would call me stupid for saying no, but thanks anyway."

"Pride is a dangerous thing. You need the help; let me give it to you."

She stands and grabs her purse. "You remember what I told you about my dad?"

Of course, how could I forget? "Yeah."

"I don't want to be him."

I blink, shocked and equally proud that Eve would take charity as an absolute last resort, if at all. She's doing everything in her power to stay on her feet or go down swinging: a girl after my own values.

She takes a few steps closer, head tilted and eyes on me. "I'll figure this out and do what I need to, but it has to be me."

I hate it, but, damn, I fucking admire it. "Fine." Standing, I pull her into my arms. "But you promise me if you're on the verge of losing the roof over your head, you take my offer."

"I can't—"

I squeeze her tightly. "Yvette."

"Fine." A long sigh slides from her lips. "Bossy."

"Atta girl."

Her body melts into mine, and I grin at how even the slightest positive enforcement seems to affect her. And even with the weight of her body in my arms, decompression lightens my chest again. For a split second, my legs wobble with the force of it, and for the first time since the last time I dropped, I worry this lightening will knock me off my feet.

TWENTY-FOUR

EVE

"This is bad ass." Ryder throws an arm around my shoulder for a side hug. "I can't believe I'm backstage at The Blackout."

I tilt my head back to see his face. Even though he's only seventeen, he's at least six inches taller than I am. "I'm happy it worked out and we got you in."

Tonight's a double whammy of awesomeness because this a rare Saturday night show for Ataxia at The Blackout. They usually headline the club on Sunday nights, but tonight they're opening for a bigger band that has drawn an insanely huge crowd.

Backstage is exactly how I imagined it'd be. Band members throw back beers, talk too loud, and curse even louder. Groupies are staggered throughout the room in their microminis and five-inch heels. All of it screams rock-n-roll and promises a night to remember.

"Seriously, Eve, this is so fuckin' cool." Ryder's eyes dance around the room, taking it all in as if he's recording it to be stored in the I'll-Never-Forget-This-Night file.

"Hey, don't thank me." I nod to Rex, who's sitting on the couch across the room, tuning his guitar. "He put you on as a roadie to get you back here."

Ryder's hold tightens for a quick couple seconds. My chest swells with warmth, and I look at Cameron, who has his eyes trained on his son in a sweet, but still glary, stare.

Cameron motions across the room with a chin lift. "Might want to go ask the guys about settin' up, Ry."

"Yeah, totally." He grins down at me and then his dad before he lets me go and heads over to Rex.

Another arm drops to my shoulders, this one bigger and familiar. It's been only a week since we outed our relationship status, and things have been pretty good. Being jobless has freed up a lot of my time. Days I spend figuring out what I want to do with my life, and my nights are spent with Cameron.

I had to take a substantial loan from Raven, which I fought like crazy to avoid, but when I laid out all my options, I couldn't turn down what she was offering. She inherited a ton of money from her dill-hole dad and has sworn to give every bit of it away to help others get on their feet. I swear I'm going to pay her back. She swears she won't accept a dime.

"He's in heaven." Cameron watches as Rex gives Ryder the rundown for setting up and breaking down their equipment.

"I'm glad." I tilt my head back to see his face. "You only turn eighteen once."

Cameron's jaw gets hard, but this time I expect it. There've been a few times that Ryder's birthday has come up, and every time seems to get a negative reaction out of both men. I want to ask, but I also want him to volunteer the information when he's comfortable sharing. Ryder's actual birthday isn't for another few days, and this little impromptu gift couldn't have come at a better time.

"We should go find somewhere to sit. The place is filling up fast." I don't want to interrupt so we slide from the room without saying bye and head out into the crowded club.

Cameron tucks me to his side. The bar is already packed. We squeeze through the multitude of people to get to the tables that run along the standing-room-only section near center stage. Once we emerge from the crowd, we spot Blake,

Layla, Mason, and another guy who looks familiar at two high-top tables that they've pushed together.

"Room for two more?" I hug Layla and playfully shove Blake, who's built like a damn tank, so isn't affected at all.

Layla gives me a sad smile. "I wish Ataxia would play somewhere else. I hate it here." She speaks softly enough for only me to hear.

"I know it's hard." I give her another hug, wishing like hell it would be enough to wipe that sad look off her face.

She's been so worried about her friend Mac, who was a bartender here and suddenly disappeared. She left a note saying it was time for her to move on, but Layla thinks there's something more going on. I don't blame her. I could never skip town without at least saying goodbye to Raven. Although Layla and Mac weren't as close as Raven and I, my gut sours at the thought of going through what Layla's going through. Being left behind without so much as a goodbye is the worst kind of rejection.

Feeling eyes on me, I look up to a scowling Mason. "Mase."

He nods toward me in recognition. Polite, but I know he's figured things out. He may look like nothing more than a perfect body with a tan and a smile, but the guy's no idiot.

Cameron squeezes my hand and gets my eyes. He leans down and drops a kiss on my jaw. "Don't worry, babe. He'll get over it."

I nod and he pulls back.

"Wade, I didn't know you ever left the gym." Cameron addresses the other guy at the table before he flags down a waitress.

"Thought I'd get out and see what all the fuss is about." He takes a swig of his beer and jerks his head toward Blake. "And this fucker wouldn't take no for an answer."

"Bull crap, man. Ever since you moved to Vegas, you've been dying to weasel into my old stomping ground and pick up where I left off."

"Well, that shouldn't be hard to do." Layla's voice and expression is all fake sugar and acid. "Figure he plays Eeny Meeny Miney Mo and he's got a ninety-nine percent chance of nabbing a chick who you've seen naked."

Blake's cool-guy expression turns bitter, and I muffle my laugh. I absolutely adore the fact that Blake found a woman who can stand toe-to-toe with his shit talk.

He pulls Layla to his side and kisses the top of her head. "Don't remember any naked women, Mouse. Your sexy ass has burned away the memory of all the other women."

She goes soft and leans deeper into him.

I can see the make-out session brewing and swing my gaze to Wade. "That's where I know you from. You fought Blake last month, right?"

"Wade, this is Eve." Cameron introduces us.

"Nice to meet you. Yeah, Blake got lucky. Won't happen again."

"Talk all the shit you want, man. We'll get a rematch soon enough. Don't come crying to me when I knock you out. *Again*," Blake says.

Cameron interjects and Mason jumps into the conversation, which soon leads to a who's-fighting-next debate. I tune them out when I see people moving around on stage. I focus on Ryder, who fits in perfectly up there with his punk rock hair, eyeliner, and jeans that seem tight but still sag off his hips.

"…when Cameron gets his fight."

The words stab through my concentration.

I turn to Mason. "What did you say?"

Cameron's body tenses at my side.

Mason's mouth lifts with a small grin that doesn't look all that friendly. "Cam's fighting Faulkner."

Layla's eyes are wide on Blake, who suddenly finds the label on his beer bottle the most interesting thing in the room.

"When do you find out if the board approves the fight?" Wade chimes in. "Be a kick-ass card, man."

The waitress swings by, dropping off new drinks and setting down a scotch for Cameron and a Corona for me.

Cameron shrugs. "I've been approved, but official word waits so they can announce it at a press conference."

I jerk my head to Cameron. "What are you talking about? You're going back into the octagon?"

"He is," Mason says, "pending medical and board approval."

Medical? I keep my eyes on Cameron. "What does that mean?"

Cameron opens his mouth to answer.

"Brain damage is no joke, Eve." Mason jumps in, earning a scowl from Cameron. "Gotta make sure his noggin can take another hit, or they'll be signing his death certificate."

Death.

Cameron drops his chin, and his knuckles go white around his glass.

I lean in. "Hold on. Explain—"

The lights flash and electric guitar blasts through the speakers. A roar from the crowd makes the rest of this conversation impossible, and I hope I can calm my nervous stomach enough to enjoy the show.

Cameron back in the octagon. Why would he do that? Raven told me once that a thirty-year-old fighter is a retired fighter. It was something she was looking forward to so she wouldn't have to worry about her husband. I'm sure there are exceptions, but Cameron is thirty-eight.

Back into the octagon. With them throwing words like brain damage and death around, I have too many questions and not a single answer. I watch Ataxia play but don't hear the music. My thoughts are on the man at my side and why the hell the president of the UFL would even consider taking this kind of risk.

CAMERON

"Good show, huh?" It's my third attempt at conversation since we left The Blackout. She's blown me off twice, and if she refuses to acknowledge me this time, it's three strikes you're out.

Mason—that little shit—and his convenient confession at the club didn't seem to fuck up the night completely. Eve still seemed to enjoy the show well enough. She didn't bounce around and sing into her thumb as I've seen her do in the past.

Ryder did his duty as roadie like a champion and was flyin' high when he left the club to hook up with some friends, probably intent on bragging his ass off while celebrating his birthday. Eve really hooked it up for my boy.

I pull into my garage and throw the Maserati into park. She doesn't move, her head still turned away from me and gazing out the window, this time at nothing but the interior wall of my garage.

"Yvette."

She jerks her head around to face me, eyes tight.

I fight the urge to grin at her expression. A pissed-off Eve is feisty Eve, and damn, she's fun when she's feisty.

"Talk to me."

"I hate it when you call me that."

"I know."

"But you do it anyway."

I scratch my jaw. "What can I say, doll? I like pissin' you off."

"Psht." She shakes her head and turns back to her window.

"You wanna sit starin' at the wall all night or go inside and talk to me about what has you so upset?"

Mason bringing up my fight with Faulkner was clearly done to get under Eve's skin or, more specifically, to drive a wedge between us. The fact that everyone at those tables knew about the fight except her clearly isn't sitting well with my little ball buster.

"You're gonna fight?"

There it is. "Yeah."

She turns to me. "Why?"

"Old rival, back from the dead, callin' me out—"

"You could say no."

I chuckle, surprised she doesn't know me better by now. "Never turn down a challenge."

"What did Mason mean—?" She smacks her hands on her thighs. "Would you stop looking like someone farted in your face every time I say his name?"

I roll my lower lip into my mouth to keep from smiling. "Go on."

"It got me to thinking. You know you've never really talked much about your career."

"Talking now."

"Why do you need medical approval?"

"It's mandatory. All fighters have to pass a basic physical." The lie tastes sour on my tongue. "I haven't fought in a while. They just want to make sure I'm healthy enough." *Lie, lie, lie.*

"What about the brain-damage stuff?"

Damn. I take a deep breath. "It's not a big deal."

"That's a non-answer."

This isn't a conversation I'm ready to have, but what she's probably thinking is worse than the truth. "Back when I fought for the UFL, I got a chipped tooth. Pretty common, didn't think much of it. I went to have it taken care of and moved on. A few months later I started getting headaches, fevers, just didn't feel right. Blew it off, thinking it was a bug. I remember being so damn tired, and then it was like I couldn't communicate. Someone would ask me something. I'd answer them, but the words would come out all fucked up."

Her hand goes to her chest. "That had to be scary."

"I thought it was fatigue."

"So what was it?"

"One night I woke up, and my body was flopping around in the bed. I remember thinking I was having a seizure, but I couldn't speak or stop the movements. Like being prisoner in your own skin."

"Oh my God."

"D'lilah called 911. An ambulance ride, MRI, and a biopsy later determined I had an infection in my brain. They had to go in and remove the damaged brain tissue. Didn't know what part of the brain was fucked up, so they couldn't predict how I'd come out."

"How did you come out?"

"I had to relearn how to speak, walk, write. Luckily the brain compensates, and it didn't do anything too permanent, but I was in rehab for a long time before I could even consider going back to work."

"Why didn't you?"

"UFL didn't need the liability. They had concerns about what a concussion would do to my already fucked-up head. They let me go."

"So this infection that you had no control over ended up robbing you of your fighting career?"

And my daughter. "Basically."

"How were you not angry?"

"Oh, I was." The memory of the rage I felt after losing my career and my daughter in the same day makes my hands shake. "But that anger lit a fire under my ass. I swore I'd make it back into the octagon no matter what it took."

Her head swivels from side to side. "That's why you took Gibbs's job."

"Yes. This puts me a lot closer to the cage than promoting ever did."

"Smart. *Stupid*, but smart." She chews on her bottom lip. "Wait, if you're rehabilitated, why won't the board just let you fight?"

"I still struggle with certain things. Memory, impulsiveness, shit like that. They're also worried if I fight I'll damage my brain further."

"Is it life threatening?"

"Afraid that's part of the unknown, doll."

"Oh." She looks down her hands balled in her lap. "Were you going to tell me?"

"Probably not. Not a fan of exposing my weaknesses."

"Not that. About Faulkner."

"I haven't even talked to Ryder about the fight yet. Then I'll have to tell D'lilah." And with our history, she'll be all over my ass. And now Eve, who I'm sure will give me her opinion on the matter whether I want to hear it or not.

I rub my eyes, so damn tired and envious of my early years with the UFL when I never had to answer to anyone. Every decision I made was based on what was best for my career. Nothing else. But look where that got me.

"Yeah." She turns a sad smile to me. "I understand. They're your family. They should know first."

"Babe…" I don't know what to say, but I hate the way she's slumped in on herself, head tucked and hiding behind her hair.

An angry Eve is fun, but a hurt Eve is torture. Her dad did damage of which I've only managed to scratch the surface. I've seen the devastation flash in her eyes, and I don't want to be the reason for that look.

"Inside, doll." I pull her hand to my lips. "Need to get those clothes off you and put you in my bed."

Her eyes flare and a tiny smile ticks her lips. I push back my victorious grin. I've never in my life been with a woman so sidetracked by sex. It's the one thing I've learned that she'll drop anything for.

My mouth all over a naked Eve is the best way to put an end to this conversation. I wonder how many orgasms it'll take for Eve to forget our talk altogether. Sex-induced amnesia? It's a cheap shot, but I'm excited about the challenge.

TWENTY-FIVE

CAMERON

I'm dreaming. I must be because I know I'm in my bed. I fell asleep with Eve curled to my side with her head on my chest, but the sound resonating in my ears is something I'd never expect to hear in my own damn bed.

I cringe as a foul song sung by a high-pitched voice pulls me from sleep.

Soft feminine moans come from my side seconds before I lose the heat of her body. I blink my eyes open to find Eve, ass in the air, top half of her body hanging over the side of the bed. Damn, what a view. I grin through my sleep haze and put myself into a mental choke hold for allowing her to put panties back on last night.

She reaches toward the ground and the source of the sound then sits up with her phone in her hand. The ridiculous noise stops. Her eyebrows pinch together as she studies the caller ID and then pop up when the sound begins again.

"Interesting ring tone."

Her gaze swings to mine, an uneasy expression on her face. "It's Timbo." She hits a button and lies back down just as the phone starts ringing again.

"Don't know who Timbo is, babe, but if you don't make it stop, I'm breakin' the fucker."

Her chest rises on a big shaky breath. What the hell?

Before I can ask, she hits a button and presses the phone to her ear. "Please tell me you're not dying."

I turn my body toward her and prop my head on my hand.

"Um...maybe because I haven't heard from you since Christmas?" Her eyes are fixed on the ceiling, but her mouth is held tight and her jaw hard. "It's July, Mother."

Ah, well this makes sense. I keep my eyes trained on her face, watching for any physical evidence that she's hurting. If so, that phone is mine.

She closes her eyes and shakes her head. "No, I'm not giving him money anymore."

Shit. Guess her dad's not the only POS in the family.

"Well, I'm sorry to hear that, Mom, but he's your ex. You married him; you deal with him."

My fingers itch to rip the tiny cell from her hand and tell her mother exactly what I think of her choice to reproduce with Eve's fuck-head father. Although if she hadn't, Eve wouldn't exist. The thought alone is depressing.

"Sounds good. Talk to you next year." She doesn't wait before hitting *End* and tossing the phone to the foot of the bed.

"Everything okay?"

She nods and rolls to fit herself along my side. I pull her in and sift my fingers through her hair.

"That was my mom."

"Gathered that."

"My dad called her and told her that I'd abandoned him since he didn't get a single cent of my last paycheck."

"Nice guy." A growl rumbles in my chest. What the fuck is up with these people?

"Ha. Yeah, my mom doesn't want to deal with him, so she's trying to get me to kick him something so he'll leave her alone."

"You think he'll show up at her place? Clean her out like he did you?"

She shakes her head, her fingers tracing a pattern on my abdomen. "Nah, she lives in North Carolina. If he had the money to track her down, he'd gamble it before he made it to the airport."

"Sounds like she had the right idea getting away from him."

"Mm."

"Why didn't you go with her?"

"I wasn't invited. She left when I was a kid."

My stomach churns, and my fist clenches into her hair. I force myself to loosen my grip. "Sorry to hear that, but sounds like you're better off without her."

She nods into my chest again. Abandoned by her mother, raised with a dick for a father, the only real family she had growing up was her best friend and a teacher.

No wonder she seems older than she is. She's lived the kind of pain and abandonment that would lend to an edge in her demeanor: a street-taught maturity that only comes from pulling through the shitty dredges of life's circumstances. Warmth spreads through my chest. She's been delivered the hits, taken them blow for blow, and she's still standing.

"When did your last check come in?"

"Friday. Why?"

"You think your Dad will come snoopin' around since you didn't pay up?"

She shrugs. "He's called. I didn't answer. No clue what he'll do, but I wouldn't put it past him to show up."

"Right." I smack her sweet ass and she jumps with a squeak. "Get up, babe. I'm taking you to the training center. Next time you come face to face with your pops you'll be able to lay him to the ground if he steps foot in your place."

She tilts her head back and rests her chin on my chest. "You're gonna teach me how to kick some ass?" An excited smile pulls at her lips.

"I am." I lean down and brush a soft kiss across her lips. "Need to know if he shows up you'll be able to handle yourself until I get there."

If he puts her in a position where she has to protect herself, I will kill him.

———

EVE

We're standing in the middle of the octagon, and I don't care how sexy he looks sweaty. He's crazy if he thinks he's going to win *this* fight.

"Quit your bitchin' and put 'em on." Cameron shoves the pair of lightly padded gloves at me again.

"No way." I hold my hands up and back, shaking my head. "You've tortured me enough. I'm done."

This was a mistake. I thought we'd head to the training center and he'd teach me how to kill a man using some fancy *jui-jitsu* nerve pinch. I was wrong. It wasn't until he pulled me through the doors of the weight room when he informed me in his usual bossy way that we were going to work out. *We.*

After I not so politely explained that I don't work out, he threw my ass on the treadmill to warm up. I figured it would be over sooner if I cooperated. He took me through a list of things with ridiculous names: deadlifts, burpees, and something called cat-vomit crunches, which sounded ridiculous until I did them and realized they're aptly named. At last when he explained I'd done enough, he shows me to the octagon where he's going to teach me something. Now. After an hour of misery? Nope. Not happenin'.

"Hardly torture, doll." He's grinning his not so big but totally big for him grin.

"Uh, yeah. It was." I throw my arm out toward the weight room door. "For the love of God, Cameron, you made me run!"

He shoves the gloves toward me again, his lips twitching. "We're not done."

"Oh." I cock a hip and wave a finger in his face. "We so are." I point to my damp hairline. "You made me sweat!"

He tugs his bottom lip between his teeth clearly trying to hide his amusement.

"My body feels noodley." I pick my shirt with two fingers. "And I'm all wet!"

His smile dies, and his eyes narrow into a heated glare that makes my tummy flip. He dips his chin and looks at me from under his eyebrows. "Put 'em on."

I take a step back, and my blood races when he advances toward me.

"Not putting them on, Cameron."

He tilts his head, and damn, I feel that look between my legs.

Another step. "It's my responsibility to make you wet and exhausted." One more step. "Let me do my job."

My back hits chain link. He closes the space between us, and I'm practically begging for him to touch me. "No."

"Yvette."

I roll my eyes.

"On." He holds out the gloves so that they brush against the tip of my breast.

A slow shiver runs down my spine and across my sweat-dampened skin. He's glaring down at me with eyes that promise a reward if I obey. I hold out my hand and he slides one glove on before the other with a smug look of satisfaction on his perfect face.

He kisses my forehead. "That's my girl."

I close my eyes, suck in a shaky breath, and allow the warmth of his approval to wash over me.

"Eyes open, doll."

They pop wide at his firm command, and I watch in awe as his large powerful body moves to the center of the octagon. With a flick of his wrist, he waves me over before sliding circular pads on each hand.

My shoulders slump, and I drag my overly exerted and now aroused body to meet him in the middle of the cage. When I meet his eyes, something looks different. This is a different Cameron. The heat of his glare is dark and determined. His jaw is clenched and his body's standing firm, feet planted, and prepared. I don't have a single doubt as to who I'm looking at now. This is UFL Heavyweight Cameron Kyle.

Embarrassingly, this Cameron shoots a straight shot of we-need-to-get-naked straight to my veins.

He holds his padded hands up like targets. "Let's see how you hit." He nods to my gloved hands. "Make a fist. Bring 'em up."

I do as I'm told.

"Higher. Too low and they do you no good."

I raise my fists higher, every command from his gravelly voice impossible to ignore.

"Good. Now"—he brings the targets up—"focus. Hit."

Nervous but determined, I throw a punch and connect with his hand. Damn, that felt great.

"Again."

I do it again and again until I'm breathing heavily.

He steps back, rips the pads off his hands, and tosses them aside. "Not bad, but probably not enough to fight off an attacker." He waves me closer.

I move in, so close I can feel the heat radiating off his massive body and see every detail of his stubbled chin.

His dark gaze drops to my lips; it traces the line of my jaw back to my eyes. "I'm gonna put my hands on you now."

Yes, please do.

"Fight me off."

I nod, not trusting my voice to hide how insanely turned on I am. He reaches for me, and I try to dodge his grip, but he's too fast. His hands lock around both my wrists, and I jerk back, away from his unrelenting hold. I pull harder, tug against him, but he's too strong. Throwing my entire body weight back, I try to wrench my arms free.

"Enough." He lets me go. "You're doing exactly what I'd expect. You're pulling away."

I look from side to side. Is he joking? "Well, yeah. You told me to fight you off."

"Right, but the key to a good defense is actually stepping into the hold." He waves me back into position. "Let me show you. Come at me."

Gladly.

I reach forward and grab his wrists just as he did mine. He steps close, twists into my hold, and I'm airborne.

I land on my back in the cushion of his arms. "Whoa!" I blink up at him. "What was that?"

His mouth gets soft and he leans in close. "Takedown."

"There's no way I'll be able to do that."

"Sure you can."

"But you're way bigger than me. Way stronger."

"The most effective self-defense moves are joint manipulation. I rolled into your hold, took advantage of the angles. Only time I used my strength was to catch you, which by the way you won't do in a self-defense situation."

I glare at him and shove him away from me. "Okay, smartass. Teach me that."

He pulls me to my feet, and we work through the moves a few more times until I'm able to twist into him enough to make him grimace and let go.

I grin huge and watch him shake out his arms. "I did it!"

"You did. On to lesson two." He moves behind me. "Let's say you get grabbed from behind." He locks his arms around my chest, his warm breath at my ear. "Fight me."

A shiver races down my spine and goose bumps rip up and down my arms. A low, approving chuckle vibrates his chest.

I pull against him, but his grip only tightens. Dammit. He told me to step into the hold. I need to lean back. Shifting my weight, I press my back to his front.

"Atta girl, Eve. Think. Use your mind to fight."

My mind. Right. I close my eyes and feel his big, powerful body wrapped around me. I could stomp on his feet. I've seen that in moves before, but I don't think that would be enough to get him to let go.

His hold gets tighter. "Side step."

I do what he says.

"One more."

I take another step to the side.

"Now, reach back with your left leg and hook behind my knee."

Our legs almost side by side now, it's easy to push back with my leg and hook his.

"Exactly, baby. Now throw your weight behind that leg and—*shit!*" His arms peel away from my body, and he stumbles a few steps. "That's it."

"I did it?"

"You did it. And I wasn't making it easy on you." Pride shines in his eyes, and a small grin dances across his lips.

"Can we do it again?" I'm practically tingling with excitement as power surges through my muscles.

I don't know if the feeling is more from being able to execute the move, or if it's from the look on his face that is still shining at me.

My guess is the second.

"Let's do it." He steps in close and wraps his arms around me from behind. "Focus. Orientate yourself."

I nod.

"Right, now break free from me."

Never.

TWENTY-SIX

CAMERON

Seven twenty, seven twenty, seven twenty…

My pen traces the numbers into my notebook on repeat. The twentieth day of July. One of two days I never need to write in my planner to remember.

Today is the twins' eighteenth birthday.

It hit me before I woke up as if I'm on some fucked-up alarm system that only remembers the worst shit imaginable. Every cell in my body and ounce of blood pumping through my veins could never forget the day I held my kids in my arms for the first time.

Life was so fucking promising back then with the entire future at our feet. And Rosie, she had enough life for the two of them. Always squirming, she hated being wrapped up tightly the way most babies loved. It was as if she knew there was so much waiting for her out there and she couldn't wait to get at it.

Three years. All she got was three fucking years.

I Frisbee my notebook across the office, amazed I was even able to do that when my body feels as if it's filled with concrete.

The phone on my desk buzzes. "Hey, Cam?" Layla's voice is tentative, having probably heard me toss my planner.

"Yeah."

"The guy from Cage Freak wants to know if he can set up a meeting with you today. I saw you cleared your schedule, but I wanted to make sure I wasn't looking at it wrong."

"I'm leaving at noon." Before I take Ryder out to dinner tonight, I have a few errands to run, and every one of them is going to be unpleasant.

"Oh, sure, okay, I'll set him up for tomorrow." The intercom clicks off.

I should write that down somewhere. In scribbled words, I make a note and stick it to my computer screen.

The intercom buzzes again. "Sorry to bother you, but there's pretty little blonde out here whose mouth will put what's written on a truck stop bathroom stall to shame."

Eve? What's she doing here?

"Want me to send her in?"

"Please."

I stand and move around my desk just as the office door swings open. Eve saunters in all smiles and swaying hips. For the first time today, I'm able to take a full breath.

"Surprise." She holds out her arms, grimaces, and curls her arms around her chest. "Ouch." Her fingers rub circles into her triceps. "I'm still sore from the other day."

"That's good. We'll have to get you back in the weight room." I pull her close for a hug, dragging her sugar-and-spice-scented hair deep into my lungs. "What brings you by?"

"Oh, I had to tell you. I just had a job interview."

Well, that explains why she's dressed up, but this kind of a long summery get-up with a deep vee that shows off her ample cleavage isn't something I'd consider interview material.

"Where?"

"Pool at Mandalay."

I guess sexy beach casual makes more sense.

"How'd it go?"

She shrugs, and I release my hold enough so she can back up a step, but I keep my arms around her waist. Being in the same room with her is calming, and touching her is even better.

"Good, I think." She worries her bottom lip. "I'm not really sure. I applied for one of the supervisor positions, but told them I'd take first available even if that means I have to pounce around in a G-string and sling drinks to drunks."

A low growl hums in my chest. "Don't know how I feel about that, doll."

That's not true. I'm good and fucking sure I hate that.

"Money is money. I'm just trying to earn enough to feed myself, pay the bills, and hopefully have enough to get a pizza from time to time.

Slinging drinks in a G-string? Nope. Not happenin'. "Layla's going on maternity leave in two months. Until then, I've got enough going on to keep you both busy."

She backs away, her big and very wide eyes on me. "You'd… but you don't know anything about me."

I lift an eyebrow and feel the side of my mouth curve. Leave it to Eve to get a smile out of me on today of all days. "You sure about that?"

Her cheeks flush. "Oh, no, I mean…yeah, you know me like…naked or whatever, but you don't know anything about my work ethic or how I operate under pressure. You've never seen me handle a challenge or problem solve."

"Sure as shit have. You want the job; it's yours. It'll give you plenty of time to train with Layla so when she's gone it'll be a smooth transition. She can take as much time as she wants, and it'll give you some valuable work experience on your resume."

She's staring at me, her jaw hanging on its hinges. Her eyes flutter and she shakes her head. "Has anyone ever told you that you're a genius?"

I shrug. "Yeah, I hear that a lot."

She launches herself into my arms. "Thank you, Cameron. I swear I'll work so hard. I'm a fast learner." She smothers my neck and jaw with quick kisses. "Thank you, thank you, thank you." With a quick, jerk she leans back and covers her mouth. "Oh, but no kissing the boss, right? Sorry."

"Fuck, doll, if there's no kissing, then I revoke my offer."

She slaps my chest just as Layla pops her head through the cracked door.

"Sounds like we're celebrating."

"Cameron's going to hire me while you're on maternity leave." Eve jumps up and down clapping her hands.

The girls hug and start talking about how much fun they'll have, and for a second, I wonder if there'll be any work going on between them or if it'll be mainly gossip and chick talk.

I grab my notebook off the floor and move around my desk to check the time. Almost noon.

"Let's go to lunch and celebrate." Eve's eyes swing to mine. "Is that okay? Or do you have fighter boss shit to do?"

"Yeah, I've got some things I need to take care of before tonight." I drop my gaze to my desk because I know if I make eye contact she'll see I'm not giving her everything. And knowing Eve, she'll pry until she gets it.

"Aw, poop." Her brief disappointment is soothed when Layla describes the new sandwich place that opened up down the street.

I grab my keys and shut things down for the day while listening to them moan over what they're calling "fancy chicken salad."

"Eve, babe, I'll pick you up at six-thirty." I brush a small kiss against her lips and roll my eyes at the gooey-girlie sound that Layla makes.

Once out of my office, the oppressive weight is back.

Seven twenty, seven twenty, seven twenty…

The day I was handed everything I'd never appreciate until I lost it.

———

Suicide isn't always quick. For some, it's slow, dirty, and more complicated than a bullet through the skull or a belly full of pills: a daily decision to syphon any fight they have left, drown it in substance and depression. Death by sheer will to be done with this world combined with the weakness to fucking man up and end it.

Sitting in my old living room and staring at the door that leads to the empty pool that drained my little girl of the life she was meant to live, D'lilah pours herself another glass of cheap vodka. For the first time in a long time, I relate to what she's feeling.

My body aches and I'm tired. So fucking tired. I fist my hands into my hair and try to pull to the forefront all my reasons for needing to stay strong, but fail. This isn't about me, shouldn't be about me, but it hurts so badly.

"What did they say?" D'lilah slurs from her slumped position in the chair across from me.

I peer up at her and take in her dirty clothes and tangled hair. Her pallid skin and bloodshot eyes prove her slow suicide mission is working.

"She's going downhill." I swallow back the ache in my throat that hasn't disappeared since I left the nursing home. "No longer responding."

"Huh." She takes a swig of the clear liquid and drops her head back. "Probably for the best."

I grind my teeth and rein in my temper. "Whatever the fuck that means, 'Li." Easy to say from her hiding place at the bottom of a bottle.

She laughs a deep guttural sound of intoxication and surrender to the inevitable. "Never should've put her in that place."

My lips pinch together to keep from saying all the things I've wanted to say but never could.

"Just drawing it out, ya know?" She shrugs and takes another gulp.

"Says the drunk who wrote her off," I say, shocked at the intense growl that punctuates my words.

This is fucking stupid. I need to get the hell out of here before I make today worse than it already is.

She glares at me through one eye. "I tried to go; you wouldn't let me."

"Too little too late."

"What does it matter anyway? She's gone, Cam! What's the point? So I can stare at the shell of a girl I don't know?"

Unthinking, I hook the lip of the coffee table and flip it on end. "You selfish bitch!"

She shoots to her feet, stumbling before she finds her balance. "Fuck you! Get the fuck out!" Her face blooms red with anger, and her nostrils flare.

I shake my head and storm from the room, ignoring the foul rant that she's spewing to my back. If living in denial, wallowing in her own pain until she dies is what she wants, I'll leave her to it. My stomach knots as the obligation to make right all I've done wrong washes over me.

Dammit. Fuck! I turn, throw my fist, and smash through the dry wall. My chin drops with the weight of regret. I lean my forehead on wall and try to slow my heaving breath and racing heart.

"Cam—"

"Not now." I hold my hand out to keep her back and close my eyes. *Calm down. Think.*

"I'm sorry. Today sucks for all of us."

I push off the wall but avoid her eyes. "I have to go."

"You don't have to leave—"

I whirl around and fix my eyes on hers. "Sober up, 'Li. You need to be there for our son tonight. Do *not* fuck this up."

She jerks as if my words were a sucker punch to the gut. *Good.* Maybe that'll help pull her head out of a liquor bottle long enough for her to show up to her son's birthday dinner.

TWENTY-SEVEN

EVE

I'm uneasy, and it's not for the reason I'd think. Walking through the Planet Hollywood Casino to The Striphouse restaurant on Cameron's arm is attention getting enough. He's somewhat of a local celebrity now that he's taken over as president of the UFL. I curl my fingers into the starched fabric of his navy blue dress shirt and feel the tension in is muscles.

Something is off.

And I don't think it has anything to do with the fact that we're having dinner with his ex-wife and teenage son. This feels bigger than that. There's a vibe of anxiety or tension that charges the air around Cameron and has been since he picked me up. I felt a similar agitation from him before, leading up to Ryder's birthday. But tonight it's intensified to the point that my skin tingles with the power of it.

"Mr. Kyle, the rest of your party is here." The hostess motions for us to follow her through the old Hollywood-style restaurant.

The deep red upholstered walls are covered in old black-and-white photos of actors and actresses from decades ago. Chairs and booths are in the same dark red leather, which lends a sophisticated and classy ambiance. The scent of melted butter and rich meat swirls in the air, and my mouth waters despite the off mood of my date.

"Here you are." She stops at large half-circle booth where both D'lilah and Ryder are waiting.

Cameron gives a grunt of acknowledgement.

"Took you two long enough." Ryder flashes a teasing smile. I've noticed he's ditched the old faded tees for a nice plaid button-up shirt.

"Sorry, that was probably my fault." I shift on my feet at the feeling of D'lilah's eyes eating me up from heels to hair. Luckily, I wore my favorite sleeveless white fit and flare that's just short enough to be sexy rather than skanky and a pair of black pumps that make my legs look twice as long as they are.

"Sorry to keep you waiting." *Oh, he speaks.* Cameron guides me into the booth next to Ryder and slides in after me to take the end.

"No, not at all." D'lilah takes a sip, or more like a gulp, of her wine. "Although, some of us aren't getting any younger." Her eyes never leave Cameron. "Isn't that right, Cam?"

"Mom, you promised." Ryder's fixed on his mom, and Cameron's glare is directed at her too.

The air is heavy with the silence between them. I fidget in my seat, wanting desperately to melt back into the booth and become one with the pleather.

"Welcome to The Striphouse, my name is Tarryn, can I get you two something to drink?"

The waitress's bell-like voice works like a whistle to call time out between the three at the table. This is going to be a long night.

Cameron orders a bottle of wine, and the mood is a little airier by the time we get our glasses.

"I'd like to make a toast." I raise my glass and everyone follows suit. "To Ryder, you're now a legal adult. Don't do anything stupid and get yourself killed."

Ryder's eyebrows come down low over his eyes. Cameron drops his head a little, and D'lilah's face goes pale. Everyone is silent, staring. So much for the lighter mood.

"Cheers?" I hold my glass to the middle of the table, and slowly Cameron taps my glass. The rest of the family follows his lead. I try to make eye contact with Cameron, but he seems content to look everywhere but at me.

"How long do you think we'll be here?" Ryder checks his watch. "I told the guys I'd meet them at an eighteen-and-over club."

"We'll make it quick." Cameron waves for Tarryn.

I take a long draw from the full-bodied red wine and pray that the booze goes straight to my head so I can get through the next hour because Lord knows I'll need a buzz to do it.

"Are you ready to order?" Tarryn is back, and I scramble for the menu that I haven't even had the chance to look at yet.

"We'll split the Kobe steak, creamed spinach, and Au Gratin potatoes." Cameron doesn't even look at me even though he clearly just ordered for me. He snags my menu from my hands and gives it to the waitress.

What the fuck? First, he's clearly got a stick up his ass. He's been communicating like a damn caveman, and now he's taking away my options for dinner? I take a deep breath and chain up my shitty remark that would no doubt make a crap situation worse.

Besides, tonight is about Ryder, and although the poor guy looks as if he'd rather be at a One Direction concert rather than dining at the table-o-tension, I can pull my shit together for him.

"What's the name of the club you're headed to?" D'lilah says, her eyelids drooping a little.

Ryder goes into his plans for the night, and we all listen attentively and pretend it isn't uncomfortable as hell.

"Mm, sounds like fun." She shrugs. "Maybe I'll go with you."

"'Li, it's his birthday for shit's sake," Cameron says on a growl.

"I realize it's his *birthday*. But I'd like to go have some fun too, seeing as I'm the one who *birthed* him."

"It'll be nothing but a bunch of kids, 'Li. That's ridiculous."

"Ha, but hanging out with kids"—she leans across the table toward him, the deep neckline of her blouse exposing the tan strap of her bra—"seems to have worked for you."

A low grumble charges the air, and I slide my hand to Cameron's thigh on instinct. His muscles are rock hard as if he's gearing to use them to spring across the table at his ex.

"Not another fucking word," he says so deep and low that it raises gooseflesh on my arm. "Tell me you hear me."

D'lilah's eyes narrow, and she opens her mouth to speak.

"Wait, just stop." I pull my napkin from my lap and put it on the table. "I shouldn't be here. It's making things tense, and Ryder doesn't need this on his birthday. I'll go—"

"No fucking way, babe."

I give his leg a squeeze. "Cam—"

"Eve, I invited you here," Ryder says. "It's my birthday, and I say you stay."

"Yay." D'lilah rolls her eyes into her wine glass.

I'm rethinking my idolization of D'lilah Monroe.

"She's staying." Cameron throws back the rest of his wine and pours himself more.

I make a mental note that a grumpy Cameron equals me having zero say in shit! I rip my hand from his thigh only to get the glare of all glares and a jerk of my hand back to his thigh.

Asshole.

After a few minutes of silence, it's clear that no one at the table is going to even *try* to salvage the rest of the night. I remember my talk with her on the Fourth of July. She seemed to calm and even become pleasant when we talked about her modeling. I'll give it a shot. Worst she can do is tell me to go fuck myself.

"So, D'Lilah, tell me about living in Milan when you were a teenager. That must've been pretty cool."

Her eyes flash to Cameron's and something she sees in his expression makes her relax a little. Slowly and between sips of wine, she opens up about her glamorous life as a model. She pours herself another glass, and I'm afraid if she doesn't eat we're going to be carrying her out of here.

The food arrives right on time, and I struggle to push food down past my anxiety.

Cameron must catch on to me pushing my food around my plate because I look up to find him glaring down at me. "Eat."

I sigh and turn to my food, making sure to shovel in every last bite. After a couple bites, Ryder launches into a story about his night playing roadie for Ataxia. Everyone laughs and responds in the right places, and soon my appetite returns. The waitress asks if we want a dessert menu, but Ryder declines, his eyes still glued to the time.

"No way, you have to make a wish," I insist. "It's your birthday."

"It's fine, really." His gaze swings between the time on his phone and the exit. "I'm a little old for restaurant sing-a-longs."

"What? You're never too old for those, dude." I pull over the small candle from the middle of the table. "Here. This'll do."

I start to sing happy birthday, and after the first few words, D'lilah joins in. I notice Cameron passes on joining the celebration, but that doesn't surprise me, especially given the mood he's in.

I watch as Ryder fills his cheeks with air and blows hard to turn the flickering orange flame into a slithering column of smoke.

"There. Now can I go?" He smiles.

"What did you wish for?"

"Yeah, right. I can't tell you that or it won't come true."

I laugh and turn to the rest of the table, almost falling out of the booth at what I see. D'lilah's face is wet with tears, and Cameron's eyes are soft on her. *Soft.*

"'Li."

She shakes her head. "I can't do this."

"Mom." There's no sympathy in Ryder's expression, just irritation.

"It's okay."

What's okay? What in the hell is going on with this family?

"I can't." She leans over and places a kiss to her son's cheek. "Happy birthday, baby. I have to go." She slides out of the booth and hurries to the exit.

"Fuck." Cameron moves to chase after her, but jerks back into his seat like he just remembered I'm there.

"It's okay." I place my hand on his forearm. "Go see if she's okay."

He looks conflicted, his gaze swinging back and forth between where I'm sitting and where she disappeared.

"Right, well, I'm outta here." Ryder scoots out of the booth. "Thanks for dinner, Dad."

"Ry, go check on—"

"Not tonight, Dad. If there's ever a day where I don't have to live in someone else's shadow, I pick today." He turns and follows the direction his mom left.

Shadow?

"Cameron, what the hell just happened?"

He buries his face in his hands. "Not now, Eve."

Eve? Not doll or babe? *Shit.*

My heart cramps violently and familiarly. I'm losing him. My body's alarm system screams for me to run, as if distance will protect me from the looming heartbreak.

Something happened between this morning and tonight that robbed me of the Cameron I know and replaced him with a man I feared he would become. He's thrown up a glass wall between us, and I don't know how to bust through.

I take a deep breath. "It's okay. Go after her."

He looks at me, eyes held in a tight glare and yet totally expressionless. "I'm not leaving you." His voice doesn't carry the conviction of his words.

"I'll grab a cab." I feel my grip on him slide away as my heart succumbs to its fears.

"Eve." There's no fight in the way he says my name. No desperation or even the bossy control I've heard in the past.

"Really." I tilt my head to the front of the restaurant. "She shouldn't be driving." *Don't leave me.*

"Shit." He shakes his head. "I didn't even think about that." His eyes find mine. "You sure?"

I nod. *Take me with you.*

He pulls out his money clip and drops a wad of hundred dollar bills on the table. "This should be enough for dinner and a cab." He leans over and kisses my forehead.

Not my lips. I almost hear an audible crack of my heart.

"I'll call you later."

And then I watch him walk away.

———

CAMERON

Fuck. I should've known this would be a disaster: Eve and D'lilah at the same dinner table the night of our twins' eighteenth birthday. Mourning all that we've lost while celebrating our son's launch into adulthood is a mixed box of shit that I don't even want to attempt to sort out.

I quicken my pace through the lobby and outside to the valet. Pushing through the doors, I'm hit with a wall of desert-summer heat. I scan the busy *porte cochere*. People jump in and out of cabs, while others load and unload suitcases. A flash of blond catches my eye.

You've got to be kidding me. D'lilah's leaning up against the wall in the designated smoking area with a few guys half her age. They're all talking too loud and using wild hand gestures.

'Li catches my approach and her drunk smile falls. She takes a long drag off her cigarette and stares right at me.

"Come on, beautiful. It'll be fun," one of the dicks says.

"I'd love to." She practically purrs and looks right at me.

"The fuck you will. You're going home. Now." My muscles are so tense I could split my damn shirt.

I'm so sick of following her around, taking care of her out of duty or obligation. I told myself as soon as she got on her feet, got herself sober, I'd walk away. I always thought it was what I owed her for what I'd taken from her. But this is bullshit. It's been fourteen years, and she's worse than she's ever been.

"D'lilah. Now."

One of the douchebag guys whispers something to his limp-dick friends about getting the hell out of there. Smart.

"No, Cam." Her eyes glisten with tears. "No way. I don't want to go home. I can't go back there. I can't." Drops slide down her face to cascade off her jaw.

The guys slowly back away, and I step in closer to her. "Don't do this. Not now. Not here."

"Don't make me go back there. I can't." She shakes her head, her body crumbles in on itself, and I move quickly to keep her from dropping to the ground.

Hell, this is an impossible position. I'm so angry at her, but also feel too responsible to walk away.

"Shh, it's okay. Let me take you home."

She nuzzles into my chest as sobs rip from her throat. "I can't go there tonight. I…I miss her. My baby." Another wave of tears and her body quakes with the force of it.

My heart seizes behind my ribs, and I pull her closer and hold on with all I have. It's not her I want to be holding, but fuck if I don't grip something I'll drop.

"Sir, can I get your car?" The valet who took my keys when I got here shifts uncomfortably, and I notice that we've drawn a small crowd.

I nod, and he moves quickly to pull up my car, which thankfully was parked right up front. He leaves both doors open.

"Car's here, 'Li." I rub her back and try to get her to loosen her hold on my waist. "Come on, you can stay at my house for the night."

Her arms let up a tiny bit, just enough for me to get my hands on her shoulders and peel her off the front of my body. She keeps her head ducked, and I usher her to the passenger side of my car. My skin prickles with the feeling of eyes on me from all angles and whispers of who I am and what's going on.

Once inside the Maserati, I point it toward home. Damn, this is going to be a long night. And if I know Eve, my little ball buster's going to have a few choice words for me once I call her.

This is crazy. I need to come clean and tell Eve everything about my past, but there's no way I'm doing it over the phone. I need to be there to lock her in my arms if she tries to run away after she finds out I'm responsible for robbing my daughter of a future.

—

EVE

Everything's blurry and my throat burns. No matter how hard I try to stop the tears from falling, they ignore me. I can't breathe.

Fuck, what was that? I left to grab a cab only to see Cameron and D'lilah hugging so tightly they looked like lovers. She seemed upset, but he was comforting her in such a physical way a stab of jealousy shot right through me.

They're sharing something. Most likely mourning the death of their marriage. Being together as a family with me there must've hammered the point home that they're over. I can't shake the feeling that he isn't telling me the whole story where she's concerned. Tonight, surrounded by their family, it was obvious they're all aware of something I didn't have the privilege of being a part of. But what?

Do they still love each other?

He says no, but that's the only explanation I have for the tender way I watched him rub her back and tilt his nose into her hair, just as he'd do to me. Oh God, how could I've been so damn stupid? He's not over her. And the worst part of it all is that I can't blame him. They share a past and a love that brought about a child. They're the same fucking age!

As soon as D'lilah leaves the same way I showed up—in Cameron's car with him—I push through a crowd of whispering onlookers. I hum loudly to avoid hearing what they're saying word for word. I don't want to know what they're assuming because it's probably the worst and most likely the truth. A row of cabs is my escape and I hop into the first one I reach.

I can't do this: wonder how long it'll take before he leaves me, waiting for the day I push him too hard and send him into the arms of someone else. So many things can go wrong, and if history proves correct, they will. Eventually.

"Where to?"

My gaze drifts out the window, and without thinking, the words slip from my mouth, "Stone Hearth Country Club. I'll direct you from there."

A nervous flutter in my belly is quickly soothed by the need for answers. Why does he insist on treating me as if I'm the only woman in the world and then turn around and treat me as though I'm only one of many?

No. I told myself I'd never be this desperate again. I'd rather be single than play second. It's time he hears that from my lips.

TWENTY-EIGHT

CAMERON

D'lilah cried the entire way home, and as badly as I wanted to veer off the freeway to her place and drop her there, I couldn't stomach leaving her alone in that house like this. She may not be my wife anymore, but she's Ryder's mom, and I owe it to him to take care of her. Especially when she's this messed up.

She drops like dead weight onto the couch, hiccupping still from her sadness. I unbutton my tear-soaked, makeup-streaked shirt and slide it off.

"The guest room is made up. I'll grab you something to sleep in." I move to the hallway to grab her a tee and some boxers.

"I can't do this anymore," she whispers.

"You just need a good night's sleep." I take another step toward my room.

"What happened to us?"

What the fuck? I turn on my heel and study the crumpled-up woman on the couch, who is a mere shadow of the woman I married. "I don't think you need a recap of our lives, 'Li."

"No, I know. It's just...You've dated women in the past, but you're different with this Eve girl."

I blink and step closer, curious. "Different how?"

"She's making our son breakfast." She wipes beneath her eyes. "Showing up at his birthday dinner. She's special to you."

"What's your point?" This is bullshit. I don't owe D'lilah a breakdown of my feelings, and I'm not at all comfortable with the lust swirling in her drunken gaze. Sooner she passes out, the better.

She pushes up from the couch and moves to me, stumbling at the seductive swing she's attempting to throw into her hips. "We had some fun, didn't we? Back before things got so complicated?" She stops inches from me; her drunken gaze eats up my bare chest.

"'Li—"

"Remember our honeymoon?" She tilts her head. "We couldn't get enough of each other back then."

She was breathtakingly gorgeous, but I never connected with her beyond the physical. Back then I thought the strongest kind of attraction was sexual. Animalistic need. Since Eve came along, I realize how much better sexual attraction is when I'm also attracted to the many facets of her personality.

"We got pregnant on that trip." She presses her palm against my chest. "Remember—"

I grip her wrist. "That was a long time ago."

"It doesn't have to be, Cam." She bites her lip seductively. "It can be just yesterday. For one night, we can pretend that I'm still the woman you fell in love—"

"No, 'Li." I pull her hand from my chest. "I'm sorry."

"No? But I'm offering you a chance to be that guy again. You were so powerful, so smart." She pulls my hand up to place it against her chest.

I step back. "And now I'm not. Is that what you're saying?"

Her eyes narrow. "I know you miss the old you. The old us."

"I don't, not even a little."

She flinches.

"I'm sorry, but it's the truth." I move toward the hallway. "It's been a long day and an even longer night. Grab something to sleep in from Ryder's room. We'll get your car in the morning."

I'm halfway to my room when she grabs my elbow from behind. "Cam, wait."

I tug my arm from her hold. "Walk away, 'Li. I know what's going on, and it's not going to work. I'm with Eve."

Her attempt at a sexy quickly morphs into confrontational. "She's a child. It's disgusting."

"Watch it. I'm not above getting you a cab back to your place if you insist on insulting her."

She shakes her head. "You're nothing like the man I married."

"Why, because I won't fuck you? Because I refuse to be a part of this game you're playin'? You want to feel better about yourself? Sober up. Get a job. Make a difference in your kids' life. For once, make a healthy decision."

"Says the guy who lost everything." She grits the words through clenched teeth.

"Sleep it off, but make sure you're gone in the morning." I turn my back on her and slam my bedroom door behind me.

Fuck, this woman is a damn mess. I've tried too hard to fix her, to make up for all I'd taken from her, but no amount is ever enough. I can't replace all that she lost, no matter how hard I try.

—

EVE

"Give me a second. I'll be right back." I put the cab on hold while I head up to Cameron's house, not sure if I'll be staying and worried finding another cab in this ritzy neighborhood will be impossible.

I've had little time to concoct my speech beyond the forward "What the fuck?" Flutters explode in my belly as I make my way up the drive. The smell of fresh cut grass from the golf course and warm desert air does nothing to soothe my nerves. There are no exterior lights on. I wonder if he's even home? What if he's at D'lilah's house? Visions of what they could be doing together flicker through my mind a second before I squash them. No, I'm not going there.

Once to the door, I see through the front window into the living room. I lean over and peer inside, nearly falling backwards at the image that slams me in the chest.

Cameron's shirtless and standing just a few feet away from where D'lilah's seated on the couch. They're talking, or she's talking and he's listening. My eyes lock on her blouse that is gaping off one shoulder. She gets up and sashays to him. Her hand rests against his chest and his on her hips. I swallow the thick ball of emotion that clogs my throat. I spin around, my back pressed against the door, breath coming in harder and being chased from my chest by the power of my racing heart.

How did I not see this coming? I was always a toy to him. His Doll. A plaything to keep him occupied until he and D'lilah could reconcile. No one would ever choose me over a supermodel. My own mother chose her life over her daughters. My father chose addiction. And Vince, well he was never in it for me. I wasn't good enough then, and nothing has changed.

Cameron's voice filters from behind the door. Is he headed this way? I sneak one last peek, panicked that he'll walk out the door, but gasp at what I see. Cameron strides into the hallway toward his bedroom with D'lilah on his heels.

I struggle to catch my breath and race back to the waiting cab. "Go, please!"

The driver jumps, but luckily my outburst has the cab rolling forward. "Where?"

"Anywhere but here."

Fuck! It happened again. I can't believe I put myself in this position again. I actually thought Cameron was different. I groan and lean my forehead against the grimy window of the cab. Isn't that what I think of every man who's ever destroyed me?

I'm sick; my stomach threatens to unload. I hate him. I hate all of them, every fucking one.

Or do I hate myself?

I mumble my address, and it seems as if lifetimes pass before I'm finally in my bedroom, stripping off my dress and pulling on an old pair of sweatpants and a tank top. I wash my face, brush my teeth, and pull my hair back. I move through it all by rote until I fall in defeat to my bed.

The familiar burn of tears wells in my eyes, but I will not cry again over a man. I'd worked so hard to build up my barrier, and Cameron broke it down that first night we met in less than an hour. That shit won't happen again.

I'll make sure of it.

TWENTY-NINE

EVE

At first I thought I was dreaming. The repetitive knock could've been the water pipes from my elderly neighbor's bath time, but it's the middle of the night. I lie still and focus to hear what it is that woke me up.

Knock, knock.

There it is again. It takes a few seconds for my brain to catch up to realize someone is knocking on my front door. My pulse speeds so much I can hear it thumping in my ears.

Cameron?

It has to be. Whoever is knocking is doing it softly enough to not wake up the neighborhood, but firm enough to get my attention. It has to be him.

I rip the covers off and stumble to the door as if my body is acting on its own accord. If he's here to see me in the middle of the night, maybe I misinterpreted everything I saw in his living room. He wouldn't come over in the middle of the night to break up with me, not with D'lilah still warming his bed.

I pull open the door. "Cameron, what're you—"

"Nope. Not Cameron." There's man I've never seen before leaning against the doorframe.

I hurry to slam it closed, but don't make it in time before he blocks it with his foot.

"Now that's no way to treat a guest. I suppose you learned your manners from your father." The last word comes out on a snarl. His seedy gaze traces the curves of my body.

"If you're looking for my dad"—the shake in my voice is unmistakable—"he's not here."

"I know he's not here. Just got finished having a very unpleasant conversation with him where he gave up this address." His lips curl back over yellowing teeth. From the looks of him, I'd say this guy has seen his fair share of the inside of every casino in Vegas. Stale cigarette smoke wafts off his body in nauseating waves, coming not from his clothes but emanating from his skin. Hell, even the dirty brown and gray color of his hair matches that of smoke.

"Oh, you're friends with my dad?" I need to think, devise a plan. My thoughts jumble, and I struggle to think through my fear.

"Not anymore." His foot is still in the door. "Now he owes me money and told me you hold on to it for him."

I shake my head. "I'm sure it's no surprise to you that the man is a compulsive liar. I don't have any of his money." Shit, the way this guy is looking at me makes me think money isn't the only form of payment he'd take. I swallow back the surging stomach acid.

"Your pops owes me five grand, and he told me I could come here and collect." The man tilts his head and studies me. "'Fraid his problem is now your problem."

Shit.

That greasy no good piece of shit.

"Five thousand dollars, huh?" I don't even know what I'm saying as long as it buys time. His foot is still in the door, so I can't really slam it and grab my phone. "I don't have that kind of money on me." Oh God, what am I going to do? I have nowhere to run but inside, and he'll only chase me down. I think back to Cameron's self-defense lesson. *In order to fight someone bigger, stronger, you reel them in rather than run away.* Bringing him inside my house seems insane, but it's my only chance. "You know what? I can make a healthy payment tonight, and then I'll put a call in to my dad tomorrow to get things squared away."

He seems to think over my suggestion before nodding. "That'll work. Besides, if I don't get paid the remainder…I know where you live."

My hands shake as I force them to do what seems too risky to chance and open the door. "I have a safe in the kitchen."

Shit.

I'm dizzy as all the blood rushes from my head to my stomach. If I can get to the kitchen and to my keys, I might have a running chance to get to my car.

He pushes the door open, and I step deeper into my house with him, closing the door behind him. My arms and legs are wobbly, my pulse raging in my ears.

"I keep the safe up there." I point to the cupboards above the refrigerator and grab my car keys. "There's a stepstool in the utility closet." I pretend to fumble through my keys, searching for the right one for a safe that doesn't exist.

He's shoulders deep in the closet, fishing out a stepstool. Here's my chance. In a spring action, I run.

Fear powers my muscles. I fling open the front door.

"You fucking bitch," he says from still inside.

Dammit! His car is parked behind mine. I split in the opposite direction, through the neighbor's yard. My legs burn; bare feet ache as I race to find somewhere to hide. All the desert trees are nothing but sticks. He's gonna find me, fuck! I bolt across the street, pushing my legs as hard as I can.

Strong arms wrap me from behind. "No!"

"Gotchu', bitch."

I buck and kick, but he doesn't let up. Panic seizes me. I jerk hard. Pain lances through my shoulder. "Fuck!"

I slump in his arms as heat and burn blaze up my neck. Did he stab me?

I've been held like this before when Cameron was teaching me self-defense. If I can break free of his hold, I can surely get away from this weaselly fuck.

I lean my weight back. Take two steps to the side, throw my knee behind his and sweep his legs out from under him.

He drops his hold and falls.

I take off toward a big apartment building. There has to be somewhere to hide at least long enough for this guy to give up. Maybe he'll go back to my place and toss it looking for money. That's my only hope. I scurry under a low staircase that's tucked in a dark corner.

With no phone, just my car keys, I crouch down in the tiny space. My lungs burn with the effort it takes to slow my breathing. My legs shake with fear and the strain of trying to hold still. I don't move and pray like hell he doesn't find me. My dad sent a fucking loan shark to my house, and the worst thing about that is I should've expected it. Dammit, why the hell did I open the door?

Because I thought it was Cameron.

The air drains from my lungs in one long defeated breath. Cameron never even called, and I would've known because I kept the damn phone with me in bed. And he didn't stop by. I mentally beat myself up for being so naïve.

Minutes pile on top of each other until my legs go numb. I have no concept of time, but a deep purple hue bathes the sliver of courtyard I can see from my hiding spot.

There's no way I'm going to risk going home. He could be hiding anywhere waiting for me. Even an attempt to get to Raven's is a risk. Going anywhere near my house, even if it's only to get my car, is a piss-poor idea. So what then? Knock on doors?

Hiya, I'm your neighbor, and I'm being chased by a psycho loan shark. May I come in?

I've driven by this apartment complex a million times, and I think there's a pay phone behind the back parking lot. If I call the cops, they'll want me to file a report and my dad could go down, or worse, if these guys want retaliation, he or I could end up in a dirt grave. Jonah and Raven are my only chance.

I wait a few more minutes and close my eyes to tune my hearing. It's silent and I'm alone as far as I can tell.

With a deep calming breath, I slide out from under the stairs. Crouched low, I wait another few seconds. Still quiet. Starting slow at first, I creep out into the courtyard, making sure to stay to the sidewall and the camouflage of the shadows.

Once I make it through to the rear lot behind the building, I glue my back to the wall before turning the corner. I hope the pay phone I think I remember is real.

Please be there; please be there.

A dog barks. Panic fuels my legs as I beat feet to the phone. *Yes!* I rip the phone from its cradle and press it to my ear. Think, Eve, think! With a shaky finger, I dial the one, eight-hundred, and now I have to spell collect.

My finger slips. Shit! I hit the lever, look over my shoulder, and try again. Concentrating as if my life depends on it, I dial the damn number and follow the prompts.

"Please hold while we attempt to contact…"

I spin around to keep a visual on my surroundings, and wait. My breath quickens, and even though there's not a soul walking the streets, I'm terrified he'll jump out at any minute.

I wait, listening to dead air. Come on, Rave. Pick up, pick up. My heart hammers in my chest, and my eyes dart around the open space.

If that jerk was around, he'd nab me no problem. Out here, I'm a sitting duck.

"Your call is connected." There's a small click.

"Eve, oh my gosh, Eve? Where are you?" Raven's voice is deep with sleep and heavy with concern.

"A man came to my house. My dad sent…" I can't breathe. The words rush to the surface and none of them make sense.

"Where the fuck are you?" Jonah's voice comes roaring through the phone.

"Oh God, Jonah, I'm hiding. I'm…" Why can't I breathe?

"Eve. Calm down. Listen to me."

"Mm."

"Are you home?"

"No. I ran."

"Close to home?"

I nod a couple times before I realize he can't see me. "Yes, the apartments."

"Okay, listen. You hear that?"

There's a grumble in the background. An engine?

"That's the truck. I'm on my way to you."

"Okay, okay, okay. Yeah."

"Breathe, Eve. I'm on my way. You stay on the phone with me until I get there. Won't be long."

"Yeah, but what if he finds me out here."

"Fuckin' shit." I hear the sound of his hand gripping the phone tight. "Who the hell's after you?"

"I…I don't know. Dude just showed up. I ran, hid, didn't know who else to call."

"You did the right thing. Just hang tight."

"Okay, but hurry."

"I'm three minutes away. You good?"

"I'm scared."

"Yeah, I get that. Stay on the phone."

"Okay, I'm...okay."

"Two minutes, babe."

I don't answer verbally, but the swell of tears I've been holding back begins to well. He's almost here. I'll be okay. I blow out a long breath of relief when I see his lifted black truck squeal around the corner.

I run out into the middle of the street to flag him down, not even bothering to hang up the pay phone.

THIRTY

EVE

"Here, this should help." Raven hands me a steaming cup of herbal tea.

I haven't been able to stop shaking. The tremors at the pay phone only got worse once I was safe in Jonah's truck. It's as if my body was waiting until I was safe before it hit me hard with the trauma shakes.

"Thank you." I wrap my trembling hands around the warm porcelain mug.

Jonah enters with the phone to his ear. "Thanks. I'd appreciate that. We'll be by to move her out tomorrow. No, that's it. Thanks, Dave."

I grip my tea to keep my hands steady. "What did he say?"

Jonah called his police connection on the way home after I told him what happened. The on-duty cops swung by my place and reported to Dave what they found, and Jonah just received that call.

He leans his hip against the island counter and pulls his robed wife into his arms. "Dude tossed the shit out of your place."

"Dammit." I drop my chin and try to keep my emotions in check. "I know he didn't find any money. Did they say if anything was missing?"

"Eve, the guy cleaned you out: jewelry, TV, your phone. Safe to assume anything you had of value is gone."

Raven slams her palms to the countertop. "That motherfucker!"

My eyes dart to her. She never used to curse until she married Jonah, and now she does on occasion, but I've never heard her drop an em-effer.

"It's okay, Rave. You know nothing I have is worth jack crap. Whatever he made out with will probably buy him a couple twenties at the pawn shop."

"Hate to state the obvious, but you need to move out. Get a PO Box for your mail, and go unlisted for a while. Probably wouldn't hurt to get a new phone number too." Jonah rubs his wife's back. "You know, when you get a new phone."

"Yeah, I think that's a good idea." My situation comes crashing over me in an all-encompassing downfall. "Shit."

I have nothing. No job, no money, and now what little I did have, was stolen from me. How am I going to start over with nothing? There's the job with Cameron, taking over for Layla, but chances are after he breaks my heart he'll renege on that offer too.

The weight of Jonah's stare lifts my gaze to his. I self-consciously wipe my mouth. "What?"

"You've been here for over an hour."

"Oh, yeah, sorry." I start to stand, but don't have the slightest idea where I'll go.

"Why haven't you called Cameron?"

The air grows heavy with tension. I drop back down to my stool. "Oh, um…"

"Noticed you called me instead of him." Jonah's head tilts, eyes narrow.

Raven's eyes do the same.

"We, um…We broke up."

"What!" Raven stands up only to have her husband place hands on her shoulders and lower her back down to sitting.

I shake my head. "Don't freak out; it's okay." No, it's so, *so* not okay. "It's for the best."

Jonah keeps quiet, but his intense glare seems to inspect my every word.

"Pretty sure the guy still has feelings for his ex." I paint on my most carefree smile. "I'm not mad. We were just hanging out anyway."

Silence ticks between us.

Raven clears her throat. "You sure?"

"Mm-hmm." I sniff away the burn of held-back tears.

Her scowl tightens. "You're exhausted. Let's get you to bed." She comes around the counter and grabs my tea. "Come on. I'll get you settled in with some pj's in the guest room."

I look down at my filthy tank and pants. "I need a shower." I stand and swing my eyes to Jonah. "Thanks. You saved my ass big time."

"You're family," he says, but he doesn't smile. His jaw ticks, and I get the feeling he's either thinking about revenge on the guy who did this or a firm talking-to with Cameron. My chest warms from the power of his concern, which only goes to illustrate his point.

We are family.

Raven and me, now Jonah and the baby.

Not the man who's used me for money since I was old enough to make it. Or the woman who moved across the country in search for the better life she deserved, but apparently didn't think her only fucking daughter deserved the same. Not the countless men who have come and gone and made promises they never kept.

Jonah and Raven, Blake and Layla, hell even a pissy Mason feels like family.

And Cameron. He and Ryder felt like more once. But not now.

No, I know who I can trust.

I lie in Raven and Jonah's huge guest bedroom, sprawled out like a starfish on the king-sized bed. Staring at the ceiling, I finally feel rested. I have no clue what time it is, but the sun is high, and I have a lot to do today, which includes making this guest bedroom my new temporary residence.

A small knock sounds on the door. "Good morning, you up?"

"Yeah, Rave. Come on in."

She pushes through the door, and judging by the robe she's still wearing, I'd say she hasn't been up long either.

"What time is it?"

She drops down on the bed with me, her head on the pillow next to mine. "Almost eleven."

I groan and throw my forearm over my eyes. "I haven't slept in this late since after I stayed up for three days at that Electric Dance Festival."

"You needed your sleep." She doesn't quite sound like her perky self. Maybe it's the lack of sleep or possibly the pregnancy hormone stuff, but either way my friend is off.

"Same to you." I roll to my side and prop my head in my hand. "You're sleeping for two, ya know."

Her hand goes to her belly, and a tiny grin pulls at her lips as she looks down at the baby. "Don't need a reminder. Jonah makes it very clear all that I'm doing and *not doing* for two." No more smile.

"Uh-oh. What now?"

She shakes her head. "You don't want to know."

"I just asked you, pisslicker. Tell me."

With a groan, she scoots her pregnant body down and flips toward me on her side, mirroring my position. "He won't let me do anything already, but after last night?" She shakes her head.

"Oh, is this about driving the Nova?"

"Yeah, I mean I conceded that point about the Nova and its safety. I agreed I wouldn't drive it until after the baby is born. He informed me this morning before he took off that he'd 'prefer' I tell Guy I'm done with work until further notice."

Wow, that's a bit controlling. It's like when Cameron ordered my drink and my meal for me last night at The Striphouse. It was torture to sit there like a good little submissive while he took all my choices away from me, but there's something to be said for man who'll make the hard calls, risk pissing her off if it means keeping her safe and happy.

"So no work, no car. Anything else?"

Her serious blue-green eyes fix on mine. "Yes, he tells me what to eat, what not to eat, when to take my vitamins, even what brand to take. I can't go near Dog's litter box anymore, and he's obsessed with having no soft cheese in the house."

I don't know much about pregnancy, but this all seems a little extreme.

Raven sniffs and rests her hand on her belly. "I know he's worried about the baby and me."

"He loves you, Rave. Just tell him he's being a jackass."

She shakes her head and picks at the terry robe. "No, I understand why he's scared. I mean losing his Dad so tragically he's afraid something will happen to the baby and me." She flips and drops back to the pillow. "I'm sorry. I'm totally making this about me."

"Please, I'd much rather talk about your fucked-up life than mine." A shadow of a smile tugs at my lips. "Kinda feels like old times."

Life has been so good for Raven lately, but there was a time, years and years of time, where we'd just drive and vent about our shitty lives. She'd always be complaining about her mom; I'd be bitching about my dad. It worked out great because the second I wished I had a mom around I'd listen to Raven bitch about Milena and decide maybe a mom's not all that cool. I'm pretty sure my dad stories did the same for her.

"Remember that night senior year when we drove all the way to Barstow?"

I can't help but laugh at the memory, and it feels so damn good. "We had big plans, huh?"

She dissolves into full-belly laughter. "That song."

"Oh my gosh, Raven, the song! Yes." We'd written a song on the way there and swore we could sell it in Hollywood and make millions. "I still remember the words."

"You and me were lovers at fi-irst, you and me were fi-irst lovers, oh…"

We both double over, holding on to each other's arms and laughing until tears stream from our eyes and our bellies cramp.

Raven catches her breath. "Holy crap! That was so much fun. We had the world at our fingertips that night."

"Yeah…" I wipe the laugh-tears from my eyes. "Until we got hungry and decided we'd try again another day but bring more food."

Her eyes go unfocused, and she swings her gaze out the window as if she's seeing that night vividly in her mind's eye.

"For all the shit that was thrown at us, Rave, we made it through all right."

She turns toward me, a peaceful expression softening her features. "Yeah. I'd give anything for even a little taste of the freedom we had that night."

I hate seeing her so down, and after the night I've had, I think we could both use a little freedom. "So?" I raise an eyebrow. "Let's go for it."

Her eyes go wide, and she shakes her head. "Oh, no, Jonah would kill me."

"Is he here?"

"No, he's at the training center." She chews on her fingernail, letting the idea marinate. "He won't be home until tonight."

"A ten-minute cruise around the neighborhood." A flutter of excitement ignites in my belly. I sit up cross-legged. "We'll roll the windows down, blast your crappy fifties music. It'll be just like old times."

"I don't know, Eve."

"Oh come on! It'll be fun. And just think. You'll get it out of your system, and you won't get pissed at Jonah anymore."

"Fine."

"What? I mean"—I shake my head—"are you serious?"

"Yes, dork!" She stands up from the bed and holds her hand out. "But I'm not going to hide it from Jonah. I'll tell him tonight when he gets home. He'll be pissed for a second, but I'll take the tires off of it and put it on blocks if that's what it takes to convince him that I'll never do it again."

"Yes!" I hop off the bed. "Can we grab a coffee while we're out?"

She rolls her eyes. "Fine. Now get dressed and meet me in the kitchen before I change my mind." Without another word, she races from the guest room, and I race toward my...Crap. I have no clothes.

"Wait, Rave. I need something to wear!"

"I'll bring you some!" she calls from down the hallway.

A slow smile pulls at my lips. This is exactly what I need. Being like this with Raven, having this little taste of our history, reminds me of how much I need her, and she me. Here this whole time I thought that Jonah and the baby would fill the spot I occupy in her heart. But is it possible that spot is sectioned off for only me? That there's enough room for all of us to co-exist? Maybe she gets something from our friendship that she won't get from her husband and kid.

With our Nova ride at the forefront of my thoughts, I forget that I still haven't heard from Cameron or that the way we left things last night and the subsequent position he was in with his ex in his house does not equal good things for us. Okay, so maybe I remember all that, but I don't dwell on it.

Instead, I gear up for some time with my best friend, doing what we do best: laugh, sing, and pretend things don't suck.

THIRTY-ONE

CAMERON

Today is for shit.

Not only did I wake up late and end up racing through the training center doors still buttoning up my shirt, but I never did get a chance to call Eve. I managed to send her a text but had to bullshit the dude I was in the meeting with and say I was crunching numbers on my phone in order to do it. It was short, but I hoped it was enough to let her know that I was thinking about her.

It's just after eleven and still no reply.

She's pissed. That's the only explanation. I wasn't thinking clearly yesterday. With so much emotional turmoil, it was nearly impossible to do or say the right things. Now that I've survived another one of the twins' birthdays, I can see that it was a mistake to leave Eve at the restaurant last night. I should've left D'lilah to her own devices.

"Did you reschedule the announcement?"

I look up and Layla's standing in the doorway, holding up my printed schedule for today.

"What? No, why?"

She shakes the paper at me. "Um, because the announcement meeting started ten minutes ago."

Shit! I push back from my desk and grab my planner that clearly is zero help if I don't actually look at it.

"Forgot." I pass her and head toward the conference room where all my local fighters should be waiting.

"Figured that." Layla slaps a folder to my chest that should have all the information I need for this announcement. "Go get 'em."

Damn, this woman is assistant gold.

I push through the conference room door. "Gentlemen…"

There's a feminine clearing of throat: Camille, my first fighter in what I hope to be a very successful female UFL division.

"And lady." I drop the folder at the head of the table in front of an empty seat. "Sorry I'm late. Hopefully what I have to say won't take long."

It's funny. I can't pinpoint the exact reason why I looked up to find Jonah in the crowd, but I do, and when I do, there's no doubt in my mind that I must've felt his glare before I saw it. My muscles tighten in a defensive response to the aggression that's rolling off him and aimed directly at me.

What the fuck is his problem?

"Anyway, the reason I called this meeting is to announce that the day after tomorrow there will be a press conference announcing my fight with Rusty Faulkner."

The room is silent except for a few whispered "oh-shits" and "motherfucks."

"For those of you who know my history, I'm taking this fight on fully aware of the dangers, so don't corner me in the locker room with your Come-to-Jesus talks, all right?"

I go into a few details of the fight and field a few questions.

"What happens if you die?" Reece leans back and interweaves his fingers behind his head. "Who's gonna take over for you?"

My temper's running close to the surface, and I push back what I really want to say to Reece. "Not dying, so there's no need to discuss that."

"No disrespect, Cam." Blake leans forward with his fore-arms on the table. "But we got fucked, lube-free, from the last douchebag-dick that ran this place. Figure we deserve to know what happens if this fight doesn't go as planned."

Blake's sitting next to Jonah, who is still glaring at me as if the sheer power of his eyes could destroy me.

"My plan is to stay on my feet and waltz out of that octagon a winner. Shit goes bad, the board will get a guy in here that's probably a hell of a lot nicer than I am."

Blake shrugs. "Good enough."

Reece glares at me. "Right, so if you'll—"

The sound of a cellphone ring echoes through the room. Are these guys kidding me? I groan and drop my forehead only to look up and see Jonah on his cell.

"Yes, she's my wife. What the fuck is going on?"

The room falls silent with tension with the seriousness of Jonah's demand. My muscles crank up even tighter, every sense on high-alert. I know that tone. I've heard it in my own voice, and the sound of it still haunts my worst nightmares.

It's anger born of unadulterated fear.

Oh shit.

He stands up and sends his chair back against the wall hard. "Tell me she's okay!" His voice cracks with emotion.

Something happened to Raven. Oh shit…the baby.

Jonah bolts to the door. "Where is she? I'm on my way." He knocks into the doorframe and staggers down the hallway.

Without even thinking to do so, I'm right behind him, treading the steps he's taking. He still has his phone to his ear. I'm two steps behind him and about to reach out and grab his arm to stop him when he drops.

Slowly, so fucking slowly, he drops to his knees.

Falls.

Oh God.

He curls in on himself and a groan-like roar of agony billows through the hall, practically shaking the walls. Panic seizes my thoughts, and I'm overcome with a singular mission to help.

"I'll drive." I hold out my hand to help him up. "Just tell me where."

He tilts his head back, and his eyes are rimmed red. "Desert Springs Memorial."

"Got it." I pull him to his feet, and we charge out to my car.

I don't know what the fuck is going on, but memories from the past are knocking to get in. I need to stay focused and get Jonah to his wife and unborn baby. Before it's too late.

THIRTY-TWO

CAMERON

The car is still moving when Jonah jumps from the Maserati in the hospital's emergency driveway. I leave the car there and run after him. The sterile scent of the room ignites a flood of memories that mix with current events and have me struggling to stay in the moment.

This isn't Rosie. Not Rosie.

"My wife, where is she?" Jonah looms over the young girl at the admissions desk. "She's seven months pregnant."

The girl's eyes are wide on him, most likely scared shitless by the 250-pound fighter who looks as if he's about to rip someone's arms clean off their body. "Oh, um…I need a…name, sir?"

"Fuck, just tell me she's okay." Jonah shoves his hands through his hair. "Jesus, God, please, they need to be okay."

He looks seconds away from completely losing his shit and tearing the walls down to find his woman.

I push him aside and go to the desk. "Hi, um"—I read her nametag—"Carol, her name is Raven Slade. She's seven months pregnant and was brought in about twenty minutes ago."

She nods and types a few things on her computer. "Yes, she's um…" More typing.

"Where the fuck is my wife?" Jonah's question thunders off the walls and slick floors, attracting the attention of security guards nearby. They start to close in.

I hold out my hand to them and turn toward Jonah. "Slade, cut that shit out."

His eyes dart around the room, unfocused, tears brimming. Fuck.

I stand up tall so we're roughly the same height. "Look at me. Hey." I slap him lightly in the face to get his attention, and he turns a hateful glare at me. "Pull your shit together now. You'll do your wife no good by getting arrested. You want to help Raven and the baby; you need to fucking man the fuck up and be strong; you hear me?"

He blinks a few times, and some of the rage behind his eyes dissolves.

"That's right. There you go. This is title-fight time; bring your fucking A-game. Do you understand?"

He nods.

"Good, now stop scaring the piss out of this poor girl, and let's get a lockdown on your woman."

"Yeah." He nods a few more times. "Right."

Still a mess, but at least he's not looking murderous.

I turn back to Carol, who hands us a few pieces of paper. "If you could fill these out—"

"No, first you tell me where the fuck my wife is." Jonah's growled words make Carol's hand shake.

"Sir, your wife, Raven?" She shifts on her feet and eyes me nervously.

Oh fuck, this can't be good.

Carol clears her throat. "All I know is she was involved in a hit and run. T-boned pretty bad."

"No." He shakes his head and stumbles back a step.

"Jonah, man. Dig deep for it," I say loud enough for only his ears.

"She was unconscious when they brought her in, and they rushed her right into surgery, but that's all I know."

Jonah's jaw is tight, his mouth in a thin line, and a single tear escapes his eye.

Hands on my hips, I drop my head with the weight of what Jonah's feeling. I know it, have lived it, and fucking live it every day of my life. Pain, regret, anger.

She puts the papers down and shoves them toward him. "If you could—"

He turns his back on her and storms outside.

I pick up the papers and grab a pen. "Thank you. I'll get these taken care of."

She nods and flashes a sad smile that makes me hurt even worse for the heavyweight fighter.

"Do you know if the woman Mrs. Slade came in with has any relatives? We can't seem to—"

"Woman?" My head goes light, and my spine tingles. I brace my weight on the desk. "She wasn't alone?"

"No, she had a passenger in the car with her." She looks at her computer screen. "A woman by the name of Yvette—"

White noise. Total static. I don't need to hear the rest of what she has to say. Eve's hurt. The room tilts on its side, and my knees buckle. I wobble but hold tight to the desktop, refusing to fall.

"What happened to her? Is she okay?"

She checks out her computer screen and makes a few clicks. "Are you family?"

"No, but"—I point over my shoulder to the doors Jonah stormed out of minutes ago—"we're the closest thing she has to family."

"I'm sorry, sir, I can't give any information out unless you're related."

I lean forward, desperate for something. Anything. "Please, just…can you give me something? Is she…?" I swallow hard. "Is it bad?"

Her eyes dart to her computer screen then come back to me. "I can't—"

"Carol, please."

A long sigh escapes her lips. "Her injuries are internal. Doctors are waiting on the results of an MRI."

Internal, meaning she's okay. Right? God, please let her be okay.

"Thank you." My pulse pounds in my ears.

I spin around, dizzy at how quickly things went from bad to fucking worse, and spot Jonah through the sliding glass doors. He's sitting on the curb with his head in his hands, his shoulders shaking. My chest cramps, and I move into the waiting room to give him privacy to breakdown and plead to God for a miracle.

It's been two hours, and the hospital waiting room is practically alive with the tension of pacing fighters. After word got out, Blake, Mason, Caleb, Killer, and even Rex showed up. They maintain their distance from Jonah, but stick close enough to keep him from putting his fist through a wall, or worse, through someone's face.

I rub my eyes, pushing at the headache that started the second we got here and hasn't quit. My past collides with the present, and even though I can somewhat relate to what Jonah's going through, that's not what's fucking me up the most. Maybe it's the added weight of watching one of my fighters face the possibility of losing his wife and unborn baby.

Whatever it is, one thing is clear. My feelings for Eve are way more serious than they should be.

Eve's managed to become important to me without me even knowing. Like a muscle you don't even realize you have until it's sore, she slid right in undetected, and hearing that she's hurt twists a pain deep in my gut. When did she become more than someone who makes things light or whose bad attitude is the best comedy? She's not a woman who I keep around because it's easy or convenient as I first thought. She's so much more. And fuck, but I never gave her permission to be all that.

She deserves better than the dregs I have left to offer. And what little I do have, I don't want to give. Because I know what happens when I love people more than myself, care more for them than I do anything else. When they're gone, the pain is unimaginable. And Jonah hunched forward with his head in his palms is a disturbing illustration of exactly what I don't want. Just looking at the guy is like a nut-shot to the chest that pisses me the fuck off.

The walls are too close and the air's too heavy. I can't breathe. I don't bother excusing myself and move toward the double sliding glass doors to get some air.

"Sir, I realize that you *say* you're her father, but without an ID, we can't relinquish details of Miss Dawson's condition."

My head jerks to the admission desk.

"Go ahead and ask her. She'll tell you. I'm her dad. Cass Dawson. Ask her."

No shit? What in the motherfucking hell is this asswipe doing here?

This guy looks old enough to be Eve's grandpa: gray hair and a wrinkled tee that hangs off bony shoulders and exposes frail arms. Looks as if the gambling Vegas lifestyle has aged him more than his years.

"You're welcome to wait until she gets admitted into a room, sir. But without a valid ID, I can't help you."

I sidle up less than a foot from him, and his eyes dart to me. His weak sneer turns to panic when his gaze focuses over my shoulder. I don't have to look over to know that Jonah's standing at my back. I can feel the tension of his anger behind me.

"You've got some nerve showing your face here after what you did to Eve." Jonah steps around me and growls down at the puny man.

Mr. Dipshit's eyes move back and forth between Jonah and me before they finally widen in recognition. "Ah, you must be Raven's guy."

Jonah steps closer to the man at the sound of his wife's name.

"Easy, Slade." I don't dare lay a hand on the fighter, who's clearly been pushed passed his tolerance. "You've got better things to do than take out the garbage."

Eve's dad takes a step back while Jonah seems to contemplate my suggestion.

"Hey, I don't want any trouble." He holds his hands up and shakes his head. "I'll uh…I'll just catch up with my daughter later."

"Find it fucking hilarious that you've got the balls to call her your *daughter*." Jonah's practically vibrating with anger. "Last night you threw your daughter to a fucking shark."

I whip my glare from Cass to Jonah. *What the shit?* "Fuck you talkin' about, brother?"

Jonah doesn't take his eyes from Eve's dad. "Picked Eve up on a fucking street corner this morning after she was chased out of her own damn house by some loan shark." He tilts his head, glaring through the man who's about to taste his own blood. "Middle of the night, dude shows up to collect on your debt. She was hiding for hours under stairs in her pajamas, motherfucker."

My vision swims in red. He did fucking what? "Tell me he's wrong." The last word fades into a snarl. My fists clench and I wait.

The scumbag has the decency to look ashamed.

"Listen to me." I lean in close, so much so that I smell booze and stale cigarette smoke wafting from his body. "I'm gonna walk you out. You will not come back here. You will not contact Eve, and from this point on"—my teeth grind together painfully—"you don't have a daughter."

"Listen. You're hearing lies from the girl." He holds his hands up and stumbles back a step.

"The *girl* is no longer your concern." I jerk my chin toward the doors. "Now, let me help you find your car." My lips pull back over my teeth, and I'm salivating at the opportunity to throat punch this pathetic excuse.

"I don't want any trouble," he says in a whisper meant only for me.

Jonah pushes closer to me. "Want, no. But you've fucking earned it. You mess with Eve again, those loan sharks will look like guardian angels compared to the shit we'll put you through."

His tiny brown and bloodshot eyes dart between us. "You guys threatening me?"

"Bet your ass, we are." I swing my gaze to Jonah and he nods. "Right, so let's get you on your way, Cass." My muscles coil. Ready. "Come on." I head outside and don't look back, but as I walk away, I sense Jonah's shifted to stand behind Eve's dad, most likely breathing down his neck so that he doesn't have any other choice but to follow me out.

Seconds later, the little shit skirts by me in a full sprint. He's running just as fast as his feeble legs can carry him.

"Nice try, bitch." I hook him by the elbow and search for a more private area.

"Teach him a lesson he won't forget," Jonah says to my back. "Want good news to share with my girl when she's out of surgery."

He digs his heels into the ground. "Wha—no!"

"Ten-four, man." I continue to lead—drag—him outside and tell myself I can't kill the guy.

"Hold on, I…" He bucks in my hold as we turn toward the alley behind the hospital. "What do you want? I'll pay you—"

I stop, whirl the lanky shit around, and throw him against a brick wall. "With what? Your daughter's money?"

He claws at my fists, which are gripped into his shirt. "What? I don't know what you're—"

"You lying sack of shit. I picked up the pieces of the girl you left behind after you robbed her." I slam him against the brick again. "Your own damn daughter!"

"I was desperate!" His voice is high and shakes with a fear that fuels my irritation.

"You're her dad! You're all she has, and you steal food from her mouth." My hand flies, knuckles first, and I backhand the little bitch. "What the hell's wrong with you?"

He spits blood, and his forehead beads with sweat.

"She needed you. Every kid needs their dad." My heart cramps, and I slam him into the wall again. "You abandoned her. Never looked back, did you?" A lump swells in my throat. "It's because of you she's locked up in the hospital all alone." My nose burns and my legs wobble.

"Let me go—"

"She's lived her entire life without a family because you weren't strong enough to take care of her. And now she's dying and totally alone!" Fuck! I release Eve's dad and take a few steps back. My eyes prick with emotion.

"Eve's dying?" he whispers.

Hands on my hips, I breathe deeply. "No. She's not." I push both hands through my hair and try to relax.

What the hell just happened there? One second I'm talking to Eve's dad, and the next minute I'm yelling at an older grayer version of myself.

Am I really all that different from Cass?

A wave of what-the-fuck numbs my legs, and I lean against the wall for support. The answer comes in a torturous trickle of self-realization.

He put his addiction before his daughter, and I put my crusade to regain my career before mine. He's written her off as if she doesn't exist and I…Fuck. How did things get so fucked up? At what point did I lose focus on what matters?

Whatever shit's going on in my chest when it comes to Eve is working like a magnifying glass and forcing me to inspect my life.

This isn't me. I don't want to be the coward who runs from his problems or the guy who insists on living in the past. I can't fix what was, but I can fix this for Eve.

"How much will it take?" The words rasp from my lips and Cass jumps, but his eyes spark.

"I don't under—"

"How much!"

He steps close. "Total? Fifteen grand."

"How much more will it take for you to leave your daughter alone?"

He opens his mouth to answer then slams it shut. I don't miss the lack of offense in his expression but not the twitch of excitement in his jaw.

"Don't fucking act like you don't have a number going through your head, man. You and I know good and damn well that you do."

He shrugs one shoulder. "Double what I owe."

Just like that. Pathetic.

Disgusted, I reach into my pocket and pull out my card. "Call me. I'll wire the money first thing tomorrow."

He snatches the card from my fingers, but I can't bear to look up to see what I know is going to be the pure delight in this man's face: the expression of a father who just sold any chance of having a relationship with his daughter for less than it costs to buy a car.

"You're not messing with me, are you? His voice shakes.

"You take this deal." I push up to my full height and move in close, tucking my chin to keep his eyes. "She's dead to you. You get me, motherfucker? I pay you. You back off. Forever. You don't, and my boys and I will annihilate you."

"Deal." He nods frantically and holds out his hand for me to shake.

I glare at his hand. "Get the fuck out of my face."

He blinks up at me.

"Now!"

His spindly body jerks and he takes off running.

Forty-five grand is a small price to pay to know that Eve will be safe from her father and his lifestyle, but the peace that brings is short-lived when I remember what waits inside the hospital.

I head back into the waiting room and see a doctor approaching Jonah with his hand outstretched in greeting. He's wearing scrubs along with a matching hat that they use in surgery. His facemask is hanging around his neck, and his eyes are locked on Jonah.

"Mr. Slade." The doctor shakes Jonah's hand. "I'm Dr. Kapatia."

Jonah responds with a stiff nod.

"Let's have a seat, and I'll explain how Raven and the baby are doing and answer any questions you might have."

The heavyweight fighter's chin drops to his chest, and his shoulders sag as he lets out a long, relieved breath. "They're alive."

"Yes, they're alive and stable." The doc motions to the seats and sits down, but Jonah stays standing, his arms crossed over his chest, hands tucked into his armpits.

Blake is nearby with a sobbing Layla wrapped up tight in his arms. Rex is a few seats down, elbows on his knees and head hanging low between his shoulders. A few of the other fighters are keeping a safe distance. My stomach churns with anxiety. Stable is good, but it doesn't mean Raven and the baby are going to make it. At least, not in the way that Jonah might think. Stable means breathing. But the body is a complex machine, and a major trauma could fuck it up enough to turn it into a shell of what it should be.

I should know. I live it every day.

"Raven was hit on the driver's side of a car that wasn't strong enough or equipped with the modern safety devices that newer cars have. Lap belts alone aren't—"

"Fuck!" Jonah interlaces his fingers behind his head. "Don't say it."

The doctor looks to me and then to Blake with a question in his expression. He swings his gaze back to Jonah. "I'm sorry, don't say what?"

"The Nova. She…" He scrubs his hands over his face. "I told her not to…"

"I don't know the make of the car she was in, only that it was older and has a soft top, which is why—"

"Fuck!"

Blake steps close to Jonah and leans in to say something to him under his breath. Whatever it is works, and Jonah calms down. "Go on."

"The impact broke a few of her ribs, fractured her arm, and she's got a nasty concussion. But the reason we took her into surgery was because she suffered placental abruption."

Jonah's eyes are to the floor, his hands fisting into his hair. I wait for him to ask a question, seek the details, but it looks as if he's lost to his fears.

"What does that mean for the baby?" I ask and hope like hell the next thing out of this doctor's mouth is good news.

"The placenta detached from the uterus. The baby can't survive in that situation. We took Raven into surgery to check on some internal bleeding and to take the baby."

Jonah's head snaps up; his shoulders crank back. "My baby's here?" His eyes dart to the long hallway that leads into the hospital. "But it's too early. How? I mean is he or"—he swallows what must be a massive ball of emotion—"she…? It's too early."

The doctor stands up and holds out his hand to Jonah. "Mr. Slade, congratulations, you have a very tiny, but feisty, baby girl."

A girl.

Jonah stumbles back as if the good news delivered a solid punch to his chest. "A girl."

"She's early—too early—but we're doing everything we can to mature her lungs and get her weight up. Girls are incredibly strong, and this little one is demonstrating she's a fighter just like her Dad."

"I have a daughter." Jonah sucks in a shaky breath and everyone around him gives him silent congratulations in the form of a thump on the back.

The doctor clears his throat. "Your daughter—"

"Sadie," Jonah says. "Her name is Sadie."

He nods. "Sadie. She's in the Neo-natal Intensive Care Unit. I'll send a nurse down to get you, and you can go see her."

"And my wife?"

"She's in recovery. After a couple hours of observation, we should be able to get her into a room. You're welcome to go back and see her, but everyone else will have to wait until she's out of the ICU."

Before the doc says another word, Jonah's moving down the hallway, followed by the doctor, to see his daughter for the first time.

My head gets light. I wobble on my feet and grab the back of a chair. Fuck. I rub my eyes, brushing off my dizzy spell to exhaustion and stress.

"Two down. One to go," Layla says quietly to Blake, who only nods.

One to go.

Eve.

THIRTY-THREE

EVE

I blacked out.

Don't remember anything after waking up this morning until I woke up in a hospital bed with the worst headache of my life.

The nurse explained that Raven and I had been in a car accident. Hit and run. I was knocked out immediately, or at least that's what they're telling me. No matter how hard I try to pull up the memories, my mind is blank, a black hole that gapes between this morning and now.

I wish I had answers, but all I know is that Raven was rushed into surgery, and that's enough to keep my mind occupied and my heart racing.

If anything happens to the baby, she'll never recover. And if anything happens to her, I'll never recover.

My eyes slide shut, and I cry out another plea to God. Please, let her and the baby be okay. They have to be okay.

The sound of heavy footfalls pulls me from my prayer. I jerk to sit up and my vision swims. The splitting cramp in my side and stabbing pain above my right ear send me back to the pillow. Fuck!

I roll my head to the side, surprised I'm even able to do that since it seems to weigh six hundred pounds, to see Jonah pushing past the curtain.

"Jonah." My voice is shredded with worry and lack of use. "The baby?"

He lifts his eyes to mine, and I gasp at the pure heartache I see in them. Oh no.

"Raven and the baby…" I blink to clear my vision and unleash tears that sting my cheeks. "Tell me they're okay."

He moves to the chair close to my bed and drops into it, his head in his hands. "They're okay. She's in recovery. Broken ribs, arm. Fuck, Eve, what the fuck were you guys thinking?"

A whisper of relief filters through my body but is quickly drowned out by confusion. "I don't…" I lift my hand to the bandage on my head. "I don't remember anything."

His bloodshot eyes find mine, and I suck in a breath. A man like Jonah, who's usually so strong and confident, now resembles a broken and fragile boy. "She promised me she'd stay away from the Nova," he whispers.

I shake my head as much as I can without wincing. "She'd never take out the Nova. She told me she promised you, and she'd never take it out."

Wait, but I remember trying to talk her into it weeks ago. Was that weeks or…?

He laughs, but the sound crackles with confusion. "You girls got T-boned in the Nova, Eve." His eyes meet mine, determined. "So tell me"—he leans in, his glare turning into something feral, dangerous—"what the fuck were you guys thinking!"

I press back into my bed, wanting to escape the agony I hear in his voice and see in his expression. "I…I don't know." More tears fall and drip off my jaw.

Reaching back into my memory, I try to sort out what must've happened. After seeing Cameron at his place with D'lilah, I was upset. Then my Dad sent that guy to my house, looking for money. Jonah picked me up, I spent the night with them, and then…nothing.

"I can't remember. I'd tell you if I could, but..." My fingertips press into my temples.

"This is so fucked!" he roars. "My wife is recovering from surgery while my daughter is in a fucking tiny oven keeping her warm with tubes coming—"

"Daughter?" Goose bumps dance down my arms. "The baby's here? She's a...she?"

A softness touches Jonah's expression, finally melting some of the anger he arrived here with. "Sadie."

"Sadie." I test the name on my lips then blink up at him. "It's perfect."

"She's fucking perfect, but, Eve"—he shakes his head, his face twisting in pain—"she's so damn small."

"I'm so sorry. I wish..." What can I say? "I'm sorry."

He nods once. "Raven made me promise that when the baby was born I'd make sure to keep them together. She didn't want to be separated for even a second. Now my wife is on a different level of the hospital from our daughter. She's sleeping, but when she wakes up..." He shakes his head. "I should be grateful that everyone's alive, but fuck, I told her to stay the hell out of that car!" He digs his hands into his hair.

Silence hangs heavy in the room for minutes or hours. The concept of time is lost on me, and I wish like hell I had answers.

"Right, well." He stands up and rubs the back of his neck. "I wanna be there when Raven wakes up. She's gonna be confused as hell."

I nod. "Yeah."

"I'll check in with the nurses, see how long until they'll let you go home. My guess is we'll probably be here with Sadie a few days longer than you."

"Can't go home. That much I remember."

He glares at me. "Our home."

"Jonah, I can't stay with you guys. Raven, the baby, you don't need a houseguest."

"No, but I'll need your help. And Eve, she's gonna need you."

Need me? But I thought after the baby came her family would be complete. She wouldn't need the makeshift family we formed together. "She'll need her family. Her mom, you, Sadie—"

"And her sister."

The warmth of his words goes straight to my chest and it's like I can't breathe. "Are you sure—?"

"Eve."

I'm family. I pick at thread of my blanket. "Thank you."

He doesn't say another word and leaves the room along with leaving me with more questions than I have answers to.

What the hell happened?

———

CAMERON

As I pace the hallway of the hospital, I'm assaulted by the fear from the past. I try to force the anxiety away, but fuck if this place doesn't make me remember all the shit I'd hoped I'd forget.

The dread that overcomes you at the possibility of losing a child.

Guilt from knowing I could've saved her if I'd just paid attention.

Shit, this isn't about me. It's about Eve.

Jonah sent everyone home a while ago after he explained that Raven and the baby are both doing well. Raven's mom,

Milena, showed up sobbing and, according to Jonah, refuses to leave the baby alone for a second. They're in good hands.

But Eve…*fuck.*

I stop pacing and stare at the door to her hospital room. Maybe I should just go home. I shove my hand into my hair and pull. Don't be such a pussy!

Fact is for the first time since the day Rosie drowned, I'm fucking terrified. The shit stirring behind my ribs when it comes to this girl is something I'd swore off ever feeling again.

I've fallen for Eve.

Hard.

I can't get my thoughts straight, and compounded with the memories of losing one of the only other people I've ever loved in my life doesn't make this shit any easier.

"Mr. Kyle?" The nurse from the circular desk who gave me directions to Eve's room approaches me. "You're right; that's the one." She nods toward the door I've been pacing in front of for the last ten minutes. "Room 452."

"Great, thank you." Now go away so I can figure my shit out, please.

She opens Eve's door wide and peeks inside before looking back at me. "You're lucky she's awake."

How wonderfully fucking helpful is she? I groan. So much for sorting my shit. I take a deep breath and move into the room.

My gut clenches. Eve's tucked beneath the sterile-looking hospital blanket, her head wrapped in white gauze. She's turned away from the door, gazing out the window. She looks so tiny, fragile.

The nurse motions for me to go in before she leaves, but my feet are frozen in place as I take in the beauty and tragic sadness of the room. No family, not even a good friend. Just me. And her dick of a father who probably would've spent visiting hours tossing the room for cash.

Her eyes dart to mine and widen. I suck in a breath at the bruises and cuts that pepper her gorgeous face. Blackened eyes, stitches along her cheekbone, and a split lip. My fists clench.

Her jaw goes slack. Shocked to see me?

"Hey." I step deeper into the room, and immediately the walls close in and anxiety pricks my nerves.

"You're here?"

I nod and move a few more steps toward her bed. "I am."

"W-why?" Her gaze swings over my shoulder and to my side. "You alone?"

She sees I'm alone, so I ignore her question. "Your head."

Her fingers gently press to her gauze-covered temple and run down to smooth her tangled hair. "Oh, yeah, I guess my head went through…I don't know, maybe the side window? Or…" Her fingers trail from her cheek to the length of her jaw, stopping to read each cut and tender spot. "I don't know."

She doesn't remember, something I know more about than I'd ever let on.

I take another step and sit at the foot of her bed. The mattress dips with my weight, and her hand flies to her ribs and she cringes.

I jump up. "Shit, I'm sorry."

"No, it's fine. I just braced a little too hard when I saw you sit." She breathes deeply and motions to the end of the bed. "Please, it's fine. Sit."

I drop slowly to make sure there's no sudden movement and watch her expression.

She takes a slow but deep breath. "I'm good."

"You don't remember the accident."

Her jaw gets tight. "No. I remember waking up at Jonah and Raven's this morning and then waking up here."

Jonah had mentioned she stayed the night with them after she got run out by some piece-of-shit lowlife looking for her dad's payoff. "Heard you had a visitor last night." What I didn't hear was why the fuck she called Slade instead of me.

Her ocean-blue eyes fix on mine. "How did you know that?"

"Been sitting in a waiting room with Slade for the better part of the day."

She blinks and her eyes narrow. "What are you doing here, Cameron?"

What am I...? What does she think I'm doing here? "You were in a car accident. You think I'd let you go through this shit alone?"

The answer is probably "yes" considering the man in her life who did a shitty job teaching a young Eve how she deserved to be treated. I should've chased after his ass when he ran even if only for one good crack to his jaw.

Her nose scrunches up in what looks like disgust before her head falls softly back to the pillow. Her gaze slides to the window. "Ah, makes sense, I guess."

Makes sense she guesses? I look around the room thinking she's got to be talking to someone else. "I missin' something?"

Her chest jumps with what's supposed to be a burst of non-funny laughter, but it must hurt because she grinds her teeth with a grunt.

"You need me to get a nurse?"

She pinches her eyes closed. "Go home, Cameron."

No fucking way I'm leaving. Why the hell would she want me to?

My blood races and I try to keep my jaw locked so I don't say some shit I can't take back. I bite my lip and study the loose stitching of the blanket on her bed.

"Not trying to be a bitch, really, it's just...I know what's going on here, and I don't want any part of it."

My eyes snap to hers. "What's going on here?"

"I'm stupid, I get it, but unfortunately for you, I'm not *that* stupid."

"I don't have the slightest fucking clue what you're talking about."

"Really." The sarcasm is so thick in that one word it's nearly impossible to keep me from responding on impulse.

I keep my lips clamped together.

"Only lost my memory for a day, Cameron, sorry to say." She rolls her head against the pillow. "If I could forget what I saw, I swear to God I would."

"You call the cops on him?"

Confusion carves into her injured face. "What?"

"The guy who showed up at your place. If he's a loan shark, he might have a record. If you could identify him—"

"Stop." She places her fingertips to her eyelids, like she wants to press in, but knows it'll hurt like a bitch.

God, this is frustrating as hell. It's not enough that being in this room is making me want to jump out of my skin. She's laid up in a hospital bed, head wrapped up, bruised and angry red cuts marring her perfect fucking face, and now she's talking as if she's gone damn crazy. I run both hands through my hair, pulling with the hope that the scalp sting will calm my urge to roar "What the fuck are you talking about!" I blow out a long breath.

"You fucking left me for her." Her voice hitches with emotion.

My eyes snap to hers. This is about last night? "No, I chased after 'Li to get her drunk ass home, which, by the way, was a huge fucking mistake." Wait...my eyes get tight. "You told me to go after her. Practically shoved me after her."

"I went to your house to talk to you after you left."

"Okay, so why didn't we talk?"

She pushes herself up about an inch, but the effort it took to do so has her panting. "I *saw* you. With her."

I don't know if I'm more insulted or pissed off about what she's implying. "There's no fucking way I'd touch D'lilah like that again. Whatever you think you saw is a mistake."

What kind of clusterfuck is whipping up in that pretty and broken head of hers?

"You didn't have a shirt on, she had her hand on your chest, and then she followed you back to your room. Do you…?" She sucks in a breath and swallows hard. "The way you were looking at her, Cameron, I see it in Jonah's eyes when he looks at Raven and hers when she looks at him."

I almost want to smile and how ridiculous her ideas of what she saw are. "You didn't see what—"

"Will you stop treating me like I'm stupid! Fuck, I know what I saw."

"*Think* you know what you saw."

"At least have the decency to tell me the truth."

"Eve—"

"I'm in a damn hospital bed, and I can't even remember how I fucking got here. If you care about me at all, you'll give me honesty. You're in love with her."

"You don't know what the fuck you're—"

"Just say it! Stop fucking lying."

"I'm not lying. Shut up and let me explain—"

"I saw it!" She points to her face. "With my own fucking eyes. You're in love—"

"Yes! Fine! Fucking feel better?" I push up and ignore the gasp that shoots from her lips when I shove a chair hard enough for it to hit the wall.

"I knew it." Her voice is hard.

I whirl around, glaring. "You don't know shit because you won't shut the fuck up long enough to listen. It's not her, it's—"

"Get out."

"Fuck that. I had to sit here and listen to you blab about shit you know nothing about. It's my turn to talk, and you're gonna listen even if that means I need to gag you to get you to do that."

Her eyes widen in shock. "You wouldn't."

"I would, and I'd enjoy the shit out of it." I pace the small room. "You're the most infuriating woman I've ever met."

"I know what I saw."

"What you saw was me listening to a very sick and sad woman."

"Shirtless."

I whirl on her, and in one long stride, I'm at her bedside. I lean over and brace my weight on the bed just above her shoulders so that our noses are mere inches away. "Final warning, Yvette. Shut. Up."

She rolls her lips between her teeth but glares in defiance.

I push back up to standing and gaze down at her. "I took my shirt off because it was soaked in her tears. She pulled some fucked-up shit on me that I was not having. I was upset, told her to get the hell home, turned to go to bed, and she followed—"

Her mouth gapes.

"Don't fucking do that. Do not go there in your head."

Her swollen eyelids flutter.

"You want to know what I was thinking last night, what you saw on my face? I was thinking about you. How I should've never left you at that restaurant." I watch and wait for what I've told her to sink in. "If I wanted her, why would I be here? Don't you get it? I'm here. With you."

"But you're here because I'm her. You want to fix her, and I remind you of her, so you want to fix me too."

I shake my head and step to the edge of her bed. "No, doll. I told you before you're not her. Not even close. I'm here because you're you."

She chews on her lip for a moment. "I went home thinking you were done with me, and when someone showed up at my door in the middle of the night, I thought…"

She thought the loan shark was me? Makes sense; it's exactly what I would've done had I been able to drop 'Li off. She opened the door, expecting me. If I'd called her, explained what was going on, she never would've answered the door and let that piece of shit in.

Dammit, this is exactly the kind of crap I worried she'd be signing herself up for by being with me. No matter how hard I try, my head will always be a few steps behind. She's lucky she was able to get away from that guy last night. If she hadn't, who knows what he would've done in order to get his money?

Holy fuck! If I'd called her last night or maybe never left the restaurant to chase after D'lilah, Eve would've been home safe with me all night and never would've gotten in a car accident.

Jonah's wife would still be pregnant, their baby growing in the safety of her mother's belly rather than a plastic box hooked up to a dozen tubes. My pulse pounds in my ears. My knees go MIA, and I hold the guardrail of the hospital bed to stay standing.

This is my fault. Not outwardly, but I made decisions last night that set a series of shit in motion. Just like with Rosie. Holy fuck!

"I'm sorry." The apology is weak, puny in comparison to what I've done. "I never should've left you at the restaurant. If I hadn't…" *None of this would've happened.*

"I was so sure it was you banging on my door, but when I realized it wasn't…" A visible shiver wracks her body. "Thank God Jonah came when he did."

Now I know why she called Jonah instead of me. She thought I was hooking up with D'lilah. Dammit! I can understand why Jonah was giving me a look that he wanted to kill me during the meeting before he got the call about Raven.

"Anyway, I'm moving in with Jonah and Raven for a little while."

They'll keep her safe. She deserves that, and yet disappointment tightens my chest. "That's a"—I clear the words I really want to say from my throat—"good idea."

"Raven and I were talking about it"—her eyes go unfocused over my shoulder and then narrow—"this morning when we were…" She stares thoughtfully at nothing. "We talked about our song."

"Eve?"

"Barstow and then…" She blinks rapidly. Her chest rises and falls faster. "Oh God. No." Her face goes pale.

"What is it?" I cup her good cheek, the skin clammy against my palm. "Are you in pain?"

"I think I…" Tears slide over her lower lids and mark trails down her cheeks. "No!"

I cup her face with both hands to force her eyes to mine. "Talk to me. What?"

"I…The accident." Her breath comes faster and faster. She's going to hyperventilate.

"What about it?"

Her expression goes from slack to twisted in agony. "It was me." She chokes on a sob. "The Nova was my idea."

THIRTY-FOUR

EVE

I'm being crushed from the inside. Heart, lungs, and stomach compacted in the vise grip of my memory.

It was my idea to take out the Nova. Raven only agreed to make me feel better. Music. I remember the music was loud. The crash was quick. I can almost see it in slow motion. We were hit hard. My head slammed into the side window, and then everything went black.

"Eve, doll, talk to me."

I look to the voice without seeing.

"Let's go for it."

"Oh, no. Jonah would kill me."

"Is he here?"

"No."

"A ten-minute cruise around the neighborhood. We'll roll the windows down, blast your crappy fifties music. It'll be just like old times."

"I don't know, Eve."

"Oh come on! It'll be fun."

"Fine."

"Are you serious?"

"Yes."

"I talked her into the Nova," I whisper.

The bed shifts, but I don't feel any pain...only regret and stifling guilt.

"Eve, listen to me right now."

I blink up to sympathetic...no, *empathetic* eyes?

"This isn't your fault. You couldn't have known you'd get hit."

"The Nova. Jonah didn't want her driving it because it's not safe. I talked her into it. She said no, but I talked her into it."

The panic wells in my chest. Sweat breaks out over my skin. I can't suck in enough air. I'm dizzy. The baby. What if she doesn't make it or if she has complications because of the accident? Raven will never forgive me. I'll never forgive me.

"I have to get out of here." I pull at the monitoring wires. "I need to go." Tears flow freely down my face.

"Hold on; just calm down." Cameron's hands come to my shoulders.

"No! Let me go." I swing my legs over the bed and search for a way to get to air. "I can't stay here. I can't breathe." I stand and take quick steps toward the door before the sting of my IV stops me.

Strong arms wrap me up from behind, and a splinter of pain twists in my side, but it's nothing compared to what I deserve. I savor it and take my punishment.

"There's no air." A soul-deep sob rips from my throat; my body shakes with the force of it. "My chest hurts."

"Shh, I know." He rubs soothing circles on my back. "I know."

I pull back and look him in the eyes. "You don't know, Cameron! You have no fucking clue. I did this. The baby could die because of me."

His face gets hard.

"How am I going tell Jonah it's my fault he almost lost his wife and baby?" I press against my breastbone, the pain slicing through. "How will I explain that it's my fault that he almost lost his wife and baby the same way he lost his father?"

The entire weight of my body sinks, but I don't hit the ground. Cameron's hold keeps me upright, even though my legs are completely limp beneath me.

"They're my family." I hiccup through my bawling and my head throbs. His arms drop around my waist, and he buries his nose in my shoulder.

I cry with uncontrollable wails and pain. So much pain.

Oh, God, what have I done? They'll never forgive me.

CAMERON

A nurse rushes into the room, her eyes wide on me. "What's going on?" She quickly studies the beeping machine and then Eve, who's falling apart in my arms. "Get her to the bed." She jogs out of the room.

"Come on, Eve." It's a waste of breath to speak because she's so lost in her sadness and guilt that she's not hearing a damn thing outside of her own agony.

I lift her up as gently as I can, and her arms wrap around my neck, holding on while she whispers remorse-laden prayers into my neck. A sense of déjà vu makes my chest heavy, and the urge to run is overwhelming. Every cry from her lips pulls at a part of me that I've hidden deep. A part covered with years of avoidance and a shitload of work.

The regret.

Guilt.

Loss.

I lower her to the bed just at the nurse comes back in with a syringe. My first instinct is to crouch in front of Eve to protect her from the sting of the needle, but I know the anguish she's going through. I've felt the same things she's feeling.

The nurse steps forward. "Hold her steady." She injects what I'm assuming is a sedative into Eve's IV. "That shouldn't take long to kick in." She crosses the room to drop the syringe in the sharps box. "I'll be back in a minute, after she calms down."

Eve's eyes slide closed and her breathing slows.

"I won't be here." There's no way I can do this shit.

I've spent the last fourteen years of my life with my back to the pain. I'm not ready to turn and face it now.

Not even for Eve.

I'm not brave enough.

The nurse checks Eve's vitals, and it's clear the meds have kicked in and she's fallen asleep. "What set her off?"

"She remembered the accident."

"Mm, okay, I could see how that would be disturbing." She tucks Eve in and hits a couple buttons on the machine at her side.

"What's your name?"

The nurse smiles in a way that, combined with her salt-and-pepper hair, reminds me of a grandmother. "Rose."

A vicious stab slices through my gut. I stand and fight to breathe through what I'm about to do. "Do me a favor?" I pull a wad of twenties from my wallet, no clue how many, but enough. "Make sure she has a ride home when she's discharged." I pull out more cash. "And some clean, comfortable clothes."

Rose fingers through the cash and tries to hand it back. "Sir, I can't—"

I hold up my hand. "Please. She doesn't have family and"—I clear my throat and swallow the burn of remorse—"I won't be around."

Her lips form a tight line, but she nods. "Okay."

She's not stupid. I'm sure she can sense the coward in me running away with my tail between my legs.

My gaze slides to Eve. She looks so peaceful now, not at all as she did minutes ago when the world was crumbling down around her. I lean in and place a soft kiss to her lips, mindful not to disturb her. God, I'm going to miss her.

"Thank you." And without another thought, I turn from the room and pat the dirt on the shredded and now recovered emotions from my past.

She'll realize after the drugs wear off that none of this would've happened if it weren't for the decisions I made last night. Then she'll hate me. Resent me. And we can both go back to being where we were when we started.

She has people in her life who will take care of her: people who care for her like I do, but won't fuck her up like I will.

Like I already have.

—

EVE

Midnight and not a word from Cameron.

After waking up from my drug-induced nap, I expected to see him here. I expected to open my eyes to him scowling at me from the corner. I expected...

And ain't that the shit that screws me over every time.

I blink heavy eyelids and know that although my body demands rest my mind is too busy for it. Instead, I study the long triangle of light that slices through the dark hospital room floor. The eerie silence with the occasional murmur of nurses from the hallway lulls me to self-inspection.

The accident was my fault. Guilt's oppressive weight constricts my chest. Raven and the baby are alive, but they shouldn't even be here. If I hadn't been so caught up in my own life, my own pain, I never would've pushed so hard to take out the Nova.

The low grumble of a man's voice, followed by the soft whisper of a woman's, filters in from the hallway. I shove up on an elbow, and my heart pounds wildly in my chest.

Cameron?

His shadow drowns out the light as he trudges through the door and into my room. I fish around my blankets for the remote that turns on the light and grunt through the throbbing in my shoulder.

"You're back." *Ah-ha!* There it is. I click on the light to illuminate the towering fighter. "Oh, Jonah. Hey." The hollow in my chest aches.

He doesn't speak but crosses to a chair that sits near the window. He drops down and slouches into the seat, his forehead to his palm.

"What happened?" My breath freezes in my lungs. "Is it Sadie?"

He scrubs his face and sets tired eyes on me. "No, they're good."

I exhale a heavy breath that releases the tension in my muscles. "What's going on?"

"Raven told me what happened."

Stomach acid churns, and I clutch the hospital sheet to my chest. "Jonah, I—"

"Too late. What's done is done." He shakes his head and looks out the window to the city lights. "She knew. I told her every day how fucking scared I was at the thought of losing her or Sadie." He pinches the bridge of his nose. "How could she do this?"

"Jonah, no, it…" I swallow my panic and summon the courage to tell him the truth. "She wouldn't."

"But she did."

"Because of me." I swallow the lump forming in my throat. "She didn't want to take the Nova. I talked her into it."

His eyes slide to mine, and confusion works behind them. "Why would you do that?"

I fill my lungs with a steadying breath. "The chances of anything happening in that car were so slim. She knew you'd be upset, but she wanted that little taste of freedom again, just like I did."

His tortured expression morphs into something terrifying. "I thought you said you didn't remember."

"I didn't. And now I do." I drop my chin, unable to hold his glare. "She didn't want to go. I convinced her."

Silence.

"I wouldn't let up until she agreed."

I give that a moment to sink in and wait for the onslaught of fury that I know is coming.

But it never does.

I peek up to see Jonah's eyes pointed back out the window. "Jonah, I'm sorry. If I could take it back, I—"

"The worst day of my life was the day we got the call that my dad wasn't coming home. I remember being sad, really fucking sad." He blinks and turns toward me. "But what I remember the most is being scared, fucking terrified, because for the first time in my life, I saw the agony in my mom's face. I remember thinking the pain would rip right through her flesh. She screamed, beat the walls, and crawled like a dying animal as the pain shredded her. I…" He leans forward and cradles his head in his hands. "I just want her safe. I *need* her to be safe. Always."

The sting of fresh tears in my wounds blares its agreement. "Me too. I can't take back what happened, and I understand if you can't forgive me." I sag deeper into the bed. "I can't forgive myself."

"You want to blame yourself, I get that. But Raven knew better. Anyway, what's done is done." He pushes up from his chair and heads for the door, stopping just before the privacy curtain. "I'm not happy about any of this, but it doesn't change anything. We're family." He doesn't look up but continues out of the room.

I cough on a sob as it makes its way up my throat. How can he say that after all I've done? The only explanation is it hasn't sunk in. Surely once he realizes I almost ripped his wife and daughter from his life, he'll forbid Raven from having anything to do with me.

He can't possibly care enough to see past my offense.

Can he?

THIRTY-FIVE

EVE

"You have all your shit ready to go?"

My skin crawls, and I want to turn around and choke Mason with my old IV tubing. "I don't have shit, Mase. All I have is what I have on."

It isn't even mine. My nurse, Rose, brought me a Target bag filled with yoga pants, tank top, flip flops and a couple different sports bras. I should've been a little creeped out that there were even panties in the bag and strangely they were my size, but I'm too angry to be creeped. I just want the fuck out of here.

It's only been thirty-six hours, but every hour I've had to endure after waking up to no Cameron has been a whirling-fucking-dervish of emotional upheaval. He hasn't stopped by again, called, nothing. I'd call him, but my phone was snagged by that piece of shit that showed up at my house last night.

I grip my discharge papers to my chest. "I'm ready."

He nods to the wheelchair. "The orderly will be here in any minute to wheel you down. Get in."

"No way."

"Come on, Eve." Mason's pale blue eyes are set on mine. "It's hospital protocol. You have to." He's trying to be cool, but there's a hint of that anger I saw the last time we were together that still lurks behind his eyes.

I groan and drop into the stupid thing. "Fine. This is stupid. I'm not a cripple for cryin' out loud."

"Damn, you're a regular Disney Princess. Now put your feet on the foot things."

I do what he says but make sure to slam my feet in so he knows I'm not at all happy about his sarcastic humor or having him push me around in this grown-up stroller.

As much as I appreciate Jonah working out a ride for me, after my last visit with Mase at The Blackout, I think I'd rather walk.

Where the hell is Cameron and why does it feel as if I've been cast aside? I thought after our talk things were better. I mean I know shit got ugly when I remembered the accident, but he was so sweet and considerate. What made him change his mind?

This guessing game I've been playing with men—"Does he like me? As in, like-like me?"—is getting so fucking old. Why can't a guy just be upfront? Say what he means and mean what he says?

My inner asexual roars her return. Men can go to hell. All of 'em.

A guy wearing scrubs shows up and pushes me down the hall, and I give a small wave to the nurse's station as we pass. Once inside the elevator, Mason rests his hand on my shoulder, and I swear if I were a dog I'd turn around and bite him.

"You hungry?" He slides his fingers behind my neck and massages the tense muscles there.

Even that kind act on his part only manages to piss off my inner-bitch even more. All I need is an invitation and I'm going to lose it. "Like you care."

He tips his chin to look down at me. "What the fuck is up with you?"

Invitation received.

I turn to him as much as I can, considering I'm chair-bound, and grit through a tiny wave of nausea the movement causes. "What is it with men? You guys get your fucking panties in a bunch, and you're totally justified in being complete assholes. I was in a hit-and-run accident that put my best friend and her baby in the hospital, my head feels like it's being squeezed between The Rock's thighs, my face looks like I was attacked by zombies, and my ribs are constantly on fire, and you want to know what the fuck is up with me?"

The orderly clears his throat and—*is he laughing?* I'm about to whirl around and ask him when the elevator stops and the doors slide open. Probably best since I can't move without doubling over in pain. A couple enters, and they must sense the tension because they move as far away from us as they can in the small space.

The doors slide closed and I lean toward Mason to be heard, even though I have no intention of whispering. "You were a total dick to me at The Blackout, Mase. You didn't see me climbing up your ass, asking you why. Show me the same courtesy."

I expected he'd be angry at me for airing his assholeness in front of strangers, and it's confirmed when his glare tightens. "Oh, excuse me for not jumping for joy over your new relationship status with my fucking boss. *My* boss who you met when you were on a date with *me*." He shakes his head, looks around, and then swings his gaze back to mine. "I mean fuck. I can't even beat his ass for the cockblock because he's—*ta-da*—my boss!"

"Oh yeah, and did Frankie pull your hair and wipe a booger on your homework, Mase?" I shove my finger into his chest. "Grow the hell up!"

"So I'm good enough to take you out, but not good enough to be exclusive."

"We went out on one date. One. And you knew. You fucking knew I wasn't interested in you like that."

"Oh yeah, I knew, Eve. I fucking knew because I've been after you for months and you don't give me the time of day. Cam just looks at you, and you're all over his shit."

Is he right? I mean, yeah, Mason's been flirting and asking me out for a while now. I turned him down a lot, not because he's unattractive, but because…he's so nice.

But Cameron. He was a dickhead the first night we met. Taking my drink, giving me shit about not buying my own drinks and I…Damn. I slept with him.

The elevator door pings again, and the couple scurries from the car. My head gets light and I rub my temples.

"Shit, I'm sorry, Eve." Mason's hand comes to the nape of my neck and rubs small but firm circles there. The elevator opens to our floor. "Let me get you home."

I want to protest, to tell him "fuck no" and jog home to prove I don't need him or Cameron or anyone for that matter. But shit, I'm exhausted and my head spins.

I'm wheeled out into the lobby to Mason's waiting truck. Once inside, he turns the truck toward Jonah and Raven's, and I drop my head back and close my eyes with the hopes of falling asleep and avoiding any more conversation with him, especially if it's going to involve Cameron.

Thankfully, he takes my not-so-subtle hint and remains silent the entire drive. He pulls the truck up to the front door.

"Eve, listen. I'm sorry about the way I treated you at The Blackout. I've always been a jealous guy, and seeing you two together turned out to be harder than I thought."

Now he's back to sweet. Jekyll and Hyde much?

"It's funny, you know. I always thought it would be easy to walk away from a woman who doesn't want me. I mean why waste time on a girl who isn't interested?" He moves his gaze from me to out the front windshield, his tan skin and sun-kissed hair making him almost look like a boy rather than the man that his biceps and bulging chest give him away to be. "Not as easy as I thought."

Warmth blooms in my chest. I've always known that Mason was a good guy, but I'm starting to realize that we have more in common than I thought: pining after people who don't want us.

"I know what you mean. If only it were that easy to turn it off." If only we could all learn from Cameron, who doesn't seem to have a problem shutting people out.

Specifically me.

D'lilah on the other hand…shit.

He nods, looks to his lap, and when he brings his eyes back to mine, he seems different: less weighed down. "Let's get you inside." He slides from the truck then moves around to help me out.

Yeah, he's a good guy. And what is it about good guys that I seem to find so irritating? I mean I don't deserve a man who'll open doors, hold onto crushes, and be willing to piss off his own boss just because he can't stand to see me with someone else.

Mase and I have never even kissed.

He deserves a woman who'll be that, do all that, for him.

Once inside, I go straight to the couch while he walks through, turning on lights and checking things out. Dog, the cat, stands from his curled-up spot on the end of the couch and crawls onto my lap, purring.

"Everything looks good. You need anything before I take off?"

I shake my head, so ashamed at taking advantage of Jonah and Raven's kindness by staying here in their home combined with the guilt of not being able to give Mason what he wants after all he's done for me.

"Eve."

His voice is close. I look up and he's standing less than a foot away.

He holds his hand out. I put Dog down on the couch with minimal feline protesting and take his hand so he can help me up. Once he does, I'm in his arms, my hands holding on the back of his shirt and my cheek to his chest.

"I'm sorry," he says, and I feel the press of his lips to the top of my head.

"Me too." I close my eyes and absorb his comfort. I imagine for a second that it's Cameron's arms I'm in, his support that's warming my insides, his lips that rest against my hair.

He pulls back, and the fantasy is ruined by his shining Caliboy good looks. Nothing like the angry, hard edges of Cameron. I squeeze my eyes closed, trying to banish the thought.

"Hey, you okay?" Mase slides his arm around my waist.

"Yeah, just tired. A little dizzy." I blink up at him. "I think I need to lie down."

"Yeah, of course." He guides me back on to the couch, and I toe off my flip flops before he pulls my legs up onto the couch. "Get some sleep. I'll leave my number by the phone. Call me if you need anything."

I long yawn pulls at my jaw. "Okay, I will." My eyes drift shut.

"I'll lock the front door on my way out."

"Mmm."

Such a sweet guy. I should love him. I really should.

The last thing I hear is the door closing before I fall to sleep to dreams of Cameron.

———

CAMERON

My cell rings. Jonah's number lights my caller ID. "Slade."

"She's home."

"Good." I take a relaxing breath. I knew she was being released today, and I'd hoped the good nurse would follow through with my instructions to ensure she got to Jonah's safely. "She get clothes and a cab?"

"Clothes yes, cab no. I had Baywatch bring her home."

A low growl vibrates in my chest before I silence it. I have no reason to get possessive over Eve. After all, I'm the one who walked away. Hell, if I were forced to handpick a guy for her to date, I'd kill the person forcing me to pick, but in my head I'd consider Mason.

"I get why you're doing this, man. She deserves to come first. For what it's worth, you're doing the right thing by walking away."

"Yeah." It might be right, but it feels like someone's ripping my lungs from my chest. "How's she doing?"

"Mase said she's throwin' 'tude like a damn champ, so I'm guessin' she's feeling good."

Fuck. I rub my eyes and try to force back the jealousy at the thought of Eve throwin' sass at anyone other than me.

I forced her into this situation, so I need to lie in the bed of shit I made.

"Sadie and Raven?"

He clears his throat. "Doing good. Raven's milk came in. Sadie's nursing. All is right with the world, ya know?"

"Any word on when they'll be discharged?"

"Shouldn't be long now."

"Good news, brother. Take as long as you need. We'll be here when you're ready to get back to work."

"'Preciate that, Cam."

"Later."

The phone disconnects, and I rub my face, hoping to extinguish the cloud of doubt that's been following my ass around since the day I walked out of Eve's hospital room. It doesn't do shit except keep my hands busy so I don't throw my phone across the room.

Eve will eventually fall for Mason. He's a good fighter, a decent guy, and he fuckin' loves the shit out of her. He's a lot closer to her age and could give her the kind of life she deserves.

Me? Ha! She'd end up having to remind me of my own name. That is if I didn't end up forgetting something that resulted in burning the damn house down. I couldn't give her the family she deserves. Not strong enough to put a baby in her belly and watch it grow, hoping to God I didn't do something that would...*fuck!*

This is a waste of time and not what I should be concentrating on. I have a fight coming up that I need to train for. Luckily, the board is taking over most of the promotions so I can focus on training.

I groan and lean back in my office chair. This woman has burrowed in deep, ripping through my insides and making a permanent mark on my fucking soul.

Did I make a mistake by walking away? If Mason makes his move, I'll rip his throat out. No. Dammit.

My phone vibrates on my desk, a welcome distraction to the direction of my thoughts. "Yeah?"

Throat clearing. "Cam?"

I close my eyes as disappointment washes over me. "'Li, what's up?"

"I know you don't want to talk to me, but Ryder just told me you're...Are you...? I mean you're not returning to the octagon to fight Rusty, are you?"

"I am."

"Why?"

"He challenged. I accepted."

A few seconds of silence pass between us, and I have a feeling she's trying to formulate a response that won't piss me the fuck off.

"But you don't fight anymore."

"I've never stopped training, 'Li. Fighting's my life."

"Your life. Right. Are you, um…?"

Fuckin' hell. "'Li, you got something to say?"

"I don't want you fighting."

"You're not my wife anymore, so you don't get a say in what I do. Ever."

"But Ryder—"

"Is a grown man. I'll always be there for my boy, but he doesn't get a say either."

"Rosie—"

"Stop right there."

"Cam—"

"No, you don't get to throw her in my face, D'lilah. Not anymore."

I'm met with silence.

"I'm fighting Rusty. You can be supportive, or you can mind your own damn business. I gave up everything the day I left the UFL. I did it with the hope that I could take care of you, of Ryder. Make amends for my fucked-up head. Realized last night that nothing I do will make you better, bring her back."

"You're giving up on me?"

"It's been fourteen years. Ryder's grown up and off to college soon; you're worse off than ever. Nothing I do is fucking working."

"I'll try harder—"

"No, I'm taking the fight. I need this. For me."

"So that's it."

"'Fraid so."

"Don't expect my support."

Is she fucking kidding me? I've been wiping puke off her face, paying for her to live in a house that's ten times too big, supported her through multiple stints in rehab. Hell, I left the only woman I've ever really cared about alone at a restaurant and vulnerable to a loan shark so I could chase after D'lilah's drunk ass.

Heat roils in my gut. I grip my cell tighter to stop the tremors that wrack my hands. As if light is shining on my situation for the first time, everything seems so clear. I can't do this anymore. I'm not helping D'lilah get better; I'm only supporting her getting worse.

"This is over." I bite back fourteen years of rage that fights to spill from my lips on impulse.

"What's over?"

"You've got three months. Sober up, get your shit together, and move on."

"Okay, fine."

"No, you don't get it. I'm selling the house in three months, 'Li."

"But—"

"You've got twenty-eight days to get sober and another two months to get a job and find a place to live. I'll help you until then, but at the end of three months, the house goes on the market and I walk away."

"Cam—"

"Non-negotiable."

"What am I supposed to do?"

"I'd get lookin' for a rehab facility. Fast. You want my suggestion? Call Raven's Nest. They have people you can talk to who'll be able to point you in the right direction."

"Raven's what? Wait, why are you doing this?" The panic in her voice is palpable.

"Because you've done nothing but suck the fucking life out of me, D'lilah, and I let you. I offered it to you with open hands and you took. Now I'm done. I have nothing left for you. Three months, 'Li, and you're on your own."

I hang up the phone at the sound of her muffled sobs. She'll cry, turn to the bottle, get blitzed, and then call me back to lay into me and remind me of all the ways I've failed her. Running on an endless loop since forever, we've tortured each other by allowing this shit to continue. Ryder being thrown in the middle, he's now a casualty of this disgusting war we've waged against ourselves: both of us grinding through the self-torture as a way to pay penance.

I never saw it clearly before. Sometimes it takes losing someone to put life into perspective. Sort out priorities.

I've lost close to everything I ever loved, and I'm only now seeing shit for what it really is: a series of tragic mistakes that have ruined lives.

And I've had the power to put an end to it all.

THIRTY-SIX

Two months later...

EVE

"Don't, seriously, I will kick each and every one of you in the balls if you sing." The high pitch of my voice and the fact that I can't stop smiling is probably the reason why everyone sitting around the table has started singing "Happy Birthday."

I shake my head with a grin that I know is gigantic because my teeth are getting cold.

They serenade me in a wretchedly beautiful rendition that has me pulling back tears. Raven, Jonah with Baby Sadie in a sling across his chest, Blake, a very pregnant Layla, Owen and his wife Nikki, Caleb, Wade, and Mason. Everyone except Rex, who rarely shows up for anything that isn't UFL related anymore.

They finish off the final word to the song, stretching out "You" in the most obnoxious way possible, which shoots right to my heart. My throat swells, and my eyes burn as I use the last of my strength to keep from falling apart.

A single tear escapes, but I dip my chin to look at the home-made chocolate cake that Raven and Layla made for me. The finger swipes through the decadent frosting have me giggling through my tears, making me feel crazy and loved all at the same time.

"Make a wish, babe." Mason nods to the cake, a genuine smile across his perfect face.

I suck in a long breath and close my eyes. The words go through my head, just as they do every single night in my prayers. It's the same thing I've always wished for, the only thing I've wanted so badly that it's turned into an obsession.

I want to stop loving Cameron Kyle.

The words carry through my mind, and I blow the twenty-two candles out, sending a cloud of smoke into the air. Everyone cheers, and I give myself a second as the sinking feeling in my chest reminds me that my wish is only that.

A wish.

I haven't seen or heard from Cameron since the day he came to see me at the hospital. I went from being hurt, to angry, to furious, and now content. The most Jonah will give me is that he's doing well, trained up for his fight, and totally focused on that. He always said fighting was the most important thing in his life. He made it clear that he could lose his own wife and not blink but that giving up his career sent him to his knees.

Now he has his fighting back. I'm happy for him.

"Here ya go, birthday girl." Raven hands me a piece of cake on a paper plate.

Things have been good since she was released from the hospital. Sadie is gaining weight and was given a clean bill of health; even the doctor said she's very strong for a premie. With her father as heavyweight champion of the UFL, most think Sadie gets her fight from him, but I know better. She gets it from her mom.

Raven came out of the hospital, ready to take on the world. We talked about the accident, and I explained my feeling responsible, but she refused to place blame. We hugged and cried and hugged some more. We've never spoken of it again.

There are times when the guilt hits and I'm overwhelmed with gratitude for all that my best friend and her husband have done for me. More than I deserve. But they assure me that my helping out around the house, babysitting Sadie so they get alone time, and often getting up with the baby in the night so they can sleep, is worth more.

"What time do you have classes tomorrow?" Layla says through a bite of birthday cake.

"I have a seven forty-five anatomy class then a lab at three." I've been taking some classes at the community college to see if anything interests me outside of the restaurant business. So far I'm finding that science is my thing. Who knew?

"You guys hear about the show this weekend?" Caleb leans back in his chair and takes a pull off his beer.

"Yeah, Ataxia is opening for Five Finger Death Punch at the House of Blues." Blake curls an arm around Layla. "Biggest show they ever played."

"That's gonna be a kickass show. Can we still get tickets?" I watch Mason move across the room and drop into the seat next to me.

He leans in close, and I fight the urge to lean away.

"Happy birthday, babe." He slides a white envelope into my lap.

"No way, you got me tickets?" I should've known he would. He's always trying to win me over with gifts and gestures, but my heart will never belong to anyone but Cameron. I throw my arms around Mason's neck and hug him tight. "Thank you."

He buries his nose into my neck through my hair. "You're welcome."

I pull back to avoid him holding on too long and getting the wrong idea. I know he thinks I'll come around, regardless of my constantly telling him that I won't.

"There's two tickets in there. It's your present, so you're free to take whoever you want." He shrugs and peeks up at me through eyelashes that are long for a guy. "If you need a ride though, I'll take you."

"Oh." I study the envelope as I turn it over a few times in my hand. "I mean…yeah." I swing my gaze to meet his. "Of course."

I'd much rather go with Raven, or hell, I'd even rather go by myself than with Mason, but I can't tell him no. The problem is, in the crowded club, he'll take the opportunity to touch me. It'll be innocent enough, but his mind will conjure up ideas about us being together, making the goodbye at the end of the night awkward.

Something I've learned over months of experience.

The sound of Sadie crying pulls my eyes to Jonah.

He's patting the sling and swaying from side to side. "I think this party girl is ready to hit the sack."

Raven turns to her husband with a forkful of birthday cake in her mouth.

"Hey, you guys enjoy the rest of the party." I stand, grateful that I now have something to do that will break up my conversation with Mason.

It's such a bitchy thing to do, but the alternative is to hang out with him longer, and that could lead him on, which is even bitchier.

"I'll put Princess to bed." I hold out my hands to Jonah, who places the little dark-haired angel into my arms. "Hey, Sadie girl." I kiss the top of her head. "You ready for bed?"

I leave the party in the dining room and move into the kitchen to pull a glass bottle of breast milk from the fridge and pop it into the bottle warmer. Sadie kicks her tiny little feet and squirms in my arms.

"I know you're hungry, baby. It's almost done. Hang in there." Finally, when the light indicates it's ready, I test the milk temperature on my wrist. "Perfect."

I pop the bottle into her mouth and move through the house and into my bedroom, where there's a rocking chair. "Shh." I hold Sadie close and watch her tiny little lips suckle and her eyes start to droop.

It's times like this, in the silence of a dark room with nothing but gentle baby grunts, I reflect on my life. It hasn't been easy, and I've seen my fair share of heartache, but I wouldn't change a day of it because it meant getting me here.

Right now, this moment.

Holding my niece, living with the only family I've ever known, a room full of friends who've taken the time to come celebrate my birthday. It's the closest thing to perfection I've ever known.

The one person who would make it perfect is Cameron.

But who deserves perfect? I certainly don't, so I'll choose to embrace the close-to-perfect kind of life I'm living.

It's more than I ever expected.

And better than shitty.

CAMERON

I don't know how I got talked into this shit. Layla tends to be persuasive when she wants to be. I don't see why she thinks going out to a crowded club with a bunch of kids half my age would be more fun than what I'm doing. That being working my ass off, going home to a have dinner in front of the TV, and then crashing.

Rex's been slowly coming back from the dead for whatever reason, and I do want to support his band. I don't know what the big deal with this band that he's opening for is, but the

House of Blues is a pretty decent venue, so I get that this is a big deal for him.

Thankfully, being the kid's boss got me on some kind of VIP list, so I didn't have to wait in line, and I got access to a private bar that's a little less crowded than the main one. My muscles are tight and equally exhausted from all the hours I'm putting in at the training center. Jonah's been training with me, which has been great, but knowing that he's living with Eve makes it hard not to ask about her every time we're training.

I'm pretty sure he purposely doesn't talk about her with me, but he's slipped up a few times, and I've gotten little glimpses into her life. I know she's taken to Sadie like second nature, which doesn't surprise me at all. She'll make a great mother someday. I grit my teeth and slug back a mouthful of scotch. I know that she's in school and working hard to get back on her feet after she lost her job and her house.

I also know it was her birthday last week.

No one invited me to the party, and even if they did, there's no way I would've gone. Those messages she'd left me for a few weeks were torture. Listening to her cry and beg for answers to why I left and never turned back was pure soul-splitting agony. Shit, I had to lock my phone in my car every night for a month straight to avoid calling her. There was no way I could make contact with her because I knew if I ever touched her again, ever allowed her voice to penetrate, I'd never let her go, consequences and all.

But loving her means I have to stay away. It's what's best for her.

The bartender nods to my empty glass while dropping drinks off to a couple of girls next to me.

I push the glass away and nod for another. When the hell is this shit going to start? My watch says it's ten minutes past nine.

I grab my new drink and turn my back on the bar to watch the stage. There's music playing through the speakers while the band sets up. Thank God. Setting up is a good step in the right direction to getting this show over with.

Fuck, I sound like my old man.

My eyes scan the room, noting the colorful variety of people in attendance. The rockers with their black clothes, gelled hair, tattoos and piercings like Ryder. Then there are the women who could probably care less about the music and are here for the attention. Long legs, big shoes, bare midriffs, and an overabundance of cleavage. Finally, there're the guys, the ones who also probably care less about the music, but followed the girls inside and are hoping to get laid.

I shake my head, but it stills when something familiar draws my eyes to the dance floor. What is that? I push off my barstool and move to a waist-high railing that separates the bar area from the rest of the place. It's hard to see through the bodies that surround her, but I can tell by the serpentine way she moves and her hair that's the perfect shade of gold.

Eve.

My mouth goes dry, and my blood floods with adrenaline. She's not dancing alone, and as the people who surround her ebb and flow with the music, they part enough where I can see her. She's with another girl.

Their legs are staggered together, hands sliding up the other's arms slick with sweat. Eve rolls her hips to the beat of the music that seems to match the pulse that pounds in my ears. She flips to give the girl her back and then raises her hands into all that long blond hair. Just like the first time we met, watching her dance has my dick hard and aching. Every move she makes has me imagining her doing the same straddled over my lap while I'm buried deep inside her tight body.

I grip the railing to keep from lunging at her and ripping that tiny skirt up to her waist. Fuck. Her hips swivel, and with her hands in her hair, a slice of skin at her belly button shows. The girl she's dancing with slides her hands around and trails her fingers higher…higher. Eve's head drops back to the girl's shoulder.

The eager girl cups Eve's breast. Oh, fuck no.

As hot as it is to watch and as fired up as this little dance of seduction is making me, this is Eve. No one fucking touches her. Jealousy rips through my chest, and before I can put together a coherent thought, I'm prowling toward the dance floor. I shove through a crowd of horny assholes that have formed a semi-circle around the pair of girls, probably hoping to get in on their show, but they're sorely mistaken.

I reach them and grab Eve's hand hard. Her head jerks up along with her wide blue eyes. I take moment to study her gorgeous face now healed and as vibrant as it was before the accident. With her eyes on me, I want to savor the moment, but what I need to do, what my body demands, is riding me with an urgency that I've never felt before.

A symphony of shit talk and booing comes from the small crowd as I drag Eve to the back of the club and into a dark hallway with a lighted red Exit sign above it. I shove open the door and spill out into the back alley. I whirl her around and push her back against the wall, caging her with my body.

"Camer—"

My mouth comes down on hers in a punishing kiss, hard, demanding, and unforgiving. Fisting her hair, I tug her head back and to the side, pressing in so we're touching chest to hip, my knee between her legs. She gasps, and my tongue dips deep inside the warm cavern of her mouth.

A low moan rumbles up from her throat, and her body melts into mine. I growl my approval and flex my hips into hers to show her exactly what her little fucking dance did to me. What she does to me.

Two months of not having this mouth spew sass and shit talk, this body tempting me with the simplest of sways. A wild, almost savage urge to fuck her hard right here roars through my blood.

I use my knee to spread her legs and push her tiny skirt up to her waist. Her nails rake up my arms, over my tee, and into my hair, pulling me deeper into her mouth. Fuck, yeah. She wants this.

With a swift tug, I pull her shirt up over her breasts. I run my thumb over the pale purple lace and watch her chest rise and fall faster. I slide my fingers beneath the fabric and pop out one breast before doing the same with the other then lean back to take her in. She's pinned to the wall, shirt to her neck, gorgeous tits bared and moving with the force of her quickened breath. My dick strains against my jeans.

I try to be gentle, focus on not hurting her as my hand moves to the damp panties between her legs.

"Fuck, doll, you miss me as much as I missed you?" I run my fingers back and forth against her, wishing it was my dick that was feeling the wet heat of her arousal. "It better not be that bitch that got you this wet."

I look down at her and groan at how sexy she looks: swollen lips ripe from my sucking, heavy lids, flushed cheeks.

"Tell me what turned you on, Eve." I growl the words against the tender skin below her ear.

"Y-you…I…It's you."

I slide her panties to the side and bury two fingers into her. "Missed this; missed you."

"Don't stop."

I taste the length of her neck, drinking in the warm sugar scent of her skin. Her body writhes against my hand, desperate for more.

"Cameron…"

"Yeah?"

"Please…"

"Come home with me."

"Can't wait." Her hips press down on my hand and she rubs herself on my palm.

So fucking hot I could come right here from just feeling it. "You want it here?"

"Yes."

I unzip my jeans, and it doesn't take much to free my hard-on. Fisting it tightly, I press the head into her so she can feel how fucking serious I am about giving her what she wants right fucking now. "Last chance."

She hikes one leg over my hip and leverages her back against the wall. "Now or I swear I'll die."

Raking her panties as far to the side as I can get them, I press inside her body. "Hell, baby, you feel too good."

She rocks her head back against the wall, her hands holding onto my biceps, and legs locked around my hips. "No such thing as too good. Now move, Cameron."

"Missed your sassy mouth." I pull back and thrust in again. Back and forth again and again, punishing her for letting me go, and for not showing up at my door and demanding we stay together.

I quicken my pace, sliding my hand down between us to feel us connected and reminding myself that this is real. I need Eve like I need a damn hole in my head, but fuck if I can live without her. The woman sends me from zero to a zillion in a heartbeat; she brings out the worst in me and makes me feel completely out of control. She makes me feel alive. Gives me a taste of something I can fight for, something worth working my ass off to keep.

No way I'm letting her go again.

"Tell me you're still on the pill, baby."

Her head is back, eyes closed, lips parted.

I lean in and suck her bottom lip into my mouth and release it with a firm tug of my teeth. "Eyes open. Answer me."

She tilts her chin down, gazes up at me through sex-fogged eyes, and pulls me to her lips in a long wet kiss that has me fighting to hold back my release.

"Yes." She whispers against my lips so seductively as if she's answering a lot more than my question with that one simple word.

I drop kisses along her jaw and hike her up a little higher to suck one pink nipple into my mouth.

Her hands tighten into my hair making my scalp sting. "I lo…Cameron, I—" The orgasm rips through her body with such force that I have to use both my hands to hold her steady. I feel her pulse and the vibration of her moan against my forehead, which I've buried into her neck.

Her body in my arms, wrapped and throbbing around me, I fall right over the edge after her, my hips jacking forward with the force of it. My fingers dig into the heavenly flesh of her bare ass, and I swear to myself I'll do whatever it takes to keep her.

We're panting hard. The music from the live show blares all around us and makes it impossible for anyone to have heard what just happened.

"You good, baby?" I kiss a path from her collarbone to her lips.

She nods, and I slide out of her before easing her down to her feet. Once she's steady I focus on righting her panties, which has my dick forgetting that it just came seconds ago. I tuck it back into my jeans and pull Eve's skirt down, to cover her while she adjusts her bra cups and straightens her shirt.

She looks up at me, and I can't explain what it is about her expression that makes me uneasy, but it's like there's a shadow there that wasn't there before. I don't like it.

"Look, I…" I run my hand through my hair and study the brick wall just over her shoulder. "I'm sorry about coming after you like that."

She shakes her head and opens her mouth to say something, but her body language is freaking me the fuck out, and I don't want to hear the words that are going to accompany it.

"Before you say anything, can we go somewhere and talk?"

"I can't. I, uh"—her eyes dart out toward the backdoor of the club—"I need to go."

"No." I step closer with the hope that my body size alone will be enough to keep her from running. "You don't. I'm not letting you get away again."

Her eyes narrow and her jaw gets hard. "Letting *me* get away? *Again?*"

"If you'll let me explain—"

"You had your chance to explain, Cam."

Cam? She's never called me by my nickname before. Hearing it from her lips shreds through my chest.

"You called me doll, soothed me, and told me everything was going to be okay, and then you left me in a hospital bed. I haven't heard from you in two months. I called you, crying, begging you to talk to me. And now you want to explain?"

"You have every right to be pissed, doll—"

"Don't fucking call me that!"

I need her more than I've ever needed anyone in my entire life. It took me too long to realize it, but I realize it now, and the fact that she's pulling away from me is making me crazy.

"I'm trying to explain to you why I had to walk away."

A short burst of laughter shoots from her lips as if she intended it to strike and kill. "It's too fucking late! The damage is done."

No, no way. "I refuse to accept that."

"Ask me if I care."

"You seemed to care when I had my dick buried in your body." Dammit. I cringe against my own words.

Her mouth gapes and then closes before her eyes narrow. "That was a mistake."

"The fuck it was. You don't beg for mistakes, Yvette." Again, probably not the smartest thing to say, but damn she brings the shit out of me.

"I didn't beg."

I lean in close. "The fuck you didn't."

"Step away, Cameron."

"I can't. I'm in love with you."

Her entire face goes slack, and she sucks in a quick breath. "That's a cheap shot." There's malice in her words, but her eyes well with tears.

I cup her cheek and swipe at a single tear that slides down her face. "Not cheap, doll. I am. I love you."

She shakes her head, and her eyes dart up in what looks like an effort to look anywhere but at me. "Let me go, Cameron."

"I can't; that's what I'm trying to tell you."

Her expression fluctuates between pained and steely. "I don't believe you."

"Don't believe me. Let me show you. I'll prove it to you."

She coughs on a sob, and I pull her into my arms. My chest swells as she melts into my body, and her arms wrap around my waist. We stay like this for minutes, and I wish we could stay like this for hours, weeks, years. Just like this, her head on my chest, and my nose buried in her hair. We fit perfectly together like this, and once I share all my secrets with her, if she chooses me, we'll be able to work through everything else.

I just need that chance. One more chance.

THIRTY-SEVEN

EVE

What the hell did I do? One minute I'm lost in the music, thinking about Cameron and wishing it was his hands on my body rather than some random chick looking for attention. The next thing I know he's there, pulling me into the back alley as if he'd read my thoughts and searched my fantasies.

He's bigger than he was two months ago, proof that the whispers about him training for his fight with Faulkner are true. His shoulders, back, arms, all of it strains against the thin cotton of his black tee. Biceps that pull the fabric tight accentuate the cuts and swells of his massive muscles.

The epitome of power, strength, and protection, and yet he abandoned me. But I had sex with him anyway.

This is so fucked up. Cameron may not be the dick that my dad is, or the monster that Vince was, but he has more power than the two of them combined to completely destroy me. I know because I've been living it for the last two months. I've felt what being abandoned by Cameron feels like, the fear and insecurity that rushes in after he sets me up with more than I could ever hope for and then in one breath takes it all away.

How long will I put myself through this kind of pain before I finally decide it's not worth it? Every time one of them walks away, it's as if they stash a little piece of me in their pocket when they go. There's hardly anything left of me as is, and

I'm afraid that the feelings I have for him are too good, too intense. When he leaves again, he'll strip me raw. There'll be nothing left.

He's in love with me.

But words are just that. Words. Anyone can say things and even pretend that they mean them. They don't mean anything.

What *does* mean something is the fact that he abandoned me with no explanation. He just walked away and never told me why. He knew I had questions, knew I was suffering, and still gave me nothing.

I'm not an expert on love, but I've been living under a roof where it's expressed daily, and what Cameron did to me isn't love.

I squeeze him to me one last time, knowing this is going to be the last I ever get of him, and soak in as much as I can. It's time. Finally, for the first time in twenty-two years, it's time for me to take care of myself and make choices that protect my heart rather than constantly sacrifice it.

On that thought, I pull back enough to nuzzle against his pec and place a kiss over his heart.

He runs his hand through my hair and cups the back of my head when I tilt back to look up at him. "We good? You coming home with me so I can explain?"

I turn my head and kiss the inside of his wrist then press my hands against his abs for him to step back.

He does, and confusion washes over his expression. Fuck. That kills.

"Yes, we're good." I shake my head. "But no, I don't need to hear you explain."

"Eve, I—"

I cup his strong jaw and press my thumb to his lips. "It's okay. I know you want to protect me, but I need you to know that I can take care of myself now. You think you love me,

Cameron, but you're mistaking caretaking for love. A few months ago I would've been happy with that. It would've been more than enough for me, but not anymore."

"Don't do this. Don't walk away from us."

"I have to." I close the space between us and push up to my toes to wrap my arms around his neck.

He doesn't make me work for it and pulls me by the waist, lifting my feet off the ground in a hug so tight it almost makes me smile. Almost.

"Think about what you're doing," he whispers in my ear then sets me back down on my feet. "Don't do it."

I release his neck, but pull his face down to mine so our foreheads are touching. I take a deep breath, close my eyes, and speak what's been on my heart since the first day I met him.

"I love you, Cameron Kyle, but I'm not strong enough to hold on to you."

His big body goes loose, and I take the opportunity to get away before he says something that makes me change my mind.

I turn my back on him in the alley, and even though my heart, my body, every single thing in me is screaming for me to turn around, I do what's best for me and walk away.

And I'm not at all surprised that he doesn't chase after me.

—

CAMERON

I'm dragging my ass to work on the Monday after making love to Eve. It was spontaneous, primal, raw, but it was love. I felt it with every slide of our bodies, the connection of so much more than two animals seeking out pleasure, but two souls finally coming together.

Rather than hitting the weights first, I head toward the heavy bag, hoping to blow off some of the frustration that's been building since Eve blew me off. She's wrong if she thinks I'm going to just let her turn her back on us. I'm going to get her back, but after this weekend I've realized how fragile she is and need to have a plan.

I love you, Cameron Kyle.

Her words ring through my head on a loop as they have been since she said them.

I'm not strong enough to hold on to you.

But I can be strong enough for the both of us.

I pop in my ear buds and find the playlist that suits my mood. Social Distortion's "When She Begins" blares in my ears so loud it feels as if my ears will bleed. Good, anything to push the memory of Eve to the back of my head.

Gloves on, I throw my first few punches to warm up. Every hit, the resistance of the bag, pushes back and makes me hit harder. *Left—right—left—right.* I step back, kick. Lean in, punch. Back and forth, I beat away all the shit that plagues my mind in search for the clarity and simplicity that only comes when I train.

Sweat dampens my shirt, drips down from my temple. I hit harder, concentrating on getting the most behind every throw. The music drives me. Finally warmed up, I move quicker. Duck. Hit. Lean. Hit. Kick.

An earbud pops free from my ear. What the fuck? I stop and look to see Blake standing next to me with a satisfied grin.

"Daniels, what's up?" I rip off my gloves and pull out my other earbud.

"Think the real question is what's up with you?" He crosses his arms over his chest. "Looks like you're trying to strike gold on that heavy bag, man." His eyebrows drop low.

"This is what real training looks like." I toss my gloves to the side. "Might wanna take notes."

He shrugs. "I'll give you that because I know you're pissed."

"Who says I'm pissed?"

He tilts his head, as if he's trying to read me. "My woman said you and Eve aren't speaking."

Shit. I guess I shouldn't be surprised that Layla's noticed. Now that I think about it, I find it strange that she hasn't asked. She's usually nosey as hell.

"Your woman would be right." No use in lying. Chances are the whole story has made it through the gossip chain already.

"Probably for the best." He shoves the heavy bag. "Eve's been through hell already, and you're a moody son of a bitch."

Been through hell? First Jonah and now Blake.

I wipe my forehead with a towel and take a swig from my water bottle. "You talking about her pops?"

"Nah, I'm talking about Vince."

Vince? Who the fuck is that, and why is this the first I'm hearing about it?

"You mind elaborating?"

His eyes narrow. "She hasn't told you?"

I grind my teeth and my muscles tense. "She told me, you think I'd be askin'?"

"Huh." His gaze drops to the floor, as if he's thinking about whether or not to share, and then shrugs. "Figure you'll find out sooner or later. Vince was Dominic Morretti's right hand."

My fists flex at the idea that someone who even breathed the same air as a sadistic fuck like Morretti was anywhere near my girl.

"Dominic needed to get the inside scoop on Raven; best way to do that was through her best friend." His jaw gets tight. "He sent Vince to do the job."

What the fuck does that mean? He needed information out of Eve so he what? Held her captive? Tortured her? My thoughts whirl into a tornado of horrific scenarios. "Go on."

He recoils, but it's slight. "Guessin' you lookin' like you're gonna kill someone shows Eve didn't share this shit with you."

I don't answer.

"Right, well, best guess is he saw her weakness, preyed on it."

"Meaning?" I hope it's not what I'm thinking.

"He seduced her."

The breath rushes from my lungs in a quick burst.

"Told her all the fluffy shit chicks like to hear, weaseled his way in there, and when I say in there, I mean in there in every way a man can be. Her home, her bed, her body."

"Fuck."

"That's not the worst of it."

My chest aches and my body readies for a fight.

"Dickhead roughed a dude up pretty bad at a club one night for talking to Eve, dragged her and Raven's asses out, let Eve go so he could kidnap Rave. Luckily Jonah showed up, but not before Vince marked Raven's neck up with bruises."

"Fuckin' hell."

"Worst part is Eve was jealous of that shit. Vince was lying to her the whole time, using her body, taking all she offered, but his eye was on the prize and that prize was not Eve."

"Where's he at?"

He chuckles. "Know what you're thinkin', but you can rest easy he's getting his. He's servin' a life sentence in prison."

"Not good enough."

"Yeah, I agree. But he's also living in prison without a dick thanks to Jonah's flawless aim with a Desert Eagle."

"No shit?" I cringe and adjust my junk at the thought. "He shot his dick off?"

"Pretty much. Dude kidnapped his woman, tried to rape her. Jonah made sure he paid."

How the fuck did I not know all this? I'd read the story the media put out, but I never knew Eve was this involved. And why the fuck wouldn't she share this shit with me?

Maybe because I never asked.

Fuck!

"Advice?"

No thanks, asshole. I bite my tongue.

His expression gets uncharacteristically serious. "If you're not a million percent sure about Eve, then you should leave her alone. She's been fucked with enough to last a damn life-time, and she's got a whole lifetime in front of her. If anyone deserves easy, Cam, it's her. If you can't give that to her let someone who can have that shot."

"Sounds like you're not speaking figuratively."

He scratches his cheek and shrugs. "Baywatch is crazy about her."

Fuck, fuck, fuck!

"She feel the same?"

"Eve needs to relearn some shit. She's been taught how she deserves to be treated by a man. Unfortunately, she was taught by the wrong man. Mase is trying to show her different. She's not there yet."

Whatever the motherfuck that means. If Mase knows what's good for him, he'll keep his hands, mouth, and dick away from my girl.

"We done?" I'm barely able to keep the rage from my voice.

He nods and turns to go, but stops short to crank his neck around. "Sooner or later a man has to decide. You wanna be the man she wants, or can you find it in you to be the man she needs? Figure that shit out, or bow out, and let a better man move in."

"Yeah, you can fuck right off."

He grins. "Glad we understand each other."

I turn and swing hard into the heavy bag then wince at the sting in my knuckles and glare at a retreating, but laughing, Blake.

No fucking way I'm stepping aside so Mason can have his shot at the woman I love. I'll get her back. I just need to figure out how.

THIRTY-EIGHT

EVE

This is the hardest part, the final crawl to the top. Sweat drips from my hairline, and desert dust coats my skin. I hook my toes in and use my hands to grip rock and pull myself up. My muscles shake with exertion. One more pull and a healthy heft and I'm up and over. I pant for breath, relief.

I'm at the top. I glare at my handsome hiking partner, who's squatting down looking every bit the Ralph Lauren model and nothing like the sweaty mess I appear to be.

"Thanks for waiting, dickhead." I smile sweetly and ruffle his thick blond hair. Jeez, it's not even sweaty! What the hell.

Mason laughs. "Took you long enough. I was seconds away from building a shelter and hunkering down for the night."

"So funny I forgot to laugh." I drop down next to him, my spandex-covered ass directly against the rocks and dirt because I don't have the strength to hold myself up as he does.

I take a deep breath and can practically smell autumn moving in. I turn my head slowly from one side to the other, taking in the panoramic view of the city. Funny how brown Vegas is from this perspective. In the light of day, looking down on the city, you'd never guess there's anything special down there. If anything, it couldn't look more ordinary. But I know better. I know that once the sun dips behind these mountains the entire city turns into a carnival of lights and action that is unequal to anything else in the world.

"So pretty up here."

"I was thinking the same thing."

I look over to see Mase isn't looking at the view, but rather directly at me. It's like a sucker punch to the gut.

"Mase, that's sweet, really, but you know I don't—"

"Feel that way about me." He turns his eyes to the view and flicks a rock over the edge. "Yeah."

I rock into him with my shoulder. "Hey, you know I care about you, right? As a friend."

"Friend zone." He groans and drops his chin to his chest. "Awesome."

"You have no idea how badly I wish I could make myself love you that way, Mase. Honest to God, it would make my life so much easier."

"Yeah, I know that too." He throws a rock over the ledge. "Why is that? I mean why do girls like guys who treat them like shit?"

I shrug and wrap my arms around my bent knees. "It's not like we intentionally go for assholes. It's just that sometimes we can't ignore the pull of our hearts."

"I'm familiar with that feeling," he mumbles.

A twinge of guilt twists in my chest. "But Cameron isn't an asshole. That night at The House of Blues—"

"The night you had sex with him in the alley?" His jaw ticks, and I can feel the intensity of his stare from behind his sunglasses.

"Yes, that night. He told me he loved me."

"He doesn't. No man who really loves a woman would tell her while fucking her in an alley."

"Mase—"

"I'm sorry, Eve, but you've got to drop these delusional thoughts about Cameron suddenly turning into a nice guy.

He's a player, and for whatever reason, that shit seems to turn you on."

I don't want to argue with Mason. I can't because technically he's right. Cameron did tell me he loved me right after he had sex with me against a dirty wall in an alley. Ugh, that really does sound awful. Why did it feel so real? Like the power of those words could cure diseases, mend broken hearts, and heal old wounds? Pointless to think about it now.

"Anyway, I walked away from him that night."

"I remember. You didn't tell me until after the show, but I could tell when you found me in the crowd that you seemed… different."

I nod and draw swirls into the dirt with a stick. "I was different. It was the first time in my life that I turned my back on something I wanted."

"And that felt good?"

"It did. I mean I've never had control of much in my life, but telling Cameron goodbye was like swallowing medicine. Yeah, it tastes bad, might even give me a bellyache, but I know doing it is eventually going to make me feel better. Make me healthy."

"I could do that for you." His voice is soft and so sincere.

"Thank you, Mase. Honestly, I don't know what I'd do without you in my life."

He smiles, but it's tinged with sadness. He throws his arm over my shoulders and pulls me to his side. "Yeah, you little shit. I'll always be here for you."

We sit like that for a while, looking at the view and enjoying the simple act of being. Living in the moment.

My thoughts wander, as they often do after Mason and I have conversations like this. Could Mason be like the city view? Uninspiring from one perspective, but if I got a better look, maybe took the time to see him at a different angle, could he be unequal to anyone else in the world?

Or will I always be the girl, as Mason says, who's hopelessly devoted to assholes?

———

The drive back to Jonah's from our hike is a silent one. Mason's given up for now, and I appreciate him giving my defenses a break. He hits the satellite radio and "Chasing Rainbows" by No Use for a Name fills the car.

I've always loved the song, but something tells me he purposely put it on just for me. I peek at him out of the corner of my eye, but he keeps his gaze forward.

Whatever. So he hasn't given up; he's just changed tactics. Fantastic.

Having slipped my dusty hiking shoes off before we got in the car, I prop my socked feet up on the dash and listen to the music, choosing to not concentrate on the words, but the instruments alone.

As we get closer to the city, billboards that advertise all the latest Vegas shows and events start coming into view and popping up one after the other. Celine Dion, O by Cirque de Soliel, Blue Man, they flash by the window and start to lull me to sleep.

My eyelids droop behind my sunglasses when a flash of a familiar face that's ten feet high jerks me awake and upright in my seat. "Whoa!" I turn around to see the back of the billboard disappearing behind us. "Was that—?"

"Yep. It was." Mason sounds a little annoyed.

That's no surprise.

I drop back into my seat, fighting back the urge to scream "Turn around so I can get a better look."

In the quick glance I got, I could tell it was Cameron on one side of the billboard and another guy who I'm assuming is his opponent, Faulkner, on the other. Cameron's image was intense: his gorgeous dark eyes set in a glare, flawless tan skin oiled up and accentuating his tattoos, fists raised. I also caught the flash of white text. Big and bold—*UFL: Rival Revolution*.

"When is the fight?"

Mason doesn't take his eyes from the road; his jaw ticks. "November."

"That's next month. Is he ready? I mean are you guys making sure that he's trained and—?"

He swings his gaze to mine, irritation with a hint of pain working behind his eyes. "You seriously asking me this shit, Eve?"

"Well, yeah, I mean I know you don't like him personally, but he's your boss. Are you guys making sure he's not going to get hurt or get hit—?"

"Fuckin' hell" he mumbles and shakes his head.

"Don't be a dick. This is serious."

He turns angry eyes on me. "You think I don't see that?" His gaze travels around my face with a look of disgust. "You're about to jump out of this truck and run to his rescue after seeing a damn billboard."

Am I? I let out a lung-full of air and sink back into my seat. "Sorry."

He shakes his head, and his knuckles are white on the steering wheel. "He'll be fine, Eve. He's a good…No, he's a phenomenal fighter." The compliment sounds as if he had to drag it from his throat.

"How do you know? He hasn't fought in forever."

"Everyone knows that." He stares forward. "You've never seen videos of his old fights?"

"No."

His eyebrows shoot to his hairline. "Really?"

"No, Mase, I mean it's not like we sat around reliving the glory days when we were together."

"Huh. If I were him, I'd brag about that shit to anyone who listened."

Really. Why have I never thought to Google Cameron's fighting career? Funny, it's not something he'd ever bragged about, and come to think of it, anytime we talked about his fighting it was always me pressing him for information. He never shared it willingly.

If he's as good as Mason says, why would he hide it?

"So he was pretty good, huh?"

"No, he was the best. Fighters like that never lose their touch. It's in their blood."

"Wow, be careful there, Mase. It almost sounds like you're giving the guy a compliment."

"Yeah, well, he's not a *total* asshole." He cringes, slight but noticeable. "I'll give him credit for getting your dad off your back and for being—"

"Whoa, what?" My heart pounds harder in my chest. "What about my dad?"

His eyes dart from the road to me. "You don't know?"

"Know what?"

He mumbles "shit" under his breath.

"Mason!"

"At the hospital, after your accident, your Dad showed up."

I gasp and cover my mouth.

"Cam stepped up, told the dude he wasn't welcome, and then ran him out of there. Spent some time with your pops outside, not sure what all went down, but Cam came back in looking like he'd just fucked a dude up."

He did that for me? "That doesn't make any sense." Why would he go to the trouble to threaten the father of a woman he's about to walk out on? Unless…

I study Mason's profile, and for the first time in a long time, the guy won't even spare me a glance. "Mase?"

"Hm?" He keeps his eyes pinned to the road ahead of him.

"What else aren't you telling me?"

His gaze darts to mine but doesn't commit. "What're you talking about?"

"What is it?"

"Fuck."

"Tell me!"

He finds something interesting outside his driver's side window. "Can't believe you're hearin' this shit from me."

Are Cameron and D'lilah back together? Does he have a new girlfriend? What the hell is so damn important that he's hiding it? Fear grips my stomach as I wait for a confession that will most likely kill me.

"Cam took care of your dad's debt."

"What?" The single word falls from my lips on a whisper.

"According to Jonah, Cam asked your dad how much it would take to get him off your back. Your pops gave a price." He shrugs as if it's no big thing that the man I'm in love with forked over a generous amount of his own money so that I could live free without the extra burden of my dad.

"Oh my…" I think back over the last few months. "My dad hasn't made any attempt to contact me. I figured it was because he didn't have my new number or know where I was."

"Cam lined his pockets, paid off the loan shark who fucked up your place, and sent him off with a pretty serious warning from what I hear. Your dad's a lush and a loser, babe, but he's not an idiot. My guess is he knows exactly who Cam is and what he's capable of. Even if you don't."

"Wow."

"Great." Mason's sarcastic tone is obvious. "So much for you movin' on, huh?"

Stunned, I swivel back to facing the highway stretched in front of us. He paid off my dad's debt and sent him packing with money. All for me. Warmth spreads through my gut and my chest and revives the cold lifeless part of my heart that I'd reserved for Cameron. The corner of my soul that was determined to keep my feelings for him locked away bursts free and brings hope.

But the question remains. Why did he walk away at the hospital? I suppose if I'd given him a change to explain when he'd tried to at The House of Blues I would have the answer.

THIRTY-NINE

CAMERON

"Dad. Dad, wake up."

I blink open my eyes to Ryder shaking my shoulder.

"Ry, what's…you okay?"

"Someone's at the door."

I curl up to sitting and check the clock. "It's the middle of the night."

"Yeah, no kidding. That's why I'm waking you up."

The sound of someone knocking on the front door has me up and moving. I don't think it would be D'lilah. After almost fifty-six days in rehab, she graduated from the program sober and even managed to get a job working the reception desk at a high end spa and seems to love it. Ryder's home, so unless that's the cops banging my door down…The knock sounds again.

I move down the hallway with Ry on my heels. Unfortunately, the way the front door lines up to the street, I can't see if there's a car in my driveway, and I don't have a peephole because, fuck, why would I need one?

The knock sounds again, not loud or urgent, only persistent.

I swing open the door and almost stumble backward.

Eve.

"Why'd you do it?" Her eyes are on mine, focused to the point of delirium.

"Eve, what're you doing—?"

"Answer the question." She takes a quick step toward me, her hands clenched tightly. "Why? Why did you do it?" Her voice is louder now.

"Come inside." Seeing her like this in the dead of night, clearly upset and wearing pink flannel pajama pants, an oversized UNLV sweatshirt, and slippers sets me on high alert.

"No." She shakes her head, and her eyes travel from my bare feet up my drawstring sleeping pants to my stomach and linger there. "Um…" She blinks and drags her gaze slowly up to my chest, shoulders, and then her blue eyes hit mine, and, fuck, I like what I see by the time she gets there.

Her big blues are wide but foggy from her appraisal. Big full lips are slightly parted and her cheeks flush.

"Eve." It's a warning, a reminder, and a plea.

She blinks and shakes her head, clarity mixed with something off kilter returning to her features. "You paid off his debt, and I know how much that was, Cameron."

My muscles tense. "Please tell me that slimy fuck isn't bothering you. He promised he'd leave you the hell alone if—"

"I haven't heard from him since the night he cleaned me out. Not him or the guy looking for money." She blinks slowly and tilts her head. "How much did you pay him, Cameron?"

"Doesn't matter. I'd have paid whatever it cost to get him to leave you alone."

"Why would you—?"

"Because I'm in love with you."

She stumbles back a step, eyes staring up in disbelief. "But you left…"

"Yeah, I fucked up, and even though I've got reasons for doing what I did, they don't matter now, but I'm paying the price by giving you space, praying you'd show up at my doorstep."

Her eyes narrow. "You knew I'd show up?"

"Hoped, prayed…but I didn't know."

"Right," she whispers, chews on her bottom lip, and drops her chin.

It's so fucking cute I can't hide my smile, but something tells me my grin is more for the fact that she isn't running away. "You coming in or are we having a conversation in the doorway?"

"Did I wake you?"

"It's the middle of the night, and I'm standing here in my sleepin' pants, doll. What do you think?"

Her eyes dart to mine. "Oh, yeah, I mean, if that's okay with you, or I could…" She points over her shoulder with her thumb. "Another time—"

"You show up on my doorstep because you've got something to say. I don't give a shit if it's to tell me your favorite brand of beer is on sale. I'm waking up to hear it."

A tiny grin pulls at her lips, and it sends a straight shot of warmth to my chest and my groin.

She tucks a long strand of her bangs behind her ear, a slight blush colors her cheeks. "That was really sweet, and I'll have to remember to do that next time my favorite brand is on sale."

"Sounds good." I step aside and swing the door open wider, and she follows me in and down the hallway to my room. I flick on a lamp and drop down on the couch.

Eve's hesitant, standing close to the door and tugging on the hem of her shirt.

"Have a seat." I nod to the club chair across from me.

She moves to it and takes a seat. "Cameron, I'm sorry. I should've called or waited until the morning, but I couldn't sleep, and all these questions were running through my head. I don't know. Now that I'm here, it all seems so pointless and stupid."

"The last time we saw each other, things were...intense. I stepped back to give you some space, time to figure things out. Now you're showing up at my door in the middle of the night. You will not see me complaining about that shit, doll."

A slight pink colors her cheeks, and she grabs her ponytail, splitting it down the middle, and then pulls each handful tightly. "Why didn't you tell me about the money? I mean hearing it from Mason—"

"What were you doing with Mason?" The words stir up from my gut in a growl.

"Huh?" Her nose scrunches up. "Hiking."

I groan and rub my eyes with my thumb and forefinger. "A date."

"No, not a date, we usually hang out once or twice a week, and today it was so nice out we decided to go hiking."

"Once or twice...dates, with an 'S'."

She tilts her head and studies me as if she can see straight through to my soul. "It's not a date or dates. He's one of my best friends, and I love hanging out with him."

Love.

"He your man?" Fuck, the words kill to get out, but lucky for me my lack of impulse control wouldn't allow them to be held back.

"No, he's not my *man*. Jeez, Cameron." She points at me. "And don't you go changing the subject. I came here because I need information."

Her face is so serious I can't help the low grumble of laughter that bubbles up from my chest.

"*Need information?* You interrogating me?"

Her eyes roll to the ceiling. "Stay with me on this one, would you?"

I nod.

"After you confronted my dad at the hospital, offered to pay off his debt, which must've been substantial"—she blows out a long breath, her eyes wide—"you came to my room, but then you disappeared. Why?"

"Seeing you hurt, all the shit you were going through, made me realize that if I'd never left you at that restaurant to go after 'Li that night you'd be safe and warm in my bed rather than running from a lunatic to your girl's house and then riding in that damn car when you got hit."

"You…You thought all that was your fault?"

"Just because I wasn't the one driving the car that hit you doesn't mean I didn't cause it." Like Rosie, I didn't throw her in the pool that day, but she ended up there because of me. "Sounds stupid, but I left because I thought you'd be safer without me. No shit, you have no idea the pain I've caused others without even trying."

She blinks. "Wha—What does that mean? Pain you've caused others?"

If I want a shot at being with Eve, I've got to let her in, but fuck if I can bring the words to my lips.

"Not big on talking about my past, Eve." Elbows on my knees, I drop my head into my hands and rake them through my hair.

"We can't build something based on secrets."

I cough on the irony of her words. "Like you don't have secrets." Fuck, but right as the words leave my lips, I instantly regret them. I feel what I'm doing, know I'm pushing her away to avoid having to tell her the truth, but even as I know it, don't want it, I'm doing it.

"You said you love me." Her eyes narrow. "You said you'd never let me go again. Now you're shutting me out. No more walking away."

My head pounds, and as much as I want what she's offering, I know I'll lose her if I tell her the truth about Rosie. But I could lose her if I don't tell her. Shit.

"Cameron, there's nothing you could tell me that would change the way I feel about you."

"You say that now, but you have no idea what you're asking for."

She swallows hard and blows out a long breath. "The last guy I dated kept secrets. He was not a good man."

"I know about Vince, doll. Bein' honest, not real excited to hear about this pecker sucker who fucked over you and Slade's girl, but I'm even more *not* excited to hear it from your sweet mouth."

My jaw falls loose on its hinges.

"I see this is a surprise to you."

"Who? When?"

"Daniels and a while ago."

She shakes her head slowly, and her eyes roam the room before coming back to mine. "Don't you think I'm disgusting?"

"Never think that about you."

"But I was in love with him."

He shrugs. "You thought you were, but, Eve, I know you. After the hell your pops put you through, no way you wouldn't jump all over a guy who showed you a little attention."

I cringe. "That's not nice." The words are barely a whisper.

"Not nice, but true."

"Is that what I did with you?"

He shrugs. "Maybe, but the difference is I don't throw away what you give me." He thumps his chest with a fist. "Feel that shit in here."

My breath catches in my throat. "But you threw me away."

"Thought I was protecting you. Walkin' away didn't mean I left you. Brought with me everything you gave."

"Why is this thing between us so hard? It feels like, if it were real, it should be easier."

"Never asked for easy. Best things in life are worth working for. You're worth it." He tilts his head. "Question is…am I worth working for?"

Before the question is out of my mouth, she bobs her head up and down.

"Not gonna lie. Until I get some shit settled, work through some crap I've been putting off for way too long, there's going to be a lot between us that'll piss you off."

"Cameron, I—"

"You're going to want to run, walk away. The shit will beat you down and make you…"

"What?"

"Hate me."

She shakes her head. "No. Never."

My eyes scan the room, but see nothing. "Rosie, my daughter."

"You have a daughter," she whispers.

"Eve—"

"Why didn't you tell me?"

"Because once you know the story, you'll never speak to me again."

Her hand flies to her mouth. "Did she…?" There's an audible swallow.

"I…" I run a hand though my hair, and push up from the couch with so much force that the air shifts between us. "Fuck!" I pace the room.

"Just tell me, because my imagination is probably making it worse." She trails behind me.

I hold up a hand. "Please, stay back."

She ignores me and steps closer. "No. Whatever this is, let me carry the burden with you. Share it with me."

Sheer panic races through my veins. "I'm not fucking around, Eve."

"I know that." She nods and steps closer, the heat of her hand on my forearm makes me flinch. "Sometimes the best defense is to step toward what scares you, not run away from it. You taught me that."

I focus on her hand on my arm. "Why are you doing this?"

"Because I love you."

The words push from my gut. My head knows releasing them will mean freedom, but the fear in my chest holds them back. "You said you weren't strong enough to hold on to me."

"I've been working out." She shrugs one shoulder. "I think I can manage now."

I drop my chin to my chest, and a desperate groan falls from my lips. "You sure you can handle it?"

She steps closer and dips her head to meet my eyes. "I'm sure."

My heart beats frantically and I'm terrified. I roll my head back, my thoughts vacant except for five little words that are my confession.

"I took my daughter's life."

FORTY

CAMERON

Eve's face drains of color. Her lips part and tears swell in her eyes. A myriad of emotions flashes in her eyes.

Shock. Disappointment. And finally disgust.

"You still think you're strong enough to hold on?"

She stumbles back, and her hand slips from my arm. Her head swivels from side to side in a slow shake that won't do anything to erase my confession. This I'm sure of because I've done it myself more times than I can count.

She swallows hard. "No."

I drop my chin to my chest, unable to hold her gaze when all I see in it is my failure. "You get the information you needed?"

"I...How?"

"Does it really matter?" I rub my eyes with my forefinger and thumb. "She's gone because of me."

"I don't know what to say," she whispers. "I..."

"Good night, Eve." I can't bear to look at her, but I hear the shuffling of her feet as she leaves the room.

And closes the door behind her.

EVE

I move numbly down the hallway to the living room, lost in my thoughts, sorting through my feelings. I expected a thousand different stories, but never did I imagine the truth would be so hideous.

I took my daughter's life.

His confession rings through my head, the desperation, sadness, guilt and agony, all so evident in his voice. If only—

"Eve."

I jump at the sound of Ryder's voice. He's leaning against the couch, shrouded in the dark of the living room.

"I'm, ah"—I fumble to pull up the right words, to think clearly—"sorry for waking you up."

He closes the space between us, his eyes narrowed on my face. "You okay?"

"Am I?" I rub my forehead, pushing my bangs back. "I think so. I just found out about…"

"Ah. So Dad finally opened up, huh?"

I jerk my eyes to his. "Um…"

"About Rosie?"

"Rosie." Her name. His sister. My heart cramps for the pain he must feel at her memory. "Yeah, I guess he did. I'm…I had no idea."

"Yeah, he doesn't like to talk about the accident." He shrugs and crosses his arms over his chest. "I don't really see what the big deal is. I mean it happened; can't hide that shit, ya know?"

I cringe at the easygoing way he speaks about his sister's death at the hands of his own father, even if it was an accident. "How, uh, how long ago did she die?"

His eyebrows drop low over his eyes. "Hmm." He looks down the hallway toward Cameron's bedroom then swings his eyes back to me. "You got any plans right now?"

I shake my head. "It's almost two a.m."

"Right. Let me grab my shoes. You drive."

I watch him disappear down the hallway and into his room. Drive? Where the hell are we going? Not that it matters. I've got nowhere else to be, and after Cameron's confession, I'll get no sleep with all the questions filtering through my mind. And something tells me Ryder has all the answers.

——

CAMERON

It's the middle of the day and my concentration's for shit. After Eve's visit last night, I've gone back and forth between showing up at her door and throwing myself at her mercy or locking myself up in a padded room. The more she knows about me and the further away she runs, the more I want to chase her down and keep her forever.

I flip through my notebook again, absently taking in the list of to-dos and don't-forgets, but only see her face, fear working behind those big blue eyes. A kind of fear I've never seen on the strong woman I've come to care for. The resilient woman I've come to love.

A knock sounds on my office door. "Come in."

Killer mopes in, his eyes downcast. "Hey, Mr. Kyle."

"Killian, what's up?"

It isn't until he gets closer that I realize he's not just looking down, but he's trying to hide his face behind long shags of hair. He takes a seat and keeps his head down, but that doesn't keep me from seeing the color on his cheek.

"Whoa, what the fuck happened to you?"

His shoulders slump, and he lifts his chin to reveal a black eye and pretty decent knot on his forehead. "I probably should've come to talk to you sooner, but…"

My muscles tense. "Who the fuck did this to you?"

"Thinkin' you already know who." He swallows and avoids my eyes. "I overheard Reece and some of his guys blabbing a few months ago. They were talking shit about the UFL and how they were only here for a little while until they"—he motions with air quotes—"get what they need."

"This back when they started fucking with you?"

"I tried to talk to them about it, ya know, get them to see things my way? These guys, Reece and his friends, they don't respect the century-old fundamentals of MMA. To them, this UFL stuff isn't a sport. It's, I don't know, a way to become famous by beating people up."

Damn, I seriously dig where this kid's mind is at. "So you confronted them."

"Yeah, I told them they need to have more respect for the organization or go fight for someone else."

"Shit, Killer. They're bullying you because you're defending *their* sport." I grind my teeth and withhold the rapid-fire curse words itching to be released.

"They got pissed I'd heard whatever it is I heard." He scratches his head. "I don't even know what they were talking about, but ever since then, they've been threatening me, roughing me up if I talk."

"So they're only here to get what they need. What does that mean?"

"I don't know. That's why I didn't come talk to you sooner. I thought once they realized I didn't hear shit they'd back off."

"But they didn't." I motion to his face.

"I walked into the locker room, and they were in there with a camera, like the handheld video kind?"

I nod.

"I told them they can't have that in there, UFL rules, and I don't know…They snapped."

What the fuck were they doing in there with a camera, and why would being reminded of league rules cause them to beat the shit out of an eighteen-year-old boy?

"Makes me wonder what's on that camera." I scratch down a reminder in my notebook to call in Reece and the boys for a little talk and then let them all out of their contracts effective immediately.

"No clue. Lopez took off and ran with it right after he finished videotaping."

My eyes snap to his. "He recorded the beating?"

Killer's forehead drops again. "Yeah."

As if an ass kicking isn't enough, but they insist on humiliating the poor kid too? I'm fed up and ready to put an end to this shit.

I hit the intercom on my phone. "Layla, get Reece and Lopez in my office now."

A soft knock on my door and Layla steps in with her eyes trained on a post-it note in her hand. "Vanessa gave this to me. It's a message, but"—she hands me the little yellow note—"it's kinda vague, not that I'm surprised." Her eyes roll to the ceiling. "Vanessa's as helpful as an STD."

In bold handwritten letters, the note says "URGENT" and below it is an address. It takes a quick scan of the address for me to know exactly who the note is about. I'm on my feet and fishing my keys out of my pocket before I make it to the door of my office.

"Give me an hour," I call over my shoulder to Killer and Layla as I move down the hallway.

My pulse throbs in my veins, is audible in my ears, and makes my heart race. There's only one reason I'd be called to the nursing home, and God...

I'm not ready to lose her.

FORTY-ONE

CAMERON

My tires squeal as I pull into the parking lot of the Horizon Care Facility. Adrenaline fuels my muscles, and I sprint through the lot then squeeze through the sliding glass doors before they're fully open. The sterile scent of the place turns my stomach and worry dampens my palms.

Pam, who works the front desk, looks up with wide eyes. "Can I help—Oh, Mr. Kyle."

"Yeah, hey…"

"We didn't expect you 'til Sunday." Her easy smile doesn't communicate anything close to urgency.

"I got your message." I lean over to peer down the hallway. "Is she okay?"

"Message?" She looks around her desk as if the answer is lying around haphazardly on some scrap of paper.

"It said 'urgent.'" I scour the area for any sign of disruption, my pulse pounding.

"I'm sorry. I don't see anything here about an urgent message."

"I received a message with this address."

"Oh, well it wasn't from us. Rosie's just fine."

I hear her words, but they don't calm the fears. "I'd like to see her."

"Yes, of course." A soft smile curves her lips. "Rosie's very popular today. I'll take you back."

Popular? I move around the circular desk to a door that leads to a long hallway: a hallway I've walked a million times, but today seems different somehow. Maybe it's the leftover panic that still has my muscles twitching.

I follow Pam to the door with a nameplate on it that says "Rosie" in script. "So you didn't leave a message with my secretary today?"

She shakes her head. "No, but I might have an idea who did." She dips her forehead toward the square window in the door.

My mind whirls and my gut tightens. I step up to the closed door and peek in through the window.

The air around me stills along with my lungs. My daughter, smaller than the average eighteen-year-old, sits in her chair, head and legs locked into place by soft straps.

But she's not alone.

Eve.

Emotion clogs my throat, and I force myself to swallow. She's in a chair, leaning forward so that her long hair veils most of her face. She has one of Rosie's hands between her own, and she's talking.

My eyes track movement on the other side of the room. I look over to find Ryder, his eyes on mine through the window, and a pleased smile on his face.

Without the conscious decision to do so, I push open the door and move into the room.

Eve's head swivels toward me. Her big blue eyes are red-rimmed and puffy, cheeks painted with tears. "I didn't know."

"Now you do." It's all I can say, the only thing I can get out before I brace for her reaction: her disappointment, anger, revulsion that because of me my daughter's living out her life brain dead in a hospital. All because of me.

Eve turns sad eyes back to Rosie. "She's beautiful, just like her mom."

I nod, even though she can't see me, not trusting my voice.

She holds Rosie's curled-up hand, rubbing comforting circles on her knuckles, and the visual threatens to drop me. I look away and blink as my eyes focus on my son.

"Hey, Dad." Ryder plops down on Rosie's bed, hands behind his head. "So I take it you got my message, huh?"

I dip my chin toward Eve. "You do this?"

He shrugs one shoulder. "It was time. Rosie and I were sick of watching you fall apart, so we took matters into our own hands." He looks at his twin sister. "Ain't that right, Rose?"

"We? You haven't been here in—"

"Guess my secret's out too." Ryder steps closer to whisper. "Just because I haven't been coming with you doesn't mean I haven't been coming."

Pride floods my chest with warmth. Here I thought he'd been abandoning his sister, but instead he's been forging his own relationship with her. "How long?"

"Couple months. I stopped coming with you and I missed her. I decided to come visit, and I liked it better being alone with her. When I used to come with you, it was so depressing."

"Sorry, son." I rake a hand through my hair. "I...I don't know what to say."

"Nothing to say." He says it in such a casual way I have to wonder how I didn't see this before.

I turn my attention to my daughter. Eve moves away from her spot to give me room.

"Hey, baby girl." I lean in and press a kiss to her forehead before taking the seat that Eve just vacated. "Busy day, huh?"

I watch for a reaction, a flicker of her eyelids, twitch of her lips, but get nothing. Her deep blue eyes stare blankly at me.

I notice a picture lying on her lap. "What's this?" I pick it up. It's of me, Eve, and Ryder from the night Ataxia played at The Blackout. "Your brother bring you this?"

"It's a great picture," Eve says in a soft way that gets my eyes. I get lost for a moment at the tenderness I see in her expression.

"One of my favorites, although"—she reaches to a framed picture on the table next to her—"this one is the best."

I take the frame from her, and an instant smile pulls at my lips upon viewing the image of Ryder and Rosie just weeks before she drowned. They're eating popsicles in the backyard, both of them with bright purple lips and sticky sweet dripping off their chins. Messy blond hair and sun-kissed toddler cheeks.

"That was a good day." My voice cracks with the memory.

"Why didn't you tell me?"

I shake my head. "I guess the same reason you lied about your age. I didn't want you to hate me."

She steps close, and I exhale hard with the soothing warmth of her hand on my shoulder. "I could never hate you. It was a mistake, Cameron."

"A mistake that cost her…" I swallow the lump forming in my throat and pull Rosie's hand to my lips to kiss each one of her knuckles. "I'm so sorry, baby girl."

Still no response from Rosie, but the telltale sniff of silent tears from Eve shoots straight to my chest.

I turn my head. "Now you know. It's because of me she's locked inside a body she can't control. She'll never have a life outside of this facility, and if all plays out the way it seems like it's going to, she'll die in here—"

"Shhh." Eve wipes her eyes and stands next to Rosie. "She can hear you."

"We don't know what she can hear."

Her glistening eyes snap to mine. "I know she can hear you."

"Eve, there's no way to know that. She's no longer responding."

"She responds to me." Her words seem to reverberate through the room.

"What?"

"It's true, Dad." Ryder sounds off from his place on the bed. "We've been here for hours, and a couple times she responded to us. It's subtle, but it's something."

"You've been here for hours?" I look between Ryder and Eve.

"We've been in here with her since before the sun came up."

I look between Eve and Rosie. "Can you show me?"

Eve nods and walks around to the front of Rosie's chair. She bends at the waist and brings Rosie's hand to her cheek. "Hey, Rosie. Do you remember me?"

Rosie's eyes stay fixed on nothing across the room.

"You know your dad here thinks you won't respond. I don't know about you, but I really enjoy proving him wrong. What do you say? Can you help a sister out?"

Still nothing.

Unease churns in my gut. "Eve, it's okay—"

"No, we're not giving up." She cups my daughter's jaw with one hand. "Are we Rosie? Come on. Look at me. I'm right here."

Rosie's eyes shift toward Eve ever so slightly.

"Yeah, there it is!" Eve's high-pitched voice is filled with pride. "Hey, pretty girl."

"Holy shit. You did it." I stand and place a kiss on my daughter's forehead.

"I told you." The triumph in Eve's voice is contagious and sends shock waves of excitement through my body.

"I'm proud of you, baby." I smooth Rosie's short blond hair. "You're so smart."

"She's amazing, Cameron." Eve leans into my side.

The door bursts open, and D'lilah comes rushing inside. "Is she okay? What happened, is she—oh!" Her eyes take in everyone in the room. "What's everyone doing here?"

I catch Ryder trying to hide a grin behind the back of his hand.

"Yeah, she's fine." I nod to my son. "Ry, you mind filling your mom in before you give her a heart attack?"

"Don't mind if I do, Dad." He steps forward and clears his throat. "Rosie's fine. I left the urgent messages with you guys."

D'lilah's hand on her heart, she blows out several breaths. "Ryder, you scared me to death."

"Drastic times. Here's the thing. I've been watching you all dance around each other for months. Been watching Mom slowly kill herself for years. Figured it was time we had a family meeting."

"But—"

Ryder holds his hand up to D'lilah. "Before you say anything, Mom, let me say that Eve is going to be part of our family eventually"—he fixes his eyes on mine—"as soon as Dad pulls his head out of his ass."

Eve snort-giggles at my side.

"Eve, you love my dad. Dad, you love Eve." He looks at his mom. "Mom, you've been sober now for a little while, and I know you love me. I don't need a mom, but Rosie does. She needs all the love she can get, and I'll be busy with college. It's time you guys stop living in your mistakes and start looking forward."

"How'd he get so smart?" Eve grins up at me.

I shake my head. "No fucking idea."

D'lilah slides her gaze from Ryder to Rosie. Her eyes fill up with tears. "She's grown since the last time I saw her." She wraps her arms around her stomach.

Eve holds her hand out to D'lilah. "Come look at her from over here. She looks so much like you."

'Li looks at Eve's hand and slowly takes hold of it. I step away from the women as they crouch down in front of Rosie, then move to my son who's sporting a very proud grin while watching his mom with his sister.

"You did good, son."

"Yeah, I know."

And just like the night of The Fourth of July, Eve becomes the easy that our family needed—the light that we've been missing for years—the glue that somehow holds us together.

I was living behind a translucent wall of apathy, not allowing anything or anyone that might drop me to my knees get close enough. Love has brought me the worst kind of pain imaginable, and I was so afraid of feeling that again, of losing something so beautiful I'd never be able to recover. But the risk is half the beauty of living. I'm risking my sanity by loving Eve, but the alternative is far more painful than the fear of losing her.

She shattered me, broke down the old me, and freed the possibility of a new outcome. Rewriting my future to create one I never even knew I wanted.

And as I watch my ex-wife fawn over our disabled daughter, as Eve and Ryder look on with smiles so big they could light the dark, I let go.

For the second time in my life...

I fall.

This time, by choice.

FORTY-TWO

One month later...

CAMERON

"You ready, old man?" Blake calls from his spot propped up behind me, elbows on the top of the octagon.

"You got this, Cam." Jonah's next to Blake, same position, and Caleb, Rex, Mason, and Wade are there too.

Owen's down, standing stoic with his arms crossed at his chest, game face on.

I nod to the fighters and bounce on my toes as Rusty Faulkner enters the cage.

The stadium is packed with thousands of screaming UFL fans. They chant my name and electrify the air with the intensity of their thirst for battle. An over-a-decade rivalry will be settled in five-minute rounds, or less if I have my way.

This is it. What I've lived for since the day I landed my first punch. Everything I've been scrambling to get back after I lost my chance at the title. Here, standing in the octagon with the heat of the lights on my skin and the fire of a challenge in my gut.

But this time is different. This time, my life is no longer inside the cage, but sits outside, hands locked together in support. Ryder and Eve, and the thought of Rosie, who's been showing subtle signs of improvement every day. Even D'lilah decided to show her support and is sitting in my corner, holding hands with a pretty decent dude she's dating.

"You're going down, Prez." Faulkner's attempt at shit-talk doesn't faze me.

I knew after seeing him at weigh-in that he doesn't stand a chance. He's sloppy, undertrained, and overconfident. But this isn't about me beating him; it's always been about proving myself to me. In a lifetime of unintentional failures, I'm ready for intentional success. I need to prove to myself that my career wasn't a total waste.

The ref talks, brings us together for a rundown of the rules, but I'm waiting on the word. That one word that signals it's time to throw down.

The ref's voice cuts off, and the speakers shriek as feedback, loud and piercing, slices through the air. *What the fuck?* The crowd screeches, and I fight the urge to cover my ears.

Everyone looks around in question; shock plays across the faces of the ref, the judges, and the commentators. The arena comes alive in a flurry of confusion as the jumbo screens go from shots of the octagon to static.

I glare across the cage to a very smug-looking Rusty Faulkner. Something tells me whatever this is the dickbag has something to do with it.

The sound of my own voice spills from the speakers and calls my attention to the screen.

"If you don't like it, get the fuck out!"

A video plays of me talking to my fighters the day of Rex's and Blake's fights. Who the hell is responsible for this?

"You spoiled little jackoffs!"

That's me again from the same meeting. My gaze swings to Rusty, who is now surrounded by his crew, and fuck if Reece isn't standing right there with him. *Fucking snake.* Reece was working for him this whole time? That's what Killer walked in on and why he's been catching hell ever since.

More video plays on the big screen for a crowd of over ten thousand fans. I don't need to look to know my own fighters have formed a barrier of support at my back. I can feel the heat of their anger.

The voices of my fighters questioning my ability to run the UFL filter in through the area, and I'm sure there's video to go with them, but I wouldn't know as my eyes are fixed on the traitorous bastards standing across from me.

"Man with brain damage isn't fit to run this organization."

"Once he fucks it all up, we're all out of a job."

"The dude can't remember to wipe his own ass let alone run the UFL."

"Did you hear what happened to his daughter?"

"Enough!" In two long strides, I'm nose to nose with the slimy fuck. "So this is what you were after?" I shove him hard, but his crew holds him up. "You want to publicly humiliate me?"

"Don't flatter yourself, Kyle." Faulkner's lips curl back over his teeth. "This is about giving the fans a good show, something the UFL has neglected to do for years."

"Fans aren't stupid. They'll see right through this." I jerk a thumb toward the screens. "And you're fucking high if you think this bullshit will ever sell."

"Ah, but that's where you're wrong. Between Reece, Lopez, and me, we've got enough footage to splice together a pretty interesting show. Internet fans around the world will pay big bucks to be let in on the UFL's secrets."

"Got some good locker-room conversations recorded." Reece high-fives another fighter on Faulkner's crew. "Ever wonder what people are saying about you behind your back?"

"You dirty little shit." Mason rushes Reece but is held back by Caleb and Rex.

I step into Rusty's face, and the weight of angry fighters surrounds me. "No one fucks with *my* organization or its fighters. You hear me, you weaselly prick?"

My pulse pounds in my ears, and adrenaline powers my muscles. I didn't get the fight I trained for, but it's not too late. I shove Rusty again, sending him back. His crew surges forward, and my fighters press in from behind.

"No! Wait!" A feminine but powerful voice cuts through the group, and Eve squeezes in between us.

"Slade," I growl. "Get her out of here."

Jonah grabs her arm, but she knocks him off with a few girlie slaps to his hand. "Don't you dare, Jonah Slade." She presses against my chest, demanding my eyes. "There are cameras on you right now." She jerks her head to Rusty. "His cameras. This is exactly what he wants. Don't give it to him."

"Yeah, Cameron." Rusty nods to Eve. "Listen to the little girl. Walk away in front of a stadium packed with UFL fans. Show them what a pussy you are."

"Slade. Now."

"Fuck." Jonah moves to grab her again.

"Yeah, Jonah. Get the little bitch—"

"Whoa!" Eve holds her hands up, and I'm seconds away from throwing her to Jonah so I can fuck this guy up. She scratches her chin. "On second thought"—she pushes up to her tiptoes and presses a long closed-mouthed kiss against my lips—"I think it's about time you get your fight." She looks between Rusty and me then brings her eyes back to mine. "Kick his ass."

Finally, I get my fight with Rusty Faulkner. No judges. No commentators. In less than three minutes, it's over by knockout.

Victory.

Without a single hit to my head.

EPILOGUE

Christmas Eve...

EVE

"You should see her, Eve. I found the tiniest Christmas dress with little tights and shoes. I'll send you a picture." Even through the phone, Raven's excitement is infectious.

"Yes, do that. I need some updated pictures of her for my brag album." Phone wedged between my ear and shoulder, I tape the corner of the last box I needed to wrap.

Cameron's coffee table is covered with all the gifts that we're bringing to Rosie's care facility tonight. There are even a few on the floor.

"Didn't you just take some pictures yesterday?"

"Yeah, but she grows so fast, and I need to see her in her very first Christmas dress." I pull a shimmering golden ribbon around the gift and tie it in a neat bow.

"You sure you guys won't come tonight? Jonah said he's never been invited to Rex's house, like ever. It's a big deal that he's throwing a party."

"Rex's in love. I'm not surprised he's doing things he thought he'd never do."

"Listen to you, little Miss Live-in Girlfriend." Her soft giggle is followed by a content sigh. "You sure you can't just swing by?"

"I want to spend as much time with Rosie as we can before the nurses chase us off, ya know?" Plus, I want to show Cameron his Christmas present, and I don't know how long that will take. "You should see what I did in Rosie's room: singing Santas, dancing snowmen, and a ton of colored lights hang from every surface I could reach. I swear it looks like the entire population of Whoville exploded in there."

"Sounds perfect."

"It is, Rave. It *so* is." I never knew how much I could love a child that wasn't mine, but between Sadie, Rosie, and even Ryder, they've all claimed a part of my heart in a way I've never experienced before.

"You'll be here tomorrow, right?"

"With bells on. Tell everyone I said Merry Christmas Eve and sorry we couldn't make it."

"Will do."

I end the call and put the finishing touches on my gifts.

"You went overboard." Cameron drops down next to me on the couch and props his long denim-clad legs on the coffee table, ankles crossed with socked feet.

"I know, but it's a special day." I drop back, and he wraps a possessive arm around my waist.

He pushes my hair back over my shoulder, and the move has me tilting my head, inviting his lips. "Good thing your boss pays well."

His growled words against the tender flesh of my throat send goose bumps down my arms. "That you do." My heart races and my body tingles. "You sure you want to start this?"

"Mm-hmm." He continues to assault my neck and jaw in light kisses and pulls of his teeth.

A low moan vibrates deep in my throat, and I fight the urge to push him back and straddle him right here. "We...We have to leave in thirty minutes." The breathy sound of my voice makes him groan.

"Right." He drops one last kiss below my earlobe then pushes back, but pulls me down to rest in the crook of his arm. "We'll pick this up when we get home from Rosie's."

"About that, I just...I want to say thank you." It sounds so lame, doesn't do a sliver of justice to how I really feel. "You've given me Rosie and Ryder, and hell, even D'lilah. I love you guys, and you gave me all that. I'll never be able to repay you."

"Bullshit. You're the force that brought my family together and the glue that's keeping us there."

"Cam, that's not—"

He hooks my chin and brings my gaze to his. "I love you more than I've ever loved any woman, as much as I love my own kids. Whether or not you're ready to hear this, I'm sayin' it. You're part of this family. Sooner or later I'll put a ring on that finger and make it official. If you want kids, I'll give 'em to you. Bottom line...I've fallen for you, Yvette. I ain't ever gettin' up. So you—"

I crash my mouth to his and sink into a deep kiss. His hands fist in my hair, pulling me closer and holding me there. Exactly where I want to be.

My fingers dig into his bicep, and it's all I can do to not become overwhelmed by him. But instead of sucking up every ounce of this, storing up everything he gives out of fear that it'll all be taken away, I slow down. My lips glide against his in a slow seduction, nibbling for once in my life rather than devouring out of fear that I'll never have it this good again. For the first time, I feel entitled, as if I've earned this kind of love. And that in itself is miraculous.

Everything I never had crept into my life the day I met Cameron. I swore I'd never let anyone in, built up walls to ensure my heart would be protected, but leave it to the best fighter in the UFL to shatter them.

———

CAMERON

I don't remember the last time I smiled so much my damn cheeks hurt. It's been forever since I've been able to be in Rosie's room at the care facility without sinking into a pit of guilt and depression. But now, surrounded by my kids, my ex-wife, and Eve, it's as if the world started spinning again, and it's Eve who set it in motion.

"Okay, it's Rosie's turn to open a present from me." Eve brings over a large box, and sitting in a chair across from my daughter, she places the box on her own knees.

"Hold up." Ryder raises his hand in mock offense. "The movies, the books, and now you're giving her more? I got gypped!"

We all chuckle as Eve pulls off the ribbon and rips open the bright red paper. Her hands placed on the box's lid, she smiles at my daughter. "You ready?" She pulls the lid off, tosses it aside, and lifts up a stack of magazines.

I squint and, upon D'lilah's gasp, realize what Eve's just done.

"These are all the old magazines I kept that have your mom on the cover. I'm passing them on to you." Eve turns from Rosie to a choked up 'Li. "I figured there's a lot of stories behind these images. Bet your daughter would love to hear them."

My throat swells, and my eyes burn as D'lilah jumps from her seat to hug Eve. I catch my woman's eyes and pray that she sees my appreciation.

"Eve, wow…" D'lilah takes the stack of magazines and plops them on her lap. "Oh my gosh, this photo shoot was in Japan." She flips through the pages. "Oh, see here. You can't tell, but I was so sick this day." Eve leaves the seat in front of Rosie, and D'lilah takes it. Lost in her story, she holds the photos up to her daughter. "Look at this one, baby. My hair was shorter here, like yours."

"Doll." Eve's eyes find mine. "Come here."

She glides over to me, and I pull her down to my lap.

"Fuckin' love you, babe." I run my nose along her jaw, breathing in the warm sugary scent. "Sweet gift you gave my girl."

She shrugs. "Nah, they're just magazines."

"Not just magazines. You gave Rosie…" We both look over to D'lilah and Rosie, who are now surrounded by a smiling Ryder and Rosie's nurse. "You gave Rosie her mom back."

Eve sucks in a quick breath and then hides her face in my neck. "I was hoping I could do that for her."

I run my fingers through her hair, my eyes fixed on my little girl and D'lilah's light laughter ringing through the room, when suddenly—wait, did she?

"Oh my gosh, Cam, did you see that?" D'lilah's eyes are glistening with tears.

Eve jumps off my lap and we surround Rosie.

"Yep, I saw it." Ryder ruffles his sister's hair. "That was a smile."

"I saw it too." It was unmistakable: the tiny twitch of her lip.

"Of course she smiled." Eve sounds so confident, as if the assumption that she wouldn't smile is offensive. "She's perfect."

I pull Eve into my arms and bury my nose in all that blond hair. "I can't believe it. You got my little girl to smile."

She tilts her head back. "I was hoping she would. That was my Christmas present to you."

I blink at what she just said. "Wait, so this isn't the first time you've seen that?

She shakes her head. "She did it on my last visit. I told her if she could pull that off for Christmas that would be great since

I planned on spending all my money on her and her brother. That was the only gift I could think to give to you."

"Fuckin' hell, doll." I wrap her in my arms, amazed that this incredible woman is capable of giving me so much in such a short period of time. "I love you."

"I love you too."

Falling isn't always failure. Sometimes the biggest victories only happen when we're brave enough to let go and give in to the pull.

~The End~

ACKNOWLEDGMENTS

First, thank you God for giving me the opportunity and ability to write stories and share them with the world.

To my husband, thank you for your support and for doing your own laundry when I'm stuck behind the computer, lost in the writing.

Thank you to my girls who are a constant inspiration and bring me more joy than I could imagine.

To my family, thanks for supporting me from day one and helping when I need it. Whether it's been a motivating shove in the butt or someone to watch the kids, you've never let me down.

Thank you to Evelyn Johnson for dropping everything when I need to travel, keeping my schedule so I show up places on time, organizing everything from my brain to meet and greets, but, most importantly, thank you for being a loyal and loving friend. I'd be lost without you…literally. But you already know that.

I'm forever indebted to my amazing crew of critique partners. Sharon Kay, Claudia Conner, Racquel Reck, and N.J. Layouni. Thank you for pushing me to be my best every single time. Your friendship means the world to me, and I don't know where I'd be without you.

To my partner in crime, PI Ninja, Maya Banks stalker, and all things in between buddy, Cristin Harber. Honest to goodness, my world would not spin without you in it. I cherish our friendship and our working partnership more than words could say. I will forever be ready in all black with a beanie cap for barrel rolls...anytime, anyplace.

I can't thank my PIMA, Amanda Simpson from Pixel Mischief Design, enough. You have been there from day one and are the creative force behind my brand. I'm forever grateful for everything you've taught me, but most importantly I'm honored by your friendship. If all this ends tomorrow, I know I'd have a friend for life in you. Thank you for allowing me to be your PITA.

Thank you to Elizabeth Reyes for all your guidance and advice. It's been an amazing year; meeting you and getting the opportunity to sign with you was the highlight. I cherish your friendship and look forward to many more opportunities to hang with you in the future.

To the Goddess of the Alpha Male, Kristen Ashley, thank you for your friendship. I've worshipped your writing since the beginning of your career and to think that I'd ever be in a position to call you "friend" would've seemed like nothing more than the fantasy of a romance junkie. You're the most down-to-earth person I've ever known, and it's your staying true to you that sets you apart from the rest. I'm absolutely honored to know you and blessed by your friendship.

Thank you from the bottom of my soul to every single Fighting Girl who has tirelessly pimped my books. To all the girls in The Fighting Girls Fun Cage, thank you for being there for each other, for showing the world what it means to be a woman: that we can be strong and compassionate, that we have integrity, and that we're always there to lift up someone who is suffering. Not a day goes by that I'm not proud beyond comprehension of what you girls have created in that group. The love and support you show each other is unparalleled by any other I've seen, and my prayer is that it continues and spreads like a virus because the greatest of these is love.

Thank you to all the bloggers who've supported The Fighting Series. Your promotions, reviews, and constant pimps are absolutely vital to Indie-published authors. I would not be where I am today without your support. I'm so incredibly grateful for each and every one of you.

Huge thank you to Lael Telles, Lauren McCullough, and Chris Jackson. You guys rock!

Thank you to my editor, Theresa Wegand, for taking on the challenge of this book and steering me in the right direction.

This book wouldn't be what it is without the infinite wisdom of Scott Tannenbaum at the TNT MMA Training Center. Thank you for taking the time to indulge me with my list of questions, follow-up questions, and follow-up-follow-up questions.

Last but never least, thank you to every single woman out there who has a passion for romance novels. Doesn't matter if you read mine or not; just the fact that you read them keeps the genre alive and thriving. Romance readers are the most passionate people and make this place a better world.

Love and infinite gratitude,
JB

FIGHTING THE FALL PLAYLIST

"Remember the Name" by Fort Minor
"Gone too Soon" by Simple Plan
"I Can Wait Forever" by Simple Plan
"How I Go" by Yellowcard
"Terrible Things" by Mayday Parade
"A Drop in the Ocean" by Ron Pope
"Stay on Your Feet" by MxPx
"I Wanna be a Warhol" by Alkaline Trio
"Don't Push" by Sublime
"21st Century Digital Boy" by Bad Religion
"Chasing Rainbows" by No Use for a Name
"Work Hard, Play Hard" by Wiz Khalifa
"When She Begins" by Social Distortion

ABOUT THE AUTHOR

JB Salsbury, New York Times Best Selling author of the Fighting series, lives in Phoenix, Arizona, with her husband and two kids. She spends the majority of her day as a domestic engineer. But while she works through her daily chores, a world of battling alphas, budding romance, and impossible obstacles claws away at her subconscious, begging to be released to the page.

Her love of good storytelling led her to earn a degree in Media Communications. With her journalistic background, writing has always been at the forefront, and her love of romance prompted her to sink her free time into novel writing.

For more information on the series or just to say hello, visit JB on her website, Facebook, or Goodreads page.

http://www.jbsalsbury.com/
https://www.facebook.com/JBSalsburybooks
http://www.goodreads.com/author/
show/6888697.Jamie_Salsbury

Made in the USA
San Bernardino, CA
11 November 2014